Brazen and
the Beast

"I can't risk you taking revenge."

He met her gaze without hesitation. "My revenge is not a risk. It's a certainty."

"I've no doubt of that. But I can't risk you taking it through me. Not tonight." She reached past him for the door handle, speaking at his ear, above the rattle of wheels and horses from the street beyond. "As I've said . . ."

"You have plans." He turned toward her, unable to resist her scent, like an almond teacake, sweet temptation.

She met his eyes. "Yes."

"Tell me the plan, and I'll let you go." He'd find her.

That smile again. "You're very arrogant, sir. Must I remind you that I'm the one letting you go?"

"Tell me." The command was rough.

He saw the change in her. Watched hesitation turn to curiosity. To bravery. And then, like a gift, she whispered, "Perhaps I should show you, instead."

Yes.

Also by Sarah MacLean

The Bareknuckle Bastards
WICKED AND THE WALLFLOWER

Scandal & Scoundrel
THE ROGUE NOT TAKEN
A SCOT IN THE DARK
THE DAY OF THE DUCHESS

The Rules of Scoundrels
A ROGUE BY ANY OTHER NAME
ONE GOOD EARL DESERVES A LOVER
NO GOOD DUKE GOES UNPUNISHED
NEVER JUDGE A LADY BY HER COVER

Love by Numbers
NINE RULES TO BREAK WHEN ROMANCING A RAKE
TEN WAYS TO BE ADORED WHEN LANDING A LORD
ELEVEN SCANDALS TO START TO WIN A DUKE'S HEART

THE SEASON

This is a work of fiction. Names, characters, places, and incidents are products of the author's imagination or are used fictitiously and are not to be construed as real. Any resemblance to actual events, locales, organizations, or persons, living or dead, is entirely coincidental.

Excerpt from *Daring and the Duke* copyright © 2020 by Sarah Trabucchi.

BRAZEN AND THE BEAST. Copyright © 2019 by Sarah Trabucchi. All rights reserved. Printed in the United States of America. No part of this book may be used or reproduced in any manner whatsoever without written permission except in the case of brief quotations embodied in critical articles and reviews. For information, address HarperCollins Publishers, 195 Broadway, New York, NY 10007.

First Avon Books mass market printing: August 2019
First Avon Books hardcover printing: July 2019

Print Edition ISBN: 978-0-06-269207-8
Digital Edition ISBN: 978-0-06-269198-9

Cover design by Patricia Barrow
Cover illustration by Alan Ayers

FIRST EDITION

21 22 23 LSC 10 9 8 7 6 5 4 3 2

Brazen *and the* BEAST

The
Barenuckle
Bastards Book II

SARAH MACLEAN

AVONBOOKS

An Imprint of HarperCollinsPublishers

For V.
You're my favorite thing.

Chapter One

September 1837
Mayfair

In twenty-eight years and three hundred and sixty-four days, Lady Henrietta Sedley liked to think that she'd learned a few things.

She'd learned, for example, that if a lady could not get away with wearing trousers (an unfortunate reality for the daughter of an earl, even one who had begun life without title or fortune), then she should absolutely ensure that her skirts included pockets. A woman never knew when she might require a bit of rope, or a knife to cut it.

She'd also learned that any decent escape from her Mayfair home required the cover of darkness and a carriage driven by an ally. Coachmen tended to talk a fine game when it came to keeping secrets, but they were ultimately beholden to those who paid their salaries. An important addendum to that particular lesson was this: The best of allies was often the best of friends.

And perhaps first on the list of things she had learned in her lifetime was how to tie a Carrick bend knot. She'd been able to do that for as long as she could remember.

With such an obscure and uncommon collection of knowledge, one might imagine that Henrietta Sedley would have known precisely what to do in the likelihood she discovered a human male bound and unconscious in her carriage.

One would be incorrect.

In point of fact, Henrietta Sedley would never have described such a scenario as a likelihood. True, she might have been more comfortable on London's docks than in its ballrooms, but Hattie's impressive collection of life experience lacked anything close to a criminal element.

And yet, here she was, pockets full, dearest friend at her side, standing in the pitch dark on the night before her twenty-ninth birthday, about to steal away from Mayfair for an evening of best-laid plans, and . . .

Lady Eleanora Madewell whistled, low and unladylike, at Hattie's ear. Daughter of a duke and the Irish actress he loved so well that he'd made her a duchess, Nora had the kind of brashness that was allowed in those with impervious titles and scads of money. "There's a bloke in the gig, Hattie."

Hattie did not look away from the bloke in question. "Yes, I see that."

"There wasn't a bloke in the gig when we hitched the horses."

"No, there wasn't." They'd left the hitched—and most definitely empty—carriage in the dark rear drive of Sedley House not three quarters of an hour earlier, before hiking upstairs to exchange carriage-hitching dresses for attire more appropriate for their evening plans.

At some point between corset and kohl, someone had left her an extraordinarily unwelcome package.

"Seems we would've noticed a bloke in the gig," Nora said.

"I should think we would have," came Hattie's distracted reply. "This is really just awful timing."

Nora cut her a look. "Is there a *good* time to find a man bound and unconscious in one's carriage?"

Hattie imagined there wasn't, but, "He could have selected a different evening. This is a terrible birthday gift." She squinted into the dark interior of the carriage. "Do you think he's dead?"

Please, don't let him be dead.

Silence. Then, a thoughtful, "Does one store dead men in carriages?" Nora reached forward, her coachman's coat pulling tight over her shoulders, and poked the possibly dead man in question. He did not move. "He's not moving," she added with an unhelpful shrug. "Could be dead."

Hattie sighed, removing a glove and leaning into the carriage to place two fingers to the man's neck. "I'm sure he's not dead."

"What are you doing?" Nora whispered urgently. "If he's not, you'll wake him!"

"That wouldn't be the worst thing in the world," Hattie pointed out. "Then we could ask him to kindly exit our conveyance and we could be on our way."

"Oh, yes. This brute seems like precisely the kind of man who would immediately do just that and not immediately take his revenge. He'd no doubt doff his cap and wish us a fine good evening."

"He's not wearing a cap," Hattie said, unable to refute any of the rest of the assessment of the mysterious, likely dead man. He was very broad, and very solid, and even in the darkness she could tell that this wasn't a man with whom one took a turn about a ballroom.

This was the kind of man who ransacked a ballroom.

"What do you feel?" Nora pressed.

"No pulse." Though she wasn't exactly sure where one would find a pulse. "But he's—"

Warm.

Dead men were not warm, and this man was very warm.

Like a fire in winter. The kind of warm that made someone realize how cold she might be.

Ignoring the silly thought, Hattie moved her fingers down the column of his neck, to the place where it disappeared beneath the collar of his shirt, where the ridge of his shoulder and the slope of . . . the rest of him . . . met in a fascinating indentation.

"Anything now?"

"Quiet." Hattie held her breath. Nothing. She shook her head.

"Christ." It wasn't a prayer.

Hattie couldn't have agreed more. But then . . .

There. A small flutter. She pressed a touch more firmly. The flutter became steady. Slow. Even. "I feel it," she said. "He's alive." She repeated herself. "He's alive." She exhaled, long and relieved. "He's not dead."

"Excellent. But it doesn't change the fact that he's unconscious in the carriage, and you have somewhere to be." Nora paused. "We should leave him and take the curricle."

Hattie had been planning for this particular excursion on this particular night for a full three months. This was the night that would begin her twenty-ninth year. The year her life would become her own. The year *she* would become her own. And she had a very specific plan for a very specific location at a very specific hour, for which she had donned a very specific frock. And yet, as she stared at the man in her carriage, specifics seemed not at all important.

What seemed important was seeing his face.

Clinging to the handle at the edge of the door, Hattie collected the lantern from the upper rear corner of the carriage before swinging back out to face Nora, whose gaze flickered immediately to the unlit container.

Nora tilted her head. "Hattie. Leave him. We'll take the curricle."

"Just a peek," Hattie replied.

The tilt became a slow shake. "If you peek, you'll regret it."

"I have to peek," Hattie insisted, casting about for a decent reason—ignoring the odd fact that she was unable to tell her friend the truth. "I have to untie him."

"Not necessarily," Nora pointed out. "Someone thought he was best left tied up, and who are we to disagree?" Hattie was already reaching into the pocket of the carriage door for a flint. "What of your plans?"

There was plenty of time for her plans. "Just a peek," she repeated, the oil in the lantern catching fire. She closed the door and turned to face the carriage, lifting the light high, casting a lovely golden glow over—

"Oh, my."

Nora choked back a laugh. "Not such a bad gift after all, it seems."

The man had the most beautiful face Hattie had ever seen. The most beautiful face *anyone* had ever seen. She leaned closer, taking in his warm, bronze skin, the high cheekbones, the long, straight nose, the dark slashes of his brows, and the impossibly long lashes that lay like sin against his cheeks.

"What kind of man . . ." She trailed off. Shook her head. What kind of man looked like this?

What kind of man looked like this and somehow landed in the carriage of Hattie Sedley—a woman who was very unused to being in the vicinity of men who looked like this.

"You're embarrassing yourself," Nora said. "You're staring and your jaw has gone fully slack."

Hattie closed her mouth, but did not stop staring.

"Hattie. We have to go." A pause. Then, "Unless you've changed your mind?"

The casual question brought Hattie back to the moment. To her plan. She shook her head. Lowered the lantern. "I haven't."

Nora sighed and placed her hands on her hips, staring

past Hattie into the carriage. "You get his bottom, and I'll take his top, then?" She looked to a shadowed alcove behind her. "He can resume consciousness there."

Hattie's heart pounded. "We can't leave him here."

"We can't?"

"No."

Nora slid her a look. "Hattie. We can't take him with us just because he looks like a Roman statue."

Hattie blushed in the darkness. "I hadn't noticed."

"You lost the power of speech."

She cleared her throat. "We can't take him because *Augie* left him here."

Nora's lips flattened into a perfect, straight line. "You don't know that."

"I know," Hattie said, holding the lantern near the rope at the man's wrists, and sweeping it down to the place where he was bound at the ankles, "because August Sedley can't tie a Carrick bend worth a damn, and I fear that if we leave this man here, he'll find his way loose and head straight for my useless brother."

That, and if the stranger didn't find his way loose, who knew what Augie would do to him. Her brother was as cabbageheaded as he was reckless—a combination that routinely required Hattie's intervention. Which, incidentally, was a significant reason for her decision to claim her twenty-ninth year as her own. And still, here her infernal brother was, ruining everything.

Unaware of Hattie's thoughts, Nora said, "Recently unconscious or no . . . this doesn't look like a man who loses in a fight."

The understatement was not lost on Hattie. She sighed, reaching in and hanging the now glowing lantern on its peg, taking the opportunity to cast a long, lingering look at the man in her carriage.

Hattie Sedley had learned something else in her twenty-eight years, three hundred and sixty-four days: If a woman had a problem, it was best she solve it herself.

She pulled herself up into the carriage, stepping carefully over the man on the floor before looking back at wide-eyed Nora on the drive below. "Come on, then. We'll drop him on our way."

Chapter Two

⊙ ⊙

𝔗he last thing he remembered was the blow to the head.

He'd been expecting the ambush. It was why he'd been
driving the rig, six fine horses pulling a massive steel conveyance laden with liquor and playing cards and tobacco,
destined for Mayfair. He'd just crossed Oxford Street when
he'd heard the gunshot, followed by a pained cry from one
of his outriders.

He'd stopped to check on his men. To protect them.

To punish those who threatened them.

There'd been a body on the ground. Blood on the street
beneath it. He had just sent the second outrider for help
when he heard the footsteps at his back. He'd turned, knife
in hand. Thrown it. Heard the shout in the darkness as it
found its seat.

Then the blow to the head.

And then . . . nothing.

Not until an insistent tapping against his cheek returned
him to consciousness, too soft for pain, still firm enough to
be irritating.

He didn't open his eyes, years of training allowing him
to feign sleep as he gathered his bearings. His feet were

bound. Hands, too, behind his back. The bindings stretched the muscles of his chest tight enough for him to take note of what was missing—his knives, eight steel blades, set in onyx. Stolen along with the brace that strapped them to his chest. He resisted the urge to stiffen. To rage.

But Saviour Whittington, known in London's darkest streets as Beast, did not rage; he punished. Quick and devastating and without emotion.

And if they'd taken the life of one of his men—of someone under his protection—they would never know peace.

But first, freedom.

He was on the floor of a moving carriage. A well-appointed one, if the soft cushion at his cheek was any indication, and in a decent neighborhood for the smooth rhythm of the cobblestones beneath the wheels.

What was the time?

He considered his next move—envisioning how he would incapacitate his captor despite his bindings. He imagined breaking a nose with the flat weapon of his forehead. Using his bound legs to knock the man out.

The tapping at his cheek began again. Then a whispered, "Sir."

Whit's eyes flew open.

His captor wasn't a man.

The wash of golden light in the carriage played tricks with him—seeming to come somehow not from the lantern swaying gently in the corner, but from the woman.

Seated on the bench above him, she looked nothing like the kind of enemy who would knock a man out and tie him up in a carriage. Indeed, she looked like she was on her way to a ball. Perfectly done, perfectly coiffed, perfectly colored—her skin smooth, her eyes kohled, her lips full and stained just enough to make a man pay attention. And that was before he got a look at the dress—blue the color of a summer sky, perfectly fitted to her full figure.

Not that he should be noticing anything about that, con-

sidering she had him tied up in a carriage. He shouldn't be
noticing the curves of her, soft and welcoming at her waist,
at the line of her bodice. He shouldn't be noticing the gleam
of the smooth, golden skin at her rounded shoulder in the
lantern light. He shouldn't be noticing the pretty softness of
her face, or the fullness of her lips, stained red with paint.

She wasn't for noticing.

He narrowed his gaze on her, and her eyes—was it possible they were violet? What kind of a person had violet
eyes?—went wide. "Well. If *that* look is any indication of
your temperament, it's no wonder you are tied up." She
tilted her head. "Who tied you up?"

Whit did not reply. He did not believe she didn't know
the answer.

"*Why* are you tied up?"

Again, silence.

Her lips flattened into a straight line and muttered something that sounded like "*Useless.*" And then, louder, firmer,
"The point is, you're very inconvenient, as I have need of
this carriage tonight."

"Inconvenient." He didn't mean to reply, and the word
surprised them both.

She nodded. "Indeed. It's the Year of Hattie."

"The what?"

She waved a hand, as though to push the question away.
As though it weren't important. Except Whit imagined it
was. She pressed on. "It is my birthday. I have plans for myself. Plans that don't include . . . whatever this is." Silence
stretched between them, then, "Most people would wish
me a happy birthday at this juncture."

Whit did not rise to the bait.

Her brows rose. "And here I was, ready to help you."

"I don't need your help."

"You're quite rude, you know."

He resisted the unwelcome instinct to gape. "I've been
knocked out and tied up in a strange carriage."

"Yes, but you must admit the company is diverting, no?" She smiled, the dimple flashing in her right cheek impossible to ignore.

When he did not reply, she said, "Fine then. But it strikes me that you're in a bind, sir." She paused, then added, "You see how diverting I can be? In a bind?"

He worked at the ropes at his wrists. Tight, but already giving. Escapable. "I see how reckless you can be."

"Some find me charming."

"I do not find things charming," he replied, continuing to manipulate the ropes, wondering what possessed him to spar with this chatterbox.

"That's a pity." It sounded like she meant it, but before he could think of what to say, she added, "No matter. Even if you won't admit it, you do need help and, as you are bound and I am your travel companion, I'm afraid you are stuck with me." She crouched by his feet, as though it were all perfectly ordinary, untying the ropes with a soft, deft touch. "You're lucky I am quite good with knots."

He grunted his approval, stretching his legs in the confined space when she set him free. "And that you have other plans for your birthday."

She hesitated, her cheeks pinkening at the words. "Yes."

Whit would never understand what made him press further. "What plans?"

Her ridiculous eyes, an impossible color and too big for her face, shuttered. "Plans that for once don't involve cleaning up whatever mess you are."

"Next time I am clubbed unconscious, I shall endeavor to do it where I shan't be in your way, my lady."

She grinned, that dimple flashing like a private jest. "See that you do." Before he could reply, she said, "Though I suppose it won't be an issue in the future. We clearly don't run in the same circles."

"We run in them tonight."

Her grin became a slow, easy smile, and Whit couldn't

help but linger on it. The carriage began to slow, and she peeked out the curtain. "We're nearly there," she said quietly. "It's time for you to go, sir. I'm sure you'll agree that neither of us will have any interest in you being discovered."

"My hands," he said, even as the ropes slackened further.

She shook her head. "I can't risk you taking revenge."

He met her gaze without hesitation. "My revenge is not a risk. It's a certainty."

"I've no doubt of that. But I can't risk you taking it through me. Not tonight." She reached past him for the door handle, speaking at his ear, above the rattle of wheels and horses from the street beyond. "As I've said . . ."

"You have plans," he finished for her, turning toward her, unable to resist her scent, like an almond teacake, sweet temptation.

She met his eyes. "Yes."

"Tell me the plan, and I'll let you go." He'd find her.

That smile again. "You're very arrogant, sir. Must I remind you that I'm the one letting *you* go?"

"Tell me." The command was rough.

He saw the change in her. Watched hesitation turn to curiosity. To bravery. And then, like a gift, she whispered, "Perhaps I should show you, instead."

Christ, *yes.*

She kissed him, pressing her lips to his, soft and sweet and inexperienced and tasting like wine, tempting as hell. He worked double time to free his hands. To show this strange, curious woman just how willing he was to see her plans through.

She freed him first. There was a tug at his wrists, and the ropes loosened a heartbeat before she lifted her lips from his. He opened his eyes, saw the gleam of a small pocket-knife in her hand. She'd changed her mind. Cut him loose.

To capture her. To resume the kiss.

As she'd warned, however, the lady had other plans.

Before he could touch her, the carriage slowed to take a corner, and she opened the door at his back. "Good-bye."

Instinct had Whit turning as he fell, tucking his chin, protecting his head, and propelling himself into a roll, even as a single thought thundered through him.

She's getting away.

He came to a stop against the wall of a nearby tavern, scattering the collection of men outside.

"Oy!" one called out, coming for him. "All right, bruv?"

Whit came to his feet, shaking out his arms, rolling his shoulders back, shifting his weight back and forth to test muscle and bone—ensuring all was in working order before extracting two watches from his pocket and checking their clockwork. *Half-nine.*

"Cor! I ain't never seen anyone right 'imself from such a thing so fast," the man said, reaching out to clap Whit on the shoulder. The hand stilled before it settled, however, as eyes set on Whit's face, immediately widening in recognition. Warmth turned to fear as the man took a step back. "*Beast.*"

Whit lifted his chin in acknowledgment of the name, even as awareness threaded through him. If this man knew him—knew his name—

He turned, his gaze narrowing on the curve in the dark cobblestone street where the carriage had disappeared, along with its passenger, deep into the maze of tangled streets that marked Covent Garden.

Satisfaction thrummed through him.

She wasn't getting away after all.

Chapter Three

"*Y*ou *pushed* him *out*?" Nora's shock was clear as she peeked inside the empty carriage after Hattie had descended. "I thought we didn't wish for his death?"

Hattie ran her fingers over the silk of the mask she'd donned before exiting the carriage. "He's not dead."

She'd hung out the door of the carriage long enough to make sure of it—long enough to marvel at the way he'd launched himself into a roll before springing to his feet, as though he were frequently dispatched from carriages.

She supposed that, since she'd discovered him bound in her carriage that very evening, he might well be tossed from conveyances regularly. She'd watched him nonetheless, holding her breath until he'd come to his feet, unharmed.

"He woke, then?" Nora asked.

Hattie nodded, her fingers coming to her lips, the feel of his firm, smooth kiss a lingering echo there, along with the taste of something . . . lemon?

"And?"

She looked to her friend. "And what?"

Nora rolled her eyes. "Who is he?"

"He didn't say."

A pause. "No, I don't suppose he would."

No. Not that I wouldn't give a great deal to know.

"You should ask Augie." Hattie's gaze shot to her friend. Had she spoken aloud? Nora grinned. "Do you forget that I know your mind as well as my own?"

Nora and Hattie had been friends for a lifetime—more than one, Nora's mother used to say, watching the two of them play beneath the table in her back garden, telling secrets. Elisabeth Madewell, Duchess of Holymoor, and Hattie's mother had existed together on the outskirts of the aristocracy. Neither had received a warm welcome, fate having intervened to make an Irish actress and a shop girl from Bristol into a duchess and countess, respectively. They'd been destined to be friends long before Hattie's father had received his life peerage, two inseparable souls who did everything together, including birth daughters—Nora and Hattie, born within weeks of each other, raised as close as sisters, never given a chance not to love one another as such.

"I'll say two things," Nora added.

"Only two?"

"All right. Two *for now*. I shall reserve the right to say more," Nora amended. "First, you'd better hope you are right and we didn't accidentally murder the man."

"We didn't," Hattie said.

"And *second* . . ." Nora continued without pause. "The next time I suggest we leave the unconscious man in the carriage and take my curricle, we take the damn curricle."

"If we'd taken the curricle, *we* might have died," Hattie scoffed. "You drive that thing far too quickly."

"I'm in complete control the whole time."

When their mothers had died within months of each other—sisters even in that—Nora had come searching for comfort she could not find with her father and older brother, men too aristocratic to allow themselves the luxury of grief. But the Sedleys, born common and now the kind of

aristocrats who weren't considered at all aristocratic, had
no such trouble. They'd made space for Nora in their home
and at their table, and it wasn't long before she was spending more nights at Sedley House than at her own, something her father and brother seemed not to notice——just as
they'd seemed not to notice when she'd begun spending her
pin money on carriages and curricles to rival those driven
by society's most ostentatious dandies.

A woman in charge of her own conveyance was a woman
in charge of her own destiny, Nora liked to say.

Hattie wasn't entirely certain of that, but she did not deny
that it paid to have a friend with a particular skill at driving, especially on nights when one did not wish coachmen
to talk——which any coachman would do if he'd deposited
two unmarried aristocratic daughters outside 72 Shelton
Street. It was no matter that 72 Shelton Street did not, at
first glance, appear to be a bordello.

Was it still called a bordello if it was for women?

Hattie supposed that did not matter, either, but the beautifully appointed building looked nothing like what she
imagined its male-serving counterparts looked like. Indeed, it looked warm and welcoming, shining like a bea-
con, windows full of golden light, planters exploding with
autumnal colors hanging on either side of the door and
above, in boxes at every sill.

It did not escape Hattie's notice that the windows were covered, however, which did seem reasonable, as the goings-on
within were surely of a private nature.

She lifted a hand and checked the seat of her mask once
more. "If we'd taken the curricle, we would have been seen."

"I suppose you're right." Nora shrugged one shoulder and
flashed Hattie a grin. "Well then, out of the carriage with
him."

Hattie chuckled. "I shouldn't have done it."

"We aren't going back to apologize," Nora said, waving a
hand at the door. "And so? Are you going in?"

Hattie took a deep breath. This was it. She turned to her friend. "Is this mad?"

"Absolutely," Nora replied.

"Nora!"

"It's mad in the best possible way. You have plans, Hattie. And this is how you get to them. Once this is done, there's no going back. And frankly, you deserve it."

Doubt whispered, barely there and heard nonetheless. "You have plans, too, but you haven't done anything like this."

A pause, and Nora shrugged. "I haven't had to." The universe had gifted Nora with wealth and privilege, and a family that didn't seem to mind if she used both to take life by the horns.

Hattie had not been so lucky. She wasn't the kind of woman who was expected to take life by the horns. But after tonight, she intended to show the world just how well she intended to do just that.

But first, she was required to do away with the one thing that held her back.

And so, she was here.

She turned to Nora. "You're certain this is—"

An approaching carriage interrupted, the clattering horses and rattling wheels thundering in her ears as it pulled to a stop. A trio of laughing women descended in beautiful silk gowns that gleamed like jewels and harlequin masks nearly identical to Hattie's. Long-necked and narrow-waisted, with wide smiles, it was easy to tell these women were beautiful.

Hattie was not beautiful.

She took a step back, pressing up against the side of the carriage.

"Well, now I'm *certain* this is the place," Nora said dryly.

Hattie looked to her friend. "But why would *they*—"

"Why would you?"

"But they could have—" *Anyone they liked.*

Nora slid her a look, a dark brow arching. "You could, too."

It wasn't true, of course. Men did not clamor after Hattie. Oh, they liked her fine. After all, she liked ships and horses and had a head for business, and she was clever enough to amuse during a dinner or a ball. But when a woman looked as she did and talked as she did, men were far more likely to clap her on the shoulder than they were to clutch her to them in passionate embrace. Good old Hattie, even when she'd been in her first season out and not old at all.

She didn't say all that, though, and Nora filled the silence. "Perhaps they, too, are looking for something . . . untethered." They watched the women rap on the door of 72 Shelton Street, a small window opening and closing before the door itself followed suit, and they had disappeared within, leaving the street silent once more. "Perhaps they, too, are looking to captain their own fates."

A nightingale cooed above them, answered almost immediately by another, at a distance.

The Year of Hattie.

She nodded. "All right, then."

Her friend grinned. "All right, then."

"You are certain you don't wish to come in?"

"And do what?" Nora asked with a laugh. "There is nothing within for me. I thought I'd take a drive—see if I can beat my time round Hyde Park."

"Two hours?"

"I shall be here." Nora tipped her coachman's cap and flashed Hattie a grin. "Enjoy yourself, milady."

That had been Hattie's plan all along, hadn't it? To enjoy herself on this, the first night of the rest of her life, when she closed the door on the past and took her future well in hand. With a nod to her friend, she approached the building, her eyes fixed on its great steel door and the tiny slot within that opened the moment she knocked, revealing a pair of darkly kohled, assessing eyes. "Password?"

"Regina."

The window closed. The door opened. And Hattie stepped inside.

It took a moment for her eyes to adjust to the dark interior of the building, a jarring enough change from the brightly lit exterior that she instinctively reached for her mask. "If you remove it, you cannot stay," came a warning from the woman who'd opened the door, tall and lithe and beautiful, with dark hair and darker eyes and the palest skin Hattie had ever seen.

She lowered her hand from the protection. "I am—"

The woman smiled. "We know who you are, my lady. There is no need for names. Your anonymity is a priority."

It occurred to Hattie that it might be the first time anyone had ever told her that she was a priority in any way. And she rather liked it. "Oh," she replied, for lack of anything else to say. "How kind."

The lady turned away, pushing through a thick curtain and into the main receiving room, the three women Hattie had seen outside pausing their chatter to study her. Hattie began to move to a nearby empty settee, but her escort stayed her, pushing through another door. "This way, my lady."

She followed. "But they arrived before me."

Another small smile on the beauty's full lips. "They do not have an appointment."

The idea that one might turn up at a place like this unannounced ran wild through Hattie. After all, such a thing would mean that one *frequented* the location—what would it be like to be the kind of woman who not only had access to such a place, but regularly took advantage of it? It would mean she had *enjoyed* it.

Excitement thrummed through her as they entered the next room, this one large and oval, richly decorated in deep red silks and gold brocade, lush blue velvets and silver platters laden with chocolates and petits fours.

Hattie's stomach growled. She hadn't eaten earlier in the day, as she'd been too nervous.

Her beautiful escort turned to face her. "Would you care for refreshments?"

"No. I'd like to get this done." Her eyes went wide. "That is—I mean to say—"

The woman smiled. "I understand. Follow me."

She did, through the labyrinthine corridors of the building, which from the outside seemed deceptively small for the expansive space within. They climbed a wide staircase, and Hattie could not resist running her fingers along the wall coverings of deep sapphire silk embossed with silver-threaded vines. The whole place dripped with luxury, and she should not have been surprised by it—she'd paid a fortune for the privilege of an appointment, after all.

At the time, she'd thought she was paying for secrecy, not extravagance. It seemed she was paying for both.

She looked to her chaperone as they reached the top of the staircase and turned down a well-lit corridor, lined with closed doors. "Are you Dahlia?"

72 Shelton Street was owned by a mysterious woman, known to the ladies of the aristocracy only as Dahlia. It was Dahlia with whom Hattie had corresponded in the lead-up to the evening. Dahlia who had asked her a handful of questions about desires and preferences—questions that Hattie had barely been able to answer for her flaming cheeks. After all, women like Hattie were rarely given the opportunity to explore desire or to have preference.

She had preference now.

The thought arrived illustrated—the man in the carriage, handsome in slumber and then . . . awake, undeniably beautiful. Those amber eyes that assessed and valued, that seemed to see straight to the core of her. The ripple of his muscles as he fought the bindings. And his kiss . . .

She'd kissed him.

What had she been thinking?

She hadn't been.

And still . . . she was grateful for the memory, for the echo of his sharp inhale when she'd pressed her lips to his, for the soft grunt that had followed, the sound pooling deep inside her, a punctuation as he gave himself to it. As he'd submitted to her desire. As he'd become her preference.

Her cheeks went hot again. She cleared her throat and looked to her escort, whose full lips were curved in a secret smile. "I am Zeva, my lady. Dahlia is not in residence this evening, but not to worry. We have prepared for you in her absence," the beauty continued. "We believe you will find everything to your liking."

Zeva opened a door, allowing Hattie to enter.

Her heart began to pound as she looked about the room. She swallowed against the knot in her throat, refusing to allow nerves to show despite what had once been a wild idea now becoming a concrete eventuality.

This was no ordinary room. It was a bedchamber.

A beautifully appointed bedchamber, with silks and satins, and a velvet counterpane in a vibrant blue that shone against the elaborately carved posts of the room's centerpiece—an ebony bed.

The fact that beds traditionally were the centerpieces of bedchambers seemed suddenly, completely irrelevant, and Hattie was certain that she'd never in her life seen a bed. Which explained why she could not stop looking at it.

It was impossible to ignore the amusement in Zeva's voice when she said, "Is there a problem, my lady?"

"No!" Hattie said, barely recognizing the squeak of the word, which came in a pitch reserved only for hounds. She cleared her throat, the bodice of her dress suddenly seeming entirely too tight. She put a hand to it. "No. No. Everything is perfect. This is all very expected. Entirely as planned." She cleared her throat again, still riveted by the bed. "Thank you."

From behind her, Zeva spoke. "Would you perhaps like a moment of peace before Nelson joins you?"

Nelson. Hattie turned to face the other woman at the name. "Nelson? Like the war hero?"

"Just. One of our very best."

"And by best you mean . . ."

Dark brows rose. "Aside from the qualities you requested, he is charming, knowledgeable, and *exceedingly* thorough."

Exceedingly thorough in bed, *she meant.*

Hattie choked on the sand that seemed to fill her throat. "I see. Well. What more can one ask?"

Zeva's lips twitched. "Why not a few moments to acquaint yourself with the room—"

With the bed, *she meant.*

She waved at a pull on the wall. "—and ring the bell when you are ready?"

Ready for bed, *she meant.*

Hattie nodded. "Yes. That sounds ideal."

Zeva floated from the room, the quiet *snick* of the door the only evidence that she'd been there at all.

Hattie let out a long breath and turned to face the empty room. Alone, she was able to take in the rest of it, the shimmering gold wallpaper, the beautifully tiled fireplace, and the large windows that would no doubt reveal the web of Covent Garden rooftops by day, but now, by night, were made mirrors in the darkness, reflecting the candlelight of the room, and Hattie at its center.

Hattie. Ready to begin her life anew.

She approached one large window, trying her best to ignore her reflection, considering instead the darkness surrounding her, limitless, like her plans. Her desires. The decision to stop waiting for her father to realize her potential, and instead to take what she wanted. To prove herself strong enough, clever enough, unfettered enough.

And perhaps just a little bit reckless.

But what was the path to success without a bit of reck-lessness?

This recklessness would take her out of the running as a wife to any decent man, and make it impossible for her father to refuse her what she truly wanted.

A business of her own. A life of her own. A future of her own.

She took a deep breath and turned to face a table nearby, laden with enough to feed an army: tea sandwiches and canapés and petits fours. A bottle of champagne and two glasses stood sentry alongside the food. She shouldn't be surprised—the survey of her preferences for the evening had been quite thorough, and she'd requested just such a spread, less because she cared for champagne and delicious food—though who didn't?—and more because it felt like the sort of thing a woman with experience would provide upon such an occasion.

And so, a table lay in wait of a pair, as though this place were a posting inn on the Great North Road, and the room set for newlyweds. Hattie smirked at the silly, romantic thought. But that was the commodity 72 Shelton Street sold, was it not? Romance, as preferred, purchased and packaged.

Champagne and petits fours and a four-poster bed.

Suddenly *very* ridiculous.

She gave a little nervous laugh. There was no way she was eating canapés or petits fours. Not without immediately casting them up from her roiling stomach. But champagne— perhaps champagne was just the thing.

She poured herself a glass and drank it down like lemon water, warmth spreading through her faster than she'd ex-pected. Warmth and just enough courage to propel her across the room to pull the bell. To summon Nelson. Exceedingly-thorough-like-the-war-hero Nelson.

She supposed there were worse names for the man who would rid her of her virginity.

Hattie pulled the bell—silent in the room, but ringing in

some faraway place in the mysterious building, where Hattie imagined a passel of handsome men waited to provide exceeding thoroughness, like horses at a racing start. She grinned at the wild image, at faceless Nelson—wearing a full uniform and an admiral's hat for lack of more creative imagining—leaping to movement at the sound, running toward her, long legs taking stairs two, perhaps three at a time, huffing his breath in the race to get to her.

How should she be arranged when he got here? Should she be at the window? Would he want to see her standing up? To assess the situation? She wasn't wild about that thought.

Which left a chair by the fireplace, or the bed.

She highly doubted he'd wish to converse with her. Indeed, she was not certain that she was interested in being conversed with. This was a means to an end, after all.

So. The bed it was.

Should she lie down? That seemed rather forward, though, truthfully, she'd likely passed forward somewhere between seeking out 72 Shelton Street months ago and hitching the carriage that evening. She'd fully lost sight of forward while kissing a man in her carriage.

And for a wild moment, it wasn't a faceless admiral who raced toward her. It was a different kind of man entirely. Beautifully faced. With perfect features and amber eyes and dark brows and lips that were softer than she'd ever imagined lips could be.

She cleared her throat and pushed the thought away, returning to the question at hand. Lying down felt wrong, as did sitting, ankles crossed, on this bed. Perhaps there was a middle ground? A seductive lean of some kind?

Ugh. Hattie had never been seductive in her life.

She perched on the most dimly lit corner of the bed and leaned back, wrapping an arm about the post to keep herself steady, pressing herself to it, willing herself to look like the kind of woman who did this sort of thing all the

time. A seductress who knew her desires and her preferences. Someone who understood phrases like *exceedingly
thorough*.

And then the door was opening and her heart was
pounding, and a great shadowed figure was entering, and
he wasn't wearing an admiral's hat or a uniform. Or anything remotely dapper. He was wearing black. An immense
amount of black.

He was inside then, and the light cast his perfect face in
a warm, golden glow.

Her heart stopped and she straightened, overcompensat-
ing for her shifting position, nearly tossing herself straight
off the bed.

He moved with singular grace, as though he hadn't been
unconscious in her carriage an hour earlier. As though she
hadn't dispatched him from it. Her gaze traced over him,
checking for scrapes and bruises, for aches and pains from
his fall. Nothing.

She swallowed, grateful for the low light. "You're not
Nelson."

He did not reply. The door closed behind him.

And they were alone.

Chapter Four

She should have been a needle in a haystack.

She should have disappeared.

She should have been one of a thousand women, in a thousand carriages, scurrying like scorpions through the darker corners of London, unseen by the ordinary men of the world beyond.

And she would have been just that, except Whit wasn't an ordinary man. He was a Bareknuckle Bastard—a king of London's shadows, with scores of spies posted in the darkness—and nothing happened on his turf without him knowing it. It was laughably easy for his wide-reaching network of lookouts to find the single black carriage headed into the night.

They'd been following it before he took to the rooftops. They had its location as quickly as they'd had the information they'd known he'd want. The shipment he'd been driving was gone, the outriders who had been attacked were alive, and their attackers were disappeared. Unidentified.

But not for long.

The woman would lead him to the enemy—an enemy

for whom the Bareknuckle Bastards had been searching for
months.

If Whit was correct, an enemy they had known for years.

It didn't hurt that his boys were always watching the en-
trances to the brothel. A brother protected a sister, after
all—even when the sister in question was powerful enough
to bring a city to its knees. Even when the sister was in hiding from the one thing that could strip her of that power.

Whit had easily found his way into the building and past
Zeva, pausing only long enough to discover the location of
the woman she would not name. He'd known she wouldn't.
72 Shelton only succeeded because of uncompromising discretion, and secrets were kept from everyone—Bareknuckle
Bastards included.

Because of that, he did not press Zeva. Instead, he pushed
past her, ignoring the way her dark brows rose in silent surprise. Silent for the moment; Zeva was the best of lieutenants, and kept secrets from all but her employer. And when
Grace—known to all London as Dahlia—returned to her
rightful post as mistress of this place, she'd know what happened. And she wouldn't hesitate to come asking about it.

There was no relentless curiosity like that of a sister.

But for now, there was no Grace to pester him. There was
only the mysterious woman from the carriage, full of information, the final piece to the clockwork he'd been waiting
to set in motion. The spring, waiting to be wound. She had
the names of the men who had fired on his shipment. Fired
on his boys. The names of the men who were thieving from
the Bastards.

The names of the men who were working with his es-
tranged brother. His enemy. And here she was, in a building belonging to his sister, on the land that belonged to
Whit himself.

Waiting for a man to pleasure her.

He ignored the thrum of excitement that coursed through

him at the thought, and the thread of irritation that followed. She was business, not pleasure.

It was time to get business done.

He saw her the moment he entered, his eyes finding her perched on the edge of the bed, clutching a bedpost in the darkness. As he let the door close behind him, he was consumed by a singular thought: Sitting here, in one of the most extravagant brothels in the city—one designed for women of discerning taste and promising the utmost discretion—the woman could not have looked more out of place.

She should have looked completely at home, considering she had poked him awake, carried on a full conversation with him as though it were entirely ordinary, and then pushed him from a moving carriage.

After kissing him.

The fact that she'd been headed here had seemed fully in keeping with the rest of her wild night.

But something was off.

It wasn't the dress, luxurious silken skirts exploding from the darkness in wild, turquoise waves that suggested a modiste of superior skill. It wasn't the matching slippers, toes peeking out from beneath the hem.

It wasn't the way the bodice glistened in the darkness, hugging the curve of her torso and showcasing the lovely swell above it—no, that bit was perfect for Shelton Street.

It wasn't even the shadow of her face—barely recognizable in the darkness, but just visible enough to reveal her mouth gaping in surprise. Another man might find that open mouth ridiculous, but Whit knew better. He knew how it tasted. How those full lips softened and yielded. And there was nothing remotely out of place about that.

72 Shelton Street was more than welcoming of full bodies and full lips and women who knew how to use them.

But this woman didn't know how to use them. She was stiff as stone, clinging to the bedpost with one white-knuckled hand and to an empty champagne flute with the

other, holding herself at an odd angle, looking altogether
out of place.

Even more so when she straightened impossibly further
and said, "I beg your pardon, sir. I am waiting for someone."

"Mmm." He leaned back against the door, crossing his
arms over his chest, wishing she weren't in shadow. "Nelson."

She nodded, the movement like jerking clockwork. "Quite.
And as you are not him—"

"How do you know that?"

Silence. Whit resisted the urge to smile. He could nearly
hear her panic. She was about to back down, which would
put him in the position of power. She'd give up the information he wished in minutes, like a babe to sweets.

Except, she said, "You do not match my list of qualifications."

What in hell? Qualifications?

Somehow, miraculously, he avoided asking the question
outright. The chatterbox provided additional information
nonetheless. "I specifically requested someone less . . ."

She trailed off, and Whit found himself willing to do
nearly anything to have that sentence finished. When she
waved a hand in his direction, he couldn't stop himself.
"Less . . . ?"

She scowled. "Precisely. Less."

Something suspiciously like pride burst in his chest, and
Whit pushed it away, letting silence fall.

"You're not less," she said. "You're more. You're *much*.
Which is why I tossed you from the carriage earlier—I
apologize for that, by the way. I hope you were not too
bruised in the tumble."

He ignored the last. "Much what?"

That hand wave again. "Much everything." She reached
into the voluminous fabric of her skirts and extracted a
piece of paper, consulting it. "Medium height. Medium

build." She looked up, assessing him frankly. "You are neither of those."

She didn't have to sound disappointed about it. What else was on the paper?

"I did not realize how large you were when we met earlier."

"Is that what we are calling it? A meeting?"

She tilted her head in consideration. "Have you a better term?"

"An attack."

Her eyes went wide behind her mask and she came to her feet, revealing a height he had not imagined in the carriage. "I didn't attack you!"

She was wrong, of course. Everything about her was an assault, from her lush curves to the brightness of her eyes to the shimmer of her gown to the scent of almonds on her—as though she'd just come from a kitchen full of cakes.

The woman had felt like an attack from the moment he'd opened his eyes in that carriage and found her there, talking up a storm about birthdays and plans and the Year of Hattie.

"Hattie." He hadn't meant to say it. Definitely hadn't meant to *enjoy* saying it.

Her eyes went impossibly larger behind the mask. "How did you know my name?" she asked, coming to her feet, panic and outrage pouring from her. "I thought this place was the height of discretion?"

"What is the Year of Hattie?"

Realization flashed, memory of revealing her name earlier. A pause, and then she said, "Why do you care?"

He wasn't sure of the answer, so he did not offer it.

She filled the silence, as he was discovering she was wont to do. "I suppose you're not going to tell me your name? I know it's not Nelson."

"Because I'm too much to be Nelson."

"Because you do not match my qualifications. You are

altogether too broad in the shoulder and too long in the leg and *not* charming, and *certainly* not *at all* affable."

"You've made a list of qualifications for a hound, not a fuck."

She did not take the bait. "And all that before we even consider your *face*."

What the hell was wrong with his face? In thirty-one years, he'd never had a complaint, and this wild woman was going to change that? "My face."

"Quite," she said, the word coming like a speeding carriage. "I requested a face that wasn't so . . ."

Whit hung on the pause. *Now* the woman decided to stop talking?

She shook her head and he resisted the urge to curse. "Never mind. The point is, I didn't request you and I didn't *attack* you. I had nothing to do with you turning up unconscious in my carriage. Though, to be honest, you are beginning to strike me as the kind of man who might well deserve a whack to the head."

"I don't believe you were a part of the assault."

"Good. Because I wasn't."

"Who was?"

Beat. "I don't know."

Lie.

She was protecting someone. The carriage belonged to someone she trusted, or she wouldn't have used it to bring her here. *Father?* No. Impossible. Even this madwoman wouldn't use her father's coachman to ferry her to a brothel in the middle of Covent Garden. Coachmen talked.

Lover? For a fleeting moment he considered the possibility that she was not simply working with his enemy, but sleeping with him. Whit didn't like the distaste that came with the idea before reason arrived.

No. Not a lover. She wouldn't be in a brothel if she had a lover. She wouldn't have kissed Whit if she had a lover.

And she had kissed him, soft and sweet and inexperienced.

There was no lover.

But still, she was loyal to the enemy.

"I think you do know who tied me up in that carriage, Hattie," he said softly, approaching her, a thrum of awareness coursing through him as he realized she was nearly his height, her chest rising and falling in staccato rhythm above the line of her dress, the muscles of her throat working as she listened. "And I think you know I intend to have a name."

Her eyes narrowed on him in the dim light. "Is that a threat?" He didn't reply, and in the silence, she seemed to calm, her breath evening out as her shoulders straightened. "I don't take kindly to threats. This is the second time you have interrupted my evening, sir. You would do well to remember that it was I who saved your hide earlier."

The change in her was remarkable. "You nearly killed me."

She scoffed. "Please. You were perfectly agile. I saw you tumble your way from the carriage like it wasn't the first time you'd been tossed from one." She paused. "It wasn't, was it?"

"That doesn't mean I am looking to make a habit of it."

"The point is, without me, you could be dead in a ditch. A reasonable gentleman would thank me kindly and take himself elsewhere at this point."

"You are unlucky, then, that I am not that."

"Reasonable?"

"A gentleman."

She gave a little surprised chuckle at that. "Well, as we are currently in a brothel, I think neither of us can claim much gentility."

"That wasn't on your list of qualifications?"

"Oh, it was," she said, "But I expected more the approximation of gentility rather than the actuality of it. But there's the rub; I have plans, approximations be damned, and I'm not letting you ruin them."

"The plans you spoke of before tossing me out of a carriage."

"I didn't toss you." When he didn't reply, she said, "All right, I tossed you. But you fared perfectly well."

"No thanks to you."

"I don't have the information you want."

"I don't believe you."

She opened her mouth. Closed it. "How very rude."

"Take your mask off."

"No."

His lips twitched at the unyielding reply. "What is the Year of Hattie?"

She lifted her chin in defiance, but stayed silent. Whit gave a little grunt and moved across the room to the champagne, returning to fill her glass. When the task was done, he returned the bottle to its place and leaned back against the windowsill, watching her fidget.

She was always in motion, smoothing skirts or playing at her sleeve—he drank in the long line of the dress, the way it wrapped her unruly curves and made promises that a man wished she would keep. The candlelight teased over her skin, gilding her. This was not a woman who took tea. This was a woman who took the sun.

She had money, clearly. And power. A woman required both in spades for entry to 72 Shelton—even knowing the place existed required a network that did not come easily. There were a thousand reasons why she might wish access, and Whit had heard them all. Boredom, dissatisfaction, recklessness. But he couldn't see any of those in Hattie. She wasn't an impetuous girl—she was old enough to know her mind and to make her choices. Nor was she plain, or a dilettante.

He moved toward her. Slowly. Deliberately.

She stiffened. Her grip tightened on the paper in her hand. "I shan't be intimidated."

"He stole from me, and I wish it back."

But that wasn't everything.

He was close enough to touch her. Close enough to measure the height he'd noticed in her before, nearly equal to his own. Close enough to see her eyes, dark behind the mask, fixed on him. Close enough to be cloaked in almonds.

"Whatever it is." She pushed her shoulders back. "I shall see it returned."

Four shipments. Three outriders with bullets in them. After tonight, Whit's own throwing knives, which he prized above all else. And, if he was right, more than could ever be repaid.

He shook his head. "It's not possible. I require a name."

She stiffened at the doubt. "I beg your pardon; I do not fail."

Another man might have found the words amusing. But Whit heard the honesty in them. How was she involved in this mess? He couldn't resist repeating himself. "What is the Year of Hattie?"

"If I tell you, will you leave me alone?"

No. He didn't say it.

She took a deep breath in the silence, seeming to consider her options. And then, "It is what it sounds like. It is my year. The year I claim for myself."

"How?"

"I've a four-point plan to captain my own fate."

His brows rose. "Four points."

She lifted a hand, ticking the answers off on her long, gloved fingers. "Business. Home. Fortune. Future." She paused. "Now, if you would tell me what precisely was removed from your possession, I will see it returned, and we can go about our lives without bothering one another ever again."

"Business. Home. Fortune. Future." He tested the plan. "In that order?"

She tilted her head. "Likely."

"What kind of business?" Whit had money to spare and could aid her in whatever business she wished . . . for the information he required.

Her gaze narrowed, and she remained silent. She likely had aspirations as a dressmaker or a milliner, both of which would buy her a home, but neither of which would earn her a fortune. But wouldn't this woman be better suited to a future as a wife and mother on some country estate?

That, and not one of her four points made sense in the context of the Shelton Street brothel. He pointed to the paper clutched in her fist. "What were you hoping for from Nelson, investment?"

She huffed a little laugh at the question. "Of a sort."

Whit narrowed his gaze. "What sort?"

"There's a fifth point," she said.

A clock chimed in the hallway beyond, loud and low, and Whit extracted his watches without thinking, checking the time on both before returning them. "And what is that?"

Her gaze followed his movements. "Do you have the time?"

He did not miss the teasing in the question. "Eleven."

"On both watches?"

"The fifth point?"

A wash of red flashed over her cheeks at the question, and Whit's curiosity about this strange woman became almost unbearable. And then she said, clear as the clock in the hallway beyond, "Body."

When Whit was seventeen, he'd come out of the ring reeling from a bout that had gone too long with an opponent who was too big, the roar of the crowd stuck in his ears for the heavy blows he'd endured. He'd landed in the rear alleyway of a warehouse, where he'd sucked cold air into his lungs and imagined himself anywhere but there, in a Covent Garden fight club.

The door behind him had opened and closed, and a woman had approached, a length of linen in hand. She'd offered to clean the blood from his face. Her soft words and kind touch marked the most pleasure he'd ever felt in his life.

Until the moment he heard Hattie speak the word *body*.

In the silence that stretched between them, she gave a little nervous laugh. "I suppose it's more of a first point, considering it is essential to the rest of the points."

Body.

"Explain." The word came on a growl.

She appeared to consider the possibility of not explaining, as though he would allow her to leave this place without doing so. She must have realized it, because finally, she said, "There are two reasons."

He waited.

"Some women spend their whole lives searching for marriage."

"And you do not?"

She shook her head. "Perhaps at one point I would have welcomed . . ." She trailed off, and Whit held his breath, waiting for her next words. She shrugged a shoulder. "Tomorrow, I am twenty-nine. At this point, I'm a dowry and nothing more."

Whit did not for a moment believe that.

"I don't wish to be a dowry." She looked to him. "I do not wish to be commodified. I wish to be mine. To choose for myself."

"Business. Home. Fortune. Future," he said.

She smiled, wide and winning, that damn dimple flashing, and he could not resist lingering on those lips, the feel of which he keenly remembered from earlier in the evening. They moved again. "There is only one way to ensure that I am allowed to choose for myself." She paused. "I do away with the only thing about me that is prized. I claim myself. And I win."

"And you came here to . . ." He trailed off, knowing the answer. Wanting her to say it.

Wanting to hear it.

That blush again. Then, magnificently, "To take my virginity."

The words rang in his ears.

And somehow this woman *laughed.* "Well, I can't take my own virginity, obviously. It's more a metaphor. Nelson was to do the deed."

He let silence reign for a moment while he collected a riot of thoughts. "You relieve yourself of your virginity and you become free to live your life."

"Precisely!" she said, as though she was delighted that someone understood.

He grunted. "And what's the second reason?"

The red wash again. Who was this woman, somehow both bold and also blushing? "I suppose—" She stopped. Cleared her throat. "I suppose I want it."

Christ.

She could have said a thousand things he would have expected. Things that would have kept him quiet, unmoved. And instead, she said something so fucking honest, he had no choice but to be moved.

But to move.

He stopped it before it began, holding back his desire, sliding the hand that reached for her into his pocket and extracting the paper sack there, fetching a candy from within. He popped the sweet into his mouth, lemon and honey exploding over his tongue.

Anything to distract him from her words.

I want it.

Hattie squinted at the pouch. "Are those—sweets?"

He looked down at them. Grunted his acknowledgment.

She tilted her head. "You shouldn't partake in treats if you are not willing to share, you know."

Another grunt. He extended the sack toward her.

"No, thank you," she said with a smile.

"Then why ask for one?"

Another grin. "I didn't ask for one. I asked to be *offered* one. Which is a different thing altogether."

She was incredibly frustrating. And fascinating. But he didn't have time to be fascinated by her.

He returned the candy to his pocket, trying to focus on the lemon, a tart, sweet pleasure—one of the few he allowed himself. Trying to ignore the fact that it was not lemon he desired in that moment.

Trying not to think about almonds.

He required the woman's knowledge. And that was it. She knew who was attacking his men. Who was stealing his cargo. She could confirm the identity of his enemy. And he would do what he must to get her to do just that.

"You're not going to tell me I'm wrong?" she asked.

"Wrong about what?"

"Wrong to want . . ." She trailed off for a moment, and a thread of cold fear went through Whit as he considered the possibility that she might say *it* again. When this woman said *it*, a man wanted to fill the space between those two minuscule letters with a score of filthy things. ". . . to explore."

Good Christ. That was worse.

"I'm not going to tell you you are wrong."

"Why not?"

He had no idea why he said it. He shouldn't have said it. He should have left her there in that room and followed her home and waited for her to reveal what she knew. For there was no way this woman kept secrets well. She was far too honest. Honest enough to be trouble.

But he said it nonetheless. "Because you should explore. You should explore every inch of yourself and every inch of your pleasure and set your course for your future." Her lips fell open as he closed the space between them, speaking a longer string of words than he'd offered another in an age. In a lifetime.

He reached for her. Lifting his hands slowly, letting her

see him coming. Giving her time to stop him. When she
didn't, he removed her mask, revealing her wide, kohl-
darkened eyes. "But you should not hire Nelson."

What was he doing?

It was the only option.

Lie.

She caught the mask in her free hand, lowering it between them. Fiddling with it, her fingers brushing against
him. Singeing him. "It will be difficult to find another man
to assist me without repercussions."

"I assure you it won't," he said, leaning in, lowering his
voice.

She swallowed. "You intend to find me such a man?"

"No."

Her brows shot together and he ran his thumb over the
furrow there. Once, twice, until it smoothed. He traced
the lines of her face, the sweep of her cheekbones, the soft
curve of her jaw. Her plump lower lip, as soft as he remembered.

"I intend to be him."

Chapter Five

As she'd come to 72 Shelton Street with the intention of ruination, Hattie really should have considered the possibility that the business of virginity losing might be pleasurable.

She'd never thought of it in such a way. Indeed, she'd thought it would be a perfunctory business. A ticking-the-boxes kind of business. The kind of business that was a means to an end.

But when this man touched her—mysterious and handsome and unsettling and more welcome than she'd like to admit—she was unable to think of anything but the means.

The very pleasurable means.

Very pleasurable means that took hold of her when he suggested that he be the one to assist her in losing her virginity.

But the combination of his low growl and the slow sweep of his thumb over her lower lip made Hattie think that he might do more than that. Think that he might burn her down. Think that she might allow it, incineration be damned.

And then it made Hattie think very little but *yes*.

She'd arrived earlier in the night to the promise that she would be met by an *exceedingly thorough* man who would prove a stellar assistant. But this man, with his amber eyes that saw everything, with his touch that understood everything, with his voice that filled her dark, secret corners, was more than an assistant.

This man was dominion—the kind that Hattie hadn't imagined but now couldn't *not* imagine.

And he was offering to make everything she imagined real.

Yes.

He was so close. Impossibly large—large enough to make Hattie feel small—and impossibly handsome—handsome enough to have given her pause on another, less heady night—and impossibly warm in the cold room.

And impossibly, he was going to kiss her.

Not because she was paying him; because he wanted to.

Impossible.

No one had ever . . .

The slide of his hand into her hair pushed the thought aside before it finished. "You will—"

Silence.

"—assist me—"

His fingers tightened.

"—with . . ." He held her hostage with his touch and his silence. He was making her finish the thought, dammit. The sentence. *What was the thought?* ". . . it?"

He met the word with a growl, a rumble of sound that she wouldn't have understood if she weren't so rapt. If she weren't so eager for it. "All of it."

Her eyes slid closed. How was it that a man could turn so few words into such pleasure? He was surely going to kiss her. That was how it began, wasn't it? But he wasn't moving. Why wasn't he moving? He was supposed to move, wasn't he?

She opened her eyes again, finding him there, so close,

watching her. Looking at her. Seeing *her*. When was the last time someone had seen Hattie? She'd spent a lifetime becoming so good at hiding, she'd never be seen.

But this man—he saw her.

And she found she hated it as much as she liked it.

No. She hated it more. She didn't want him seeing her. Didn't want him cataloguing her myriad flaws. Her full cheeks and too wide brow and too big nose. Her mouth, which another man had once described as horsey, as though he were doing her a favor. If this man saw all that, he might change his mind.

And that made her brazen enough to say, "Can we begin now?"

A low rumble of assent heralded his kiss, the sound as glorious as the touch when he settled his lips to hers and gave her precisely what she wanted. More than it. She shouldn't have been surprised by the feel of him against her—she'd kissed him quite boldly in the carriage before tossing him out—but that had been *her* caress.

This one was *theirs*.

He pulled her to him, tilting, tipping until they were perfectly matched, until his beautiful mouth was aligned with hers. And then his second hand came to match the first, to cradle her face, thumb stroking over her cheek as he took her mouth in little, sipping kisses, one after the other, again and again, until she thought she might go mad from the tease of them. Until he captured her bottom lip and licked, his tongue warm and rough and tasting like lemon sugar and making her . . .

Hungry.

That was what it felt like. As though she'd never eaten before and now here was food, rich and welcome and all for her.

Those licks made her wild. She didn't know how to suffer them. How to manage them. All she knew was that she did not want them to stop.

She took him in hand, gripping his coat and pulling him closer, pressing herself to him, wanting his touch against every inch of her. Wanting to crawl inside him. She gave a little sigh of frustration, and he understood, his arms coming around her like steel, lifting her, forcing her to give herself up to him, her hands sliding over his massive shoulders and around his neck, the muscles of it all corded restraint and *so warm*.

She gasped at the heat of him, and he pulled back. Was he stopping? Why was he stopping? "No!"

Good God, had she said that aloud?

"I—" Her cheeks were instantly aflame. "That is—"

A brow rose in silent query.

"I would prefer—"

And then this silent beast of a man said, "I know what you would prefer. And I shall give it to you. But first—"

She caught her breath. First, *what*?

He reached for her hand, clutching his shoulder, an embodiment of the fear that he might stop before they'd had a chance to start. He pulled it away, forcing her to let him go, but not loosening his hold on her.

What was he doing? He turned her wrist over in his grasp, and set his fingers to the line of buttons along the inside of her arm. She watched for a moment. "You're very adept at buttons."

A grunt as he worked.

"You don't even have a button hook," she said inanely, wishing she could take the words back before they'd even left her silly mouth.

He removed the glove from her hand, revealing her wrist, covered in ink stains from her afternoon at the offices, poring over lading books. She twisted the limb to hide the unsightly marks, but he wouldn't let her. Instead, he studied them for a moment, his thumb stroking over the stains like flame before he returned her hand to his shoulder. Her now-bare fingers reached for the place where his collar met the warm skin of his neck, desperate for honest touch, and he released a rumble of pleasure when skin pressed skin. The ink was forgotten.

"First that," he said.

Someone else must have replied, because surely it was not Hattie who slid her fingers into his curling black hair, pulled him toward her, and said, "And now you'll give me what I want?"

But it was Hattie who received it, his kiss claiming her as one hand lowered to pull her tight against him, to lift her thigh over his hip, to press her against the thick ebony bedpost at her back.

His tongue stroked, entered, and she met him eagerly, matching his movements with her own, learning him. Learning this. She must have done well, because he growled again—the sound of her pure triumph—and he pressed into her, rough and perfect at the juncture of her thighs, drawing her attention to the ache there, an ache she felt certain he could cure. If only he'd—

He tore his mouth from hers with a curse—a word that seared through her, making her feel wicked and wonderful and immensely powerful. A word that didn't make her want to stop what she was doing. And so she didn't, lifting her hips to his again, increasing the pressure, willing skirts gone.

His thumb pressed against her chin, lifting it high as he met her thrusts and set his lips to the soft skin there, nipping along the underside of her jaw to her ear, where he whispered, "Here?"

Yes.

He moved down the column of her neck. A glorious slide. A delicious suck. "Mmm. Here?"

Yes.

"More?"

More. She pressed against him. Was that her whine?

"Poor love," he rumbled. He lifted her higher, her feet

coming off the floor. How was he strong enough? She didn't care. He was at the edge of her dress, the fabric too tight. Too constraining. Too limiting. "This looks uncomfortable." He ran his tongue over the hot, full rise of her breasts, making them impossibly hotter. Impossibly fuller. She gasped for breath.

Not-Hattie spoke again. "Do it."

He did not hesitate to obey, setting her to the high edge of the bed, his powerful fingers coming to the edge of the bodice. Her eyes opened and she looked down, his strong hands against the gleaming silk.

Sanity returned. He surely wasn't strong enough to—

The dress ripped like paper beneath his touch, cold air chasing her shock and then—

Fire.

Lips. Tongue.

Pleasure.

And she couldn't stop watching. She'd never seen anything like it. The most beautiful man she'd ever seen, entirely at her pleasure. The breath left her lungs as she watched, uncertain of what she loved best—the sight of him or the feel of him . . .

The sight of her hands in his hair, holding him to her.

The feel of them guiding him to her pleasure.

The sound of his assent, of his *desire.*

It was beyond anything she'd ever imagined. This man was beyond anything she'd ever imagined. At the thought, she dragged him up again, her fingers thrusting into his hair, pulling him to her until they kissed again. This time, though, it was *she* who licked over his full lips. It was *he* who opened to her. *She* who plundered. *He* who submitted.

And it was *glorious.*

His hands came to her breasts, his thumbs worrying the hard tips of them, stroking, pinching, until she gasped and writhed against him, lost to him.

And she didn't even know his name.

The thought was ice.

She didn't even know his name.

"*Wait.*" She pushed back from him, instantly regretting the decision when he released her without hesitation, his touch disappearing as though it had never been there to begin with. He stepped back.

She pulled her bodice closed over her protesting breasts and crossed her arms, her hunger returning with a great, yawning ache everywhere they'd touched. Her lips began to tingle, his kiss a phantom there. She licked them, and his amber gaze fell to her mouth.

He looked hungry, too, as he watched the words spill from her. "I don't know your name."

For once, he didn't hesitate. "Beast."

She misheard. Surely. "I beg your pardon?"

"They call me Beast."

She shook her head. "That's"—she searched for the word—"ludicrous."

"Why?"

"Because . . . you're the most beautiful man I've ever seen." She paused. Then, "You're the most beautiful man *anyone's* ever seen. Empirically."

His brows rose and he raised a hand, running it through his hair and over the back of his head in something like— was it possible it was *embarrassment*? "It's rare that people point it out."

"That's because it's obvious. Like heat. Or rain. But I assume people point it out whenever they call you by that absurd moniker. I imagine it is meant to be ironic."

"It's not," he said, lowering his hand.

She blinked. "I don't understand."

"You will."

The promise sent a thread of unease through her. "I will?"

He reached for her again, cupping her cheek in his palm, making her want to turn into the heat of him. "Those who steal from me. Who threaten what is mine. They see the truth of it."

Her heart began to pound. He meant Augie.

This was not a man who punished in half measures.

When he came for her brother, he would hold no quarter.

Her brother was a proper imbecile, but she didn't want him ruined. Or worse. No, whatever Augie had done, whatever he'd stolen, Hattie would return it. And that's when she realized—the kiss they'd just shared—the offer he'd made her—it hadn't been because he wished it.

It had been because he'd wished for revenge.

It hadn't been for her.

Of course it hadn't.

After all, this man, with his controlled passion and his silent assessment, was not the kind of man who came for Henrietta Sedley, pudgy spinster with ink stains on her wrists.

Not unless she could deliver him something.

This man might not wish a dowry, but he wished something, nonetheless.

She ignored the pang of sadness that came at the understanding—pretended not to notice the sting at the backs of her eyes or the hint of unwelcome emotion in her throat. Crossing her arms more tightly over her chest, she moved past him to where she had discarded her shawl earlier.

Once she was wrapped in the rich turquoise fabric, she turned back to him. His gaze flickered to the place where the wrap covered her ripped bodice, the tear she'd demanded he put there.

She inhaled. If she could make one demand, she could make another. "It strikes me, sir, that you might be in the market for a trade."

One black brow rose in curiosity.

"I shan't deny that I know who had a hand in your . . .

predicament . . . this evening. We are both too intelligent to play at silly games."

He grunted his affirmation.

"I shall fetch what you have lost. I shall return it to you. For a price."

He watched her for a long moment. "Your virginity."

She nodded. "You want retribution; I want a future. Two hours ago, I was prepared for a transaction of sorts, so why not now?" When he did not reply, she lifted her chin, refusing to let him see her disappointment. "There's no need for you to pretend you wished to do it out of the goodness of your heart. I am no starry-eyed miss. I've eyes and a looking glass."

She had been for a moment, though. He'd almost tricked her into playing such a part.

"And you are no shining-armored knight, eager to court me." Silence. Damn silence. "Are you?"

He leaned against the bedpost and crossed his arms. "I am not."

The man could have at least *pretended*.

No.

She didn't want pretend. She preferred honesty.

"And so?"

He watched her for a long moment, those infernal all-seeing eyes refusing to release her. "Who are you?"

She gave him a little shrug. "Hattie."

"Do you have a surname?"

She wasn't going to tell it to him. "We all have surnames."

"Mmm." He paused, then said, "So, you offer the name of my enemy—though not your own—in exchange for a fuck."

"If you think to shock me with your language, it won't work." She waved away the word. "I grew up on the docks." She'd played in the rigging of her father's ships.

He narrowed his gaze on her. "You're not from the gutter."

"Are you?" *Who are you?* She wasn't surprised he didn't

reply. "No matter. The point is that I cut my teeth on the foul language of sailors and dockworkers, so I'm unshockable." She pulled the shawl tight around her and considered this man, whom she'd found tied up in her carriage, who thought her brother an enemy, and who called himself Beast. Unironically.

She should walk away. End this night before it went further. Return another time and resume the Year of Hattie with another man.

But she did not wish another man—not after this one had kissed her so well.

"I won't give you a name. But I shall return whatever you've lost." She would go home, sort out Augie's part in this play, fetch whatever it was that had been taken from this man, and return it.

"That's likely for the best."

Relief flared, then uncertainty. "Why?"

"If you give me the name, you shall take responsibility when I destroy him."

Her heart pounded at the words. Destroying Augie was destroying her father's business. *Destroying* her *business*.

She should end this now. Never see this man again. She ignored the disappointment that flared at the idea. "If you've no interest in my offer, then you should leave. I've an appointment." Perhaps she could salvage the evening.

Not that she wished for Nelson any longer.

It did not matter. *A means to an end.*

A muscle ticked in his perfect, square jaw. "No."

"What then?"

"You are in no position to make me an offer." He reached for her once more, his long, warm fingers sliding over the nape of her neck, pulling her off balance just enough for her to put her hands to his chest for stability. "I get all of it."

He caught her inhale with his lips, a firm, hot slide of pleasure. He broke the kiss.

"What is mine," he growled.

Whatever her brother had stolen. "Yes." She met his lips again. Sighed as his tongue found hers in a long, slow slide.

He pulled back. "What is yours."

Her virginity. "Yes," she whispered, coming up on her toes for another kiss.

He resisted a hairsbreadth from her. "And the name."

Never. That would bring him too close to everything that mattered to Hattie. She shook her head. "No."

One dark brow rose. "I don't lose, love."

She smiled, sliding her hands into his hair and pulling him toward her, kissing him deep. She was enjoying herself immensely. "Need I remind you that I pushed you from a moving carriage earlier? I don't lose, either."

She wasn't certain if she felt or heard the low rumble in his chest. Nor was she certain it was laughter, but she wanted it to be as he lifted her high in the air and turned for the bed once more. *To make good on their deal.* He set her down on the mattress and leaned over her to steal her lips again, and she could not contain her sigh of pleasure before he released her and kissed over her cheek to her ear, where he whispered, "Need I remind *you* that I found you?" He grazed her ear with his teeth, and she sucked in a breath. "A needle in a Covent Garden haystack."

"Hardly a needle." She stuck out like a sore thumb. Always had.

He ignored her. "Waiting for a man who met your . . . what did you call them? Qualifications?"

Her qualifications had changed. Not that he would ever know that. She turned her head, her gaze meeting his, full of fire. "I am told he is exceedingly thorough."

"Mmm," he said, before he added, "I found you first."

"Then we shall call it even." She barely recognized her breathless words.

"Mmm." He kissed her then, deep and thorough, his hands moving to the shawl that covered her destroyed dress, and she held her breath, knowing what was to come. More kissing. More touching. And all the rest. *Everything*.

But before he could undo the knot that hid her from him, a knock came, clear and firm at the door.

They froze.

The door opened barely—not even enough for a head to poke through. Just enough for words to carry in. "My lady, your carriage has returned."

Dammit. Nora. Had it already been two hours?

"I must go." She pushed at his shoulders.

He moved instantly, stepping back from her, giving her the space for which she had asked and did not want. He extracted the watches from his pocket and checked them both with such graceful speed that Hattie wondered if he even knew he'd done it. "Somewhere to be?"

"Home."

"That was quick," he said.

"I was not expecting such scintillating conversation." She paused, then added, "Though conversation is not a thing one gets often with you, is it?" After a long moment of silence, she smiled, unable to stop herself. "Precisely."

She crossed the room, collected her cloak, and turned back to him. "How will I find you? To—" *Collect*. She nearly said *collect*. Her cheeks blazed.

One side of his beautiful mouth twitched, the corner barely rising before it fell. But he knew what she had been thinking, without question. And then he said, "I shall find *you*."

It was impossible. He'd never find her in Mayfair. But she could return to the Garden. *Would*. They'd made promises, after all, and Hattie intended for them to be kept.

But she didn't have time to point all that out. Nora was below, with the carriage, and Covent Garden was no place for nighttime lingering. Augie would know how to find him. She let her smile turn full grin. "Another challenge, then?"

Something like surprise flashed in his eyes, chased away

by something else—admiration? She turned away from him and set her hand to the door handle, pleasure thrumming through her. Pleasure and excitement and—

She turned back. "I'm sorry I tossed you from a carriage."

His response was instantaneous. "I'm not."

The smile remained on her lips as she wove her way through the darkened hallways of 72 Shelton Street, the place where she had intended to start anew. To claim herself and the world that was rightfully hers.

And perhaps she had done. Though not quite the way she had expected.

Something whispered through her. Something that hinted at freedom.

Hattie exited the building to find Nora leaning against the coach, cap low on her brow, hands deep in her trouser pockets. White teeth flashed as Hattie approached.

"How was your time?" Hattie beat her friend to the start.

Nora shrugged. "Found a toff to race and lightened his pockets."

Hattie shook her head with a little laugh. "You know you're a toff, too, don't you?"

Her friend feigned shock. "You take that back." When Hattie laughed, Nora tilted her head. "Don't keep me in suspense—how was it?"

Hattie chose her reply carefully. "Unexpected."

Nora's brows rose as she opened the coach door and lowered the step. "That's high praise. Did he meet your qualifications?"

Hattie froze, one foot on the step. *Qualifications.* She patted the pockets sewn into her gown. "Oh, no."

"What?" Nora leaned in and whispered, altogether too loudly, "Hattie. You did use a French letter, did you not? I was assured they would be provided."

"Nora!" Hattie could barely summon admonishment. She was too busy panicking. She didn't have her list. It had been in her hand. And then—

The man called Beast had kissed her.

And now it was gone.

She turned and looked up at the happily lit windows of 72 Shelton Street. There he was, in a beautiful, wide window on the third floor—no longer covered. Now, it was open to the world, so all could see him, a backlit shadow—a perfect specter in the darkness.

He raised his hand and pressed something to the window. A rectangle she identified instantly.

Beast, indeed.

She narrowed her gaze. He had won this round, and Hattie didn't care for it. She turned to Nora. "Take me to my brother."

"Now? It's the dead of night."

"Then let's hope we do not ruin his sleep."

Chapter Six

$\mathcal{L}$ord August Sedley, only son and youngest child of the Earl of Cheadle, was not asleep when Hattie and Nora entered the kitchens of Sedley House half an hour later. He was very much awake, bleeding on the kitchen table.

"Where've you *been*," Augie whined from his place at the edge of the table when Hattie and Nora entered the room, bloody rag pressed to his bare thigh. "*I needed you.*"

"Oh, dear," Nora said, coming up short just inside the room. "Augie's not wearing trousers."

"This bodes ill," Hattie said.

"You're damn right it bodes ill." Augie spat his outrage. "I was *knifed*, and you weren't here and no one knew where to find you and I've been bleeding for *hours*."

Hattie clenched her teeth at the words—reminding herself that entitlement was Augie's neutral state. "Why on earth didn't you ask Russell to take care of it?" Her brother took a swig from the whiskey bottle in his free hand. "Where is he?"

"He left."

"Of course." Hattie did not disguise her disgust as she

went for a bowl of water and a length of cloth. Russell—Augie's sometimes valet, sometimes friend, sometimes man-at-arms, and constant pest—was perfectly useless at the best of times. "Why would he stay, as you're only bleeding all over the damn kitchen."

"Still breathing, though," Nora said happily, as she opened a cupboard and fetched a small wooden box, placing it next to Augie.

"Barely," Augie grouched. "I had to yank that damn thing out of me."

Hattie's gaze lit on the impressive knife cast aside on the oak. The blade was eight inches long, with a curved edge that would have shone in the darkness if it weren't so doused in blood.

If it weren't so doused in blood, it would have been beautiful.

She knew such a thought was not appropriate for the moment, but still, Hattie thought it, wanting to pick up the weapon and test its weight; she'd never seen something so wicked. So dangerous and powerful.

Except the man to whom it belonged.

Because she knew instantly, without question, this knife belonged to the man who called himself Beast.

"What happened?" she asked, coming to set the bowl on the table and inspect Augie's still bleeding thigh. "You shouldn't have taken the knife out."

"Russell said—"

Hattie shook her head, cleaning the wound, enjoying her brother's hissing curse more than she should. "I don't care. Russell is a brute and you should have left the knife in." She knocked twice on the worktable. "Lie back."

Augie groaned. "I am bleeding."

"Yes, I see that," Hattie replied. "But as you are conscious, it would make my work a darn sight easier if you were lying flat."

Augie lay back. "Be quick about it."

"No one would blame you for taking your time," Nora said, approaching with a biscuit tin in hand.

"Go home, Nora," Augie snapped.

"Why would I do that when I am so enjoying myself here?" She extended the biscuit tin to Hattie. "Would you like one?"

She shook her head, focused on the injury, now clean. "You're lucky the blade was so sharp. This should stitch well." She extracted a needle and thread from the box. "Hold still."

"Will it hurt?"

"Not more than the knife did."

Nora snickered and Augie scowled. "That's unkind." He followed the words with a hiss as Hattie began the work of closing up the wound. "I can't believe he hit his mark."

Hattie's breath caught in her throat. *Beast.* "Who?"

He shook his head. "No one."

"Can't be no one, Aug," Nora pointed out, mouth full of biscuit. "You've a hole in you."

"Yes. I noticed that." Another hiss as Hattie continued stitching.

"What are you into, Augie?"

"Nothing." She pressed the needle more firmly on the next stitch. "Dammit!"

She met her brother's pale blue gaze. "What have you gotten us *all* into?"

His gaze slid away. *Guilty.* Because whatever he'd done, whatever had put him in danger that night—it put them all in danger. Not just Augie. Their father. The business.

Hattie. All the plans she'd made and everything she had set in motion for the Year of Hattie. Business. Home. Fortune. Future. And, if the man with whom she'd made a deal was involved, it threatened the rest—*body*.

Frustration thrummed through her, making her want to scream. To shake him until he told her the truth that had landed a knife in his thigh. That had landed an unconscious man in her carriage. And God knew what else.

Another stitch.

Another.

She stayed quiet, and seethed.

Not six months earlier, their father had summoned Augie and Hattie to him, informing them both that he was no longer able to manage the business he'd built into an empire. The earl had grown too old to work the ships, to manage the men. To keep watch over the ins and outs of the business. And so he offered them the only solution a man with a life peerage and a working business had—inheritance.

Both children had grown up in the rigging of the Sedley ships; both of them had spent their early years—those before their father had been offered a title—at their father's heels, learning the business of shipping. Both had learned to heft a sail. To tie a knot.

But only one of them had learned well.

Unfortunately, that one was the girl.

So their father had given Augie the chance to prove himself, and for the last six months Hattie had worked the hardest she'd ever worked to do the same—to prove *herself* worthy of assuming control of the business, all while Augie rested on his laurels, biding his time until their father decided to hand the whole thing over to his son for no reason other than because Augie was male and that was how inheritance was done.

There was no other way to intuit the earl's reasoning:

The men on the docks need a firm hand.

As though Hattie didn't have the strength to manage them.

The shipments need an able body.

As though Hattie was too soft for the work.

You're good, girl, and with a head for it to be sure . . .

A compliment, but never spoken as such.

. . . but what if a man comes along?

That one was the most insidious. It was the one that

shouted spinster and underscored it. It was the one that effortlessly pointed out that women weren't for life if they could be for men instead.

And worse, it was the one that told her that her father didn't believe in her.

Which, of course, he didn't. No matter how many times she assured him that her life was for her alone, and not for a marriage. Instead, the earl would return to his work and say, "It's not right, girl."

She'd set out to prove him wrong. Devising strategies for increased revenue. Keeping books and tallying records and spending time with the men on the docks, so when she had a chance to lead them, they'd trust her. And they'd follow.

And tonight, the Year of Hattie began. The year when she secured everything for which she'd worked so hard. She'd just needed a bit of help setting it in motion—help one might think would have been more easily procured.

She'd had every intention of returning home to tell her father that marriage was no longer in her cards. That she'd ruined herself. She wasn't thrilled that she'd returned with her virginity still intact, but she was more than happy to report she'd found an ideal gentleman to take care of the situation.

Well. Perhaps not a gentleman.

Beast.

The name came on a hot flood of pleasure, entirely inappropriate and not easily ignored. But she did her best.

Even he had been a means to an end.

And somehow, Augie had gone and gotten himself stabbed *by the same man.*

She let her brother stay quiet while she finished stitching and bandaging him . . . a process that would have gone much faster if he'd lay still and stop whining.

She let him stay quiet while she washed her hands in the great sink, and while she sent a servant to the apothecary to fetch herbs to stave off fever.

She let him stay quiet when she returned to the table and reached for the discarded knife's hilt, gleaming and black, a silver design inlaid within, like honeycomb. While she traced the metalwork.

And then she picked up the knife, testing its weight, and met his eyes again. "You're going to tell me what you're into."

Augie was a portrait of arrogant bluster. "Why would I do that?"

"Because I found him."

His eyes shot wide as he struggled to find a reply. "Who?"

"You insult us both with that question. I also let him go."

Augie shot to his feet, wincing with the movement. "Why would you do *that*?"

"Because he was in my carriage, and we had somewhere to be."

Augie scowled at her and then Nora. "I think you mean *my* carriage."

Hattie huffed her frustration at him. "If we are parsing words, then it is neither of our carriage. It belongs to Father."

"And will eventually belong to me," Augie said, as though it were not a question.

Hattie swallowed her distaste at the words. It had never occurred to him that Hattie might do a better job of running the business. Or that she might know more about the business than he did. It had never occurred to him that he might not receive precisely what he desired the precise moment that he thought to have it. "But for now, it belongs to Father."

"And he didn't give you permission to use it whenever you like."

He had, as a matter of fact, but Hattie had no interest in having such an argument. "Oh, but he's allowed you full permission to kidnap men and leave them tied up inside of it?"

They both looked to Nora in the wake of the question.

Nora, who had moved to fill the teakettle. "Don't mind me. I'm barely paying attention."

"I wasn't going to leave him there."

Hattie spun toward her brother. "What were you going to do with him?"

"I don't know."

She caught her breath at the hesitation in the words. "Were you going to *kill* him?"

"I don't know!"

Her brother was many things, but a criminal mastermind was not one of them. "Good God, Augie—what are you into? You think a man like that would simply disappear— possibly die—and no one would come looking for you?" Hattie pressed on. "You're damn lucky all you did was knock him out! What were you *thinking*?"

"I was thinking he put a knife in me!" He waved at his bandaged thigh. "The one in your hand!"

She tightened her fingers around the hilt and shook her head. "Not until you went after him." He didn't deny it. "Why?" He didn't answer. Lord deliver her from men who decide to wield silence like a weapon. She huffed her frustration. "It seems to me that you must have deserved it, Augie. He doesn't seem the kind of man who goes around stabbing people who don't deserve it."

Everything stilled, the only sound in the room the fire beneath Nora's kettle. "Hattie—" She closed her eyes and looked away from her brother. "What would you know of what kind of man he is?"

"I spoke with him."

More than that.

I kissed him.

"What?" Augie came off the table with a wince. "Why?!"

Because I wanted to.

"Well, I was rather relieved he wasn't dead, August."

Augie ignored the warning in her words. "You shouldn't have done that."

"Who is he?" She waited.

He began to pace the length of the kitchen. "You shouldn't have done it."

"Augie!" she said firmly, summoning his attention again. "Who is he?"

"You don't know?"

She shook her head. "I know he calls himself Beast."

"That's all anyone calls him. He's Beast. And his brother is Devil."

Nora coughed.

Hattie cut her a look. "I thought you weren't listening."

"Of course I'm listening. Those are ridiculous names."

Hattie nodded. "Agreed. No one is called Beast or Devil outside of gothic novels. And even then——"

Augie had no patience for her jest. "These two are called that. They're brothers—*criminals*. Though I shouldn't have to tell you that, considering he *stabbed me*."

She tilted her head. "What kind of criminals?"

"What kind of——" Augie looked to the ceiling. "Christ, Hattie. Does it matter?"

"Even if it didn't, I should like to know the answer," Nora said from her spot by the stove.

"Smugglers. The Bareknuckle Bastards."

Hattie inhaled at the words. She might not have known what the men called themselves, but she knew of the Bareknuckle Bastards—the most powerful men in East London, possibly the rest of London as well. They were whispered about in the Docklands, only ever moving the cargo from their ships under cover of night, and paying a premium for the men with the strongest hooks.

"Also a ridiculous name," Nora said while pouring her tea. "Who are they?"

Hattie looked to her brother. "They're ice dealers."

"Ice *smugglers*," he corrected her. "Brandy and bourbon and other things, too. Silks, playing cards, dice. Whatever Britain taxes, they move beneath the Crown's notice.

And they've earned the monikers you two think are silly. Devil's the charming one, but quick to take your head if he thinks you've been doing disservice in Covent Garden. And Beast—" Hattie moved forward during Augie's pause. "They say Beast is—"

He cut himself off, looking unnerved.

Looking *frightened*.

"What?" Hattie said, desperate for him to finish. When he did not reply, she forced a scoff. "King of the jungle?"

He met her eyes. "They say that once he comes for you, he does not rest until he's found you."

A shiver went through her at the words. At the truth in them.

I shall find you.

The words made an excellent promise and a terrible threat.

"Augie, if what you're saying is true—"

"It is."

"Then what on earth makes you think you can go up against such men? That you could steal from them? That you could *hurt* them?"

For a moment, she thought he would balk at the question. At the suggestion that he was no match for these men. But he wasn't. There were few men in the world who were matches for the one she'd met earlier that evening. And that was *without* his knife in their thigh.

Augie seemed to know that. Because instead of masculine bluster, he lowered his voice and said, "I need help."

"Of course he does." The snide comment came from the stove.

"Shut up, Nora," Augie said. "This isn't your business."

"It shouldn't be Hattie's, either," Nora pointed out. "And yet, here we are."

Hattie held up a hand. "Stop it. Both of you."

They did, miraculously.

She turned to Augie. "Speak."

"I lost a shipment."

Hattie's brows furrowed and she considered the ships'

logs she'd left on her desk earlier in the day. No shipments were missing from her father's records. "What do you mean, *lost*?"

"Remember the tulips?" She shook her head. There hadn't been tulips in a cargo since—"It was in the summer," he added.

The ship had come in laden with tulip bulbs, fresh from Antwerp, already marked for estates across Britain. Augie had been responsible for the cargo and the delivery. The first he'd overseen after their father had announced his plan to pass on the business. The first her father had *insisted* Augie manage from start to finish—to prove his mettle.

"I lost them."

It didn't make sense. She'd seen the shipment marked unloaded in the books. The overland transport had been marked complete. "Lost them where?"

"I thought—" He shook his head. "I didn't know they had to be delivered immediately. I put it off. I couldn't find the men to do the job when it came in. They were working other cargo, and so I let them sit."

"In the warehouse," she said.

He nodded.

"In the dead of London summer." *Wet* London summer.

Another nod.

She sighed. "For how long?"

"I don't know. For Christ sakes, Hattie, it wasn't beef. It was fucking *tulips*. How was I to know they'd go to rot?"

Hattie thought she showed immense restraint when she wanted to say, *You'd know they'd go to rot if you'd ever paid an ounce of attention to the business.* "And then what?"

"I knew we'd have to return the payment to the customers. I knew he'd be furious." Their father would have raged, and he would have been right to do so. A full hold of good Dutch tulips was worth at least ten thousand pounds. Losing it would have cost them goodwill and enough money to matter.

But they hadn't lost it. Somehow, Augie had hidden it. Dread spiraled low in her stomach. "Augie . . . what did you do?"

He shook his head, looking down at his feet. "It was only supposed to be once."

Hattie turned to Nora, who had given up any pretense of not paying attention. When her friend shrugged her shoulders, she turned back to her brother and said, "What was only supposed to be once?"

"I had to pay the debt to the customers. Without Father discovering it. And then there was a way." He looked up, met her gaze. "I came upon their delivery route."

He took something of mine. Beast's words earlier.

Nora let out a soft curse.

Hattie sucked in a breath. "You stole from him."

"It was only—"

She cut him off. "How many times?"

He hesitated. "I paid the debt with the first one."

"But you didn't stop." Augie opened his mouth. Closed it. Of course he hadn't stopped. It was Hattie's turn to curse. "How many times?"

He met her eyes, and she saw the fear in them. "Tonight was the fourth."

"Four times." She gave a little humorless laugh. "You've robbed them four times . . . It's a miracle you weren't killed."

"Hang on," Nora said from her place across the kitchen. "How did *you* subdue *that man*?"

He scowled at her. "What does that mean?"

She cut him a look. "Augie. That man was twice as broad as you on your very broadest day. And you have a knife in your thigh."

He looked as though he might argue, then admitted, "Russell knocked him out."

Of course those two had made a mess of this. And now,

as usual, it fell to Hattie to clear it up. "It should be illegal for the two of you to speak to each other. You make each other less intelligent." She looked to the ceiling, mind racing, then said on a sigh, "You've made a hash of it."

"I know," her brother said, and she wondered if he truly did.

"What you told me about him? The Beast?" Augie met her eyes, trepidation in his own. "He's coming for you, Augie. It's a miracle he hasn't found you yet. But tonight—what you did—it was immensely stupid. What would possess you to tie him up? In the *carriage*?"

"I wasn't thinking. I'd been stabbed. And Russell . . ."

"Ah, yes. Russell." She stopped him. "He's through, too. This ends *now*. We don't sell another drop of their cargo. Where is the cargo you took tonight?"

"Russell took it to our buyer."

She cocked a brow. "Another brilliant tactician, no doubt. Who is that?"

If possible, her brother grew even paler. "I won't have you involved with him."

"As though I am not in deep enough with you?"

Augie shook his head. "You've no idea how deep you could find yourself. The man is barely sane."

"Now you find your sense of familial preservation?" Hattie resisted the urge to scream. "I suppose I should be grateful that our most pressing foe is merely vengeful, not mad."

"I'm sorry," Augie said.

"No, you're not," Hattie retorted. "If I had to guess, you're happy I'm willing to fix this. And I *can* fix this."

Augie stilled. "You can?"

"I can," she said, the plan crystallizing. The path forward. And then—*her path*. "I can."

"How?" It wasn't the worst question in the world. She looked to Nora, whose brows were nearly in her hairline in a silent echo of Augie's question.

Hattie straightened her shoulders, more certain than ever. "We make a deal for the cargo. We share the income from our shipments until he's paid."

"It won't be enough."

"It will be." She'd make it enough. She'd promise him no more hijackings. And income. With interest. If he was a businessman, he'd recognize a good deal when he saw it. Killing Augie wouldn't bring back his lost cargo, and it would bring the Crown down upon his head—something smugglers would not care for.

But money—money was real. She'd convince him of it.

She met her brother's blue eyes. "You stay out of it."

"You don't know him, Hattie."

"I know I made a deal with him."

Augie froze. "What kind of deal?"

"Yes, what kind of deal?" Nora echoed, her lips curving in amusement.

"Nothing serious."

You are in no position to make me an offer.

I get all of it.

What is mine. What is yours. And the name.

A sizzle of pleasure ran through Hattie at the memory of what he'd taken even as he'd promised that retribution. The heat of his kiss. The promise of his touch.

Augie interrupted her thoughts. "Hattie—if he agreed to see you again—whatever he said—you have to know—he's not after *you*."

She swallowed the disappointment that came with the words. Augie wasn't wrong. Men like the one she'd met that evening—men like Beast—they were not for women like Hattie. They did not notice women like Hattie. They noticed beautiful women with small, slender bodies and delicate dispositions. She knew that.

She knew it, but still . . . the unfettered honesty about her lack of allure stung.

She covered the hurt with a laugh, the way she always

did. "I know that, Augie. And now I know just what he's after. My idiot brother." She enjoyed the hot flush that washed over Augie's face more than she should. "But I intend for him to keep our agreement. And in order to do that, he will have to accept our offer."

"I'll come with you."

"No." The last thing she needed was Augie with her, mucking things up. "No."

"Someone has to go with you. He doesn't leave Covent Garden."

"Then I shall go to Covent Garden," she said.

"It's no place for ladies," Augie said.

If there were any five words that would catapult a woman into motion, they were surely those. "Need I remind you that I grew up in the rigging of cargo ships?"

Augie changed tack. "He'll do whatever it takes to punish me. And you're my *sister*."

"He doesn't know that. He shan't know it," she said. "I have the upper hand here."

Had they not parted on a challenge? One would find the other? And now . . . she knew how to find him. Pleasure coursed through her. Triumph. Something dangerously close to delight.

"And if the Beast hurts you?"

"He won't." That much, she knew. He might tease her, and tempt her, and test her. But he wouldn't harm her.

She saw Augie's acquiescence, chased like a rabbit by relief. Of course he was relieved. She was about to clean up his mess. Like always.

He exhaled. "All right."

"But Augie?" Her brother lifted his gaze and she paused, her heart pounding. "*If* I do this . . ." Suspicion crossed his face, but he did not speak. "*If I save your hide* . . . then you shall do something for me."

His brow furrowed. "What do you want?"

"Not what I want, August. What you shall happily provide."

"Go on, then."

Now or never.

Take it.

You told the Beast that you didn't lose, either.

Make it so.

"You will tell Father you don't want the business." Augie's eyes went wide as Nora let out a low whistle that Hattie ignored, frustration and determination and triumph coursing through her all at once. "You'll tell him to give it to me."

It seemed today was the beginning of the Year of Hattie, after all.

Chapter Seven

$\mathcal{T}$he next afternoon, as the sun sank into the western sky, Whit stood in the small, silent infirmary deep in the Covent Garden Rookery, keeping watch over the boy who had been ferried here after the attack on the shipment.

The room, filled with golden light, was fastidiously clean, in sharp comparison to the world beyond—a world where filth reigned—and it should have given Whit a modicum of peace.

It didn't.

He'd gone immediately to the Rookery after leaving 72 Shelton Street—come to check on the riders who had been with him the night before. Come to check on this boy, Jamie, who'd been on the ground when Whit had been knocked out, the street beneath him black with blood. Even as he'd lost consciousness, Whit had raged. No one hurt the Bareknuckle Bastards' men and lived.

Whit's heart pounded with the memory even as the door to the room opened and closed, the young, bespectacled doctor wiping his hands with a clean cloth as he entered and approached. "I've sedated him," the doctor said. "He shan't wake for hours. You needn't hover."

Whit needed to hover. He protected his own.

The Bareknuckle Bastards reigned in the twisting labyrinth of Covent Garden, beyond the taverns and theaters made safe for the London toffs, where nothing was safe for outsiders. But Whit had come up through the Rookery alongside his half brother and the girl they called their sister—learning to fight like dogs for whatever scraps they could find. Fighting had become second nature, and they'd clawed themselves higher, starting a business and pulling the Rookery with them—hiring the men and women of the neighborhood for work in their myriad businesses: swinging pies in their taverns, tracking wagers in fight rings, butchering beef and tanning hides, and running the cargo that came in off the ships twice a month.

If they hadn't secured the loyalty of the Garden as children, the money would have done it. The Bastards' Rookery was known throughout London as a place that provided honest work for good wage and safe conditions, and from a trio who had built themselves from the dirt of the Garden's streets.

Here, the Bastards were kings. Recognized and revered beyond the monarch himself; and why not? The other side of London might as well be the other side of the world for those who grew up in the Rookery.

But even a king couldn't keep death at bay.

The unconscious young man—barely a heartbeat from boyhood—had taken a bullet for them. For it, he lay in a blindingly white room against blindingly white sheets, in the hands of fate, because Whit had been too late to protect him.

Always too late.

He shoved a hand in his pocket, his fingers rubbing over the warm metal of one watch, then the other. "Will he live?"

The doctor looked over from the table in the corner of the room, where he mixed a tonic. "Perhaps."

Whit growled low in his throat, his hand fisting at his

side . . . itching for a face. For a life. He'd been so close to it the night before—if he'd woken to the enemy, he might have had his retribution.

But he'd woken to the woman instead. Hattie, eager to play at a brothel while his men fought at the hands of a surgeon. And then she'd refused to give him a name.

He watched the sleeping form, the bed somehow making Jamie smaller and slighter than he was when he was hale, when he laughed with his brothers-in-arms and winked at pretty girls as they tripped past.

Hattie would give Whit the name of the man she protected—the one who'd stolen from him—the one who threatened what was his. The one who was working with the real enemy—and who would lead Beast to him once he suffered the full force of Beast's wrath.

He'd rampage for Jamie and for all those under his protection here in the Garden, where scarcity threatened not a quarter of a mile from some of the richest homes in Britain. He'd rampage for the seven others who had come before him. For the three who had left this room and gone straight to the ground.

Another growl.

"I understand that you do not like it, Beast, but it is the truth. Medicine is imperfect. But it is the cleanest a wound can be," the doctor added. "The bullet entered and exited; we stemmed the bleeding. It's packed and protected." He shrugged. "He could live." He came closer. Extended the glass in his hand to Whit. "Drink."

Whit shook his head.

"You've been awake for more than a day, and Mary tells me you haven't had food or drink since you arrived."

"I don't need your wife watching me."

The doctor cut him a look. "As you've been standing sentry in this room for twelve hours, she had little choice." He extended the drink again. "Drink—for the cracking head you won't admit you have."

Whit took the drink, ignoring the throbbing ache at the back of his skull as he knocked it back, before swearing roundly at the taste of the rotten swill. "What in hell is that?"

The doctor took the glass and went back to his desk. "Does it matter?"

It didn't. The doctor was unorthodox, rarely using a common cure when he could mix a paste or boil a draught of something disgusting, and he had an obsession with cleanliness that Covent Garden had never seen. Whit and Devil had lured him away from a small northern village two years earlier, after he'd reportedly saved a young marchioness from a gunshot wound on the Great North Road with a curious combination of tinctures and tonics.

A man with a skill for defeating bullets was worth his weight in gold, as far as Whit was concerned—and the doctor had proven him right, saving more than he'd lost since arriving in the Rookery.

Today, he might save another.

Whit turned back to Jamie. Watched him in the silence of the afternoon.

"I'll send someone to fetch you when he wakes," the doctor said. "The moment he wakes."

"And if he doesn't?"

A pause. "Then I shall send someone to fetch you when he doesn't."

Whit grunted, logic telling him that there was nothing to be done. That fate would come, and this boy would live or die by it.

"I fucking hate this place." Whit couldn't stay still anymore. He went to the end of the room, to the exterior wall of the building, built by the best masons the Bastards' money could buy. Without hesitation, he put his fist into it.

Pain shot through his hand and up his arm, and he welcomed it. A punishment.

The doctor's chair creaked when he turned back to Whit. "Are you bleeding?"

He looked down at his knuckles. They'd seen worse. He grunted his denial, shaking out the limb. The doctor nodded and turned back to his work.

Good. Whit was in no mood for conversation, a fact rendered irrelevant when the door to the room opened and his brother and sister-in-law entered, and behind them, Annika, the Bastards' brilliant Norwegian lieutenant, who could move a hold full of contraband in broad daylight like a sorceress.

"We came as soon as we heard." Devil went straight to the bed, looking down at Jamie. "Fuck." He looked up, the six-inch-long scar that ran the length of his right cheek now white with anger.

"We're looking for his sister," Nik said as she moved to the other side of the bed, her hand settling gently on the boy's. "She'll be here soon, Jamie." Something tightened impossibly further in Whit's chest; Nik loved the men and women who worked for them like she was decades older than her twenty-three years, and they her children.

And he couldn't keep them safe.

Devil cleared his throat. "And the bullet?"

"Side. Clean through," the doctor answered.

"I almost had 'im. Left a knife in 'im," Whit added. "Aim was true."

"Good. I hope you cut off his bollocks," Devil said, tapping his silver-tipped walking stick on the floor twice—a sign of his desire to unsheathe the wicked blade from within and run someone through.

"Wait," Whit's sister-in-law, Felicity, said, coming to face him, forcing him to look down at her. "You *almost* had him?"

Shame ran through Whit, hot and inescapable. "Someone knocked me out before I could finish the deed."

Nik whispered a curse as Felicity took Whit's hands in her own, squeezing them tightly. "Are you well?" She turned to the doctor. "Is he well?"

"Seems so to me."

Felicity narrowed her gaze on the other man. "Your keen interest in medicine never fails to impress, Doctor."

The doctor removed his spectacles and cleaned them. "The man is upright before you, is he not?"

She sighed. "I suppose so."

"Well, then," he said, and he left the room.

"Such an odd man." Felicity turned back to Whit. "What happened?"

Whit ignored the question, instead catching Nik's gaze across the room. "And Dinuka?" The second outrider. Whit had sent the young man for cavalry. "He's safe?"

Nik nodded. "Got off a shot, but doesn't think it landed. Did as he was told. Came running for cavalry."

"Good man," Whit said. "Cargo?"

She shook her head. "Lost before we could track it."

Whit ran a hand over his chest, where his knife holster was missing. "Along with my knives."

Devil turned to him. "Who?"

Whit met his brother's eyes. "I can't be certain."

Devil didn't hesitate. "But you've a wager."

"All I have says it's Ewan."

He didn't use the name anymore. Ewan was now Robert, Duke of Marwick, their half brother and Felicity's once-fiancé. He'd left Devil for dead three months earlier and disappeared, sending Grace into hiding until he was found. There'd been a break in hijackings after Ewan had vanished, but Whit couldn't shake the feeling that he was back. And responsible for Jamie.

Except . . . "Ewan wouldn't have left you unconscious," Devil said. "He'd have done much worse."

Beast shook his head. "He's got two working for him. At least two."

"Who?"

"I'm close," he said. *She'll tell me soon enough.*

"Does it have something to do with the woman at Shelton Street?"

Whit's attention flew to Nik at the words. "What?"

"Ah, yes. The woman. We heard about that, too," Devil said. "Apparently you were tossed out of a carriage into a group of drunks and then followed what Brixton referred to as—" He grinned at his wife. "What was it, love?"

Felicity's mouth twisted in a wry smile. "A lady toff."

"Ah, yes. I hear you followed a lady toff into Grace's brothel."

Whit did not reply.

"And *lingered*," Nik added.

Dammit.

Whit met the Norwegian's eyes. "Have you nowhere to be? We still run a business or two, do we not?"

Nik shrugged. "I shall get the story from the lads."

Whit scowled, pretending not to notice when she brushed her hand over Jamie's brow, whispered a few encouraging words to the boy before taking her leave.

After a long silence, Felicity said, "Are we to get the story from the lads, as well?"

"I am already in possession of one inquisitive sister."

Felicity smiled. "Yes, but as she is not here, I must stand for both of us."

He scowled. "I woke up in a carriage, with a woman."

Devil's brows furrowed. "And I assume this did not occur in the excellent way that such a scenario might?"

It was the hottest kiss Whit had ever experienced, but that was not for his brother to know. "When I exited the carriage—"

"We heard you were thrown out," Felicity said.

He gave a little growl. "It was mutual."

"Mutual," Felicity repeated. "Carriage tossing."

Lord deliver him from prying sisters. "When I *exited the carriage*," he said, "she was headed deeper into the Garden. I followed."

Devil nodded. "Who is she?"

He stayed quiet.

"Christ, Whit, you got the lady toff's name, didn't you?" He turned to Felicity. "Hattie."

Having a sister-in-law who was once an aristocrat paid handsomely at times, particularly when one required the name of a noblewoman. "Spinster?"

It wasn't the first descriptor he'd assign to her.

"Very tall? Blond?" Felicity pressed.

He nodded.

"Plump?"

The word brought back the memory of the dips and valleys of her curves. He growled his assent.

Felicity turned to Devil. "Well then."

"Mmm," Devil said. "We shall come back to that. Do you know who the woman is?"

"Hattie's quite a common name."

"But?"

She looked to Whit, then back to her husband. "Henrietta Sedley is daughter to the Earl of Cheadle."

The truth slammed through Whit, along with triumphant pleasure at the revelation of Hattie's identity. Cheadle had earned the earldom—received it from the king himself for nobility at sea. *I grew up on the docks*, she'd told him when he'd tried to scare her with foul language. "That's her."

"So Ewan is working with Cheadle?" Devil said, shaking his head. "Why would the earl go in against us? It doesn't make sense."

And it didn't. Andrew Sedley, Earl of Cheadle, was beloved on the docks. His business was a source of honest work and good pay, and men who worked the Thames knew him as a fair man willing to hire anyone with an able body and a strong hook, regardless of name or country or fortune.

The Bastards had never had cause to interact with Sedley, as he exclusively ran aboveboard shipments, paid his lading taxes, and kept his business clean, with nary a whiff of impropriety. No weapons. No drugs. No people. The same rules the Bastards played by, though they played in the muck, their contraband running to booze and paper, crystal and wigs, and anything else taxed beyond reason by the Crown. And they weren't afraid to defend themselves with force.

The idea that Cheadle might have shot the first cannon at them was beyond understanding. But Cheadle and his daring daughter weren't alone.

"The son," Whit said. August Sedley was by all accounts an indolent lackwit, bereft of his father's work ethic and respect.

"It could be," Felicity said. "No one thinks much of him. He's charming but not very intelligent."

Which meant the young Sedley lacked the sense required to understand that going up against Covent Garden's best known and most beloved criminals was not to be done lightly. If Hattie's brother was behind the hijackings, it could mean only one thing.

Devil saw it, too. "Ewan has the brother doing his work, and the sister protects her family."

Whit knew the price of that. He grunted his agreement.

"She fails," Devil said, tapping against the floor again and looking down at Jamie. "This ends. We take the son, the father, the whole fucking family if need be. And they lead us to Ewan. And that ends, as well." They'd been fighting Ewan for two decades. Hiding from him. Protecting Grace from him.

"Grace won't like it," Felicity said, softly. A lifetime ago, Devil and Whit had made a singular promise to their sister—that they wouldn't hurt Ewan. It did not matter that he'd been the fourth in their band or that he had betrayed them beyond reason. Grace had loved him. And she'd made them promise never to touch him.

But Grace wasn't a part of this. Whit shook his head. "Grace will have to suffer it. He comes for more than us now. For more than his past. Now, he comes for our men."

For the world the Bastards would protect at all costs.

It was time to end it.

Whit met his brother's eyes. "I'll do it."

The words were punctuated by a knock on the door to the building, the sound muffled in the distance. Another body, no doubt. There was always someone in need of care in the Garden—and he'd be damned if he'd let an entitled aristocrat add to the body count.

The brothers locked eyes. "All of it?"

"The business, the name, everything he values. I'll bring it down." Young Sedley had crossed the Bastards, and with it, brought destruction upon himself.

"And Lady Henrietta?" Felicity said, setting Whit on edge with the honorific. He didn't like her as an aristocrat. He'd preferred her as Hattie. "Do you think she is part of it? Do you think she works with Ewan?"

No. The denial rioted through him.

Devil watched him carefully, then said, "How do you know?"

I know.

It wasn't enough.

"She'll give up the brother."

Devil regarded him in silence. "Would you give up yours?"

Whit clenched his teeth.

"If she doesn't?" Felicity asked. "What of her then?"

"Then she's collateral damage," Devil said. Whit ignored the distaste that came with the words.

Felicity looked to her husband. "Isn't that what I was, once?"

Devil had the grace to look chagrined. "For a heartbeat, love. Just long enough for me to come to my senses."

"If she's the enemy, I'll do it," Whit said.

One of Devil's brows went up. "*If?*"

You're very inconvenient.

It's the Year of Hattie.

Snippets of the conversation in the carriage.

"Even if she isn't the enemy," Devil pointed out, "she protects the man who is." He crossed his arms over his chest and leveled his brother with a firm look. "Which makes her valuable."

It made her leverage.

"You'll have no choice but to show her the truth of us, bruv," Devil said quietly. "No matter how much you like the look of her."

The truth of them. The Bareknuckle Bastards didn't leave enemies alive.

"Sort it before we have to move more product," Devil said. A new shipment would come into port within the next week.

Whit nodded as the door to the room opened, revealing the doctor. "You've a message." He pushed the door wide and revealed one of the Bastards' best runners.

"Brixton," Felicity said to the boy, who immediately preened under Felicity's attention. All the boys in the Garden adored her—half lockpicking genius, half maternal perfection. "I thought you were headed home?"

"To learn how to keep your gob shut, I hope, boy," Whit said, making certain Brixton knew Whit had heard everything the boy had told Devil about Hattie.

"Ignore him," Felicity said. "What is it?"

Brixton raised his chin toward Whit. "There's reports there's a girl in the market. Lookin' fer Beast." A pause, and then, "No' a girl, really. A woman." He lowered his voice. "The boys fink she's a *lady*."

A rumble sounded low in Whit's chest.

Hattie.

"Askin' all sorts o' questions."

Felicity looked to Whit. "Is she?"

"Aye. No' that we're answerin'." Of course they weren't. No one in Covent Garden would give Lady Henrietta Sedley information about the Bastards. That was the first of the unspoken rules there. The Bastards belonged to the Rookery alone.

"Good work, Brixton," Devil said, flipping a coin to the boy, who snatched it out of the air with a grin and was gone before Devil could add, "Seems like you won't have to find her, after all, Beast."

Whit's grunt hid the thread of disbelief that coursed through him. And the wariness. And the desire to chase her down. No, he wouldn't have to find her.

She'd found him first.

Chapter Eight

There was nothing in the wide world like the Covent Garden market.

The marketplace was massive, fronted by a great stone colonnade that gave way inside to an endless collection of shops and stalls selling anything a body could need—laden high with fruits and vegetables, flowers and sweets, meat pies and china, antiques and fabrics.

Hattie was full of pleasure as she picked through the interior of the market, weaving in and out of the vendors, tempted by the riotous colors of the late autumn harvest—flower stalls overflowing with reds and oranges, magnificent gourds piled next to bushels of beetroots in myriad colors, and heaps of potatoes still dark with the rich soil in which they'd grown.

To others, the building itself was the pride of the marketplace—an architectural marvel, massive and stunning, with immense, echoing rafters and stonework and ironwork that made this, London's largest and most expansive market, the envy of all the world.

But the building was nothing to Hattie. For Hattie, the draw of the market was the people within. And it was packed to the rafters with people. Farmers and merchants, florists and butchers, bakers and haberdashers and tinkers and tailors, all hawking their wares for a crush of customers that ranged from lowliest maid to jewel of the *ton*. If one could find their way into the building, it didn't matter where they'd come from—Covent Garden market was one of the rare places in the city where a pauper's ha'penny spent as well as a prince's—perhaps even better, as a pauper didn't have qualms about raising his voice when necessary . . . which it always was in the market.

Because beyond the color and scent of the place was the sound. A raucous cacophony of shouts and laughter, of dedicated buyers and eager sellers, of barking dogs and clucking chickens and pipes and fiddles and children laughing.

It was a pure, magnificent commotion. And Hattie adored it.

She had since she was a little girl, when her father would let her hang about on the company's ships while they were unloaded—the holds taking hours to empty, even with scores of men doing the backbreaking work. And when it was over, Mr. Sedley (he hadn't been an earl then) would fetch his eldest child and promise her a trip to the Covent Garden market for a treat of her choosing.

She thought back on those days as she lingered in the marketplace, the sun setting in the west, its rainbow of light making London—even the forgotten bits of it—magical. She thought of them, and the way she'd revered her father, the way she'd fallen in love with the ships and the business and the docks. And the way she'd loved this market, loud and raucous and covered in sawdust to soak up the stench and the filth that never seemed as off-putting as it should.

And just as she had as a child, Hattie took her time this afternoon. Recalling how she'd once dawdled at every stall, smiling at the merchants and chatting up the farmers in search of the perfect prize, she returned to the same strategy. Searching for a different kind of prize.

Beast.

She went about it methodically, finding the friendliest merchants. The apple farmer, the woman with a basket of kittens on her hip, the evenhanded seamstress embroidering a tiny pink rose on a square of linen somehow kept immaculate in the marketplace. She spoke to them, bought an apple, cuddled a kitten, ordered a dozen new handkerchiefs.

And then she asked about Beast.

Did they know him? Of him?

Did they have any idea where he could be found?

She had something of his, you see . . . and she wished to return it.

It was remarkable, though, how little her friendliness mattered. How little her patronage mattered. The moment she spoke the name—that silly, fantastical name—the merchants slipped through her fingers.

Sorry, lady, the farmer said, turning away to tempt another customer.

Ain't heard of him, the lady with the kittens assured her, *but do ye plan to buy?*

I'm sure I would remember such a name. The seamstress's hands hadn't even hesitated.

It seemed all of Covent Garden was in the market to protect the Beast.

With a sigh, Hattie took a bite from her apple, the crisp, sweet flavor exploding over her tongue as she weaved her way through the wagons, no longer piled high after a hard day of sale. The sounds in the market had quieted as the sun crept lower in the sky—people headed back to their beds to awake early and repeat the day again tomorrow.

"Flowers, lady?" A girl, no older than seven or eight, with dark skin and eager eyes, met her as she exited toward the church of St. Paul. Her black hair was tucked up under a cap, a few curls unmoored by the long day, and she wore a dress and a shawl that had seen a lifetime of mending. A shabby basket dangled from her arm, handle splintered, holes worn into its base, five lone dahlias at the bottom, wilted from a day out of water in the market square.

Hattie met the girl's dark brown gaze, recognizing the uncertainty and resignation there. The girl knew her flowers weren't what they might have been hours earlier. Knew, too, that she couldn't go back to wherever she'd come from without having sold them.

Hattie knew it, too. So she bought them, tuppence for the flowers, and another penny for the girl, who made to leave, no doubt thinking that if she didn't Hattie might change her mind. But when Hattie said, "Wait," the girl hesitated. Hattie leaned down to meet her wary eyes. "I'm looking for someone. Perhaps you could help?"

Wariness narrowed into distrust. "Don't know anyfin' 'bout anyfin', lady."

"I'm looking for a man," Hattie pressed on. "His name is Beast."

Recognition. There, in the girl's rich brown gaze. There, then gone. Hidden as the girl looked about, taking in the people lingering in the fast darkening square. Looking for someone? For spies?

"I don't wish to hurt him," Hattie added.

The girl's smile was unexpected, as though Hattie had made a wonderful joke. "No one *'urts* Beast," she said before she realized she'd given away a piece of information that she shouldn't have. Her eyes went wide, but before Hattie could press for more information, she said, "Nah, lady. Can't help ye," and scurried off with impressive speed, as though she'd never been there in the first place.

Hattie sighed her frustration and watched the girl go, pulling her shawl tight around her as the late September air lost the warmth of the sun. Did the man have all of Covent Garden on his balance sheet?

She'd have to leave soon—once it grew dark, it would be harder to hail a hack, but she had to find him, dammit. He was the key to everything—to her desires, to her plans, to her future. If she could convince him to call off his search for Augie, if she could finagle a deal with him to return what her idiot brother had taken, if she could convince him that she had the power to put an end to these severely misguided attacks . . .

If she could just *find* the ruddy man, she had a chance at everything.

Not to mention the fact that he'd made her a promise.

The thought sent fire through her, pooling deep and speeding her pulse and setting her lips to tingling with the memory of his kiss the night before. He'd promised to make good on that kiss. To make good on the rest.

And she intended him to keep it.

"Try your luck, lady?"

She turned at the sound, to where a man sat several yards away at a makeshift table of an ale cask and a wooden plank. He shuffled a deck of cards slowly and methodically, barely paying attention to the movements, his blue eyes shining bright beneath the brim of his cap, a wide, friendly smile focused on her.

"I beg your pardon?"

The soft rhythm of his next shuffle teased her. He fanned the cards across the wood, then picked them up in a single smooth motion.

She shook her head. "I don't play cards."

"Neither do I." The man winked. "Awful habit."

She laughed, moving closer. He reminded her of a fox, sly and wily, bred of Covent Garden. He was like a weed sprung from the cracks in the stone slabs of the marketplace, with strong, hardy roots that were sure to regrow no matter how many times they were pulled. A man bred in the Garden would know the king of it, no doubt. She moved closer. "Then what is it you do play?"

He spread the cards again. "Choose your three, milady."

She raised a brow and he laughed, spreading his hands wide. "Such mistrust!"

"Whyever would I think you were planning to fleece me?"

He put a hand to his chest and feigned affront. "Like an arrow in me heart."

He was *absolutely* planning to fleece her, but Hattie hadn't grown up around sailors for nothing, and she had plans of her own. She reached down and slid three cards from the spread, leaving them facedown on the table. The gamer collected the rest of the deck, setting it to one side, lifting the card from the top of the pile with a wide smile. "Nothing below board."

It was all below board, but Hattie was willing to follow.

Using the card he'd selected as a tool, he flipped the three Hattie had chosen: the three of spades, the eight of clubs, and then . . . the queen of hearts. He raised wide eyes to her. "Well, the lady chose you, it seems."

Hattie inclined her head. "And what do I receive for such a favor?"

That smile again. "The chance to play your luck, of course."

"How much?"

"Sixpence." It was an exorbitant amount—enough to prove to Hattie that he thought he had her.

And so she let him, digging into her pocket and pulling out the coin in question. She set it on the table. "And if my luck holds?"

"Why then I double it, of course!"

"Of course," she said. This man didn't lose. His entire livelihood was made here, on the edge of the market square, fleecing those who thought themselves above him. "What now?"

"It's no trouble." He smiled, turning the three cards over, returning their faces to the table. The queen's card was curved more than the others, domed to the table. "Where's the lady?"

Hattie pointed to the queen. He flipped the card, revealing her, then flipped her again. "Yer already a natural," he said with a wink. "That's all it is . . . watch the lady."

And then he began to move the cards, tossing them over and under each other, in broad arching throws at the start, so Hattie could follow the queen, then faster and faster, until the cards were moving in a near blur. A novice would be following the cards on the table, of course, watching carefully, tracking the queen.

Hattie wasn't a novice.

When the man stopped, the cards finally settled into another line of three, he turned his wide face up to Hattie and said, "Find the lady, lady."

Hattie reached into her pocket and extracted a gold crown—more money than this broad-tosser would make in a week here at the market. "Shall we sweeten the deal?"

Greed flashed. "I'm listening."

"If I lose, it's yours."

Then triumph.

"But if I find the lady . . . you tell me where I can find the Beast."

Surprise, then doubt, as though he perhaps shouldn't make the deal. But arrogance won out, as it so often did with men. To deny the offer was to admit he might lose.

He did not realize that Hattie played a much bigger game.

"A'right, lady. Ye drive a hard bargain." He waved a hand over the table. "Where's the queen?"

He expected her to choose the middle card. It was the card any good mark would have chosen if they'd been watching the cards on the table, not to mention having the domed middle they would be looking for. But Hattie hadn't been watching the cards on the table. She'd been watching the ones in his hand.

She put a finger on the card to the left.

That broad smile again. "Let's see, shall we?" He picked up the card furthest to the right and with it, flipped the card in the middle, revealing the three of spades—the card he would have let her turn over herself if she'd chosen it. "One step closer."

But he was prepared. He would ask her to move and let him flip the card for her, and in the process, he'd perform the same sleight of hand that had put the queen on the table in the first place. He waved his hand to indicate she should move away.

Instead of moving, she turned the card herself, revealing the queen.

His eyes flew to hers.

"It seems the lady did choose me, after all," she said. She lifted the crown from the table, returning it to her pocket. "According to our deal, you owe me. Sixpence and some information."

His eyes narrowed to slits as he reconsidered her, seeing beyond the bonnet and shawl that had quickly labeled her a novice. "Yer a ringer. 'At's a cheat, that is."

"Nonsense," Hattie said calmly. "I merely evened the odds. And if anything's a cheat, it's the fact that you were going to perform a buccaneer's turnover and switch my queen for the eight of clubs in your hand."

The man scowled and collected the cards in a smooth motion, quickly disappearing any hint of impropriety. "I don' deal wi' ringers."

"Please don't be disappointed," Hattie said. "I've never seen a better tosser. But fair is fair, and we did make a bet."

"Aye, but ya didn't play fair." He slid the deck of cards into his pocket and stood, revealing his small frame—at least six inches shorter than her own, and reed-thin. Still, he had no trouble lifting the tabletop and tucking it under his arm. "No deal."

She gasped as he walked away, bobbing and weaving through those lingering in the square. "I played just as fair as you did!" She followed behind. "You promised me information."

"I don' 'ave information." He sped up, slipping down an alleyway off the main square, leading deeper into the Garden.

He turned a corner, and Hattie hurried to follow. "Wait! Please!" This man had grown up on the streets of Covent Garden. He knew about Beast. She caught sight of him at the far end of another alley, making another turn.

He spun back around when she came around the corner. "Leave off!" Then resumed his retreat. Down a second alleyway. Turned into a third.

Frustration grew. She was going to lose him. "Just tell me where to find him!" she called after him. Another turn. Another.

He was gone. Lost to the labyrinthine streets.

"Dammit," she whispered to the dusk, her heart pounding, the only sound on the empty street her breath harsh in her lungs. He'd been her chance. "Dammit."

"I know where to find 'im, lady."

"Aye, me, as well."

She whirled to meet the words.

Two other men, approaching from behind. Larger than the one she'd pursued. One wore a cap low over his brow, hiding all but the tip of his nose. The other had a shock of orange hair, bright enough to see in the fast-dimming light. He smiled, baring rotten teeth. But it wasn't his teeth that made Hattie shiver. It was his eyes. Full of greed.

She took a step back. "I don't require your help, thank you."

"Och, wot a lady," Cap said. "So polite."

"And the accent—like she was born in piles o' money," Teeth replied. "Enough money that she can pay us back for wot she lost us this afternoon."

She shook her head. "I didn't—I've never set eyes on you before."

Cap sucked his teeth at that. "Nah, but ye broke our man. 'E could've worked another hour if you ain't come 'long."

The card man. He hadn't been working alone. He'd been working for these men. These men who wanted their money here and now in this empty alleyway where she'd been stupid enough to land herself. She cast about for a solution. "I'll give you what I offered him. A crown."

"A crown, she says," Rotten Teeth spat.

"She lost us wot, three times that?" came the ridiculous reply. Impossible. It would take the gamesters days to earn that amount.

It didn't matter. "I don't have that." She reached into her pocket. Extracted her remaining coin. "I've six shillings, tuppence."

They were nearly upon her.

"Aw . . . She don't 'ave it, Eddie," Cap tutted.

"Wot are we to do, then, lady?" Eddie asked. "Maybe you could work it off? Mikey don't mind big girls."

She lifted her chin. Pulled her shawl tight, one hand disappearing into the folds. "Don't come any closer."

"Or wot?"

"Maybe she'll scream," Mikey said, yellow teeth flashing as though he'd like that, the monster.

"She can," Eddie said softly, close enough to touch her if he tried. "But she won't find no savior 'ere."

Her heart pounded, fear and fury warring within. Fury won out. "Then I shall have to save myself."

Chapter Nine

$\mathcal{H}$e didn't like her in the Garden.

Beast headed for the market, keenly aware of the setting sun—of the way the place could turn from friendly to dangerous in an instant, especially for the daughter of an earl, too full of Mayfair no matter how much time she'd spent in the Docklands. She'd as well be from the other end of the world as here, where darkness came like a promise, and brought with it all manner of malice.

What if she'd left before he got there?

He increased his pace, hurrying to get to her before the last rays of light settled, weaving in and out of buildings and down alleyways, making the final turn and nearly crashing into a tiny body speeding the opposite way. He reached for the child who threatened to ricochet off his legs and land herself in the muck, taking in her empty basket and threadbare cap.

"Bess," he said once she was stable again, the drawl of the streets thick on his tongue. "What's got you racin'?"

Her eyes went wide. "Beast!" she said. "I ain't told her nuffin'! I thought she'd make a good mark for me last blooms."

Hattie.

He looked to the empty basket. "Looks like she was that."

The girl nodded, her cap going further askew. "Aye. Bought the *lot*. And for *thruppence*."

He was unsurprised by Hattie's generous spending, but made a show of looking impressed. "And now, moppet? Where's the lady?"

She shook her head. "I didn't tell her 'ow to find you. I'd *never*."

"I don't doubt it."

Her chest bowed out with pride. "Left 'er in the square, I did. Told her no one beats you."

He imagined Hattie hadn't cared for that. He reached into his pocket and extracted his bag of sweets, offering it to Bess. When she popped one into her mouth, he chuffed the girl beneath her chin and said, "Good work today, Bess. It's getting close to dark. Best find your mum." The duo would have another early day tomorrow—up at dawn to collect their blossoms and then back to the square to sell them.

If the Bastards had their way, every child in the Rookery would wake early to get to lessons, but families had to eat, and the best Devil and Whit could do was give them clean water and as much protection as was possible.

Which meant he didn't have time to protect aristocratic ladies hell-bent on adventure when he'd expressly told her he would find her, and not the other way around. He saw Bess off, then headed for the market square, crossing into it in just enough time to see Hattie on the other side, getting fleeced by one of the square's card men.

He imagined she'd chosen the dress to blend in with the Garden crowd or some nonsense, a simple walking dress in a soft, mossy green with a bonnet to match, topped with a knitted shawl pulled tight around her shoulders in an attempt to, what—make her shapeless? Whit supposed that he might have ignored the whole ensemble if not for the woman inside, who was impossible to miss and nothing near shapeless. She was taller than most and with wild curves that no one would miss. Especially not a man who'd had a taste of them the night before.

Memory flashed, her tongue meeting his in a delicious stroke, her breath coming fast at his lips, her fingers tight in his hair, as though she wished she could direct the caress.

Christ, he would allow her to direct his caress wherever she liked.

He resisted the urge to linger on what might come of it, ignoring the waking of his cock as he headed for her without hesitation, speeding up when he realized she wasn't getting fleeced. *She was doing the fleecing.*

The broad-tosser stood, anger clear on his face, collected his table, and turned away—heading for the nearest alleyway. And Hattie followed . . . not knowing she was being led into the darkness to be set upon by thieves.

Whit began to run.

He followed down the dark, empty lane where they'd disappeared, turning down one alleyway, then another, searching the dead ends that peeled off the path—each a perfect place to rob a toff. To do worse to them. He cursed, loud in the darkness.

"Don't come any closer!"

No, he didn't like Hattie in the Garden. He didn't like her boots in his filth, or her voice ricocheting off his stone walls. But he absolutely didn't like the fear in it.

He'd break anyone who touched her.

He was at a flat run at that point, desperate to get to her. Telling himself, as he tore down the street, that he only rushed to protect her because she was the key to his enemy's demise.

Protect her.

Around the final corner, still in the shadows, Whit discovered the Doolan brothers—proper Garden thugs, homegrown from the muck of the place and far stronger than they were smart—backs to him.

Facing Hattie.

Whit couldn't see her face behind the duo's thick shoulders, but he could imagine it, and he hated it. Pale with her violet eyes—that impossible color—wide with fear, and her full lips open as her breath shallowed with panic.

Rage coursed through him, setting his heart pounding.

Protect her.

He couldn't see her. But he knew she'd be inching away from the stink of the brothers, from the rot of their teeth and the scars on their faces and the filth on their hands.

Wait.

She wasn't inching away from them. "The way I see it, gentlemen," she said, her voice ringing out, steady as a steel, "you've misjudged my ability to fend for myself. I don't think you'd like to see how I would do it."

She'd had a small knife in her pocket in the carriage last night—a blade sharp enough to cut the ropes at his wrists, but too small to strike fear in the hearts of the Doolans, who'd been on the threatening end of far more dangerous weapons. And still . . .

They were inching away from her.

What in hell? Whit edged closer in the shadows.

"Where'd you get that, gel?" Eddie Doolan asked. Was his voice wavering?

"You know it, then?" She was surprised.

"E'ryone in the Rookery knows it," Mikey said, his panic undeniable.

She came into view, lit from above by a shaft of reflected sunlight, and Whit nearly rocked back on his heels at the sight of her. Tall and strong, her shoulders back and her jaw set like a warrior. And in her hand . . . a blade that promised wicked punishment.

Punishment Whit knew without question, because he'd meted it out a hundred times. A thousand.

The woman held one of his throwing knives.

Shock was chased by a thrum of anticipation when Eddie asked, words reed-thin with fear, "Are you Beast's?"

Whit ignored his instant reaction to the question.

"I have his blade, do I not?"

Clever girl, brazening it through.

"Shit," Mikey spat, "I ain't no part o' this." He scurried off like the street rat he was, there, then gone.

She turned surprised eyes to Eddie. "Rather disloyal of him, don't you think?"

Eddie swallowed. "You ain't tellin' Beast, are you, lady?"

Whit answered for her, stepping out of the shadows. "She won't have to."

Hattie gasped as Eddie spun toward him, hands already up as Whit advanced. "We weren't doin' nuffin', Beast. Just scarin' 'er a bit. Just enough so she don' mess wi' our card men again."

He came closer. "What are the rules, Eddie?"

The other man's throat worked, searching for the answer that wouldn't come. "No hurtin' gels. But—"

Whit hated the word. There were no qualifiers to the rule. That single syllable made him want to tear the other man apart.

Eddie's eyes went wide as Whit came closer, his fear spilling stupid words into the dusk. "We didn't expect 'er to pull a knife, Beast. If you fink abou' it, the lady started it."

What a fucking imbecile.

He nodded. "Started it by running from you."

Eddie's minuscule brain clamored for a reply. "Runnin' *after* the card man. Lookin' fer you." Thinking he'd struck on something valuable, he smiled. "We were protectin' *you*, see?"

"Oh, please," Hattie scoffed from over Eddie's shoulder, but Whit refused to look at her, afraid of what might happen if he did.

Instead, he reached for Eddie, clasping Eddie's grubby

lapels in his hands and pulling him close. "If I ever see you threaten a woman again, I'll show you just what that blade feels like. Remember, I'm everywhere. I see everything."

Eddie swallowed, sweat beading on his forehead. Nodded.

"Do you have something to say to the lady?"

"S-sorry," the filth whispered.

Not good enough. "Louder."

"Sorry, lady. Beg pardon. Sorry."

Whit did look to Hattie then, her own eyes wide with surprise. "Yes. All right." She slid her gaze to his, and he didn't like the uncertainty there. "I accept. He appears to have learned a lesson."

"Get out." He threw Eddie away from them, not watching as he fell to the ground and scrambled immediately backward, rising to a run. Instead, Whit turned to the rooftops and whistled, long and piercing, to the night. "Find me Michael Doolan. Tell him he'd best find me at the fights. And if he doesn't come to me, he shan't like what happens when I come for him."

He turned back to Hattie, whose uncertainty had turned to curiosity. "Do you make a habit of speaking to buildings?"

"I'll stop when they no longer do my bidding."

"The stones will fetch this man to you?" When he didn't answer, she added, "So it's true what they say?"

Who had spoken to her? What had they said?

He grunted his reply, ignoring the rage that whirled through him at the idea that she might have been hurt here, on his turf. Ignoring the deeply unsettling idea that he might not have been able to protect her had he been a few minutes later. Whether or not the woman held his knife.

Speaking of. He extended a hand. "Give me the weapon."

She tightened her grip on the onyx blade, and he imagined the warmth of her palm against the design there, the softness of her gloves polishing the fine ridges of steel that kept a grip firm and ensured a straight aim and a true strike. "What are the fights?"

His only solace. Ignoring the question, he said, "The blade, Hattie."

She looked at it. "They were afraid of it."

He did not reply, waiting for her to say what she really meant.

"They were afraid of *you.*"

He tried to find the disgust in the words. She was softness and shine—cleaner and fresher in her starched bonnet and her white shawl than this place had ever been. She was nothing like it, and shouldn't be here. And she should be disgusted by what she'd witnessed. By the coarseness of it. By the filth.

By him.

"No, not you," she said, and for a wild moment, Whit imagined she'd heard his thoughts. She lifted the blade, inspected it in the fast-disappearing light, and added, in a whisper, "They were afraid of the *idea* of you."

"All fear is fear of an idea," he said. He knew that better than most. Had been weaned on terror and learned to survive it. The tangible was bearable. It was the intangible that would steal breath and sleep and hope.

She tilted her head, considering him. "And what is the idea of you?"

Beast. He didn't give voice to the word. To the promise of it. For some wild reason, he didn't want her thinking of Beast when she looked at him.

He didn't want her looking at him.

Lie.

"Where is your chaperone?"

She blinked. "What?"

"It makes sense you didn't have one last night—no need for chaperoning at a brothel—but you're a woman of means, Henrietta Sedley, and there are any number of people in the marketplace who would have cause to recognize you."

Her lips, wide and full, opened on a surprised gasp. "You know who I am."

He didn't reply. There was no need.

"How?" she pressed.

Ignoring her question, he said, "You still don't know who I am, if you thought seeking me out was a good idea."

"I know they call you Beast." He'd told her that. "I know your brother is Devil." Uncertainty whispered through him. What else did she know? "Which makes me question the naming protocol in your family."

"He's my half-brother. We named ourselves," he said, hating the speed with which he replied. Hating that he replied at all.

Her face softened, and he hated that, too, irrationally. "I'm sorry for that, if those were the names you chose. But I suppose the Bareknuckle Bastards deserve names that deliver a blow."

He took a step toward her. "For someone who claims not to know anything about how I came to be unconscious in her carriage last evening, you know a great deal."

Those sinful lips curved into a smile, the expression like a blow. "You think I would not ask questions after our encounter?"

He should have scowled. Should have pounced on the evidence that she had a close relationship with the enemy that had shot his man and stolen his shipments and knocked him out. Should have held her family and its business to the fire and promised to set it aflame if she did not give him the information he desired.

He should have. But instead, he said, "And what else did you discover about me?"

What the fuck was he doing talking to her?

Her smile turned to secrets. "I am told that once you come for someone, you don't stop until you find them."

That much was true.

"But I wasn't certain you would come for me."

Of course he would have. He would have come for her in

her Mayfair tower even if she didn't have the information he desired.

No. Whit resisted the thought—an impressive feat until she added, that punishing dimple flashing in her cheek, "So I came for you."

He would never admit the pleasure that coursed through him at that confession. Nor would he admit to the pleasure that came when she reached for his hand, lifting it in one of hers.

"What happened to your hand?" The kidskin gloves she wore did not stop the sting of her heat as she stroked her fingers over his knuckles, red and stinging from the blow he'd put to the wall earlier. "You're hurt."

He sucked in a breath and removed his hand from her grasp, shaking it out. Wanting to erase her touch. "It's nothing."

She watched him for a moment, and he imagined her seeing more than he wished. And then, softly, she said, "No one would tell me about you."

He grunted. "That didn't stop you asking. Which returns us to the issue of your chaperone. Any number of toffs could have seen you. And I imagine any number of toffs would have questioned your lack of subtlety in asking for me."

Her lips twisted in a wry smile. "I am not known for subtlety." There was something more in her tone than humor, though—something he found he did not like.

He refused to show it. "I can't imagine why. I've known you for less than a day and during the time I was not unconscious, you were frequenting a brothel and threatening to knife a pair of Garden criminals."

"It's not as though you're a Mayfair gentleman yourself." She smiled. "Or did you forget the bit where I made an improper arrangement with you yesterday?"

Arrangement. The word sizzled through him with the memory of the night before. Of the taste of her. Of the feel of her in his arms. Of the damn look of her—like a banquet.

"Why not make one with one of your toffs?"

She seemed to consider the option. *Don't consider it*, he willed silently before she replied, "Well, first, I don't have a single toff, let alone more than one." *Because toffs were fucking imbeciles.*

He grunted. "No choice but to slum it."

Her eyes widened. "I don't consider it . . ." She couldn't repeat the words. Christ, she was soft. ". . . that."

"What, then?"

She tilted her head. "I don't care if you're not a gentleman. I don't require someone who knows their way around Mayfair. I see no reason why our arrangement should have anything to do with your ability to waltz or your knowledge of the hierarchy of the peerage."

But he did know all those things. He'd been trained to be a peer. He'd spent two years learning the intricacies of the aristocracy. Of their shit world. And but for a single moment two decades ago, he might have been a different man. He might have met her under a different circumstance. If Ewan had lost and Whit had won—he would have been a duke.

And he could have come for her in another way entirely.

Not that he wished to. All he wanted was to get her out of Covent Garden.

What was it they'd been talking about? "The chaperone."

She lifted a shoulder and let it drop beneath that finely knitted shawl that he imagined would never be white again after an afternoon in the muck. "I don't require one."

His exhale might have been shock if he were a different sort of man. "Yes, you do."

"No, I don't. I am not a child. I am twenty-nine years old today, which, by the way, would usually merit some kind of felicitation."

He blinked. "Happy birthday." Why in hell had he said that?

She smiled, bright as the damn sun, as though they were in a ballroom somewhere, instead of a back alley. "Thank you."

"You don't need a chaperone. You need a jailer."

"Literally no one cares a bit about where I go."

"I do."

"Excellent," she said smartly, "as I came for you."

It was the second time she said it, and the second time he liked it, and he did not wish to repeat the experience. "Why?"

She extended the knife to him then, opening her palm to reveal the hilt, dark against the pale glove she wore—a glove he wished wasn't there, so he might see the ink stains on her wrists and read the story they told on her palm. "This belongs to you," she said simply. "I promised you I would return it."

He looked to the weapon. "Why do you have it?"

She hesitated, and he loathed the pause—the idea that this woman, who was full of honesty and truth, had hidden her reply.

"Because I promised I would return it," she repeated. "I'm sorry."

He took the knife. What did she apologize for? Was it as simple as the knife? As the set from which it had come? Was it the attack on the shipment the night before? The ones that had come earlier? Did she know they'd taken thousands of pounds? That they'd threatened the lives of his men?

Or something else?

Was it Ewan?

Fury and disbelief roared through him at the idea. And something else. Something like panic. If she was anywhere near Ewan, Whit wouldn't be able to keep her safe.

He pushed the thought away. She wasn't working with Ewan. He'd know if she was betraying him so keenly, wouldn't he?

He struggled to tear his gaze from her, hating the way the light thieved her from him, the narrow streets of the Garden disappearing the sun prematurely, and his frustration had him reaching for her, taking her hand, and pulling her through the maze of streets, back to the market square, where white stone was aflame with the last vestige of orange.

He released her the moment they stepped into the clearing. "There. Back where you began."

She turned to him. "It's not just the knife."

"No," he replied. "It's not. The sheer amount of what has been taken from me is far more than this knife."

"I know that now. I didn't last night."

He believed her because he wanted to, even as he knew he shouldn't. Even as he had absolutely no reason for it. "I want a name, Lady Henrietta."

Prove you're not a part of it.

Tell me the truth.

She shook her head. "Surely you can understand why I might not be able to give it."

"Able? Or willing?"

No hesitation. "Willing."

She was more honest than anyone he'd ever met. Far and away more honest than he was. "And so we are at an impasse."

"We aren't, though." She turned a bright face toward him, full of truth and a simplicity that Whit wasn't certain he'd ever exhibited on his own. "I have a solution."

He shouldn't have given the words even a moment's thought. Should have stopped her from speaking and ended whatever madness she was about to suggest right there, as the sun set on the market square.

Instead, he said, "What kind of solution?"

"Reimbursement," she said, happily, as though it were all perfectly easy, and trotted off toward the market, leaving him no choice but to follow her.

He did, like a hound, knowing that the spies on the rooftops above wouldn't hesitate in reporting his actions to his brother and sister and Nik. Knowing, and somehow not caring. Instead, he followed Hattie toward the market stalls, staying several steps behind her, watching, until she crouched to inspect the contents of a basket at the feet of an older woman from the Rookery. Hattie looked up, an unspoken question on her open, friendly face, and received the only reply such an expression elicited. *Yes.*

Reaching into the basket, Hattie extracted a tiny, squirming puppy, coming to her feet to cuddle the black ball close to her chest and croon to it softly. Whit approached then, something tightening in his chest—something he did not wish to feel, and certainly did not wish to remember. Hattie didn't seem to care about that, however, turning her bright smile on him to say, "I love it here."

The words were a blow, this woman so unexpected and out of place on his turf, so impossible to ignore, with a soft joy in her voice that was impossible to miss. He didn't want her to love it here. He wanted her to loathe it. To leave it.

To leave it, and him, alone.

But she didn't. Instead, she elaborated. "When I was a child, my father would bring me to the market."

It wasn't a surprise. The market was a destination for London's upper class—a way to play in the muck of the Garden without having to risk getting dirty. Whit had seen hundreds of nobs coming down from up on high in the market. Thousands of them. As a boy, he'd fleeced them, picked their pockets, led them astray. He'd watched the men with their pristine black suits and the women with their impossibly white frocks and the children, built in the image of their perfect parents.

And he'd hated them.

Hated that, but for an infinitesimal twist of fate, he might have been one of them.

He'd taken great joy in fleecing the rich. He'd lain awake at night, imagining the shock and anger and frustration on their faces when they discovered their pockets sliced, their purses cut, their money frittered away. Their money might rule the world, but in those moments, here, it was no match for Whit's cunning. For the Bastards' power.

"Before everything changed," she said to the dog, and to him. Before Sedley had been given his peerage, he imagined she meant. He knew what kind of change that would have wrought. He'd wished it for himself once upon a time. More than once. A thousand times, even as he'd stood in this square and spit on the idea of it.

But now, as he watched this woman, cuddling a ball of black fur in her arms, he wondered if he'd ever seen her. If he'd ever watched her from the rafters above, or from behind a market stall. If he'd ever wondered at her strange violet eyes. If he'd ever seen her wide, winning smile and envied it. There had been days when his stomach was so empty of food that he'd fed on envy—and he would have envied Hattie her clean dresses and her happy smiles and her doting father.

He would have envied her life as much as he would have wanted to be a part of it.

Not any longer, of course. He didn't have time for the daughter of an earl, with a life in Mayfair, slumming in the Garden.

Hattie rubbed her cheek against the puppy's smooth head, a soft smile on her lips, and he resisted the desire that coursed through him at the idea of that soft touch on him. "There was a farmer who had an ancient stall . . . and in the spring he sold the sweetest, crispest French beans." She laughed, the sound a pretty sting. "My father would buy me a sack full of them and I'd never get further than the entrance to the market before I had it open, munching away." She paused, then, full of embarrassment, "He still calls me Bean."

Whit didn't want that story. He didn't want to be charmed by it. He certainly didn't want to know the silly name her father called her. He didn't want to think of that little, fair-haired girl, with too-big eyes and a taste for French beans, he didn't want the memory of those beans somehow on his own tongue.

She bent down, returning the puppy to the basket. His mouth watered.

She straightened, offering a wide smile to the older woman. "Thank you. That was lovely."

The saleswoman nodded. "Would you like 'un, lady?" She looked to Whit, expectantly, as though a hound was a perfectly ordinary impulse purchase.

"Oh, I would love one," Hattie said, softly, longingly, as she stared into the basket like the child he'd just been imagining.

For a wild moment, Whit considered buying the whole lot of them, dammit.

"But not today. Today, I merely needed a stroke."

He nearly choked at the words, so innocent and sweet, and somehow, so fucking filthy in his mind. He growled low and reached into his pocket, extracting a bob and passing it to the older woman. "For you, Rebecca. For humoring the lady."

The woman dipped a curtsy. "Thank 'e, Beast."

He caught her eye. "You and I both know those pups shouldn't be far from their dam just yet. If you and Seth are struggling, you come to Devil and me."

"We don't need your charity, Beast." The words were stern and full of pride. Rebecca's only son had lost a leg in an accident a year earlier, and the woman grew older by the day, but there were ways to ensure the pair was able to eat.

"I'm not offering charity. We'll find you both honest work."

The old woman's eyes went glassy and her lips thinned as she held back her response; she ultimately nodded once and reached down to collect her basket, setting it on her hip and making her way home through the square. Whit watched for a moment before turning back to Hattie, with her unyielding violet gaze.

He resisted the urge to look away—to hide from those eyes that seemed to see everything. Resisted, too, the urge to ask her what she saw.

She didn't tell him. Instead, she said, "I have the power to ensure your reimbursement."

He believed her, even as he knew others wouldn't. She wouldn't lie to him. But still, he asked, "How am I to know that?"

"I know enough for both of us," she said, as though she'd had this conversation a dozen times before. *And perhaps she had.* Uncertainty threaded through him as she continued. "I know four shipments have been thieved. I know they were worth nearly forty thousand pounds. I know the wagons hijacked were filled with contraband—liquor and fabrics and paper and glass, all smuggled up the Thames and out of Covent Garden without tax and beneath the eye of the Crown." He hid his surprise from her, remaining silent as she added, "And I am prepared to return those funds."

Why?

He resisted the urge to ask her. Instead, he crossed his arms over his chest and rocked back on his heels. "And where will you find forty thousand quid?"

She narrowed her gaze on him. "You think I cannot?"

"That is precisely what I think."

She nodded and looked around them, darkness finally having cloaked the market square, making it impossible to see farther than a few feet. She stepped closer—so he could see her? Or so others couldn't?

"I'll find it where I found the knife I returned," she said.

That damn knife. The meaning of it. The message. Had she pulled it from the thigh where he'd seated it? Had she cleaned it? How deep was she in her brother's actions? How involved was she in Ewan's? Possibly more than he'd thought if she was here now with no protection and Whit's throwing knife.

And yet . . . when her hands moved to the opening of her shawl, gripping the soft white knit there, he leaned forward, drawn to the movement, to the waft of almonds that came with it. *Was she cold?* Without thinking, he was reaching for his own coat, to shuck it and give it to her.

She spoke before he could, soft and teasing, and with a touch of . . . was that triumph? "And where I found the others." She opened the fabric, revealing the dress beneath, the perfect moss green now gray in the twilight, a quiet color befitting a spinster doing a market shop.

But it was not the pale color of the frock that sent want thrumming through Whit, stealing his breath; it was the black leather overlaid on it in thick, sturdy straps. Leather he knew like second skin, because it was *his* second skin.

Christ.

The woman was wearing his holster. Filled with the rest of his knives, gleaming in the twilight as though they belonged with her—a warrior queen.

And the sight of her, proud and strong and stunning, threatened to put him to his knees.

Chapter Ten

She should have panicked at the way his eyes narrowed when she revealed the rest of the knives. She should have quaked at his penetrating stare, at the way he stilled, like a wild animal, tuning every one of its senses to the racing heartbeat of its prey.

And Hattie's heart did pound. But not from fear.

From excitement.

She raised a brow and lifted her chin, knowing she tempted fate. "Do you believe I have the power to negotiate a deal now?"

A low growl sounded in Beast's throat before he said, "Where did you get them?"

She couldn't tell him that, of course. "I'm here to return them, just as I promised I would return the rest. Every pound."

He came closer, reached for the edges of her shawl, his rough fingers brushing over her gloves, making her wish she wasn't wearing them. Her breath was shallow as he pulled it closed around her, hiding his knives and looking about, just as she had done, as though searching for witnesses.

As though this man called Beast might reveal the precise origin of that name.

"You know not what you play at, Lady Henrietta."

A shiver went through her. She should have been terrified. But she wasn't. She put her shoulders back. "I've no interest in playing. I came to find you, and to apprise you of my plans."

The Year of Hattie.

He didn't hesitate. He grasped her hand and pulled her through the marketplace, back the way they'd come. She had a dozen things to say and even more questions to ask, but she remained quiet as he led her down a dark cobblestone street, curving away from the market square, to a sole lantern swinging happily above a painted sign. The Singing Sparrow.

"Is this place named for *the* Singing Sparrow?" The world-renowned singer was revered by Londoners, and was said to have been birthed here, in Covent Garden, where she still sang when she was home from her legendary travels.

With a grunt that might have been confirmation, Whit pushed through the door into the dark tavern, past a handful of men, listing on their chairs. Hattie craned to see the space, tugging at Beast's grip even as he tightened it, not slowing down as he passed the bar, behind which a great blond man stood, wiping a pint glass. "All right, Beast?"

Another grunt.

The man, who sounded American, turned to Hattie. "All right, miss?"

She smiled brightly. "He doesn't speak much."

The American blinked his surprise. "No, he doesn't."

"I speak enough for both of us."

"There's no both of us," Beast growled, before opening a door on the far side of the room, pulling her inside, and closing them in—and the barkeep's laughter out.

She took in the large stockroom filled with crates and

casks, illuminated by a small torch high in one corner. "Do you make a habit of commandeering tavern storage rooms?"

"Do you make a habit of commandeering men's weapons?"

"I hadn't, until now. But I will admit, they came in quite useful." His gaze narrowed on her, intense enough to steal her breath. He stepped toward her, and she wondered if he could hear her heart beating in her chest. It seemed he should. It seemed all of London should be able to hear the thunder of it.

"Take them off."

The growl sizzled through her, and for a wild, mad moment she thought he meant something other than the knives. Something like her clothes.

For a wild, mad moment, she almost did it.

Thankfully—*thankfully?*—she returned to her senses.

Or did she?

"Not yet." The reply didn't seem sensible at all. Not as the words flew from her lips and certainly not when he stepped closer, close enough for the heat of him to envelop her. It had been the first thing she'd noticed about him, that warmth, and now he threatened to incinerate her.

She let her shawl fall open, revealing his weapons, but the movement did nothing to alleviate the heat. If anything, baring herself to him only made her hotter. His gaze tracked the complicated web of leather that held her in its wicked embrace, the weight of the weapons a tempting ache.

He leaned in, the scent of his lemon sweets making her mouth water with memory of their taste. Of *his* taste. "Not yet?"

She could close the distance between them without effort. All it would take was a little stretch—just enough to press her lips to his. Would he welcome it? He didn't look like it. He looked . . . irritated.

In for a penny, in for a pound, Hattie supposed. "Not until you agree to the arrangement I'm offering."

"You are mistaken if you think you are in a position of power, Hattie."

She swallowed. "M-my father owns a shipping company. You surely know that."

A grunt of acknowledgment.

"I'm to inherit it." Surprise flashed through his eyes, there, then gone as quickly as she could name it. This was it. Her first deal as the head of the company. The beginning of the Year of Hattie. It didn't matter that it was happening in the back room of a Covent Garden tavern with a man who was more criminal than customer.

What mattered was that Hattie would make the deal, and then she would make good on it. The thought cleared her mind. She straightened her shoulders. Lifted her chin. "I'm prepared to give you fifty percent of the income on our shipments until we return the forty thousand. Plus . . . ten percent interest."

A dark brow rose. "Thirty percent."

It was an enormous amount, but Hattie refused to show it. "Fifteen."

"Thirty."

She pressed her lips into a thin, disapproving line. "Seventeen."

"Thirty."

Exasperation flared. "You're supposed to be negotiating."

"Am I?"

"Do you not run a business?"

"Of a sort," he said.

Obstinate man. "And as part of that business, do you not negotiate?"

He crossed his arms over his broad chest. "Not often."

"I suppose you just take what you like."

A black brow rose in reply. "I might remind you that it is your penchant for taking what you like that has landed us here, Lady Henrietta."

"I told you, I had nothing to do with it. I am only here to repair the damage."

"Why?"

Because that business is the only thing I've ever wanted in my life.

"Because I don't like thievery." He watched her for a long moment—long enough for her to become uncomfortable. She shifted on her feet and said, "And so . . . twenty percent."

He did not move. "So far, you've offered me nothing I would not have taken without your offering it. Indeed, you've offered less than I intend to take."

She blinked. "More than twenty percent interest?"

He was enormous in the quiet space. "More than money, Hattie."

She cleared her throat. "The deal is for money. Money and your knives."

She regretted the words as soon as they were out, his amber gaze on the leather braces crisscrossing her chest making her wish she hadn't removed her shawl.

"Then it isn't a deal," he said. "A deal implies that I get something in return. So, I ask again. What do I get from this deal that is so far simply a repayment of funds and a return of goods thieved, with no assurance that your company will avoid interaction with my businesses in the future?"

Your company. She didn't miss the words, smooth and certain on his tongue. Didn't miss the pleasure of them rioting through her—hers. She was so close to it all. The future she'd always wanted. She wouldn't let him take it from her. "You have my assurance."

"And I am to believe your father wouldn't repeat himself when he decides he needs money again?"

Defensiveness flared. "It wasn't my father." He did not react to the words. She narrowed her gaze on him. "But you know that."

"Tell me why you protect the truth."

Because he's my only chance at the business. That had been the deal with Augie. She made this disappear, she kept him safe, and he would tell Father to give her the business.

Everything was on the line. And this man—his acceptance of her offered arrangement—was all that stood between her and her future. But if she told him that, he would hold all the power. And she couldn't allow that.

So, she stayed silent.

He closed the distance between them with predatory grace that would have set any number of men on edge. And it did set her on edge as he lifted a hand, reaching for her. Her breath caught in her throat. What would he do? *Would he touch her?*

He didn't touch her. Instead, he set a single finger to the thick leather strap at her shoulder, the one leading down to his knives, tracing it with barely-there pressure. "Tell me why he gave you my knives and sent you into my world."

The touch traveled lower and lower, over the ribs of the blades seated deep in their leather scabbards. Her breath came harsh as he followed the second strap, the one that crossed beneath her breasts, over the buckle connecting one half of the holster to the other.

"Tell me why he sent you to me, like a sacrifice." His touch lingered on the brass, his thumb coming to stroke over it once, twice. On the third pass, his fingers splayed over her torso, and she simultaneously craved and feared the caress—at once hinting at immense pleasure and hot embarrassment. After all, Hattie was not exactly lean, and there, where leather crossed her body, there was a swell of flesh that she would prefer he not notice.

She took a step back, hating the loss of his touch even as she found the breath that had been impossible for her to catch. She lifted her chin, drawing strength from the cool oak door behind her. She willed her voice firm. "He didn't send me anywhere. I am the heroine of my own play, sir."

"Mmm. A warrior in your own right." He advanced, his nearness pressing her more firmly into the door. "So it is you who offers me these poor terms. Money that was mine to begin with and none of the retribution I intended to exact."

"Retribution is a silly goal," she said. "It's intangible. It's air."

"Mmm." The low rumble of assent was at her ear, so close she imagined she could feel the breath of it on her skin. "Just like air. Essential. Vital. Life-giving."

She leaned away at that, twisting to see his eyes, cursing the darkness in the dimly lit room. "Do you believe that?"

He was silent long enough for her to believe he might not reply. And then he replied, soft and dark, "I believe that we spend all our lives fighting for our due. Air or otherwise."

The words struck true. Lord knew Hattie had spent her fair time doing just that. Fighting for autonomy, for future, for her father's approval and her family's business. She'd been born a woman in a man's world, and spent her entire life battling for a place in it. Desperate to prove herself worthy of it.

But this man—when he spoke of fighting for air—Hattie did not think he was speaking in metaphors.

Unable to stop herself, she lifted a hand and, moving slowly enough that he could stop her if he wished, she set her palm to his cheek, the warmth of it searing through her glove as the rough day's growth of his beard caught on the soft kidskin. "I'm sorry," she whispered.

It was the wrong thing to say. The muscles of his jaw tightened and his entire body turned to steel. She dropped her hand the moment he caught her gaze in his. "You suggest I wait for my funds to be returned, just as I wait now, for my knives to be so. Just as I was to wait last night—for the culmination of the arrangement we made."

The agreement that he would take her virginity. That he would ruin her for all others. She didn't need it now. Not if

Augie was going to support her bid to run her father's business. She didn't need him or ruination.

But she wanted it. At this man's skilled hands.

Her gaze dropped to the hands in question, fingers loosely curled as though, at any moment, he might have to do battle. She remembered the feel of those fingers on her skin. The rough calluses on his palms. The way they set her aflame.

She wanted them again.

"I don't care for waiting, Lady Henrietta." The low words, spoken a breath from her ear, sent heat coiling through her. "So let me ask again. What do I get from your deal?"

Last night, it had all seemed so simple. He'd agreed—albeit under duress—to take her virginity in exchange for his missing items. But last night, Hattie hadn't known the missing items included forty thousand pounds in smuggled goods.

Dammit, Augie.

And now—she knew she lacked both leverage and power. This man called Beast somehow did not need the funds her brother had stolen, and he did not require the goods that had been parceled off to wherever they'd been sent. This was not about reimbursement, but about restitution. And that made him more benefactor than business partner.

Which meant Hattie had no choice but to surrender everything for the sake of the business. For the sake of her family. She took a deep breath and met Beast's gaze, and sacrificed her only desire—a desire she hadn't known she had until the night before. "I release you from last night's negotiation."

He remained silent, revealing nothing of his thoughts.

Did he even understand?

"My—" Hattie waved a hand. "Affliction."

A dark brow rose.

"My virginity."

Again, no reply.

He was going to make her say it. Lord knew Hattie had said it before. But did she have to say it to him? To this man who'd kissed her and made her feel like he wished it? "I understand that such an event . . . with me . . . is not exactly . . ." *Ugh.* This was awful. "I know you were being kind. Offering. But you needn't—that is—I am well aware of the kind of woman I am. Equally so, the kind of woman I am not. And the kind of man you are . . . well, you prefer the kind of woman I am not."

She closed her eyes tightly, willing him to disappear. When she opened them, he was, sadly, still there, still as stone. Which was unbearable.

"And what kind of woman is that?"

Like that, his presence was quite bearable, because that question became the new definition of unbearable. She drew the line at answering it. At saying any of the words that sprang to mind and tongue. *Overlarge. Unappealing.* "Never mind."

Miraculously, he did not press. "No deal."

Frustration flared. Frustration and anger and no small amount of disappointment. She'd worked for this business for her entire life, and here she was, on the precipice of losing it all. "Thirty percent."

He did not reply.

Hattie lost her temper. "Fifty-two thousand pounds and a promise to never reveal your silly-monikered crime ring to the Crown—which would surely like to hear of it, by the way."

"Is that a threat, Lady Henrietta?"

She sighed. "Of course it isn't. But what more would you like from me? I've returned your knives and offered you money and the opportunity to be rid of me for the rest of time."

"You still wear my knives."

She reached for the fastening of the holster, unbuckling the leather with quick, economical movements, sliding it off her shoulders and ignoring the unsettling sense of loss of the weapons' strange embrace. She dropped the knives at his feet, unceremoniously, resisting the urge to wince at the carelessness of the action.

"There. What more do you want?"

"I told you; I want retribution."

"We go around in circles, then, sir. As I told you; I shan't let you punish him."

"Is he your lover?"

Hattie choked at the question. "No."

A long stretch of silence ended with a nod and he turned away from her, stalking away, through the labyrinth of crates and casks.

"Why do you care?" she called after him. And why in hell had she asked such a question?

He considered a nearby crate, branded with an American flag. "I don't make a habit of fucking other men's women."

Her heart began to pound at the word and the way it painted wicked, wonderful pictures. Not that she was willing to reveal such a thing. "Am I to think it noble that you ascribe to some nonsensical view of women as doe-eyed chattel who cannot make their own decisions about their bedmates?"

His attention shot back to her.

"Because, let me be clear, sirrah," she said, coming off the door and heading for him without thought, unable to keep the haughty irritation from her voice. "If I were here on behalf of my lover, you'd do well to note who possesses whom in such a descriptor."

His tight jaw slackened in the heavy silence that came on the heels of the words, but Hattie didn't have time to be proud of the hint of his shock. She was too busy being surprised herself. She stilled, flanked by heavy casks of ale. "And besides, I have released you from the chore of ridding me of my virginity, so you may rest easy on all accounts, and tell me what it is you require so you may let me go and I may return to my well-laid plans."

He turned away, his gaze falling to the crate once more.

His shoulders rose and fell in a smooth motion, and Hattie thought she might have been dismissed.

She thought wrong. Because when he turned back to her and spoke, it was low and dark and with a promise of something absolutely devastating. And possibly very delicious. "Know this, Henrietta Sedley. Ridding you of your virginity will be no kind of chore." He approached her in slow, smooth movements—movements that had her retreating even as the promise of his nearness thrilled her. "And if you think to renege on that part of our arrangement, you have not yet learned what it is to transact with the Bareknuckle Bastards."

Her breath caught in her throat, and still he advanced, coming for her. *Yes, please. Please come for me.*

And still he spoke, more words than she'd heard him speak altogether before then. Low, lush promise. "You may not have been anywhere near the hijackings. You may not have seen a shilling of the money that the men you protect stole from us, but you are here now, and they are not, and you have put yourself in my path, and I do not lose."

She lifted her chin. Brazened it out. "I don't, either."

"I saw you brandish my blade earlier, warrior." A ghost of a smile passed over his lips then—even the hint of it dazzling. Or was it the word he used for the second time? *Warrior.* She would like to be that. She would like to match him in that.

As though she'd spoken aloud, he said softly, "We shall be well-matched. Here is your deal—the only one I shall agree to."

Hattie was in over her head, at once desperate to run from this place and hole herself up in the safety of her home far from here, and eager to stand her ground and welcome this man who promised her everything for which she never knew she could ask.

"I get it all. Everything you offered. Everything I demand. Including you." Heat flooded her, rioting over her cheeks and pooling deep in her. She gasped—how close was she to get air in this room, with him filling it like smoke, promising to burn the place down and her with it? And still, he talked. "You thought I would let you go? On the contrary. You owe me, Hattie. You owe me in his stead."

Yes. *Yes.* Whatever he wanted.

He was there, now, reaching for her, the fingers of one strong hand curving at her nape, the other hand finding her waist, pulling her close. His thumb tilting her chin up. For his promise. "You owe me, and I intend to collect. In myriad ways."

Triumph flared. She'd get it all. He'd accept the payment she offered, the return of his blades, the return of the security of his business, and Augie would tell their father that Hattie should run the business. And Hattie would finally have the life she'd planned. And, somehow, she'd get this man, too. Or at least a taste of him. She'd get his kiss and his touch and he'd show her the full experience he'd promised her the night before.

The Year of Hattie had only just begun, and it was proving to be properly auspicious.

She couldn't help her smile.

"You like that?"

She nodded.

"You don't know what you agree to."

Hattie ignored the dark promise in the words. Instead, heart pounding, she came up on her toes, unable to stop herself from reaching for him. From making him keep that promise. He pulled back just before their lips touched. "Not here."

"Why not?" The words were out before she could stop them, embarrassment hot on their tail.

"It's not private."

She looked about the room. "The door is closed, the light is dim, and the place is silent as the grave." She stopped before saying outright, *Kiss me, dammit.*

"This is one of the most raucous taverns in Covent Garden, and will soon be filled with scores of people all waiting for the nightly entertainment. Calhoun will require access to his stockroom the moment they start to drink. It's not private."

Hattie had the unreasonable instinct to stamp her foot. "Then where?"

"I'll find you when it's time."

She blinked. "You're sending me home?"

"I am."

Hattie was not a fool. She'd lived a full twenty-nine years and knew a thing or two about a thing or two, not the least of which was this: If a man was interested in tupping a woman in the taproom of a Covent Garden tavern, then he would likely get the job done there and then. Unless, of course, he wasn't entirely interested to begin with. "I see."

"Do you?"

"Very well." She cleared her throat. She would not be disappointed. She certainly would not be *sad*. Instead, she would be irritated. Irritation seemed feasible. "You cannot seduce the name from me, if that's what you intend. Imagining it as a possibility insults us both. I shall send you a bank draft the moment our next shipment is paid for." She collected her shawl from the sawdust-covered floor, shook it out, and turned on her heel to head for the door.

As her hand settled on the handle, he said, "Henrietta."

She stilled. "No one calls me that."

Silence. Then, "Hmm." Close. Too close. He'd followed her. And then he touched her, one finger tracing down her spine, sending a thrill through her. No. Not a thrill. She wasn't thrilled.

She stiffened, wrapping her arms about herself. Closing herself to the pleasure of his touch. "You needn't condescend to touch me."

"You think I do not wish to touch you?" The words were hot against the back of her neck.

"I think that men who have an inkling to deflower women—twice—do not send them home—twice—without proper deflowering." She turned her head. "It would be one thing if you were a Mayfair gentleman. But we both know you're not that."

She hated the words the moment they were out of her mouth. She didn't care that he'd never set foot in Mayfair. Lord knew most of the aristocratic men she knew weren't gentlemen in the least. Not when the world wasn't watching. "I'm sorry."

"Don't be."

"I didn't mean . . ."

"I was raised in the gutter."

She met his gaze instantly. "That doesn't mean anything." When he did not reply, she turned back to the door, embarrassed.

"I'm no kind of gentleman," he said at her ear, a dark promise. "I've never pretended to be." He slowly traced her spine back up to her shoulders, lingering on the exposed skin of her neck, and whispered, "And when I deflower you, it will be very far from proper."

And, like that, she was aflame. Out of her depth. And still, doubt whispered. "But not tonight." She sounded petulant. She knew she did. But she had been quite hopeful for the evening, and it was, after all, her birthday, and now she was to go home and who knew when he'd turn up again. Probably never.

More interminable silence, long enough for her to fidget beneath it. And then, "Hattie?"

She did not look at him. "What?"

"Shall I tell you what kind of thoughts I am thinking?"

She lifted a shoulder. Let it drop. Willed him to think she didn't care one way or another. Willed him to tell her every word he was thinking.

"I am thinking that your skin is the softest I've ever touched," he said, that maddening finger moving in perfect circles. "I'm thinking that when I get you alone—fully alone—I'm going to strip you bare and test its softness everywhere."

She sucked in a breath as the finger dipped to her shoulder, tracing the skin of her back, along the line of her dress. "I am thinking of how you feel here, soft like silk, and somehow, even softer elsewhere. I am thinking of how your breasts feel," he said, the slow, languid tenor of his voice making them aching and heavy. "Softer, still, and their tips—" He growled. "I'm thinking of how they feel against my tongue." She whimpered as the tips in question hardened, straining for him even as he resisted touching her but for that one, wild place where his fingertip stroked her shoulder.

"Of how they taste, like sugar and sin." He was at her ear, and she swayed at the words, at the way they threatened her. "Of how you bowed to my touch yesterday. Do you remember?"

She closed her eyes, wanting it again. Nodding.

"Say it."

"I remember."

"Mmm." Every one of this man's rumbles was a riot over her skin. Through her body. "And you want it again."

Another nod.

"Aloud."

"Yes." Breath, not sound. She swallowed. Spoke louder. "Yes, *please*."

"Touch them."

She jerked at the command. "I—What?"

"You want them. You want my hands on you. Show me how."

She shook her head. "I can't."

"You can. Touch them. They ache for it, for your touch."

No, she wanted to cry, *they ache for yours*.

And then, as though he'd heard the thought, "Think of

your hands as mine. That's what I am thinking. I'm thinking of holding them, of feeling them spilling out of my palms, of lifting them and taking them in my mouth. Of licking and sucking them until you are weeping and wet."

She whimpered at the words, her hands rising to the door, her fingers splaying wide on the wood, holding her upright against the onslaught of his thoughts. How could he say such things? This man who dealt in silence and grunts? How could he stand here, in a place he had declared not private enough, and say such filthy, wonderful things?

How could she want more of it?

How was he so calm? He destroyed her with every word, and somehow, he remained cool, his breathing even as ever, his only movement those small, devastating circles over her shoulder, across the back of her neck. "And you are wet, aren't you, Hattie?"

There was nothing he could say that would make her confess *that*.

"I'm finkin' 'bout what it'll do to me when you say it, Hattie." Nothing but that low growl, slipping into his Covent Garden accent. Nothing but the idea that even the thought of her desire for him might lay him low.

She bit her lip and pressed her forehead to the door. Nodded.

"Fuck." The curse came on a whisper. "Out loud."

"Yes."

"Say it."

"I am—you've made me—"

"Wait." His groan interrupted her, and suddenly it wasn't just one finger painting her skin with circles, it was his whole hand, running over her shoulder, down her arm, threading his fingers into hers. Tugging her around to face him.

And when she faced him, she saw the truth that his accent had hinted. He wasn't calm.

He was wild.

"Finish it," he growled. "What 'ave I made you?"

"Wet," she said, and the word seemed to strike him like a blow, setting him to his knees on a long, devastating curse.

He sat back on his ankles and stared up at her, his hands balled into fists on his thighs. He lifted one, running the back over his lips, like a man starved. Dear God, he was stunning. The sight of him there, on his knees, turned her into need. Pure, aching desire.

She shook her head, confused. "Please, Beast—"

"Now, I'm thinkin' you should lift your skirts."

And like that, with that single, hinted command, sanity fled. She did it, her hands under his spell as he watched the hem of her dress rise, as though by sheer force of his will. Or perhaps it was her will. Because when the skirts passed her knees, she didn't stop. She kept going. And he kept swearing, a litany of soft, filthy words in the quiet room.

"More, Hattie. Further. Show it to me. All of it."

His hands at her thighs, spreading them until he found the open slit of her drawers. The sound of ripping fabric decadent and indecent, and she didn't care even though she knew she should, and he was leaning forward, lifting one of her legs over his shoulder, and his fingers weren't on fabric anymore but skin, and words . . . they spilled from him like a rainstorm.

"That's it, love, such a pretty pussy."

"You—"

"Mmm?"

"You shouldn't use that word."

"Would you like me to use another?" He blew a lazy stream of air against her.

She gasped in surprise and pleasure. "Do you know very many?"

"Mmm. Very, very many. And I shall teach you all of them, but tonight—right now—you are so soft and wet, and I want a taste so badly—let me have a taste?"

She was too eager to be embarrassed. She was wanton and wanting and it didn't matter that she knew of this particular act only from the songs the sailors used to sing in the rigs when they thought she wasn't listening. Later, she would marvel at the way her body seemed to know precisely what he would do to her. At the way her fingers found his hair, at the way his breath caught when she fisted them and he released a long, slow curse at the soft skin of her thigh. At the way she spoke up. "Yes, please."

At the way he responded, his mouth like heaven.

He parted the folds and gave her what she'd asked for, setting his tongue to her, licking slow and steady, his tongue a magnificent gift, exploring every inch of her in long, firm strokes that had her gasping for breath. He growled against her, the vibration bringing her up on her toes with pleasure, her fingers tightening in his hair. "Mmm," he said against her. "Show me where you like it."

She shook her head, the hard oak door at her back a comfort in the storm he wrought. "I don't know," she whispered, gasping when his tongue found a glorious spot.

He stilled, then said, his voice filled with satisfaction, "I do."

And he did. He worked at that spot, his tongue flat against her, rubbing softly back and forth, again and again, until she felt as though she might scream from the pleasure. Until she was rocking against him, her grip holding him to her, lewd and lush.

"Please," she whispered, unable to summon more than that word. "Please."

And he stopped. The man *stopped*.

"No!" Her eyes flew open and she looked down at him. "Why?"

He didn't reply. He was too busy looking at her. "This . . ." he said, softly, setting that wicked, wonderful finger to her. Stroking over her most private part—the part that seemed to no longer be hers, but his instead. The part she would cede to him happily if only he'd finish what he started. ". . . is the prettiest thing I've ever seen."

She closed her eyes at the words. "Beast—"

He leaned forward and licked her, long and lush, lingering at the bud he'd been tempting. Stopped again. "This is what I was thinking about," he said. "This wet heat. This straining clit—so eager for me, innit?" He did look up to her then, his beautiful eyes full of heat and promise. "Aren't you?"

Her hips moved in lieu of her answer, undulating into his touch.

That barely-there smile of his flashed. "Mmm. Wild thoughts, indeed."

And then he resumed his kiss, spreading her wide as she pressed herself to him, and he was licking and *sucking*, and his wonderful tongue had her nearly—

The wall behind her moved. No. Not wall. *Door.*

She squeaked, her hand coming down to slap the wood behind her. He was still working at her, and she was still coiling, and there was—

A knock sounded at her ear.

She stiffened. "Stop."

"No." He redoubled his efforts.

She gasped at the immense pleasure, plateaued and now rising once more. "Yes," she whispered. "There." A delicious growl vibrated through her. Her fingers found his hair again. "Yes. Oh . . . oh, my . . . yes."

"Oy! Beast!" the American was shouting from scant inches away, beyond the door.

He pulled away from her, growling his impatience before raising his voice to say, "Not now, American."

Through the door, the barkeep said, "You've rooms of your own not one hundred yards away."

His eyes found Hattie's when he replied, "I was proving a point."

And well.

A pause. Then, amused, "Sounds like there is a *both of us* after all, Bastard—make it quick—and bring a crate of bourbon when you come."

Hattie's eyes went wide. "He knows what we're doing."

"Mmm." He leaned in and kissed her again, until she sighed. "Do you care?"

"Not—entirely." She rocked against him. "More. There."

He growled, his tongue stroking hard, in circles, firmer and tighter until he was working the place where she was desperate for him, and she was on her toes, shaking with a pleasure beyond any she'd ever felt. He was devouring her, eating her alive, and she didn't care as long as he gave her what she—

She flew apart, her hands in his hair, her hips grinding against him, and her whispered words as wild as the sounds he made, pure sin at her core. He stayed there, on his knees, against her, gentle and firm, until she released the long breath she'd held at the end, her grip relaxing from his hair, and the strength stealing from her legs.

He caught her in his arms as he stood, one strong hand capturing her face and tilting her up to him so he could kiss her. She tasted the sweet tang of herself on his lips, and he growled when she opened for him, licking deep until she was whimpering from the pleasure of the kiss.

When he lifted his mouth from hers, it was to say, "In my wildest thoughts, I didn't imagine you'd taste like that."

She dipped her head, embarrassment stealing through her. And still, she couldn't stop herself from asking, "Like what?"

He kissed her again. "Delicious." It was he who was delicious, she wanted to say, but he was kissing her again, stealing the words and the thought. "Wanton." She was wanton. What more would he show her?

So much more, if his next kiss was an indication, deep and lingering—long enough for them both to gasp for air.

He stared down at her, his chest rising and falling with his harsh breath, one hand tangled in her hair, and said softly, "Fucking dangerous."

A thrill shot through her at the words, filling her with pleasure and something far more intoxicating. Was this what people spoke of when they spoke of sexual pleasure? Did it always end with such a heady sense of . . . power?

She wanted more of it. Immediately.

But before she could say that, he was reaching down to pick up the shawl that she'd dropped in the excitement. He passed it to her and immediately turned away to collect his knives, sliding out of his coat and slinging it over a nearby cask before pulling on the holster and fastening it with ease, as though he'd done it every day of his life.

Which he likely did. *Why?* What kind of danger had a man wearing eight matching throwing knives like they were boots or breeches? How often had he used them? How often had they failed to protect him?

She didn't like the idea that he might be hurt.

She didn't like the idea that he might be hurt, and she'd never know.

She didn't say it, though. Not as he flexed beneath the leather straps, welcoming them like skin. Not as he pulled his greatcoat on over them, the heavy weight of the fabric hiding them from view and somehow doing absolutely nothing to make him look less dangerous.

Fucking dangerous.

The memory of the words on his beautiful, kiss-stung lips whispered through her. He was dangerous. More dangerous than she'd ever imagined.

She wondered if the danger made him feel powerful, too.

But she didn't ask that, either.

Not as he lifted a nearby crate—the one with the flag—with one arm, as though it were made of goose down, and pushed past her to open the door to the tavern beyond. He

stood back to let her exit ahead of him, the only indication
that he even remembered she was there.

The man he'd been—the one who'd devastated her with
pleasure—was gone. Returned was the silent Beast.

Beast.

"I still don't know your name," she said softly.

He didn't seem to hear the words. At least, she assumed
he didn't for how he herded her from the room. He barely
stopped to place the crate on the bar with a nod for the
American as they exited the tavern, already full of people
and merriment, the noise inside making the curving street
beyond cacophonously quiet.

The silence from both street and man made Hattie want
to scream.

But she didn't as he hailed a hack and opened the door,
not touching her—not even to hand her up into the conveyance.

He didn't touch her, and he didn't speak.

That is, until the door was nearly closed. And then he
said a single word, one she thought perhaps she'd misheard
for the way it came on graveled disuse, as though he was
saying it for the first time.

"Whit."

$\mathcal{A}$ low, surprised whistle sounded behind Whit as he stood in dark gardens of Berkeley Square, watching Warnick House, considering the bright lights pouring through the windows of the town home.

Whit reached into his pocket and extracted his watches. Half past nine. He returned them to their place as his unwelcome visitor approached.

"I heard you were here, but I had to see it to believe it."

Whit did not reply to the dry words, but that didn't stop his brother from continuing. "Sarita told me you were wearing formalwear—poor girl had stars in her eyes." Devil sent his voice into a high register, mimicking one of their rooftop network. "'You won't believe it! Beast is wearing a cravat!'"

The already irritating accessory seemed to tighten around Whit's neck, and he resisted the urge to tug at the elaborate folds.

Devil whistled again. "I didn't believe it, and yet, here you are. My God. When was the last time you tied a cravat?"

Beast narrowed his gaze on the house across the street, watching as a stream of nobs made their way to the ball within. "I wore a cravat to your wedding. To a woman whom you do not deserve, I might point out."

"God knows that's true," Devil replied happily, twirling his walking stick, its silver lion's head handle gleaming in the light from the lamps around the square. "Who helped you with it? It's so . . . elaborate."

"No one helped me. I remember the lessons."

It had been twenty years, and still, he remembered the lessons. Devil did, too, he imagined. Their bastard of a father had drilled them into his sons, insisting that they be prepared for entry into the aristocracy just as soon as he decided which of the three bastards—born to different women on the same day—would be the one who took up his name and assumed life as his heir. And the others?

Cravat tying hadn't come in handy on London streets. Waltzes hadn't put food in their bellies. Knowing the proper fork for the fish hadn't made for straw under their heads. And still, Whit remembered the lessons.

And he remembered how much he'd wanted the life their father had dangled in front of them, forcing them to do battle for a chance at it. How much he'd wanted the control it offered. The safety and security it could have provided the people he loved.

But the contest had never been for Whit. The prize had never been for him, the smallest and quietest of the three brothers. Devil had been sharp-tongued and Ewan full of cunning and rage, and their father had liked those traits more than those of Whit, full of nothing but a desire to protect the people he loved.

He'd failed.

But he still remembered the fucking lessons.

And so he stood here in the dark, cravat tight about his neck, watching the *ton* exit their carriages and enter a ball where, but for a single twist of fate two decades earlier, he might have belonged, waiting.

"Do you have plans for the evening beyond standing in

Berkeley Square in a perfectly tied cravat?" Devil paused. "Where did you even get a cravat?"

"Keep at the cravat, and I shall use it to strangle you."

Devil's grin flashed white in the darkness as he turned back to the town house. "So we wait for someone?"

"*I* wait for someone. I don't know why you are here at all."

Devil nodded, watching the house for a long moment before moving away, to a nearby linden tree. He leaned against the trunk, crossing one black boot over the other. Whit did what he could to ignore him.

Devil was not one to be ignored. "I assume we await Lady Henrietta?"

Of course they did. Whit did not reply.

"I only ask because you've gone full fop."

"I have not." Whit wore all black, from his boots to his hat, with the exception of his shirt and the cravat they were not discussing again.

"Sarita told me your topcoat is embroidered in gold."

Whit snapped his attention to Devil, horrified. "It is not."

Devil grinned. "But you're wearing a topcoat, which has no place in the Garden, so—clearly we are trying to impress."

"I should like to impress my fist upon your face." Whit turned back to the house, where a new carriage had arrived, footman leaping down with a block to help its inhabitants to the ground. Out came an older man, who immediately donned his hat.

"Cheadle," Devil said, as though he understood.

He didn't. Whit barely understood why he was here in Mayfair, in formalwear, watching Hattie's father. Not that he'd admit that. "I told you I'd take care of it, didn't I?"

"Indeed you did. Are you here for the father or the son? You know you cannot knife them in a Mayfair ballroom, don't you?"

"Don't see why not," Whit responded.

Devil grinned wide and tapped his walking stick against

his boot. "You should have told me you were planning a show; I would have searched out formalwear, as well."

"Nah. Someone has to keep up appearances," Whit said, watching as the footman handed down a dark-haired woman in a brilliant orange frock, who turned to inspect the rest of the assembly, her bold smile full of confidence and lacking caution.

"Lady Henrietta, I assume?"

Whit's brows knitted together. "It's not her." He took a step toward the street. *Where was she?*

"It's been a long time since I've seen the inside of a ballroom, but you can't simply walk across the street and engage the enemy, Beast."

The name brought Whit back. He turned on Devil. "That's not Hattie."

One of his brother's dark brows rose. "Ah. We wait for *Hattie* after all."

The emphasis on the diminutive set Whit on edge. Irritation flared. "I didn't say that."

"You didn't have to," Devil said, tapping a rhythm on the side of his boot. "Brixton told me you brought *the lady toff* to the Sparrow—"

"If our eyes on the rooftops don't have enough to do, I'm happy to find them more work."

"They have plenty to do."

"Watching me isn't part of it."

Devil didn't reply. "I might note that the last time they weren't watching you, you were knocked unconscious and disappeared."

A grunt. "Not disappeared."

"No, I suppose not. Thank heavens for the lady toff." Whit clenched his teeth. Had Devil always been such an ass? "Calhoun told me the two of you got lost in the storeroom—which, who among us hasn't lost their head over a woman at the Sparrow—though the stockroom isn't exactly dressed for seduction—"

Fucking hell, his brother could talk. "I haven't lost my head."

Devil stopped. "No?"

"No. Of course not." She was a threat to their business—their best link to Ewan. He hadn't even come after her until tonight. She'd found him unconscious in her carriage. She'd come to *his* turf. To Shelton Street. To the market square. She'd followed criminals into *his* darkness.

All he'd done was follow her. To learn more about the enemy.

To keep her safe.

He pushed the thought aside. It was nonsense, after all. The fact that he'd been unable to keep his hands from her once he'd reached her was irrelevant. As was the fact that he couldn't stop thinking of the feel of her skin beneath his touch, her lips against his, the sting of her fingers tightening in his hair, the sound of her cries when she came on his tongue. The taste of her. *Christ. The taste of her.*

"So, you stand in the darkness for . . ."

Her.

"Her father's business offered to repay our debt."

One of Devil's black brows rose. "Why?"

"I assume because the son stole from us, and they fear our punishment will be crippling."

"And will it be?"

"That's up to the earl."

"What's the plan?"

"He gives me Ewan's location or I take his business. The son, too."

"And the daughter?" For a moment, Whit let misunderstanding come, imagining what would happen if he took Hattie as well. If he made her his—a warrior queen. If together they ruled over the Garden and the docks. Pleasure thrummed through him for a moment before he pushed it away and shook his head. "She has nothing to do with it."

"Not smart enough to be in on it?"

She was fucking brilliant. "Not malicious enough."

Devil's walking stick tapped twice against his boot, his tell, terrifying to those who did not understand it and infuriating to those who did; it meant there was something he was not saying. "Well then. I assume you'll sort it out?"

Whit grunted.

"And well?"

What did that mean? Had they not come up together from the muck, built a business from the filth, and become kings together? Had Whit not always chosen their history over all else? "Yes."

"And quick? We've another shipment arriving—"

"I know when the shipment is arriving," Whit growled, unreasonably irritated by the reminder. "It's my business as well as yours. You needn't be such a fucking nag."

A long silence. Then, entirely casual, "And so you meet him here, dressed for dancing, instead of at his offices, dressed for damage, why? Because you love Mayfair so very much?"

Whit didn't reply. He loathed Mayfair. Loathed the excess of it and the performance of it. Loathed the people of it—this place that might have been his if his father hadn't been such a monster.

Devil leaned in close and said, "Your lady has arrived."

Whit spun back toward the house, where the carriage that had deposited Cheadle drove away. The woman in orange was still there—Hattie now by her side. Hattie, tall and blond and bright-eyed, her hair up to reveal her long neck and her curved shoulders, bare above the line of her lush, wine-colored dress, the golden glow of the house turning the silk to embers. She carried a dark shawl in one hand, but didn't seem to mind standing before all London without it artfully draped around her. She never tried for artfulness.

Which, he supposed, was why she seemed so much like

art. Like a mosaic tile that took up a courtyard, every bit of it worthy of inspection. Like music, filling every crevice of a room. Impossible to ignore.

Magnificent.

She shook out her skirts, the bending movement tightening her bodice, making her breasts more prominent. Whit's gaze tracked to the perfect swell, his mouth suddenly dry. He wondered if her skin had pinkened in the cool air— she was so easy to flush, he couldn't imagine it hadn't. He had a wild vision of stripping off his coat and crossing to her, wrapping her in its warmth. Stealing her away. Warming her.

Instead, he watched her—taller than her father, her companion, and the others assembled outside the house. Bigger, yes, and more open. More honest. Too authentic for Mayfair. He remembered her in the Garden, teasing the broad-tosser, brandishing a throwing knife, cuddling a damn puppy, seeming to blend in with the world.

Here, though—she didn't blend in. She stood out.

She was focused on her friend—he'd have laid money on them being the best of friends for the ease between them and the way the dark-haired woman smiled without artifice, listening as Hattie talked.

And, of course, Hattie was talking. Whit focused on her mouth, watching those beautiful lips move with fascinating speed. Wondering what she was saying, hating the distance between them and the way it kept him from hearing her.

Her friend laughed raucously, loud enough to carry, and Hattie relaxed into a broad grin of her own, the dimple in her right cheek flashing. Whit's cock woke as he watched and he growled his irritation, a thread of jealousy coursing through him. He wanted those words. The full force of that smile. Those violet eyes on his.

He wanted her.

He stilled at the thought. Of course he wanted her. What man wouldn't after time with her? What man wouldn't want another sweet taste? Another lush touch? Another cry of her delicious pleasure?

But that was it. He wanted the woman's body, and her father's business.

Not *her*.

"She's not my lady," he said.

"Do you know what you are doing?"

No. "I have a plan." He stiffened, straightening his coat. "And an invitation to the Duchess of Warnick's ball."

Devil cursed his surprise. "How in hell did you get that?"

"Warnick was happy to give us a favor." The Duke of Warnick owned a distillery in Scotland that made a fortune aging whiskey in American bourbon barrels, provided to him at a premium by the Bareknuckle Bastards' overland transport business. Of course, getting bourbon from the States into England beneath the usurious taxation of the Crown was not as easy as one might think, and moving empty barrels was an added risk for the smuggling operation—something Warnick knew.

The enormous Scotsman had provided Whit's requested invitation immediately, with a single caution. *If you embarrass my wife, I'll end you.*

Whit had refrained from pointing out that the Duchess of Warnick was one of the most scandalous figures in London society—the subject of a nude painting that was currently traveling Europe on exhibition—not that anyone in the *ton* spoke of it, for fear of upsetting her enormous husband and taking a beating for it.

Whit had no intention of embarrassing the duchess tonight. He had other plans. Other points to prove.

I don't care if you're not a gentleman.

In twenty years, Whit had never angled for the descriptor. He'd resisted it at every turn. He'd claimed Beast and built himself in the image, filling his days with the Rookery and his nights with the ring. He'd taken pride in his ability to move a hold full of smuggled goods in a seamless two hours, and even more in his ability to punish anyone who got in the way of the Bastards' work, or their people.

There was no place for gentility in the Covent Garden filth, and that was the stuff from which he'd been made— built from the muck into what he was now, a Beast.

And that was why he stood in the darkness, watching her from a distance. Because everything he intended that evening ran counter to what he was. And still, he dressed in formalwear. A cravat. The trappings of gentlemen.

And he watched her, desire coursing through him, reminding him that she was right. That he was nothing like a gentleman. That he never would be.

But he could play the part.

"Not a favor for *us*," Devil said, his smirk in his tone. "Walking into a pit of aristocratic vipers is not a thing I ever intend to do."

"You married an aristocrat."

"No," Devil said. "I married a queen."

Whit resisted the urge to roll his eyes at his brother's reply. When Devil had met Lady Felicity Faircloth outside a ball very much like the one in the house across the street, she'd been queen of the outcasts—tossed to the edge of society where she was expected to fade into obscurity. But Devil hadn't seen an outcast; he'd seen the woman he would love, marry, and worship for the rest of his life.

They'd married, shocking society, which hadn't mattered in the slightest to Felicity, who'd happily eschewed the world into which she'd been born, becoming more and more a Covent Garden lass each day.

"How you landed her is beyond understanding," Whit said.

Devil's smile was nearly audible. "I wonder at it every day." A gust of wind blew, and he dipped his head into the collar of his greatcoat, bouncing on the balls of his feet. "I'd be lying if I didn't wish for a warm bed with her instead of whatever this is."

Whit offered a disapproving grunt. "I did not require such an image. Christ. Go home to her then."

"And miss watching you enter society like a fucking mark?"

He looked to his brother. "You wanted vengeance. This is part of it."

Except it wasn't. It was a way for him to get to her. To show her that she was not the only one who could find a needle in a haystack. He imagined the surprise in her eyes when he approached her in the ballroom. Imagined the confusion when she found him on her turf. Imagined turning her world upside down, just as she threatened every time she arrived in Covent Garden.

"I always want vengeance. But I want to carve it out with a blade. Not . . ." He waved a hand to indicate Whit's attire. "Whatever this is."

"You didn't carve it out with a blade when it came to your wife." Felicity had been an act of vengeance before she'd become an act of love.

Devil turned knowing eyes on him. "Is this a comparable situation?"

Shit. "No."

"Whit—you haven't been inside a ballroom since we were twelve."

It hadn't been a ballroom then; it had been a torture chamber. It had been the man who'd sired him reminding Whit with every misstep that his future lay in the balance. His future, and his mother's.

It had been full of anger and fear and panic.

Whit reached into his pocket, grasping one of the two pocket watches within, running a thumb over the warm metal face. "I remember it all."

Silence, and then, softly, "He was a fucking monster."

Their father. Spreading his seed throughout England, not knowing that the three sons he sired on different women would become his only chance at an heir. And then his own wife made any legitimate sons impossible, putting a bullet into his bollocks just as he'd deserved, and the Duke of Marwick had come looking for them, not caring that their illegitimacy should have saved them all from the horrific tests he put them through. Thinking only of his name and his line.

Thinking only of himself and not the scars he would leave on three boys, and the girl who'd held the place before them.

Memory flashed. Of the last night at Burghsey House, the country seat of the Dukedom of Marwick. Of Grace— the placeholder—the girl baptized a boy so all of England would think the duke had a legitimate heir, her red hair in tangles, shaking, as the monster she'd always thought was her father told her the truth—that she was expendable.

Then he'd turned to Devil and Beast and told them the same. They weren't good enough. They weren't worthy of the dukedom. And they, too, were expendable.

But nothing had hurt more than when the old bastard had directed his attention to Ewan, the third brother, born of a fourth woman. Ewan, strong and smart and with fists like iron. Ewan, determined to change his future. Ewan, who'd once promised to protect them all.

Until their father had told him to do just the opposite.

And then they'd had to protect themselves.

Whit looked to Devil, the wicked scar down his brother's right cheek gleaming white in the darkness, evidence of their past.

They had protected themselves that night, and every night since.

Whit didn't speak the thought. He refused to resurrect the memory. His brother didn't ask him to. Instead, Devil's attention stayed on Hattie, and Whit found he couldn't resist joining him, watching as she entered Warnick House, the swing of her wine red skirts tempting him, sweet and sinful like the drink itself.

"Here is my question." Devil asked quietly, "In your mind, how does this end? The woman is protecting a family and a business that has come for our own, which makes her at worst the enemy, and at best a blockade between us and Ewan."

Whit did not reply. Devil didn't have to speak what they both knew was true. What threatened the Bastards' business threatened all of the Rookery. All of Covent Garden. And all of the people who relied on them.

The people he had vowed to protect.

"How does it end?" Devil repeated, softly.

She was gone from view, the edge of her skirts disappeared, blocked by a new group of revelers, eager for entry. He hated that he couldn't see her, even though her withdrawal from view made it easier for him to go after her. To straighten his shoulders and smooth his sleeves, and say, "Revenge."

He had nearly made it to the street when Devil called out to him, soft from the darkness. "Whit."

Whit stopped but did not turn back.

Not even when the Garden slipped into Devil's voice. "You forget, bruv . . . I, too, have stood in the darkness, watching the light."

Chapter Twelve

"Tell me again why we are here?"

Hattie spoke over the crush of people clamoring to access the entrance to the Warnick House ballroom. She and Nora had lost the Earl of Cheadle in the wild mess of people, and were now caught like fish in a current, swept up the steps to the main floor of the house.

"Balls are a diversion," Nora said, tossing a smile to someone in the distance. "And I like the Duchess of Warnick more than I like most people."

"I didn't know you knew the Duchess of Warnick."

"There are many things you don't know about me," Nora said with affected mystery.

Hattie laughed. "There is nothing I don't know about you."

"I'm thinking of finding a thing or two, honestly," came the reply as Nora passed her shawl to a waiting footman, "I don't like that you're keeping secrets about your new *paramour*." She mouthed the word in an exaggerated fashion that would have allowed anyone looking to know precisely what she'd said.

Hattie didn't blink. There was absolutely no one looking. No one looked at twenty-nine-year-old spinsters, one of whom lacked beauty and the other of whom lacked tact. "He's not that."

Nora smirked. "Oh, no. Of course not. He just . . ."—her eyes went wide and she lowered her voice—"in a *tavern*."

"Oh, for heaven's sake." Hattie looked up at the ceiling and lowered her own voice. "Might we speak about this *somewhere else*?"

"Certainly," Nora replied as though they were discussing the weather. "But no one is listening. I merely think you should consider the fact that finding a man who cares for your bits before his own is rare indeed. Or so I am told."

"Nora!" Hattie's cheeks had gone crimson, and the high-pitched cry *did* summon shocked and disapproving glances from those around them.

"At any rate, I know the duchess because the duke likes to race carriages and, as it happens, so do I." Nora accepted two dance cards from a nearby footman with a delighted laugh. "Look at how clever these are. Little paint palettes. I assume we're to write the name of our dance partner in the paint wells."

She extended one to Hattie, who shook her head. "I don't require one."

Nora sighed. "Take it."

Hattie did, even as she said, "I don't dance. I haven't danced in years." Certainly not with anyone who hadn't been forced into the situation with some kind of pity. "I don't even like to dance," she said to Nora's back as the other woman waved a hand and pushed through the door to the ballroom beyond.

The ballroom was degrees warmer than the hallway, a wall of doors opened wide to the night on one side of the room unable to combat the crush of bodies within. The chandeliers high above bathed the revelers in warm, wonderful light that flickered with the breeze from outside, strong enough to send drops of hot wax to the floor below. Not that anyone would notice. The orchestra was loud and the refreshments bountiful, and the massive duke and the stunning duchess—already in each other's arms on the dance floor and far too close for propriety—were very much in love, which would draw attention from anything else.

Hattie watched them for a moment, the way the duke, a Scotsman who had to duck through doorways and towered above the rest of the room, held his wife in his arms, tucking her close, as though she might need protection. The duchess, flame-haired and beautiful—once named the most beautiful woman in all London—lifted her gaze and met her husband's eyes with a bright, loving smile, and the man's stern face went soft and loving. The expression did damage for its honesty.

Hattie wondered what it might feel to receive such a look.

To be held so well.

To be loved so much.

She swallowed around the knot in her throat, raising a hand to her chest when they reached the top of the half-dozen steps leading down to the ballroom. Nora turned and spoke to the majordomo, who announced to the entire assembly, "Lady Eleanora Madewell. Lady Henrietta Sedley."

As was to be expected, no one looked up at the names, and the two made their way down to the main room. "Good Lord, Warnick is big," Nora said casually. "If I were interested in such a thing, I could find my way to being interested in such a thing, quite honestly."

Hattie laughed. Nora's lack of interest in such a thing made her a perfect companion for nights like this—she would never insist Hattie dance with some mincing fop desperate for a dowry—and a perfect friend, as she would never insist that Hattie was mad for eschewing the idea of a loveless marriage for the sake of procuring any husband who would be had.

Not that Nora did not intend for partnership, but in the

future she planned, partnership came with love, long-term, with a woman—which was a touch more complicated for the daughter of a duke with a massive dowry and the attention of every matchmaking mother of a son in shouting distance. This particular daughter of a duke was rich and brave and beautiful, however, and half of London was wild for her bold smile and her winning charm, so Hattie had no doubt that Nora would land precisely what she desired— life with a partner who loved adventure and Nora in equal measures.

Hattie, however, did not have such a guarantee.

Indeed, as Hattie aged, as she turned away from society and threw herself further and further into her father's business, her lack of beauty became more and more of a liability, and any desire she might hold in her heart for partnership or love had been pushed away in favor of a different, more achievable desire.

The business.

No marriage. No children. Her gaze slid over the tops of the dancers assembled, lingering on the broad shoulders and dark head of the Duke of Warnick. No partner to look at her with such devotion.

She'd put the desire for those things away.

Until Beast.

The thought was barely formed when her cheeks flushed, the memory of him coming like the heat in the room. The memory of his touch on her skin. Of his kiss. Of the taste of him, sweet and tart like the candy he carried everywhere. And his *voice*, low and dark and perfect at her ear, at her lips, at her breast. Lower.

She'd wanted him to show her what she was missing. To ruin her with pleasure so she might always remember it, even if she was never able to have it again. And he'd done just that.

And promised her even more.

Of course, he'd packed her off to home instead of delivering on that promise. And now, three days later, she'd heard nothing from him. He knew her name, but would he be able to find her? Would he even come looking?

And that word he'd whispered when he'd sent her home—what had it meant?

Whit.

She shook her head, refusing to allow herself to linger on the single, graveled syllable that had consumed her since he'd spoken it. Had she heard him correctly? What had it meant? When she'd told Nora that bit, Nora had suggested that he might have been admiring Hattie's delightful sense of humor.

Considering the events preceding the evening, Hattie had difficulty imagining that. At any rate, it did not matter. Not here, where he would absolutely not turn up.

Instead, she looked to her friend, still watching their host over the throngs of people. "If you were interested in that sort of thing, he still wouldn't have you, Nora. He's far too in love with his wife."

"And no one can blame him," Nora said happily. "Champagne?"

"Let's," Hattie replied. "One must find diversion where one can."

The words had barely left her lips when the majordomo spoke from the ballroom steps. "Mr. Saviour Whittington."

There was no reason for Hattie to have heard the name. The liveried man at the top of the stairs had announced a dozen names in the time it had taken Hattie and Nora to pick their way through the room. Two dozen. And Hattie hadn't paid an ounce of attention to them.

Except this one sent a ripple through the room.

She was sure of it.

Around her, the attendees turned to look. Not only the women—first curious, then riveted, their words caught in their throats—but the men as well, their ordinary conversation turning hushed as they looked to the staircase behind her. Over the crowd, she saw the Duke of Warnick's gaze light on the entrance to the room, and caught a glimpse of the duchess's red hair rising and falling, as though the woman were going to her toes to see, as well.

Hattie wouldn't have to go up on her toes. A whisper of air came at the back of her neck—a breeze from outside, nothing more. Still, she turned, slowly, knowing who would be there, even as she should have no earthly idea. Even as she could not fathom how it was possible that a king of London's shadows had found his way here—to the bright lights of a Mayfair ballroom.

For a moment, it seemed he was a king, standing at the top of the steps, impeccably dressed, impossibly handsome, like he'd been left there by divine right.

But royalty would have no interest in a too-plain, too-large, too-old spinster, as lost as such a woman could be in the assembly. And this man was staring directly at her.

Hattie went cold, then blazing hot, willing him to look away from her, because she couldn't seem to find the will-power to do it herself. How had he even found her in the crush of bodies? She supposed she stood several inches above most of the guests—she was not a person easily disappeared in a room. But that did not mean that he should be able to find her so easily.

And it did not mean he had permission to look at her in such a way—the kind of way that made her remember precisely what it was to have him look at her when they were far from society. Alone. In a tavern. Or a brothel.

Her cheeks flamed as heads turned around them, attempting to follow his gaze, to discover its target.

Several people craned to see past Hattie, over her, around her. Not so Nora. If the smirk on her friend's lips was any indication, Nora was fully aware of the direction of Beast's attention.

Not Beast.

Saviour Whittington.

Whit.

It had been a name.

She'd asked him to tell her his name, and he'd done so. *Whit.* But now, more than that. Now, she knew the whole of it. Saviour Whittington. No title, but he looked as though he'd simply left it at home, in the pocket of another coat, exchanged for the one he wore tonight—dark and perfectly tailored, with a bright white cravat and a beautiful face and, somehow, with an invitation to a ducal ball—which no person who called himself Beast should have access to.

"Who *is* he?" The words were out of her mouth before she could catch them.

"Do you not remember?" Nora asked, teasing at her elbow as he descended the steps and the room came alive again. Hattie spun on her heel and pushed her way deeper into the crowd. Nora followed, impossible to lose. Clarifying—as though it were required—"From Covent Garden?" Another pause. "From the *tavern*?"

Hattie's reply was barely recognizable as anything but a strangled, "Shut up, Nora."

Nora did not shut up. "He looks even better in light, Hat."

He looked beautiful in the light. He looked beautiful all the time. Hattie refrained from saying such a thing.

"I told you the duchess always has interesting guests," Nora said smugly.

Hattie ducked her head and kept going, weaving through revelers, eager to get to the far side of the room, champagne suddenly feeling far more urgent. Once at the refreshment table, glass in hand, she drank deep.

Nora watched carefully, then said, "You're slouching."

"I'm too tall."

"Nonsense," Nora said. "You're the perfect height. Everyone loves an Amazon."

Hattie slid her a look. "No one loves an Amazon."

"Seems like Mr. Whittington doesn't have much of an

aversion to them." Nora grinned. "Especially since he's here for you."

He called me a warrior. Well. She wasn't going to tell Nora that, as she'd never hear the end of it. She settled on, "He is *not* here for me."

"Hattie. That man has never set foot in a Mayfair ballroom before."

"You don't know that."

Her friend cut her a look. "You honestly believe a man like that could casually attend society events and the mothers of London wouldn't find it worthy of gossip? Filthy, wonderful gossip? My Lord, Hattie, we had to sit through six hours of listening to Lady Beaufetheringstone regaling us with which waistcoat colors were worn by the unmarried gentlemen of the season the last time we were forced to tea with her."

"It wasn't six hours."

"Wasn't it? It felt like *sixty*." Nora drank. "Point is, Hattie, that man has never been in society, and until this week, he'd never kissed you, either."

Hattie's eyes went wide. "The two are not in any way correlated."

One of Nora's dark brows rose in a smug arch. "Of course not."

Hattie straightened, telling herself she'd just have a peek—just a quick look to see if she could find him in the crowd. The moment she did, letting herself come to her full height, her gaze found his. It wasn't even as though he'd been looking about. She simply put up her head, and there he was. Like magic.

She immediately ducked again. "Damn."

Nora snickered. "You do realize that you cannot hide from him."

"Why not? You successfully hid from the Marquess of Bayswater for a full season."

"That's because Bayswater couldn't find an elephant if it were hidden in a doll's house. Your gentleman is rather more an even match."

He was a perfect match. That's what Hattie enjoyed so much about him—the sense that at any moment, they might spar, and either one of them could win. That's what made her heart pound. It's what fueled her desperation to head back into Covent Garden and seek him out. It's what had kept her awake all the previous night, tossing and turning in her bed and thinking about what he meant by *the fights* and what kind of trouble she might get into if she crept from her home and went to find out.

Imagining herself in his world was one thing; his actually turning up in hers was entirely different.

She grabbed Nora's hand and pulled her down the line of refreshment tables, eventually leading her out a large, open door and onto the balcony beyond. After heading away from a particularly raucous group, Hattie eventually put her back to the stone balustrade overlooking the Warnick gardens and said, "We shouldn't have come here."

"I don't know why not," Nora said. "I'm having a delightful time." When Hattie groaned, she added, "Besides, Hattie, wasn't the whole reason for your time in the"—she tossed a look over her shoulder to be certain they weren't being overheard—"brothel to begin the Year of Hattie with your own ruination? Wasn't it all to avoid the possibility of marrying?" She paused, then added, "This is your chance! March up to him and get yourself unmarriageable!"

Nora wasn't wrong. Certainly, that had been the intent at the start of this—a quick ruination and that would be that. Just enough to ensure that her father would know that marriage wasn't a possibility for her. That she would marry the business, and care for it 'til death did they part.

She shook her head. "I can't. Not until I understand why he's here. Not if he's about to change the game." She stopped. She was so close to getting what she wanted. Why couldn't the man just be agreeable? "Dammit," she whispered. "Why is he here?"

"If only there were a way you could divine that answer. By, say, asking him."

"If he tells my father everything, then Augie shall be found out. And then I won't get the business."

Nora scoffed. "Augie deserves to be set on his ass. He should have to clean up his own mess. *You* should tell your father everything. This Beast character, too. Let them deal with Augie."

Hattie looked to her. "He's my brother."

Nora narrowed her gaze, and Hattie grew uncomfortable. She knew that look. Assessing. Before she could change the topic, Nora said, "But that's not all, is it?"

"What do you mean? Of course it is. I don't want Augie hurt."

Nora shook her head. "No. You want to solve it. You want to prove you can solve it. Prove you can rectify the problems with the business by yourself. You want to prove yourself worthy of it. So your father will give it to you. Because you want his approval."

Hattie nodded. "Yes."

"And so you're willing to take on this man alone."

Nora meant *alone* in a perfectly proper sense. In the singular. Hattie managing a negotiation and repayment of the Bastards' stolen goods by herself, without the aid of her father. But when Hattie heard *alone*, she had a very clear vision of *alone* in the plural. Alone in a carriage. In a bedchamber. In a tavern storeroom. Alone, with him.

Either way, Hattie found her answer was the same. "I am."

She looked over her shoulder toward the door. Afraid he might be there. Disappointed he wasn't.

"Without help," Nora clarified.

"Without *interference*." And her father *would* interfere. Her father would tell her that she kept a tidy register and no one monitored the redistribution of a shipment better than she did, and yes, the dockworkers liked her, but to leave the business to men.

Hattie's teeth gritted. How many times had she heard that horrible retort? _Leave the business to men._

She loathed it. And she didn't want to leave the business to men any longer. She wanted the business left to women. To woman. To her.

And she might be her father's last choice, but she was the best one. And she wouldn't have Saviour Whittington making everything more complicated by turning up here and ruining it, dammit. Not when she was so close.

She lifted her eyes to Nora's, dark and curious and entertained in the way only a good friend could be. "This isn't amusing."

Nora barked a little laugh. "I am afraid it's immensely amusing; you told me he promised you your lessons, did he not? Did he not agree to aid you in your Year of Hattie exploration?"

Hattie was grateful for the darkness covering her blush. "He did."

And he called me fucking dangerous.

A thrill shot through her at the thought. What a delightful thing for someone to think of her.

"Then perhaps that is why he is here."

"It's not."

"It should be," Nora said. "From what you said, he rather missed out on the important bits."

"Nora!"

"I'm only arguing in favor of equality!" Nora spread her hands wide with a laugh. "All right, then, where do we go from here?"

"I really can't imagine how he knew I'd be here tonight. I'm never—" She stilled. Turned to Nora, who appeared transfixed by the starry sky above them. "You."

Nora looked to her. "Hmm?"

"You said we should come here. You pushed it. I wanted to stay home and look over the books."

"I like balls," Nora said.

"You loathe balls."

"Fine! The Duchess of Warnick sent a special note asking for me to attend and to bring you and your father. I don't like disappointing duchesses."

"You don't care a bit about disappointing duchesses."

"That's true. But I quite like this one, and she did promise a wonderful time."

Hattie pointed an accusatory finger. "You are a traitor."

Nora gasped. "I am not!"

"You are! You should have told me it was a trap!"

"I thought it was going to be another man in need of a dowry! I didn't know it was going to be a trap laden with your partner in erotic escapades!"

It was Hattie's turn to gasp.

"Not that I don't fully support said escapades," Nora qualified with a grin.

"He is not my partner in—" She paused. "Nora. This man is all that stands between me and my lifelong dream."

"And the escapades?"

Hattie gave a little sigh. "Obviously, those were quite nice." Before Nora could speak, Hattie added, "But he isn't here for that tonight. Which makes it very disconcerting to think that he's here for something else."

"You mean, like another woman?"

She hadn't, but that idea sent her stomach sinking, if she were honest. "No. I mean, here for something that would impact our negotiation. I don't know . . . information on Augie or . . . meeting my father. That *cannot* happen. I must convince him to leave immediately."

"Hmm," Nora said, the perfunctory sound drawing Hattie's attention.

"What?"

"Well, I'm not sure that's a reasonable plan."

"Why not?" Hattie said. "I'll just head back in there and . . . find him first."

"That might be difficult," Nora said.

A gust of cold air tore across the balcony. Hattie narrowed her gaze on her friend. "Why?"

Nora pointed past her shoulder, to the bright ballroom framed by the open doorway beyond. "Because he's speaking to your father right now."

Hattie spun in the direction of the other woman's finger.

Of course he was.

She'd had such wild, wonderful plans for the Year of Hattie when it had begun. And now, here she was, prepared to take the world by storm—to spend her twenty-ninth year sorting out the past so she might begin the future. And it seemed no one had told the Year of Hattie that it should cooperate with those plans.

Certainly no one had told Mr. Saviour Whittington that *he* should cooperate with those plans. "Damn," she whispered.

"Whoever he is," Nora said softly, "he's very good at this."

Her fingers tightened around the silly dance card Nora had insisted she take. It was the kind of thing that women who did not worry about business, or money, or retribution, or whether the man who'd put a knife in their (albeit deserving) brothers several days earlier might recount the entire thing to their fathers, cared about. It was the kind of thing Hattie had never cared about. And still, for some reason, in that moment, all she could do was stare at Beast's beautiful face and revel in the bite of the parchment in her palm.

Not that it would do her any good at all in the battle that was to come. Hattie might as well have been holding a violin for all the value it did her. Indeed, a violin might have been more useful, as she could have cracked him over the head with it, which would have made a scene, yes, but also would have resulted in the two men not speaking.

As though he sensed the threat in her thoughts, he lifted

his head from where he'd dipped low to speak to her father over the din of the ballroom, his strange amber gaze instantly finding hers. And then, as though he'd spent his entire life in Mayfair ballrooms, he *winked* at her.

"Interesting . . ." Nora drawled.

"No. It's not interesting at all. What game is he playing?" And why wasn't she more angry at him for playing it here, in front of all the world? She should be terrified. She should be furious. But instead . . . she was *excited*.

Warrior.

"We should go to more balls."

"We're never going to another ball again," Hattie tossed over her shoulder as she began to move, her heart pounding.

And then something gleamed in his eyes, and she recognized the emotion as the one rioting through her.

Anticipation.

He returned to speaking to her father as she pushed through the door. Under other circumstances, it would have been a comic scene: the enormous young man leaning down into the ear of the aging earl, notoriously diminutive. Her father liked to claim that it was his short stature that made him the perfect sailor, which was partially true—he barely had to duck to move about below deck on his ships. But this man—the one she no longer thought of as Beast, the one she could not help but think of as Whit despite that being entirely inappropriate—eclipsed him like the sun.

No. Not like the sun. Like a storm, come upon a ship out at sea, thieving blue skies and replacing it with silent, dark clouds.

A storm, big and beautiful and unpredictable.

What was he telling her father?

It could be anything, as it was just the two of them, seemingly oblivious to the rest of the room. Hattie quickly calculated the probability that they were discussing the mundane—weather, refreshments, the temperature of the room, or the number of footmen present.

Was it possible for something to have a negative probability?

It was far more probable that they were talking about her.

Hattie increased her speed, nearly knocking over the Marchioness of Eversley, tossing back a quick apology. If it were anyone else, she might have—*might have*—stopped to apologize, but the marchioness came from one of the most scandalous families in Britain, so if anyone would understand the need to quash whatever conversation was taking place between her father and a man who knew far too much about her dealings of the last few days, it was she.

Hattie was nearly upon them when the earl nodded, a shadow on his brow. Hattie caught her breath—she couldn't identify the emotion, but she didn't like it. And then she was there, and the words were coming before she could stop them. "That's quite enough of that."

The earl's eyes went wide and he turned to Hattie as Whit straightened and . . .

Oh, dear.

"That's trouble," Nora said softly from somewhere behind Hattie's right shoulder.

No one should have a smile that stunning. Hattie had a mad urge to throw up her hands and block the full force of it. To resist its foreign pull. *Keep your head, Hattie.*

She swallowed. "What are you doing here?"

He took the rude question in stride, extending a hand. "Lady Henrietta." The words were cultured and soft, missing their usual coarse darkness.

Hattie's brows snapped together and she tilted her head, confusion and something startlingly close to disappointment teasing through her. Was this the same man? It couldn't be. Where was the growl? The accent, grown in the Garden?

A flame lit in his amber eyes—the one that set off a twin flame deep in her.

No. He couldn't simply tempt her into docility. Her gaze slid to his outstretched hand, wary. She did not reach for it.

"Answer my question, please." When he didn't—of course *that* characteristic remained—she turned to her father, registering the censure in them. "What were you discussing?"

The earl's lips flattened. "Reconsider your tone, gel."

She swallowed her distaste at the words, barely able to consider her response before Whit spoke. "Cheadle."

There was the darkness. Warning, too, rougher and harsher than the warning that had come from her father. She turned surprised eyes on Whit, perfectly turned out and beautiful as a Greek statue, suddenly rugged as a cobbled street.

The transformation should have unsettled her, but it didn't. Instead, it comforted her.

Which almost made everything worse. She came to her full height and lifted her chin. "You don't talk to him."

Nora barked in surprise as conversations quieted around them, a collection of London's most revered aristocrats doing their very best not to look, but absolutely to listen. She cleared her throat under the weight of her parent's curiosity, and said, "That is to say, Mr. Whittington"—his lips quirked in amusement at the use of his name—"I require you . . ." One black eyebrow rose in the pause that followed the trail of the words, and Hattie leapt to add, "For a dance."

She lifted the crumpled dance card in her hand. "You're on my dance card." She turned to her father. "He's on my dance card."

An interminable silence fell. Months long. Years.

Hattie turned to Nora. "He's on my dance card."

Nora, blessed Nora, took up the thread. "Yes. That's why we're here. Clearly!"

Hattie could have done without the *clearly*, but she'd take what she could get.

"You're to dance . . . with him," her father said.

Hattie waved the card attached to her wrist. "That's what it says!"

"Does it, then." The earl seemed less convinced.

"Quite!" she said, the pitch of her voice somewhere in

the realm of a squeaky hinge as she turned to the man in question. "Doesn't it?"

He was silent, the strains of the waltz beginning behind them the only sound, a starting pistol for Hattie's worry. Perhaps he couldn't dance. No, not perhaps. He *most definitely* couldn't dance. This was the kind of man who wore holsters full of throwing knives and landed himself unconscious in carriages. He frequented brothels and Covent Garden taverns and threatened street criminals . . . he was a criminal *himself*. He might dress the part, but he did not waltz.

Which was why she lost her breath when he dipped his head like a practiced, polished aristocrat and said, all calm, "Indeed, it does, my lady."

It was just the surprise that he was willing to dance. It had nothing to do with the honorific. Nothing at all to do with the fact that he'd never called her his lady before. Not even a bit to do with the fact that suddenly those two little words—the ones that she'd heard her whole life—took on an entirely new meaning on his lips.

And then her hand was in his, and he was leading her into the crush of dancers, pulling her into his arms, her hands settling on the muscles beneath his coat, hard as steel. *Of course he couldn't dance*, the thought whispered through her. *He is made for stronger stuff than that.*

She leaned in, just enough to speak softly at his ear—ensuring no one else would hear—"If you would like, I can twist an ankle."

He pulled back, surprise and something like humor in his eyes. "I would not like that, as a matter of fact."

"But it would save you from having to dance."

His brows rose. "Are you sure it wouldn't save *you* from having to dance?"

"Of course not. I dance perfectly well," she said. "I was simply helping you, as you do not."

"And you know this because . . ."

She rolled her eyes at him. "Because of course you don't."

He nodded, his hands tightening against her, strong and firm and safe and wonderfully warm, making her wish that they were not here, in front of all the world. Her breath caught, desire pooling deep and distracting—distracting enough that she didn't notice they were moving until he said, at her ear, "I think I shall do just fine."

And he did do just fine. He did more than fine. He moved with practiced grace, as though he'd been waltzing every evening of his life, deftly avoiding the other couples as he wound her through the room. Hattie had danced hundreds of dances in her time out—in those early years her dowry had made her vaguely appealing to the men of the *ton*—but she'd never once felt like this, the way she did in mere seconds in his arms. As though she, too, had practiced grace.

Her gaze flew to find his, liquid amber, focused on her. "You know how to dance."

He grunted his reply, and Hattie took comfort in the noise—finally, something unsurprising from him. She spread her fingers over his coat sleeve, the heat of him passing through the fabric, and sighed, closing her eyes and letting herself fall into the simple sway of the dance.

Letting herself forget for a moment. Forget Augie and the business and why she was so worried—forget the deal they'd made and her dreams for her future, and the Year of Hattie. The world distilled itself in that place, in the arms of that man, his heat and his movement and his strength wrapping around her on a thread of lemon sugar.

And, for just a moment, Hattie forgot herself, too.

But a moment doesn't last. Soon, she opened her eyes to find his gaze rapt on her, and she stiffened beneath his attention, keenly aware of the things he could see—the ruddy pink of her skin—nothing like a ripe peach, nothing even close to berries and cream—her too-wide nose, her too-round cheeks, her full chin—the all-too-visible reasons why she was on the shelf.

Silence was not a friend to the unattractive woman; it left far too much time for aesthetic analysis. When he took a deep breath, she couldn't resist filling the silence. "You could have told me you knew how to dance," she said, turning away from him for a moment before realizing that he was now looking at her ear, and weren't ears the strangest parts of the human body? She'd rather he looked at her eyes. Her eyes were fairly uniform in size and of an uncommon color, and possibly her best feature. Not that she should care that he noticed her best feature.

Oh, who was she attempting to fool with that line of thinking? She absolutely wanted him to notice her best feature. She wanted him to acknowledge it as best. Not just in relation to all her other features, but in relation to everyone else's features, as well. Which wasn't possible, she knew, but she ought to acknowledge such a desire, shouldn't she? Wasn't that what the Year of Hattie was about? Acknowledging desire? Chasing it?

So there it was, she wanted him to think her eyes were pretty.

Had anyone ever used the word pretty *to describe her?*

"Why would I do that?"

She blinked at the reply, instantly thinking he was referring to her eyes and feeling oddly defensive about it before she remembered her earlier question about dancing. "Because—you must have been insulted by my insinuation that you didn't know how to dance."

He shook his head, the movement barely there. "I wasn't."

She didn't believe him. "I thought you didn't dance, which clearly you do; I thought you didn't understand the peerage, and here you are with an invitation to a duke's home, so that's utterly false, too. I underestimated you."

He was silent for a long time, the sway of the dance the only thing between them before he turned his amber gaze on her and said, "You said you didn't care if I knew any of those things."

Truth came instantly. "I didn't."

His throat worked as he considered his next words. "You didn't put value on them."

She shook her head. "I don't."

He nodded once. "Seemed you may have *overestimated* me, then."

She exhaled in a little laugh, his meaning settling in. "It does, doesn't it?" Another pause. Then, "How did you learn to dance so well?"

The tentative camaraderie that had come from their conversation disappeared, his gaze immediately shuttering. Regret flooded Hattie, along with no small amount of confusion—how had such a simple question caused such an immediate, unpleasant response?

Beneath her fingers, his muscles turned to iron, as though he were ready to do battle. She looked up at him, his eyes fixed at a point over her head, in the distance. She twisted, craning to see, expecting to find an enemy charging toward them. But there was nothing there. Nothing but silks and satins and laughter swirling like madness.

What had happened? What was wrong? She didn't know this man well, but she knew him well enough to know that he wouldn't tell her if she asked. Nor would he answer the other questions immediately on her tongue.

She looked back at his face, now ashen beneath the warm olive she'd come to expect. Concern came, hot and unpleasant. She clutched his arm with the hand there, clasped the hand in her own tighter. Lowering her voice, she said, "Mr. Whittington?" He swallowed at the name. Shook his head once, as though throwing off a foul taste. "Whit?" she said, even softer. "Are you ill?"

His breath was coming harsher now, the rise and fall of his chest impossible to ignore for his nearness. Beads of perspiration dotted his forehead and a muscle in his jaw ticked as though he was clenching his teeth, resisting whatever was consuming him.

She squeezed the hand in hers tightly. Tight enough to hurt. His amber eyes found hers. Answered the question in them.

She nodded, and they stopped dancing, but she did not release his hand, instead clinging to him tightly. Without an ounce of hesitation, she turned, and walked to the edge of the ballroom—and kept going, past a half dozen of the *ton*'s finest gossips, straight through the doors and into the darkness beyond.

Chapter Thirteen

*H*e couldn't let go of her hand.

He'd been in complete control. He'd played the part, made the noises, nodded at the gentlemen, smiled at the ladies, and spoken with the earl, issuing threats on the enemy's turf—an action designed to strike fear. He'd set the Bastards' revenge in motion.

Without Hattie.

Hattie, who had run from him the moment she'd seen him enter the ballroom, as though he might not notice. As though her running from him would make him think of anything other than chasing her. He didn't chase her. Not in the classic sense. Instead, Whit kept to his original plan and laid the groundwork for revenge.

But he'd never lost sight of her.

Not as she'd had two glasses of champagne in quick succession. Not as she'd dashed out to the balcony with her friend—a woman he now knew was Lady Eleanora, the reckless, carriage-racing daughter of a duke. And not when he'd found her father, deliberately moving them to a place where he could keep watch on Hattie, keenly aware of the possibility—the probability—that she would attempt an escape. Considering the myriad locales in which he'd found Hattie before, Whit wouldn't put it past her to scale a wall, commandeer a carriage, and make her way to the nearest gaming hell where, if he had to lay odds, he'd find Lady Eleanora nearby as sidekick and second.

If they'd tried it, Whit would have followed.

He'd been in complete control.

And he'd retained that control when she'd reentered the room and come for him, tall and strong and determined, gaze locked on him as she approached without care for the dozens of eyes that watched, considered, judged. She'd come for him, her wine red gown the color of the sin into which he intended to lead her if only she'd let him.

And she would let him. He had no doubt.

Whit had finished with her father, knowing that once she reached them, he'd lose his chance at the earl—knowledge that bore truth when she did arrive, violet eyes blazing as hot as the irritated flush on her cheeks, and he hadn't had to force the smile for that lady. It had come in earnest, and even then, he'd been in complete control.

But when they'd begun to dance, control had come tumbling down around him. He'd felt it the moment the steps had come to him, imprinted in the memory of his muscles, twenty years older but easily returning to the dance he'd once practiced, holding the darkness in his arms and imagining the beautiful woman who would fill them when he won the day and became duke.

He'd never imagined anyone like Hattie.

Hattie, who had somehow become a port in the storm of his thoughts—memories of his bastard of a father, of the competition he'd put them all through, of the sting of the duke's switch on the backs of his thighs when he misstepped. Of the ache in his stomach on those evenings when he'd been sent to his bed without food. *Empty stomachs shall make you hungrier for victory*, the monster had liked to say. How many nights had they been hungry at his hands? And how many more after they'd escaped him?

The memory had been clear and cold, and his heart had begun to pound as though he were twelve years old once more, suffering a dance lesson, control beginning to slip. He'd tried to hold on. He'd focused on Hattie, mapped her face with his gaze, taking in her golden blond hair and her full cheeks, flushed with excitement at their dance. He'd catalogued the long slope of her nose, its rounded tip, and the fullness of her lips, wide and beautiful, the memory of them impossibly soft.

Her eyes had been closed, her face tilted up to him like a masterwork—and it had calmed him. She had three dark freckles, spaced evenly apart in a little triangle on her right temple, and he'd wanted nothing more than to set his lips there, to linger and taste them. He'd taken a deep breath, enjoying the solace that came with looking at her.

She'd turned away at one point, and Whit had become transfixed by the curve of her ear, with its soft, downy lobe and dips and curls. Another freckle teased him, a beauty mark just behind her right ear at the edge of her hairline. A secret, shared only with him. One she didn't even know about—there was no way for her to ever see it herself. The woman had magnificent ears.

Eventually, she'd turned back and given him the best of all—her eyes. A wild, impossible color that was unreasonable for humans—but he'd already assumed Hattie was beyond human. Part sorceress. Part warrior. So beautiful.

And those stunning eyes—the proof of it.

A man could lose himself in those eyes.

A man could give himself up to them. Cede control. Just once. Just during the dance. Just until he could catch his breath and escape his memory.

And then she'd asked him how he'd learned to dance. And it had all come back. The memory, the discomfort. He'd tensed beneath her touch, struggling for control.

Losing.

He'd just needed a moment. A bit of air. The cool bite of the world beyond this ballroom. A reminder that his past was not his present. That he did not need that place, with its too many people and its too cloying perfume.

In that moment, however, he did need Hattie.

Because, in that moment, she saved him, taking his hand in her firm grip and leading him from the room before all London, like a hound on a lead. He'd let her. He'd wanted it. And she'd known it somehow—known that she should bring him not simply out onto the balcony, but farther, down the stone steps and beyond the light spilling from the ballroom, into the gardens. Into the darkness.

It wasn't until they were there, under the cover of a large oak, that she let him go.

He hated that she'd let him go.

Hated, too, that the loss of her touch had him struggling for deep breaths again.

Hated, more than all that, that she seemed to understand all of it.

She stood there, soft and silent and still, for an eternity, waiting for him to restore himself. She didn't push him to speak, seeming to understand that even if he wished to, he wouldn't have known what to say. Instead, she waited, watching him until he returned to the present. To the place. To her.

Hattie, whose natural inclination was to fill silence with questions, did not ask any questions. Not about his conversation with her father or about his response to the waltz. She did not ask how it was he knew how to tie an impeccable cravat.

Instead, this woman he'd known for barely longer than a heartbeat and who already haunted his dreams said, "Thank you."

The words were a shock. Should it not have been him doing the thanking?

Before he could reply, she added, "I haven't waltzed in three years. The last time I did . . . it did not go well." She laughed. He didn't like the self-deprecation in the sound. "He was a baron with an eye for my father's money, and I was nearly twenty-six and twenty-six might as well be eighty-six when London is in season."

He did not move, afraid that if he did, she might stop speaking.

"I was grateful for him, honestly. He was handsome enough, and young—only thirty. And with a smile that made me think maybe it really was for me." Whit found he had a sudden loathing for this young, handsome baron, even before Hattie added softly, "I didn't know he was a terrible dancer."

Confusion flared at that. She didn't seem the type to care about one's dancing ability. Hadn't she just said she didn't?

"There were whispers that he was after me in truth, which of course had my father satisfied—his earldom is a life peerage, you see, and Augie won't be able to pass nobility on so marriage to a baron was a boon. My father was even more happy when the baron marked himself down for a waltz. Waltzes are golden treasure in Mayfair ballrooms." She paused, taking a deep breath and looking up at the sky. "It's a sliver moon."

He didn't want to look at the damn moon. He wanted to look at her. But he did, following her gaze to the brilliant crescent low over the rooftops.

"It's setting," she said, simply.

"Yes." Her eyes flew to his, her pretty mouth falling open in surprise at his speaking. To his absolute shock, his cheeks grew warm. Whit had never been more grateful for darkness, and he'd hidden in it from soldiers of the Crown on more than one occasion.

"I stepped on his foot," she said, softly. "He wasn't a good dancer, and I stepped on his foot, and he called me—" She stopped. Shook her head and looked back to the moon before speaking again, so quiet she could barely be heard. "Well. It wasn't kind."

Whit heard her. Heard her embarrassment. Her pain. Felt it like it was his own. He was going to find this baron and fucking garrote him. He'd bring her the man's undeserving head.

The riotous pounding of Whit's heart began to calm.

"So . . . thank you for the dance tonight. You made me feel . . ." She trailed off, and Whit realized that he would happily turn over the contents of the Bastards' Rookery warehouse to thieves for the chance to hear the end of that sentence.

But she didn't finish. Instead, she waved her hand, the dance card attached to it fluttering in the breeze. He reached for it, pulling her closer to him with a barely-there tug on the fragile parchment, already crumpled from her mistreatment.

He turned it over, looked at it.

She tried to tug it back, but he wouldn't let her. "It's empty. I told you," she said defensively. "No one ever claims my dances."

Whit ignored her, lifting the pencil that dangled from the card. "I claimed one."

He could hear the smirk in her retort when she said, "As a matter of fact, *I* claimed *yours*." He put the pencil to his tongue, licking the nib before setting it to the little oval paper. "It's a bit late for claiming your waltz, don't you—"

But he wasn't claiming the waltz. He wrote his name across the whole card, claiming all of it. Claiming all of her, this woman who had rescued him, in one bold, dark scrawl. *Beast.*

Hattie looked down at the moniker, her pretty lips falling into a perfect little "Oh." He didn't respond, and she finally looked up at him and added, "That's that then."

He offered a little grunt, too afraid of what he might say if he spoke.

She filled the silence. "You're very graceful. Like a falcon."

"Like a bird?" Whit repeated, unable to stop himself. If Devil got wind of the descriptor, he would never hear the end of it.

She laughed, the low, rolling sound like a punch to the gut. "No. Like a predator. Beautiful and graceful, yes, but strong and powerful. And dancing with *you*, it wasn't like anything I've ever done before. You made *me* feel graceful." She gave a little laugh, and he could not miss the self-deprecation there. "By association, of course. As though my movements were an extension of yours. As though I, too, was a falcon, dancing on the wind." She looked to him, the lights of the distant ballroom a barely-there reflection in her eyes. "I've never felt that way. I've never had that. And you gave it to me, tonight. So th—"

He moved, finally, coming for her with the speed of the damn bird she'd compared him to. Diving for her, collecting her up in his grasp. He couldn't bear her thanking him again. Not for what had happened inside. Not for the dance he hadn't finished. He hadn't given her the dance she deserved.

Her gratitude dissolved into a pretty gasp. *Good.*

He didn't deserve her thanks. He wasn't worthy of it. Not with the plans he had for her family. For her father's business.

Not with the plans he had for her.

So he caught her words with a kiss, thieving them with his hands at those pretty, rounded cheeks, his thumbs rubbing over her cheekbones as he tilted her face up to his and kept taking, her gratitude, then her surprise, then her pleasure, licking at her full, lush bottom lip until she opened for him, welcoming him inside as though she'd done it a thousand times before. And for a moment, as he tasted her sigh, it seemed as though she had.

Whit would have sworn they'd barely begun when Hattie

pulled away, but their breath, coming heavy and desperate, suggested it had been longer than he thought—never long enough, though. Her gloved hands came to his, clutching them on her cheeks, and he wanted to tear the fabric from their hands, to feel her heat.

He almost did. Might have, if she hadn't whispered at his lips, her tongue coming out in a little maddening lick, as though she couldn't stop herself from taking another taste of him. "You always taste of lemon—even when there are no candies in sight."

He groaned, going hard as steel and pulling her tight to him, aching for her to be closer, loathing her voluminous skirts and the cage of her corset beneath the fabric of her gown—if he had his way, she'd never wear a corset again. She wouldn't wear anything that kept him from her softness, from her curves. In frustration, he lifted her up onto her toes. "You're wrong. It's you who tastes sweet." He caught her tongue and gave it a suck before releasing it and adding, "Everywhere."

He kissed her deep, rewarding the way she slid her hands over his shoulders and down his chest, exploring him. Her fingers traced over the leather straps of his knives down the quartet of blades like stays over his ribs and she pulled back, just enough for her eyes to meet his in the darkness. "You came armed."

He grunted. Then, "Attacks come from everywhere."

One of Hattie's blond brows arched. "Even in Mayfair ballrooms?"

He hauled her closer, knowing it was mad. "Especially in Mayfair ballrooms. Seeing you in this dress was an assault." His fingers curled at her back, clutching the edge of the wine silk, and for a wild moment, he considered what might happen if he ripped this dress from her and laid her down in the crisp leaves at their feet and gave her everything she'd asked of him.

His cock throbbed its approval as she said, uncertain, "You like it?"

I like you.

The thought shattered him, as devastating as the dance had been, and he released her as though he'd been singed. Her eyes went wide, and he loathed the surprise and fleeting disappointment in them as they backed away from each other, extricating themselves from the touch.

He watched as she shook out her skirts, pretending not to notice the swell of her breasts, even as he felt like a proper ass.

After a long while, he said, "I owe you another waltz."

She shook her head. "I think I shall be done with waltzes for now." She paused. "And it seems, perhaps, you should be, as well."

It wasn't a question. She didn't expect him to answer. He didn't expect to answer. And still, for reasons he would never understand, he did. "The man who sired me insisted I learn to waltz."

She straightened slowly, carefully, as though she had just discovered she was in the presence of a rabid dog. And perhaps she was. "The man who sired you."

"I didn't know him," he said, knowing he couldn't tell her everything and wanting to tell her everything just the same. "Not for the first twelve years of my life."

Hattie nodded, as though she understood. She didn't of course. No one did. No one could—except the two other boys who had lived the same life. "Where were you—before?"

The stilted, careful question came as though she'd wanted to ask a thousand of them, and that one had been the one that had fought its way out. It was an odd question, one Whit hadn't expected. He'd always thought of his life as being split in two—before the day his father arrived and after. But it hadn't simply been the day he'd met his father. And he didn't think of the time before. He didn't want to remember it.

So he would never understand why he told Hattie the truth. "Holborn."

Another nod. As though it were enough. But suddenly, it didn't seem that it could ever be enough. He reached a hand into his pocket, extracting one of his watches, the gold warm at his palm as he added, "My mother was a seamstress. She mended the clothes of sailors coming off the ships." When there were clothes to be mended.

"And your . . ." She hesitated, and he knew the dilemma. She did not want to say *father*. "Was he a sailor?"

What Whit would have done for his father to have been a sailor. How many times had he dreamed it—that he'd been born of his mother and a man who'd left to make his fortune, with a miniature of his wife and infant son sewn into the lining of his coat—a reminder of the home to which he would return when he'd grown rich on the other side of the world.

How many times had he lay abed, watching his mother hunched over a pile of dirty clothes delivered by men who'd always asked for more than mending, barely able to see her work for the scant light of the candle beside her, and dreamed that the next knock on the door would be his father, returned to save them?

And then came the day when the knock had been his father, tall and handsome, with a face that had been baked in a heat of aristocratic disdain, and eyes like colored glass. A man cloaked in a fortune he hadn't had to make, because he'd been born with it, all there on his face and in the weave of his clothes and the shine of his boots.

Twenty years, and Whit could still remember the awe he'd felt at those boots—gleaming like sunlight, the clearest looking glass in Holborn. He'd never seen anything like them, nary a scuff on them, more proof of wealth and power than if the man had leaned down and announced his name and title.

And then he had. The Duke of Marwick. A name that

had opened every door, from birth. A name that bore privilege beyond reason. A name that could secure him everything.

Everything but the one thing he wanted more than all the rest—everything but an heir.

For that, he required Whit.

"He was not a sailor," Whit said, finally. "He was nothing, until he turned up at the door to our room in Holborn and promised us the world, if only I'd go with him."

"And your mother?" There was fear in the question, as though she already knew the answer.

He didn't reply, his fist clenching around the watch. Instead, Whit turned his face to the gilded room beyond—the one rife with the privilege that had tempted him all those years before, and said, "They shall be talking of you tonight, Lady Henrietta. Leading a man into the darkness."

Magnificently, she didn't hesitate at the change of topic. Instead, she followed his gaze and smiled, the expression filled with the wry knowledge of women in the world. "You do not worry they shall be talking of you for being led?" A pause, then, "I did say I wished to be ruined, did I not?" The question might have been coquettish on the lips of another, but not on Hattie's. On Hattie's, it was honest and forthright. A clear step in the direction in which she'd decided to walk.

Admiration flared. "You should have done this years ago."

She turned to him. "There was no one who would have helped me years ago."

He reached for her, pushed a lock of her hair behind her ear. "I find that very difficult to believe." This woman could lead a good man into the darkness, and Whit was very, very far from being a good man.

She smiled, stepping back once more, straightening her shoulders, and he sensed the change in her. The determination. He'd seen it before, and the memory, combined with the determined set of her jaw and the unwavering gleam in her eyes, sent excitement thrumming through him, knowing that they were about to spar again.

He held his breath.

"What were you discussing with my father?"

He crossed his arms over his chest, the straps of his knife holster tightening around his muscles, a reminder of his role in this play—of the work he'd come to do. "Who says we were discussing anything other than a perfectly enjoyable ball?"

She gave a little laugh at that. "First of all, my father has never in his life referred to a ball as perfectly enjoyable. And neither have you."

He raised a brow. "Tonight might have changed my mind."

"If it did, it was the part that came *after* my escorting you from the ballroom that changed your mind, sir."

That much was true, and it was Whit's turn to offer up a little laugh. Her gaze flew to his. He tilted his head. "What is it?"

"It's just that . . . you don't laugh."

"I laugh," he said.

She cut him a disbelieving look. "You barely *speak*." She waved away any answer he might have found. "It's no matter. I won't be deterred. What did you tell him?"

Her father. "Nothing."

It wasn't true, and she knew it. "I told you," she said. "He's not behind the attacks on your business."

Whit knew that, but he wanted the information from her. "And I am to believe you?"

"Yes."

"Why?"

"Because it goes against all reason for me to lie to you." His brows went up at the words; true, but not something to which most businessmen would admit. "I understand that you are in the position of power, Mr. Whittington."

"Don't call me that."

"I cannot call you Beast in front of all the world."

Irritation flared. "It's not all the world, Hattie. It's an infinitesimal subset of the world. A weak subset. A useless subset. Nothing like the rest of us, who work for food and dance for joy and live our lives without fear of judgment."

She watched him as he spoke, the whole time making him wish he wasn't running his damn mouth in front of her. More so when she replied, "No one lives without fear of judgment."

"I do."

It was a lie and she heard it. "I think you live with more of it than most of us." Whit resisted the instinct to flinch at the words as she spun the conversation back to where they'd begun. "You needn't believe that I wouldn't lie to you. Believe that history does not lie. My father has been at the helm of Sedley Shipping since he returned from the wars. He sailed with an incomparable skill—one that had every nefarious businessman in Britain after him, offering king's fortunes to get him aboard their ships.

"He was approached by the worst of the world—men who wished to transport guns, opium, *people*." She shook her head, as though she'd seen the face of evil and still couldn't believe it existed. Whit knew that evil. He and Devil had received the same invitations as her father. Refused them without hesitation, just as the earl had. "Our company has had its highs and its lows, but he *never* would have authorized stealing from you. Never."

Our company. Whit had spent enough time in the world to know that daughters were too often overwhelmed with filial loyalty when it came to their fathers—but there was something more than that in Hattie's words. She did not merely defend the integrity of her father . . . she defended the integrity of a business about which she knew a great deal. *Of herself.*

And once Whit saw that, he did not hesitate. "I know."

"*Never*," she repeated, before realizing what he'd said. "You know?"

"I do. Shall I tell you what else I know?" She did not reply, and he added, "Someone made a mistake, didn't they, Hattie?"

The briefest of hesitations. "Yes."

"I believe it wasn't him. And I believe it wasn't you. And I believe you don't want me to know who it was, because you are afraid of something else."

Losing.

She shook her head. "No, because we had a deal."

That deal, the one that would kill him if he let it—the one that ended with her naked in his bed. "We did have that. And still do. But I told you that I couldn't just let it all go back to normal. There is too much on the line."

"It won't," she said, all certainty. "You shall be repaid. My father would never risk crossing you. And I only want—"

He hated the way she stopped, the words she refused to entrust to him. *Clever girl. You shouldn't trust me.* It was good that she didn't finish the sentence. If she had, he might have decided to give it to her, whatever it was she wanted.

Instead, in the wake of her silence, he said, knowing he was about to change everything, "Your father wouldn't risk it, Hattie. But your brother did."

She froze for an instant, just long enough for him to see the words strike like a blow—one he had tried to deliver softly, even as he knew the sting it would bring. She hid her surprise almost instantly, and he could not ignore his admiration.

"How long have you known?"

He didn't want her to know he'd known from the start. "Does it matter?"

"I suppose not," she said. "You promised you would discover everything."

"I did."

"Do you plan to . . ." She hesitated, and he wondered at the question—the urgent panic in it, but somehow, devoid of fear. Why had she been protecting her brother so thoroughly?

My girl Hattie is smart as a whip, the earl had told him earlier, pride in the man's rheumy eyes. *Always fancied herself heir—which was my fault for enjoying her company. The boy was never so smart. But Hattie needs to find herself a good man and have herself a good son.*

Hattie was smart—keen and clever and would make a magnificent heir to her father's business. Was it possible that that was tied up in her frustration that he'd sorted out her brother's involvement in the attacks on the Bastards' shipments?

Before he could follow the thought, her frustration flared, and she narrowed her eyes on Whit. "You negotiated in bad faith. You toyed with me. You've known all along."

"It wasn't difficult to put it all together, Hattie. I assume your brother thought he could make some quick money off us and impress your father."

"It wasn't quite so simple."

He'd known she'd been hiding it, but the halfhearted defense of her brother drove the point home, and Whit found that the tacit admission in the words was more frustrating than expected.

"No, it wasn't simple. Because he's not working alone." She stilled, surprise in her eyes. Surprise that Augie was working with someone else? Or surprise that Whit knew?

"Who is he working with?" she asked.

He didn't want her anywhere near Ewan, who would hurt her without hesitation if he knew it would punish Whit. *And it would.*

"How do you know?" she pressed.

That was an easier question. "I went looking for information about your brother the moment I learned your name, and by all accounts, he isn't very clever."

She did not reply. He was right.

Whit pressed on. "From what I hear, Augie Sedley doesn't have half the business sense of his father or a quarter of the brains of his sister."

A little twitch at the corner of her lush mouth. He'd pleased her with that. And pleasing her pleased him. But now was not the time for pleasure. "From what I hear, he has a valet who is equally unintelligent, but bears a heavy fist and is willing to double as young Sedley's personal gorilla."

She grimaced. "Russell."

He stiffened at the name. At the shudder of disgust she gave as she spoke it. Anger shot through him as he considered all the possible reasons for that disgust. Not anger. Fury. Rage. "Has he touched you?"

"No." She shook her head quickly, and the truth made him light-headed with relief. "No. He's just a brute."

"That, I believe. He packs a hell of a wallop." He lifted a hand to the back of his head, to the whisper of tenderness that remained from the night of the hijacking.

"I'm sorry," she said, as though she were responsible for the blow.

He ignored the pleasure the soft words wrought. "If this were a year ago, I'd not be worried in the slightest, because the Bastards are smarter and savvier than your brother and his thug on their best day. But four shipments have been compromised in the last few months. On three different routes. I know who is behind it, and I intend to destroy him. But I need your brother in order to do it."

There was a pause as the words fell between them, his logic clear and infallible. She nodded, seeming to understand that he wasn't asking her for help. Understanding that he couldn't allow another slight. That he wouldn't allow the ones that had already been committed, not if they were from a real enemy. From one he had to worry about more than her brother and his muscle.

"So, you went to my father," she said, softly. Of course

he'd gone to her father. His business was in peril. The world he'd built. The people who lived in it. And Hattie didn't know enough to keep it safe. "You told him about Augie."

He heard the devastation in the words. The betrayal. And damned if it didn't sting. "I did."

She nodded, but did not look to him. "You should have told me you were going to do that."

"Why?"

"Because that would have been fair."

He wished he could see her eyes in the darkness. Was grateful that he couldn't. Because he had no choice but to disappoint her. "Fairness does not win wars."

A pause. "And this is war?"

"Of course it is. It has to be."

"With me," she said.

Not if you fight on our side. Where the hell had that thought come from? He pushed it aside. "With our enemies."

"Augie is my brother."

He didn't reply. What could he say? He, too, had a brother. A sister. Hundreds of people who relied upon him. People he had vowed to keep safe. All threatened by Ewan. And by Hattie's brother. This was his only path to meting out vengeance.

She spoke in his silence. "I thought we had a deal."

He deliberately misunderstood. "You'll get your deflowering."

She exhaled, harsh in the dark night. "It's not as though he's going to hand Augie over, you know. You put a knife in his thigh—a fact my brother will happily divulge the moment my father confronts him."

She didn't know her father already knew.

On other lips, the words might have been combative. But here, on hers, they were something else. Angry, yes. But frustrated again. Fraught. Almost panicked.

He let silence fall around them—long enough for her to

fidget beneath his attention. And then he said, "What are you afraid of, Hattie?"

"Nothing."

He shook his head. "That's a lie."

"How would you know—you who have everything?" The words came like a shock. "You with your fiefdom and your world filled with people who adore you and your business an immense success, lining your pockets. You, the kind of man feared and revered by your competitors and not a single one of them doubting your skill. You're a damn king. And as though that's not enough, you're also the handsomest man anyone has ever seen—which is ridiculous, by the way." Any pleasure he might have felt at the words disappeared in their irritation, and then his own confusion when she added, "Imagine being *me*."

What in hell did that mean?

"Imagine always being the one who *never wins*. For my entire life, I've been a poor approximation of what I was supposed to be. No one longs for Hattie Sedley in their ballrooms." It wasn't true. He couldn't imagine anyone not wanting her everywhere, all the time. "I am invited by virtue of being a daughter to a rich man. A friend to a beautiful woman. Hattie, good for a laugh but too loud, don't you think? Too tall, don't you think? Can't be ignored, but needn't be considered. *Good old Hattie*. Clever enough, I suppose, but no one wants to make a home with clever . . . *And Hattie*, tacked on at the end. Like someone's dog."

Whit's teeth clenched at the words. At the hurt in them, at the madness of them from this woman he'd been unable to forget from the moment she'd touched his cheek in that dark carriage. "Who's made you feel this way?"

The question came like a threat, and it was one. Whit wanted a name. And she gave one, as though he were a child and she were explaining something as simple as sunrise. "Everyone."

There had been many times in Whit's life when he'd wanted to decimate Mayfair, but never more than that moment, when he found himself riddled with the incandescent desire to destroy the entire world that had made this woman feel somehow less than perfect. He swallowed. "They're wrong."

She blinked, and something like disappointment flashed in her eyes. "Don't. If there's anything worse than knowing you're out of place, it's being told you fit in." She gave a little laugh, one that belied the words. "And besides, when you're born the antithesis of everything the world values, you learn to adjust. You learn to be the dog. Everyone likes dogs."

He shook his head. Opened his mouth to tell her how wrong she was.

But she was still talking, this woman who never seemed to stop talking. And he forgot to speak, because he so liked hearing her. "I cannot win the game inside that ballroom. But I thought I could win another. I could win the business."

Her father had said as much, but now, on her lips, the words held him rapt, even more so when she stepped toward him, one finger brandished like a saber. "I am *good* at it."

He did not hesitate. "I believe it."

She ignored him. "And not just the books. Not just the customers. All of it. The men on the docks need Sedley Shipping to keep their hooks working and pay them well. The men who load the warehouse. The drivers who deliver the cargo. We employ a small army and I know them. To a man. I know their wives. Their children. I—" She hesitated. "I *care* for them. All of them. All of it."

She was growing more frustrated, and he understood it—the anger and the worry and the *pride* that threaded through her. He felt it himself when he stood in the Rookery, where he and Devil and Grace had built a world for people whose loyalty repaid them in spades. This woman loved her business, just as Whit loved his. She loved the Docklands just as Whit loved the Garden.

They were a match.

"You are better at it than most of the men in London." He didn't have to see it to know it.

"I can tie a sail in a high wind," she added, "and bandage a knife wound—thank you very much for nearly killing my brother, by the way—and fix any problem that possibly arises—including the one where my idiot brother went up against two of the most powerful men in London. But *it isn't good enough.*"

Now that she had started, she couldn't stop, and Whit found he didn't want her to; he wanted her to go on. He'd listen to her rage forever, even as his mind was already working to change it. To fix it. To give her what she wanted.

Impossible, if he was to do what was necessary.

She was still talking. "It's supposed to be *mine.* It's supposed to be mine and not simply because I want it. God knows I do—all of it. I want the inkpot and the ancient balance sheets and the rigging and the resin in the hold and the sails. I want the *freedom.* But more than all that . . . I earned it." She paused for breath and a vision flashed, ink stains on her wrists in the brothel. Proof of her passion, as though the way she fairly vibrated before him now was not enough. "And do you know what my father said?"

"He said you are a woman, so you cannot have it." It was bollocks.

"He said I am a woman, so I cannot have it," she repeated, narrowing her gaze on him. "My being a woman shouldn't stop any of it."

"No. It shouldn't."

She was ramping up again. "I'm so damn tired of being told it should. Being told I don't know my own mind. Being told I'm not strong enough. Not clever enough. I am."

"You are." *Christ. She was.*

"I'm strong," she insisted.

"Yes." *Stronger than any muscle in the Garden.*

"I'm *exceedingly* clever. I know a woman shouldn't say such a thing but, dammit, I *am*."

He was mad for the fact she'd said it. "I know."

"The fact that I've different"—she waved a hand over her body—"*bits* . . . shouldn't matter. Especially since these bits . . ." She trailed off. Shook her head. "Anyway."

He wouldn't trade her bits for anything. "I agree."

She blinked. "You do?"

Ah. She'd returned to him. "I do."

The words thieved the winds from her sails, leaving her breathing heavily in the darkness. "Oh."

He supposed he should have seen as much before. Should have understood it. She wanted Sedley Shipping. She wanted the boats and the docks and the world, and she should have it. "I have no difficulty believing that you can run that business better than them."

"Certainly better than Augie."

His lips twitched at her soft grumble. "From what I hear, there are some very intelligent cats on the docks that could do better than your brother. I was speaking of your father."

"Well, he did it so well they gave him a peerage."

"I am unimpressed by peerages."

She met his gaze. "I shouldn't have said what I said about you. I am sorry."

He wasn't about to allow that. "You called me handsome. You cannot take that back."

"What would be the point? It's empirical."

He knew he was handsome; she wasn't the first woman to say it to him, nor the hundredth, and yet, hearing it from her was different than hearing it from the others. As though he'd earned it from her in some way. Impossibly, heat spread across his cheeks again, and he was very grateful for the darkness. If the boys in the Garden knew that the unflappable Beast had blushed twice this evening, he'd never get another ounce of respect. He cleared his throat. "Thank you."

"You're welcome."

He should return her to the house, this woman who had rescued him and hadn't asked him to explain. Hadn't even lingered on the events inside. Instead, she'd told him about the last, miserable dance she'd had. And he'd told her nothing.

He didn't want to bring her in. He wanted to tell her something. "I think you would like my sister."

Hattie froze at the words. "I didn't know you had a sister."

"There are many things you do not know about me."

"If only there were some way you could tell me such things. Some kind of verbal communication you might attempt. Turning all your growls and grunts into discernible words. A spoken language of some kind, complete with meaning."

He grunted his amusement, and she smiled.

"Do you want to hear about her or not?"

Her eyes widened. "Absolutely."

"My sister was born a woman into a man's world. My father used to say she'd had a single purpose, and she hadn't been able to achieve it."

"A disappointment from her first breath," Hattie said, too familiar with the idea.

"And every breath after," Whit agreed, avoiding the full truth of the story. The bit where his father had never intended for the bastard girl not of his blood—useful only as a placeholder for his future heir—to live past her fourteenth birthday. Instead, he skipped to the midpoint of the tale. "When we were fourteen, Grace and Devil and I fled—to start our lives outside of his control. We arrived in the city and found our way to Covent Garden. I thought we could go to—"

To his mother. The only one of their mothers who had lived at that point.

He reached into his pocket, taking his second pocket watch in hand. Hattie's gaze tracked the movement, and for a single, mad moment, he considered telling her everything. But telling her would bring her too close. And he couldn't afford her close.

He shook his head and returned his attention to her. Cleared his throat. "Suffice to say, we couldn't have survived without Grace. She was smarter and stronger than the rest of us, by far. Bits notwithstanding." Grace might not have been their sister by blood, but she was their sister in spirit.

She smiled at that. "Where is she now?"

He didn't know. Grace had left town after Ewan had returned, knowing that he had been looking for her. Knowing that the last time Ewan had seen her, he'd tried to kill her. They'd told Ewan she was dead, and he'd nearly killed Devil for the news, then left, madder than before. She was somehow keeping her businesses running from hiding, but still, she hadn't returned.

In the silence, Hattie said, "Well, wherever she is, I am grateful that you had each other."

Don't be kind to me, Henrietta Sedley. I don't deserve it.

He forced his thoughts down a new path. "Body. Business. Home. Fortune. Future." Her eyes went wide at the echo of the night they'd met. "Body begets business. You think my ruining you will get you closer to Sedley Shipping."

She looked back to the house, where no doubt London was agog at how she'd marched him into the gardens. "We shall find out soon enough. I'm well and truly ruined after tonight."

"You're nowhere near the kind of ruined you want," he said more casually than he felt at the idea of getting her alone so he could do the deed properly. "And we'll get to that, but first, body begets business begets fortune begets future. Assuming you get the business."

Her attention snapped to him. "I'll get it."

He ignored the vow and the whisper of guilt that came with it. "And what of home? You expect your father to give you the business, but not let you stay in your family's home?"

"Of course he would. But a woman of business requires a home of her own. Filled with a life she's made for herself. One she's *chosen* for herself."

"Does she?"

"Don't you?" she asked, not waiting for him to answer before she added, "I would wager you do. Some kind of lair deep in Covent Garden. Filled with . . ." She stopped, and he hung on the pause. ". . . plants or something."

He blinked. "Plants?"

"You seem the kind of man who has plants."

"Potted plants?"

"No." She shook her head, as though this were all perfectly normal. "Exotic plants. Things a body could not find without a serious tour about another continent."

He laughed at that, surprising himself with the way she made him lighter. "I've never been outside of Britain."

Her eyes went wide. "Really?"

He shrugged. Where would a boy raised in the gutter go?

"Well then," she said, waving away the moment. "Potted plants, then."

He shook his head. "I don't have plants."

"Oh. You should get some."

He resisted the urge to continue down her mad path and instead said, "And what of you . . . do you have a home in mind? In which to keep your own plants?"

She smiled. "In fact, I do."

"Where?" He shouldn't care. But he did—he wanted to know about this dream she had—the part that went far beyond what he'd already seen. He wanted her to share it with him. To choose him to share it with.

The pleasure he felt when she did just that was immense,

filling the darkest parts of him when she reached out and clasped his hand, leading him to the far side of the gardens. It was no wonder that he followed without question.

Hattie drew him to a small stone bench several yards away, perched against the brick wall that separated the Warnick gardens from the neighbor's. Twisting her hand in his clasp, she used her free hand to lift her skirts, and stepped up onto the bench. He instantly helped her, providing strength and balance as she gained her footing there.

"Thank you." She released his hand, immediately re-offering it to him. An invitation.

He didn't take it, but joined her anyway. "This is unexpected."

She grinned, her excitement heady. "You do not spend a great deal of time standing on benches with ladies?"

He offered a little grunt in reply.

"But you've scaled a wall in your day."

His brows shot up. "Are we scaling a wall tonight, my lady?"

"I would not want to ruin your handsome attire," she teased, "but we can look." She pointed over the wall. "Look."

He did, seeing what anyone might see in such a situation. A dark garden, a darker house beyond. He didn't understand immediately—not until he looked to her, his gaze locking on her in profile, her skin glowing pale in the light from Warnick House, her eyes tracking the darkness, as though she could see every nuance of the home and gardens without need for light.

There was more than that, though. Alongside the perusal was something else entirely—desire.

"This is the house," he said.

She turned to him. "Number forty-six Berkeley Square. The former home of Baron Claybourne."

"And you want it."

She nodded. "I do."

"And you want the business."

She met his eyes, honesty clear and unyielding in her gaze. "I do."

And why couldn't she have it? Why shouldn't she? "Take it."

She cut him a dry look. "I had intended to. Augie was going to step aside and tell my father to give it to me. If I kept you from him." She gave a little shrug. "That's all gone pear-shaped."

Whit's fists clenched. He could not guarantee that if he ever met August Sedley he wouldn't put a fist directly into the man's face. What kind of a man sent his innocent sister to wage his war? The same kind of man who came for the Bastards without thinking.

No. August Sedley did not come away from this unscathed. Even if he hadn't thrown his lot in with Ewan, Augie could not be trusted to run one of the biggest shipping businesses on the docks, and run it well to keep men in work and families in health.

But Hattie . . . Hattie, who loved French beans in Covent Garden and bought day-wilted flowers for thruppence— she could be trusted.

She wanted the business and Whit could give it to her.

"And if I helped?"

Suspicion flared in her eyes. "Why would you do that?"

Because I want you to have everything you desire. "Because you should have it. Because Sedley Shipping would thrive with you at the helm. Because the docks need businessmen who know that workers make a world. And you're strong enough to be one of them."

She met his gaze. "To be the best of them."

One side of his lips lifted in a small smile. "Yes."

"You don't know that."

"I do."

"So what, you add it to the list of demands for my father? My brother gives up your true enemy, and my father

installs me as his successor, and you don't bring the whole
thing down around us?"

Clever girl. A pause fell, the truth in it.

"So I get it . . . because of your benevolence."

A thread of unease whispered through him. "For God's
sake, Hattie, who cares how you get it?"

She smiled, the expression without humor. "That is spoken like a man who has never had to prove that he earned
what he had." She paused. "I want the business on my own
merit, or not at all."

"Do you doubt you deserve it?" he asked.

"No."

"Then take it. And prove your merit as its head."

She watched him for a long moment, until Whit became
uncomfortable with her unyielding gaze. Still, he resisted
the urge to look away. He was a Bareknuckle Bastard, for
God's sake, and he refused to be stared down by a Mayfair
lady—not even one who was about to run one of London's
biggest shipping businesses.

If her father agreed.

He'd agree. Whit would give him no choice.

Finally, Hattie whispered, "You can get it for me."

"The Year of Hattie."

She smiled, bright and beautiful. "And what will that
make us? Business acquaintances?"

Why did that idea please him so much? He growled a little laugh and pulled her to him. "We already have a deal."
She gasped at the words—the reminder of the promise he'd
made her all those nights ago to take her virginity. To give
her dominion over her body.

"When?" The question was soft and sweet and full of
anticipation, and punctuated by her face tilting up to his.

In an instant, Whit was aching for her, and he growled
low and dark. "Not in a Mayfair garden."

"If it isn't soon, I shall have no choice but to find you

again. A needle in a Covent Garden haystack." The words cracked him open with their promise. When had he ever liked a woman so much as this one? When had he ever felt so well matched?

He dipped his head and sucked the full bottom lip of her smile, until she sighed.

"Soon," he whispered, when he was through. *Tonight maybe. Tomorrow.*

She did not hesitate. "Please."

What a magnificent word. "Go back to your ball, warrior," he whispered, pressing a lingering kiss to her lips. "I shall find you."

He watched her make her way back through the gardens, up the stairs, and into the ballroom, his gaze not leaving the wine red silk of her beautiful dress. And for a moment, while he watched her, Whit's thoughts wandered into places where he never allowed them to go. Places that tempted with words like *happiness*. And *pleasure*.

And *wife*.

He stiffened at the last, but did not push it away, instead letting it linger, circling over and over, until the last hint of her silk frock had been swallowed by the crowd and he was left alone, marveling at the singular feeling crashing through him—something he hadn't felt in two decades.

Hope.

The foreign word stole his breath, and he unconsciously lifted a hand, rubbing at the tightness that came with it, at the way it threatened his certainty.

There was no time for hope. Not even when it came in beautiful, brazen packages, smelling like almonds and with ink stains on its wrists and wide, dimpled smiles. He told himself that as he turned away from the lights of the house.

And found Ewan standing in the darkness.

Chapter Fourteen

We shouldn't be here.

Memory slammed through Whit at the look in his brother's eyes, a brilliant amber, identical in color to those of Whit and Devil and the duke, their father. Instantly, he was transported to the moment years ago, when he'd been guided—small and full of nerves and something like hope—into a sitting room on the Marwick country estate to find the boys who would become his brothers and allies for the next two years. He remembered them like they were here now, in this Mayfair garden: Devil—brash and bold, hiding his fear, and Ewan—still as stone, assessing eyes taking in everything, brilliant and instantly favored by their father, who never seemed to see the cold fury that burned like fire in him.

That fire wasn't cold anymore. Tonight, it threatened to burn down the world.

There'd been a time when Ewan was the largest of them—tallest and broadest and strongest. In Whit's memories, he was godlike. Full of health and arrogance. Nothing like the man who stood before him, a pale approximation of the boy he'd once been. Lean—almost gaunt, with the way his clothes hung on his long frame—and hollow, unshaven and wild-eyed. Feral.

If twenty years on the streets had taught Whit anything it was this—men who had nothing to live for were the most dangerous of animals. Warning thrummed through him, and he reached inside his topcoat to collect one of his knives.

He was comforted by the cool, heavy weight in his hand, by the knowledge of the exact angle of the throw that would instantly lay his brother low. Ewan had been the best fighter among them years ago, never sending a fist flying without hitting his target. And when they'd planned their escape from their monster of a father, they'd believed in their success because of Ewan's skill.

Twenty years of a dukedom should have evened the score. *But it hadn't.*

The last time the brothers had faced Ewan, Devil had been left for dead. If not for Felicity, Whit would have been left to battle the Duke of Marwick alone.

As he might do tonight.

"I've a boy fighting for his life in the Garden because of you." Whit let his fist fall to his side, weapon in hand. "Give me one reason why I shouldn't take my revenge right now."

"Killing a duke is a hangable offense."

"We both know you're not a duke," Whit replied, enjoying the way Ewan stiffened at the words. "Augie Sedley won't be doing your bidding anymore, bruv."

"I don't care about that; I never cared about that," Ewan said, drawing closer. Whit tightened his fist on the knife's hilt, the emotionless words unsettling. "I only cared about coming for you." His gaze tracked over Whit's shoulder, to the house. "And now I see how to do it."

To Hattie.

Something hot and terrifying coursed through Whit. "You look at me, Marwick." If he came within ten feet of

Hattie, Whit would destroy him. "I'm here, and spoiling for the fight you want to give me."

It was time to punish him. For what he'd done to them as children. For what he'd done to Devil. For what he'd done to their men.

"I want to. I want to see you bleed out in this fucking garden. But I can't." Whit held his silence. "Because of her."

Grace. The girl Ewan had loved and lost.

When they'd run, she'd made Devil and Whit vow they wouldn't hurt Ewan. She'd begged them for it. *You don't know all of it*, she'd sworn. And for two decades, they'd kept their vows. But now? With Ewan's cold gaze on the spot where Hattie had disappeared?

Protect her.

If there was to be a battle, it would be tonight.

"Grace isn't here to hold us to our promises."

Ewan's jaw turned to stone. "You don't say her name." Whit didn't respond, noting the way Ewan's wild eyes threatened something worse. Something Whit didn't want anywhere near Hattie. "You let her die. I gave her up. I let her run with you—and you didn't keep her safe."

It wasn't true. Devil and Whit had been hiding Grace from Ewan since they'd left—knowing that he would come for her, unable to keep himself from doing so. Grace, the child who had been born to the Duchess of Marwick—sired by a man who was not the duke. Falsely baptized a boy and heir. Announced a boy and heir. A placeholder for the future heir to the Dukedom of Marwick.

Grace, who, if she were discovered and revealed, could bring the whole dukedom crashing down, and Ewan with it. Falsely claiming a title was punishable by death.

Not that Grace would ever do it.

Because Grace and Ewan were forged from the same fire. The first either had loved, and the first either had betrayed. And Grace would never see the boy she'd once loved killed. Not then, after Ewan had left Whit broken on the floor and come for her at their father's bidding. Not after Ewan had raised the knife and struck nearly true. Not after he would have killed her if Devil hadn't intervened—earning the wicked scar on his cheek for the trouble.

Devil and Whit and Grace had run that night, but not before Whit had seen the reckless panic in Ewan's eyes—the fury and frustration and fear that had propelled him to come for them in the first place. The desperation to win the dukedom. To be their father's heir. All else be damned.

Whit and Devil had done all they could to keep Grace hidden—to hide her in Covent Garden and keep her from the brother who'd searched for them since the moment he'd reached adulthood, with funds and determination. The Garden's loyalty—beyond measure—had kept them all a secret until months ago, when Ewan had found them, half mad with his unending search.

They'd lied when he asked for Grace.

They'd told him she was dead.

And they'd broken him.

"You let her die," Ewan said again, coming at Whit like a rabid dog, taking hold of his lapels and pushing him back, into the darkness. "I should have killed you the moment I found you."

Whit used the momentum to turn them both, propelling Ewan into a tree trunk with a heavy thud. "I'm not the runt anymore, Duke." He raised the knife and pressed it to his brother's throat, hard enough for Ewan to feel the sharp bite of the blade. "You took the lives of three others. Innocent, working men. To what, toy with us? They had *names*. Niall. Marco. David. They were strong boys with bright futures and you *snuffed them out*."

Ewan struggled, but decades in the Rookery had made Whit stronger and faster. "Tell me why I shouldn't fucking destroy you."

He could. He could slice the bastard's neck right there.

Ewan deserved it. For the betrayal years earlier and the attacks now.

Ewan raised his chin. "Go on then. *Saviour.*" He spat the name. "Do it."

They stood in wicked tableau for a heartbeat. A minute. An hour, their breaths coming harsh and furious in the dark, in the shadow of the world they'd wanted so keenly that the promise of it had pitted them against each other.

Ewan's amber eyes narrowed in the dim light from the ballroom beyond, the only outward manifestation of their brotherhood. Where Whit was dark-haired and olive-skinned—the product of his Spanish mother—Ewan was a near copy of their father, tall and fair-haired, with a broad shoulder and a broad chin.

Whit stepped back. Released Ewan. Delivered a different blow. A worse one. "You look like him."

"You think I don't know that?" A pause. "What would you have done to kill him then?"

The truth came instantly. "Anything."

"Why not me, now?" Ewan said.

A dozen answers, none of them enough. Grace, begging them not to hurt him as a girl and then, as a woman, threatening them if they did. The threat of prison for killing a peer. The threat to Devil and Whit. To Grace. To the Rookery.

Whit watched his half brother for a long moment, taking in the hollows of his cheeks, the dark circles under his frenzied eyes. "It would be a gift," he said. "If I took it from you. The life. The memories. The guilt." Ewan's gaze grew haunted. And then, from nowhere, Whit added, "Do you remember the night in the snow?" The other man flinched. "It began with that massive dinner—yeah? Meat pies and game and potatoes and beets drizzled with honey and cheese and brown bread."

Ewan looked away. "That was the first clue. Nothing good ever came of comfort at Burghsey House."

After the meal, the three boys had been marched outside with nothing more than their regular clothing—no coats or hats, scarves or gloves. It was January and bitter cold. It had been snowing for days, and the three of them had shivered together, as their father had meted out their punishment for sins unknown.

No. The sin had been clear. They'd banded together. Allied against him. And the Duke of Marwick feared it.

You aren't here to be brothers, he'd spat, his gaze full of unwavering fury. *You're here to be Marwick.*

It wasn't new. He'd tried to break them apart a dozen times before. A hundred. Enough that they'd tried to run on more than one occasion, until they'd discovered that being caught was inevitable, and their father's punishments grew worse with each infraction. After that, they'd stopped running, but they'd remained together, knowing they were stronger together.

After he'd railed about loyalty to title above all else— above even God—he'd left them trembling in the cold with clear instructions. There was a bed inside for one of them. But only one. The first to betray the others would get it. And the others—they spent the night in the snow. No shelter. No fire. If death came, so be it.

Whit watched his once-ally's face. "When he left us in the cold, you turned to me, and do you remember what you said?"

Of course he remembered. Ewan might have stayed, but he was broken by the place just like they had been. And now he was duke, wearing their father's face and his title and his shameful legacy. "We shouldn't be here."

With the duke. At the estate. They shouldn't have followed their father's pretty promises—health and wealth and a future without care. Without worry. With privilege and power and everything that came with aristocratic benevolence.

In the wake of the pronouncement, the boys had sprung

into action, knowing from experience that they lived or died that night, together. They went for anything they could find that was dry in the snow—anything that might be warmth.

Whit could still remember the cold. The fear. The darkness as they'd huddled together. The keen knowledge that he was going to die, and his brothers with him. The desperate, futile attempts to stay alive. A child's aching need for his mother.

"But it wasn't true, was it, Duke? I shouldn't have been there. Neither should Devil. But you—you did right there, yeah? Because you're a storybook character. The boy born in the muck of Covent Garden, who landed himself a dukedom. The fucking hero of the play."

Ewan revealed no shame in the wake of the words, and that alone was enough to keep Whit going. "But that's a lie, too. You were never a hero. And you never will be. Not with your thieved name and your shit dukedom, built on the backs of your brothers." He paused, drove the point home. "And the girl you claim to have loved. Who saved us all that night."

They would have died. If not for Grace.

Grace, who had found them in the cold and rescued them, risking her own skin. And that night, a band of three had become four. "Which you seem not to remember."

"I remember," Ewan said, the words ragged and broken. "I remember every fucking breath she took in my presence."

"Even the one she took to scream when you tried to kill her?" What was left of Ewan's composure shattered, and Whit let loathing edge into his voice, along with the Garden. "Nah. Killin' is too good for you, bruv. No matter how much you deserve it. You don't get your fight."

Fury returned to Ewan's face, fury and something strangely like betrayal. "I can't kill you," Ewan said, the words coming in a frenzy. "I can't come for you." *Why?* Whit didn't say it. He didn't have to. "You two—you're what's left of her."

Grace. The dead girl who wasn't dead.

Whit met that wild gaze—so like his own. "She was never for you."

The words weren't meant as a blow, but they froze Ewan in his tracks. And then they set him on fire. "I can't kill you," he repeated, full of wild rage. "But I can end you."

Whit turned away, knowing a man lost to reason when he saw one.

And then, "You'd best watch your lady, Saviour."

Whit froze at the words, at the way they dropped like stone into the darkness between them, as though spoken by another man entirely. No longer full of explosive anger; but instead all cold menace, more unsettling than the rant that had come earlier.

More threatening.

Whit turned, heart in his throat and knife in his hand, resisting the urge to send it flying—deep into the chest of the man he'd once thought his brother. Instead, he pinned Ewan with an icy stare and said, "What did you say?"

"From what I hear, Henrietta Sedley spends a great deal of time free of the protections of Mayfair and chaperones." A pause, then a low laugh. "Which explains how she landed here tonight, making eyes and arrangements with you."

Whit's entire body drew tight as a bowstring, prepared to let fly. "You don't go near her."

"Don't make me have to."

"What the fuck does that mean?" Whit didn't have to ask. He knew.

"I saw you together. I saw the way you promised her the world. The stars in her eyes. The stars in yours. Like she was your happiness. Like she was your hope."

That word again. Like a weapon.

Like truth.

"But you'll never be able to protect her. Not from me."

Whit didn't throw the knife. He'd lost the cool calculation necessary to do it, to seat it deep in Ewan's left breast and stop his heart and this madness with a perfectly placed blow. Instead, he went for Ewan as he had when they were children, fear and fury propelling him into a fight that would have made their sire proud.

Only, this time, Whit was not the runt. He was the Beast.

He took the heir down in the darkness, rolling with him through the dirt and leaves, retaining his upper hand as he put the fist holding the knife directly into the other man's face. Once. Twice. Blood spurted from Ewan's nose. "Try it." Another direct hit, Ewan squirming beneath him. "Test me. Twenty years have made me blade sharp. And I will protect her with my last breath, Your *Grace*."

Everything shifted with the miscalculated honorific, meant to invoke another Grace, and doing just that—but making Ewan even more crazed. With madness came strength. In a rage, he fought back, coming for Whit like a runaway bull. "You don't say her name!"

Within seconds, Whit's back was to the ground, the hand holding his knife trapped in his brother's impossible steel grip. They struggled, grappling for control, until Ewan caught a break, knocking Whit's head back to the ground, where a large rock, unseen in the night, sent stars across his field of vision.

He lost his grip on the knife's hilt.

And then the blade was at his throat. He froze, his eyes opening to find Ewan staring down at him, beyond reason. "Would you know if she were dead?"

Whit's brow furrowed at the strange question. "What?"

"She's gone," Ewan said, nothing making sense. "I gave her into your keeping and she died and I didn't—" He shook his head, lost to the thought. "I would know if she were dead. And it's making me . . ." He trailed off.

Whit waited, beneath his own blade, seeing the truth.

They'd broken Ewan to protect Grace.

And now he threatened Hattie.

As though he heard the words, Ewan looked to him. "If I

don't get love, you don't. If I don't get happiness, you don't. If I don't have hope, you don't."

Heart pounding like thunder, Whit willed himself to sound calm. Unmoved. "Her destruction wins you nothing. If you come for someone, come for me."

"You were so busy hating our father that you learned nothing from him," Ewan said. "This is how I come for you. And she is the weapon I won't hesitate to use. You care for her."

No.

Yes.

"You care for her, and you'll give her up. Like I did. Or I'll take her from you. Like you did."

There, in the words, was the echo of their past. Cold, calculating Ewan, who always knew the best way to fight. The best route to triumph. Now their father, who always knew the best path to pain.

Whit's mind was already racing, unraveling the plans from earlier in the evening, restitching them to keep Hattie safe. To keep her far from him. From danger.

She'll think you betrayed her.

She'll be right.

It didn't matter. Whit strained beneath the knife, furious for this moment, once again at Ewan's absent mercy. But this time, it was not his life in the balance. It was something far more precious. "If you hurt her, I vow to you and God—duke be damned. Grace be damned. The past be damned—I'll see you directly into hell."

Ewan watched him for a moment, then said, "I am already there."

And then he raised his hand, and knocked Whit out cold.

Chapter Fifteen

"Now, that's a winning smile."

Hattie finished checking a crate of silks that had come in on the ship from France—destined for Bond Street just as soon as the Sedley warehouse marked them arrived and unharmed. With a nod to the workman, she turned to find Nora coming up the gangway, the sun bright on her grass green walking dress.

Hattie's smile widened. "What are you doing here?"

Nora stepped onto the deck. "A woman cannot see the new head of Sedley Shipping in her element?"

Hattie laughed, the description making her even lighter on her feet than she'd been earlier in the day. And the day before. And the day before that, the morning after she'd left Whit in the dark Warnick gardens with his promise of both body and business. She waved a young man holding a half-open crate of something forward. "Not head yet."

Nora scoffed at the word. "If I've learned anything about that man, it's that when he vows something, he does it."

Hattie peeked inside the open box, considering the packets of sweets within. She met the gaze of the man holding it. "There should be a dozen of these."

He nodded. "Thirteen."

She ticked the item off her list and nodded. "To the warehouse." She reached in and extracted a pack of raspberry sweets. "You've girls at home, Miles?"

The boy—no more than three and twenty—smiled. "Aye. Twins. Isla and Clare."

She pulled out two more packs and tucked them into the loose pocket in his coat. "They'll be proper happy to see their papa tonight."

The smile widened. "Thank you, Lady Henrietta."

When he passed Nora with a little nod, her friend turned to her. "Well, that was darling. And a winning strategy for the new head of the business."

"Stop calling me that. You'll curse it."

Nora waved away the caution. Of course. This was Nora, after all. "How many times do you think Augie distributed sweets on the deck?"

"I don't think Augie has ever even realized that the boats have to be unloaded," Hattie said, dryly, turning away from Nora's bark of laughter to consider a cask of Belgian ale coming up from the hold. "That can be delivered straight to the Jack and Jill," she told the man who had hooked the load. She pointed down the dock to the pub in question, past four empty ships, huge haulers that had been emptied over the last few days, their contents delivered to the Sedley warehouses.

The quiet ships were odd—owners tended not to allow boats to sit empty in harbor—especially something as in demand as a hauler—able to go long distances and with massive holds waiting to be filled. Hattie made a note to speak to the owners about the disuse. Perhaps it was time for Sedley Shipping to increase its export business.

"If I may?" Nora summoned Hattie's attention again. "I've never seen you looking so sorted." She lowered her voice. "Mr. Whittington certainly knows the way to a lady's heart."

Hattie couldn't stop the smile that came at the words, embarrassed and gleeful and full of anticipation. "My father has a meeting with him today."

Nora smirked. "How very patriarchal. Is he to ask for your hand?"

For a heartbeat, Hattie let the jest play out—imagining what would happen if the man all London called Beast marched into her father's offices and asked for permission to marry his daughter.

Though she quickly recalled that marriage meant she would never be able to own the business outright, Hattie would be lying if her first response to the fantasy hadn't been a speeding heart and a fleeting image of standing on the docks with him by her side.

"I assure you, he is not," she said, pushing the image to the side. "I haven't seen him since the night he promised to help me."

"Since the night he called you a warrior and told you that you were smarter than all the men in London, you mean."

Heat washed over Hattie's face. "*Most* of the men," she qualified.

"I'm sure he meant *all.*"

"The point is," Hattie said, looking down at the packet of sweets in her hand, running a thumb over the pretty French lettering. "He promised to find me. And he hasn't."

Nora blinked. "It's been three days. It takes time to cross off the *business* bit of the Year of Hattie."

Hattie huffed a barely agreeable sigh. Three days felt an eternity away from him. And it didn't take time to cross off the other bit. The *body* bit.

But he'd given her a taste. And that had been the most wonderful torture she could imagine. What would the rest be like? And once it was over, what would she do when she had no reason to see him?

Perhaps he'd keep seeing her.

The thought rioted through her, with a memory of his

kisses, his touches, the magnificent things he did to her in that dark room at the back of The Singing Sparrow. Perhaps he'd be willing to continue their lessons.

Three weeks earlier, Hattie had been planning one night at a brothel and now she was considering how she might tempt a man into taking her as mistress. Into letting her take *him* as mistress.

"Well. That blush is very telling and I should like very much to hear more about what caused it," Nora said, dry and quiet. "But we're about to be ambushed."

Before Hattie could follow the direction of Nora's gaze, she heard her father from a distance. "Hattie-girl!"

She waved to the earl, approaching with Augie at his shoulder. The sight of her brother, looking worse for the wear of whatever he'd done the night before, rumpled and unshaven, had Hattie steeling herself for the confrontation that was no doubt to come. She prepared for Earl Cheadle to read his youngest child the full riot act and insist on a report on how Augie had entered into criminal activity on behalf of Sedley Shipping.

She prepared for him to insist on Augie's full cooperation with Whit.

And, heart pounding, she prepared for him to announce that he was, in fact, transferring control of Sedley Shipping to Hattie.

"This is it," she whispered.

The Year of Hattie was about to begin.

"I shall be here to toast you when it's over," Nora said. "Courage."

Hattie made her way from the boat to the docks to meet her father, his silver hair shining in the brilliant afternoon sun. She willed herself calm—and failed—unable to keep herself from whispering again, this time to herself, "This is it."

This was it.

She was ready.

Except she wasn't ready for what her father said, before Hattie had even come to a complete stop. "Finish up that shipment and then come back to the office. I've sold the business."

It did not matter that Hattie was looking directly at her father when he spoke. It did not matter that her hearing was perfectly sound, as was her grasp of the English language.

She simply didn't comprehend what he'd said.

She'd clearly misheard.

Was it possible he'd spoken in another language?

No—it had been English. Clear and honest, in the firm, aging voice he used with the men scurrying about around them, that he was selling the business out from under her.

"What?" Hattie looked to Augie, whose gaze was instantly clearer, the prior evening's debauchery chased away. "Did you know this?"

Augie shook his head. "Why?"

The earl leveled Augie with a cool look. "Because if you took it in hand, you'd ruin it."

Augie's brows shot together as Hattie's heart pounded. "That's not true."

"Och," Cheadle scoffed, letting years on the water slide into his voice. "Ye never wanted it. Ye never cared for it. Aye, ye want the money it offers and the life it provides, but the business—" He shook his head. "You've never wanted the business. And I'm weary of waitin' for you to feel different." He waved a hand. "I've sold."

"You can't!" Augie said.

"I can," the earl replied. "I have. It's mine. I built it. I won't see it driven into the sea. It goes to a man who'll keep it thriving."

Confusion flared. None of this was going to plan.

She looked to the wooden slats beneath her feet, the breeze from the river swirling around them. How many times had she been here, on this very dock, where she'd used to hide in the shadows of the haulers while he finished his work? "Father—"

He cut her off, raising one wizened hand. "No, Bean." She pressed her lips flat together at the childhood name. "You're a good girl. But it was never going to be you."

The words, so matter-of-fact, took the air from her lungs, replacing it with hot fury. "Why not?"

He waved a hand in the air. "You know why."

"I don't, as a matter of fact." She lifted her chin, hating the way he avoided her eyes. "Tell me."

After an eternity, he met her gaze. "You know why."

"Because I'm a woman."

He nodded. "No one would have taken you seriously."

She stiffened at the blow from her father. "That's not true."

I have no difficulty believing that you can run that business better than them. The memory came unbidden, Whit's words in the darkness. And he'd meant them.

Or had he? He hadn't meant the rest, obviously.

This hadn't been the plan.

What had happened? Where was Whit? A thread of unease coursed through her. Was he unwell? Had something happened to him?

Unaware of the riot of her thoughts, the earl waved a hand in the air. "A dozen men on the docks. A handful of the customers we serve."

Anger rose like bile. "A *handful*?" she said. "Do you know how much I correspond with our customers? How well I know the men on the docks? How well I know the cargo, the ships, the tide tables? I've been holding this business together while you've been ailing. While he's been—" She pointed to Augie. Looked to him, taking in his wide eyes. *While he's been threatening it all.* "It doesn't matter. I'm *good*, Father. I know this business—all of it—better than anyone."

The wind caught the words and whipped them away,

along with her future. Hattie's breath came harsh with her frustration and her desire to prove herself.

Horrifyingly, tears threatened.

No. She willed them away. She couldn't cry. *Wouldn't.* Dammit, why could men rage and riot endlessly, and the moment women felt a modicum of anger, tears came on a flood?

She exhaled, her breath ragged. "This is all I ever wanted."

The earl watched her, assessing. "Bean."

"Don't call me that."

He paused. Started again. "They know you. They like you, even. You're a good match for them—with a clever brain and a smart mouth. But Hattie—they wouldn't have worked with you. Not without a man to make certain the clockwork ran smoothly."

The tears began to sting behind her nose, into her throat, where they caught in a painful knot. "That's horseshit."

The ancient sea captain in her father did not flinch at the curse. "Maybe . . ." he added. "If you had a husband."

She couldn't help the humorless laugh that came at her father's words. "The specter of a husband was always your worry, Father. How many times have you invoked the prospect as a reason I would never be able to run the business?"

"It's still a reason. I meant before. Maybe if you'd been able to find a husband before. A decent one. With a head on his shoulders. But that wasn't to happen, was it?"

No. Because no one wanted to marry Hattie. No decent man with a head on his shoulders wanted an imperfect woman who spoke her mind and had a nose for business for a wife.

Too brash. Too brazen. Too big. *Too much.*

Too much and still . . . somehow . . . not enough.

She looked down at the dock again, where her dirty boots stood stark against the wood, bleached from decades of London rain. She still held the packet of sweets, the lading papers for the ship beyond, clutched in her ink-stained fingers. When was the last time she'd seen them without stains?

How much had she worked for this? Dreamed of it?

So much for the Year of Hattie.

A single, fat tear fell to the dock.

Augie cursed softly and spoke, surprising everyone. "Why now?"

"Because I got an offer."

"From where?" This, from Augie.

A pause as her father seemed to consider his answer. To consider *answering*. And in that pause, Hattie knew the truth. She answered for him, the wind whipping around her, pulling her hair from its moorings and sending her skirts into a wild dance. "Saviour Whittington."

The earl looked down the dock, past the empty ships and the single empty berth on the far end. "You always were the smart one."

"Not smart enough for you to give me a chance," Hattie snapped.

"Who is Saviour Whittington?" Augie asked.

The earl leveled his son with a cold gaze. "You really should know the names of the men you try to fleece."

Understanding dawned. "The Bastards."

"Goddammit, Augie!" the earl thundered, drawing the attention of half a dozen men on the docks. "I ought to turn you over to them."

He didn't have to. They already knew Augie's involvement. Whit already knew. He didn't need Augie's name, or Augie himself. He was to have been paid in Augie's knowledge. That was the first of the two demands.

She reached for her father, setting an urgent hand on his coat sleeve. "Wait. He doesn't want the business. He wants Augie to tell him where to find the man pulling the strings of the hijackings." She looked to her brother. "Do you know where to find him?"

Augie shook his head. "But Russell—"

Hattie groaned. "Yes then. We need Russell. Though I rather hate the sound of that."

"Too late," the earl said. "The bastard says he doesn't require the name anymore. And so he's made me a generous offer, with the understanding that if I don't take it and get out of the Docklands, he'll pauper us."

Confusion again. None of this was what they'd agreed. Whit was to have asked the earl to pass the business to Hattie. Hadn't he praised her skill? Hadn't he understood her desire? Hadn't he told her he'd help her? "No," she said. "He promised—"

Her father and brother cut her twin looks.

"You're in bed with them, too?" She hated the disappointment in her father's tone.

Augie was a bit kinder. "Hattie. What good is a promise from a Covent Garden smuggler?"

It had been good.

His faith. His promise.

It had been wonderful. And a lie.

Confusion faded into another bout of anger. A new sort of anger—one she felt more than comfortable acting upon.

They'd had a deal. And he'd reneged on every bit of it.

Her teeth clenched.

"Goddammit, I don't know which of you is worse," the earl said, looking to Hattie. "You, for trusting a Bareknuckle Bastard's word, or Augie, for not knowing who they were in the first place."

"I've heard of them," Augie defended himself. "Of course I have."

"Then what are you doing *stealing* from them, you dankwit?" The earl scowled. "The worst bit is that Whittington didn't have to tell me. He didn't have to. I might be old, but I've a brain in my head, and I know the cargo well enough to know the difference between a hold full of tulips and one full of booze." He pointed a finger at Augie. "That's when I realized you'd never be good enough to run it."

"Maybe," Augie allowed. "But Hattie was, and you know it."

On another day, at another time, Hattie might have been surprised by and more than grateful for Augie's support. But at that particular moment, she was too busy being furious at him. And her father. And Saviour Whittington. Or Beast, or whatever the hell his name was.

These men, members of the only sex that was thought qualified to run a business, and not one of them doing a damn thing to protect it. Fury surged, and she clenched her fist, crushing the lading papers and the packet of sweets, not sure that she could suffer another moment with these men. Let them sort it out. Let them worry. She didn't want it.

Liar.

Of course she wanted it. It was all she'd ever wanted.

But she couldn't have it. So she was leaving. She was *done*.

She looked down the docks at the line of empty boats. *The boats.*

She looked to her father. "He didn't just buy the business."

He turned a frustrated look on her. "What?"

"The boats are empty." She waved a hand. "He bought the boats, too. To keep us from using them."

The earl nodded. "Aye. Ships that should have been sailing up the coast, moving our cargo. And suddenly, not one of them available to Sedley Shipping."

"We've contracts with those owners," Augie argued.

"Not with the new ones," Hattie said, softly.

"And not with any others, either," the earl added. "They've locked down every other shipping line that works the Thames. No one will do business with us. And this morning, he made his offer."

"To buy us out."

The earl nodded. "That was the option. Sell to him, or lose it all."

"Not much of an offer," Augie said.

Because it wasn't an offer. "There's nothing honorable about this."

"They're called the Bareknuckle Bastards, Hat," Augie pointed out. "They're not exactly honorable."

But they were. She'd seen it in him, from the start. Whit hadn't lied to her. In fact, he'd prized honesty between them from the start. Even when she'd refused to tell him Augie's name—his part in the play—he'd admired her loyalty.

But more than all that, he'd *believed* in her. When she'd confessed her plans—her hopes for the future, her desire for the business, her plans for it. And he'd believed in her. He'd offered to help her. Had it all been a lie?

And why did it feel like such a betrayal?

Frustration and sadness stung in her throat. "He promised he wouldn't do this."

"Bah," her father said. "He lied. Men like the Bastards always hit back, Bean. Why do you think I never tangled with them? And you've been caught."

She refused to believe that. Refused to acknowledge it. She looked to the great ship again, her gaze going soft on the warm wood of its hull. Her mind worked, turning over the events of the last several days—playing out the possibilities. She'd spent years here, working these docks, loving them.

This was *her* turf, not his.

She wouldn't let him steal it out from under her.

Bastard, indeed.

Finally, she looked up at her father. "You shouldn't have sold. Not to him. Not to anyone." Silence stretched like an eternity, the only sound the shouts of the men on the ship beyond, unloading what might be the last of the Sedley Shipping freight if the Bareknuckle Bastards had their way. "You were so afraid of letting me try. So terrified that I might fail and shame you—and you lost it all anyway."

And in that moment, Hattie realized that her father, for

so long immense in her mind, was far less than she'd ever been able to see. Smaller and slighter, white-haired, and with a craggy, weathered face, and a cowardice that he'd hidden for years . . . and could hide no longer.

This man who had built a business that had fed his family and hundreds of others with his sweat and his ethic was now tired and bested, and facing the ignoble, craven end of his legacy—because he couldn't see how his daughter might have helped to keep it alive.

Might still.

She looked to her brother, then her father.

"You may have agreed to sell, but I haven't."

Augie's brows shot up in surprise and something else— admiration?

"It's done, gel. There wasn't a choice."

"There is always a choice," Hattie said. "There is always the choice to fight."

And her father considered her for a long while, a slight gleam in his eye. A glimmer of something more than doubt. "No man has ever gone up against the Bastards and survived."

There might have been a time when she would have heeded that warning. But Hattie found she lacked the patience for warnings just then.

What was there to lose? He'd already taken it all.

"Then it is time for a woman to do so."

Chapter Sixteen

———— ❦ ❦ ————

That night, Nora and Hattie drove to Covent Garden in Nora's fastest gig.

"I've no wish to die tonight," Hattie said over the sound of the clattering wheels, clinging to the edge of the curricle as it rocketed past Drury Lane, turning left, then right, then left in quick succession. "Nora!"

"No one is dying!" Nora scoffed. "Please. I've raced this beauty along the Thames walk—and you think the Garden will do her in?"

"Let's not tempt fate, is all I'm saying," Hattie said, holding her hat atop her head as she pointed to a curved lane twisting off to the left. "There."

Without slowing, Nora steered the matched greys down the cobblestone street, darker than the roads they'd been on. "You're sure?"

Hattie nodded. "There. Up ahead. On the right."

A bright lantern hung high on the exterior of the building, illuminating the sign for The Singing Sparrow. Nora slowed the horses. "I didn't know you'd spent so much time in the Garden that you had a favorite pub."

Hattie ignored the dry commentary. "Stay here."

"There is absolutely no chance of that." Nora was down from the gig, straightening the topcoat she wore over her tight buckskin breeches before Hattie could reply. "Is he in there?"

"I don't know," Hattie said, her heart pounding as she landed on the street, grateful for her own trousers—donned to keep her from notice—and the freedom of movement they provided. "But it's the best place for us to start."

She was not leaving Covent Garden without finding him. Without confronting him.

"Do you think people will recognize us?" Nora asked.

"I don't." Though, to be honest, the last time Hattie had been in this pub, she hadn't been interested in anyone but the man who'd brought her. Heat thrummed through her with the memory of the pleasure he'd wrought here, her body tightening with the anticipation of seeing him.

No. She wasn't here for pleasure. She was here for punishment.

For confrontation.

Nora grinned. "Then I think those assembled within will see what we show them. Two well-appointed—but not overly wealthy—gentlemen. In search of ale."

Hattie cut her friend a look. "We are not here to get soused, Nora."

"I know." Nora's smile turned knowing. "We're here to find your Bastard."

"He's not mine," Hattie protested. "Though he is a bastard."

The pub was teeming with people—men and women of all walks. Hattie immediately recognized a half-dozen dockworkers, three with their wives by their sides, each ruddy-cheeked and jolly and happy to not be using his hook tonight.

Using the brim of her hat to hide her face, Hattie considered the crowd assembled, many of whom were sitting, facing an empty stage, lit by two large candelabra. No sign of

Whit in the audience, but she couldn't imagine him being interested in whatever was about to happen here.

Nora turned back to her, tilting her chin toward the far end of the room. "Is that Sesily Talbot?"

Hattie followed the direction to the dark-haired, dark-eyed woman at the bar, clad in a daringly cut, lush amethyst gown designed for anything *but* escaping notice. "Turns out there are toffs in here!" Nora said happily, approaching Sesily, who leaned over the mahogany bar, smiling broadly at the American who had been in the tavern when Whit and Hattie had been. It took Hattie a moment to recognize him, however, as his friendly face was gone—replaced by a dark, irritated scowl.

Nora sidled up to Sesily, who turned immediately, a flash of frustration in her eyes at the arrival, there and immediately gone when she recognized Nora. "Look at you!" Sesily said happily, her gaze sliding past Nora to Hattie, eyes widening just a touch as she took in the duo's attire. "And you!"

Nora leaned in. "We're in disguise."

"Of course you are!" Sesily laughed delightedly, as though the whole thing were a lark. Sesily was the last of the scandalous Talbot sisters, the one who remained unmarried and, it seemed, perfectly happy in her spinsterhood. "You look magnificent!" Her gaze traced over Hattie's coat and trousers. "You especially, Hattie. Though no one with a brain in their head would think you a man."

That much was true. Hattie had bound her breasts before coming out tonight, but there was only so much to be done when one's breasts were Hattie's. She gave a little shrug in Sesily's direction. "I only require people not notice me at all."

Sesily pursed her lips. "Whyever not?"

"Of course, it's impossible for you to imagine not being noticed." The words came on a scowl from the American, who was spending an inordinate amount of time cleaning the bartop near them.

Sesily turned a brilliant smile on him. "You've given me more than enough of the experience, Caleb. After all, you make a point never to notice me."

A muscle flexed in the man's jaw and he turned to Hattie and Nora. "Something to drink, *gentlemen*?" Recognition flared in his gaze. "Welcome back."

There was nothing scandalous in the words—but the memory they evoked had Hattie's gaze sliding to the closed door to the storage room in the distance. Her mouth went dry, and an ale appeared in front of her. "Thank you," she said, lifting the drink. "Hello again."

"You know each other?" Sesily asked.

"Hattie's been here before," Nora interjected, distracted by the crowd. "Is there to be a show tonight?"

"There is!" Sesily said, happily. "The Sparrow is performing."

Nora swiveled to look at her. "The actual Sparrow? Really? I thought she was touring Europe."

Sesily smiled. "She's returned to London."

Nora's gaze lit with excitement. "Do you know her?"

"Indeed I do." She waved away the otherwise fascinating information, turning bright eyes to Hattie. "Why are you in disguise?"

"No reason," Hattie said.

"Hattie's on the hunt," Nora replied simultaneously.

Hattie rolled her eyes as Sesily's lips dropped into a little O. "*Delicious*. For whom?"

Hattie feigned innocence. "Who says it's a *whom*?"

Sesily cut her a look. "It's always a *whom*."

Fair enough. Nora distracted Sesily with another question, and as the two women chatted, Hattie turned to the American, still lingering on the other side of the bar. "It's a *whom*."

Understanding flashed in his kind eyes, followed by something like pity. He nodded. "I'm afraid I can't help you."

"Can't or won't?"

"Can't. I haven't seen him since you . . . were here."

She was grateful for the dim light in the tavern hiding her blush. She refused to be deterred. "I have to find him." Failure was not a possibility tonight. She was through letting him run riot through her life. "It's imperative."

Caleb Calhoun scanned the crowd behind her. She followed his gaze, tracking over the men she'd recognized when she entered. "Too many strong arms here for him to be at the docks." She smiled when the American looked impressed. "I'm not a fool."

"Searching out a Bastard in the Garden would suggest otherwise," he said, but his eyes searched hers, nevertheless, for what . . . honor? She nearly laughed at the thought that someone might be concerned that Hattie was the dishonorable person in her battle with the Bareknuckle Bastards. Whatever he looked for, he found. "It's Wednesday night. He's probably at the fights."

The fights. She pounced. "Where?"

He shook his head. "I don't know. It's a moving ring. If they don't want you to find it, you won't."

Frustration flared, and she reached into her pocket, extracting tuppence and setting it on the bar. Calhoun waved it off. "On the house."

The kindness in the American's eyes was a comfort. "Thank you."

Sesily looked up from her conversation with Nora. "Caleb, you're never so nice to me!"

The bartender growled in response, turning away, even as Sesily watched him, and if Hattie didn't know better, she would have thought it was longing on the Talbot sister's face. Longing and something like frustration.

Lord knew she understood *that*.

Nora nodded in Hattie's direction. "Ready?"

Indeed. They had a fight to find.

She flashed a wide smile at Sesily before inclining her head in a formal farewell. "Duty calls."

They pushed through the crowd, thicker and more raucous than it had been when they'd arrived. Hattie had never been so grateful for the cool air in the street beyond. When they reached the curricle again, she stopped and took a deep breath. *Where was he?*

This man, whom she hadn't known, whom she hadn't *wanted* to know, and who had somehow turned her whole life upside down with his presence and his vengeance and his damn *kisses*. Hattie couldn't even be certain that she wasn't after more of those, and that was exceedingly exasperating.

Where was he?

She had things to say to him.

"Hattie?" She looked up. Nora was on the box, ready to go, looking down at her. "Where to?"

Hattie shook her head. "I don't know." And then, because she couldn't stop herself . . . *"That damn man is ruining everything!"*

Hattie's frustration echoed off the buildings around them.

When silence fell once more, Nora nodded. "We'll find him."

And the certainty in the words—the *we* there—might have made Hattie cry. Would have done, if it weren't for the words that immediately followed it, spoken from the darkness behind her. "Would you care for some help?"

Hattie spun toward the question as three women stepped from the background, each wearing a long, fitted coat over trousers and high boots, hair tucked up under caps. And there, beneath the outerwear of the tallest—the one who was nearly Hattie's height and whom she would have identified as their leader on sight—was the flash of a weapon.

Sliding her hand into her pocket, fingering the blade there, Hattie took a step back. "What sort of help?"

There was no malice in the smile the woman flashed. "Lady Henrietta, I'm more than happy to point you in the direction of Beast."

How did she know . . .

Hattie's brow furrowed. "Have we met?"

"No."

"Then how do you know my name?"

"Does it matter?"

"I suppose not, but I'd like to know anyway."

The woman laughed, low and lush. "I make it my business to know what women are looking for, and what will give them satisfaction."

"That's handy," Nora said from her place in the curricle.

The mysterious woman did not look away from Hattie as she cautioned, wryly, "Tonight is Lady Henrietta's night, Lady Eleanora. You'll get your turn."

"I couldn't agree more," Nora said, as though this were all perfectly ordinary.

It wasn't at all ordinary. But had anything been so since she'd met Whit? Since she'd found her way into Covent Garden and this wide world had been unlocked for her? Hattie would not deny the thrill of it. The woman was right—it didn't matter how she knew Hattie. What mattered was that she was willing to help. "You know where he is?"

An incline of the head.

"And you'll take us there?"

"No," she said, sending disappointment through Hattie like a shock. "But I'll tell you where to go."

Relief flooded. "Please."

Red lips smirked. "So polite. He doesn't deserve you, you know."

Hattie matched the dry tone. "I assure you, madam, he deserves precisely what I intend to deliver."

The woman's laugh was full and honest, and Hattie imagined that she was the kind of person who might make a wonderful friend if she weren't so mysterious. "Fair enough. You'll find Beast at the granary. Follow the roar of the crowd. He'll be the one winning."

Hattie nodded, a sizzle of excitement flaring as she looked to Nora.

Her friend nodded. "We'll find it."

Hattie climbed up onto the box and looked back to the woman. "Shall I give him your regards?"

"They'll be delivered along with you, my lady," came the reply from the shadows, the women already out of sight, as the gig set in motion.

It took them less than a quarter of an hour to reach the granary, with its half-dozen silos dark and ominous in the riverfront cold. The October wind whipped up the Thames, honing its blade as it wove through the uninhabited buildings. On another such night—the lack of moon making it impossible to see—there would have been no entering the space, but a half-dozen yards from the road, tucked against the corner of a building, a lit torch flickered.

"There," Hattie said, climbing down from the curricle and pulling her coat around her to block the sting of the wind. "That way."

"Now, Hattie, you know I'm always game for an adventure," Nora said, on a loud whisper, "but are you quite sure about this?"

"Not *quite* sure," Hattie allowed.

"Well. I suppose you get points for honesty."

"Fury lends itself to fearlessness," Hattie said, turning the corner by the torch, noting another one at the edge of the first silo. She headed for it.

Nora followed. "You mispronounced *stupidity*. I think we should turn back. There's no one here. We might as well summon the murderers to us."

Hattie cut her friend a look. "I thought you were the brave one."

"Nonsense. I'm the *reckless* one. That's a different thing entirely."

Hattie laughed—what else was there to do? "What does that make me?" The question was punctuated by a roar in the distance. *Follow the roar of the crowd.* Hattie looked to Nora.

"The brave one." There was no humor in it. Only truth. Truth and the kind of love that comes from one's dearest friend. "The one who knows what she wants and will do whatever it takes to get it." Nora squared her shoulders. "Well then, lay on."

Heading past a second silo, Hattie saw an orange glow around the edge of a third. Without thinking—there was no place for thought in this particular exercise—she pressed on. "You know Macduff kills Macbeth after that bit, don't you?"

"Now is not the time for literary truths, Hattie," Nora replied. "And besides, you are not the murderer I am worried about this evening." Hattie pulled up short, and Nora nearly collided with her. "Good God."

It was a fair assessment of the view ahead.

Beneath the largest of the silos, forty-odd feet in diameter and raised off the ground on massive iron legs, a huge crowd stood in an enormous circle, hands in pockets and collars turned up against the wind that searched for passage between them.

Another wild roar sounded, and a collection of arms went high in the air in celebration. Hattie moved more quickly, her breath coming faster. She knew, without question, for whom they cheered, as though the Lord himself had come to fight.

As they watched, the circle spit out a man—a loser, nose bleeding and one eye already swelling shut. No one made to follow him as he headed for the street, passing Nora and Hattie, who tried not to look too closely as he brushed past, thinking them nothing more than two men, come for the spectacle.

Hattie recognized him, nonetheless. Michael Doolan.

As requested, he'd found Whit at the fights, and been dispatched with ease. Pleasure and pride coursed through her, even as she knew it shouldn't. Whit had promised retribution. And here it was.

And had he not promised the same to her?

She pushed the thought aside. It was different. He'd made it seem that they were on the same team.

As she drew closer, the picture became clearer. Inside the outer ring of spectators, a dozen or so barrels burned, providing not near enough heat for the strange, surprising space, but plenty of flickering light to the sheltered inner circle, the location of that evening's fights.

And at the center of that circle, like the Minotaur at the center of the labyrinth, stood a man, clad only in boots and trousers, a cut bleeding on one cheek over what looked like an old bruise—even as a fresh one bloomed on the side of his torso, where Hattie shouldn't be looking, she knew . . . but who wouldn't look?

He was magnificent.

When she'd been barely into long skirts, she'd attended an exhibition at the Royal Museum, and spent more time than was reasonable considering the ridges and planes of a particular statue of Apollo.

She'd always assumed that such ridges and planes were reserved for gods and relevant depictions thereof. Not so, apparently. Apparently perfectly ordinary men like this one had them.

Was that what she would call him? Perfectly ordinary?

She swallowed, her mouth suddenly quite dry.

Hattie drew closer, her height making it easy for her to see over the clustered shoulders of the two men in front of her, shouting into the din of the rest of the spectators as Whit turned away, revealing more ridges and planes, the magnificent muscles of his back.

No, not Whit. This wasn't Whit. This was Beast, his trousers hanging low on his hips, his fists at his side, wrapped in linen that might have one day been white, but were no longer. One of the ties had come loose, and Hattie was transfixed by the way he ignored that length of dangling fabric, his hand curled into a near fist, ready for a new battle.

"Beast is on tonight, lads!" a young man no more than fourteen or fifteen called out to a raucous response. "Ye'd best wager with 'im if ye want ale tonight!" The boy tipped the brim of his cap back. Not a boy. A girl, her bright black eyes shining as she flashed a wide, winning grin that made Hattie want to open her purse as well. "Closing bets in five-four-three . . ."

The girl paused to do the business of accepting a wager. "Fank ye, sir," she said with a dip of her head. "And there it is—the next round begins! Beast against the O'Malley Trio!"

Hattie couldn't take her gaze from his shoulders, from the way they set, square and strong, as though they might spring at any time. She marveled at the power of them, right up until she noticed the sheer size of the three men approaching. Each one taller and broader than Whit, with broken noses and jaws that looked to be made of granite.

"Cor," Nora whispered at her ear. "Look at them. Like damn Cerberus."

"He can't be expected to fight all three. Surely there's someone to help him," Hattie said.

"'E'll fight all of 'em, and they'll need a surgeon for it!" came a response from one of the men in front of her. "Just you watch."

As though she could stop. The trio of men came for him, creeping closer, crouching low, and Hattie held her breath. When would they leap? Was he not going to protect himself? The crowd grew silent, and she pressed her fingers to her lips to keep in the shout she wanted to release, the one that told him to run.

They were on him in seconds, but he moved like lightning. She gasped for breath; she'd never seen anything like him as he slid beneath one man's massive fist and helped it directly into the nose of a second. And all while he kicked out into the torso of the third, sending him flying back with an ominous thud.

"Aye, Beast! Keep at it!" a woman several feet away called

out. "That's what they get for goin' up against ya!" Then, lowering her voice, she turned to her neighbor and said, "I'd like to give him a prize for this win!"

Her companion laughed her agreement, and Hattie resisted the hot jealousy that flared at the words, even as she took her eyes from him to track the spectators in the crowd. There were more than a few pretty women, eyes gleaming with lust as they watched his movements. Any one of them would offer themselves up as a spoil of this particular war. Of course they would. Hattie would, too. She was not made of stone.

And she knew what it was to be his prize.

To have him be hers.

Not that such a thing was why she was here. She was furious with him. She'd come to give him what-for.

Did he make a habit of it? Bringing these women home?

The question was lost in a wicked crack as he put his fist into the nose of one of the brutes he fought, sending the other man reeling backward and, in slow motion, to his knees. He landed on his face in the dirt like a felled tree.

The crowd screamed its pleasure. "Out cold! What did I tell ye?" the man in front of her tossed over his shoulder before adding, loudly, "One more, Beast!"

Hattie had thought the difficult part of the fight was when there were three opponents, but she fast changed her mind now that the final man standing had directed his full attention toward Whit. His enormous arms were wide and waiting, giant hands in fists that looked like stone. "Come for it, Beast!" he shouted.

It was madness.

They circled, Whit fairly dancing on his feet, until she could see his face once more, and his body, now with a new spot of blood just below his left shoulder. He was breathing heavily, and the length of linen that had come undone was still ignored, now long enough to reach his knee.

His opponent threw a wicked punch, and Whit dodged.

But it was a feint. Up came the man's other fist, straight into Whit's jaw, knocking his head back like an apple off a tree. Whit twisted away, and a second blow, aimed for his head, landed on his shoulder, sending him off balance and into the dirt.

The crowd hissed its disappointment as the enormous man put a boot into Whit's midsection, sending him rolling through the dirt.

"No!" Hattie cried out. Would someone stop the fight?

She was already shoving aside the men in front of her, one of whom was shouting, "Get up, Beast!" When Hattie squeezed through to get a better view, he added, "Oy! Get yer own space, ye git!"

Grateful for the disguise she wore, Hattie ignored him, stepping farther into the ring, toward Whit, who was already moving, rising once more. His head turned toward her and, like magic, his eyes found hers. Her heart skittered in her chest at the ferocity there. Did he recognize her?

He would be hurt. Possibly killed, the stupid man. Would he put a stop to this mad spectacle?

She didn't have time to find out, as the man behind her grabbed her arm, pulling her back. "Where do ye think yer goin'?"

She tried to pull away, but the man's grip was strong. Tearing her eyes from where Whit was coming to his feet, she looked back, letting her anger lead. She narrowed her gaze on the man, slightly shorter than she was. "Unhand me."

Anger flared in his eyes, and his fingers tightened. "I'll lay hands on ye if I want, boy. I'll put ye into the ground if you don't get out of my way."

"Oy!" Nora said, seeing what was coming. "Stop it!"

The crowd was screaming its excitement behind them; Whit must have found his footing. Somewhere, Hattie felt relief, but she couldn't look. She put a hand in the pocket of her trousers, feeling for the blade there. "Again. Remove your hand."

The man—now that Hattie could see him, she was fairly certain he was drunk—looked up to the bottom of the silo for a moment, then back to her. "I don't think so."

He drew back his fist, and Hattie pulled away with all her might, extracting the blade from her pocket as the fist came toward her.

She didn't hear Nora's scream, or the furious roar that preceded the blow that knocked her to the ground.

Chapter Seventeen

$\mathcal{T}$he fight set him free for the first time in days.

He couldn't remember spoiling for one so badly. The back-and-forth with Hattie. The guilt that racked him every time he thought of how she'd confessed her desire to run her father's company. Of what he'd promised her. His rage at Ewan's threat. His fear of it. His faith in it. And the self-loathing that came when he thought of the way he'd betrayed Hattie to keep her safe.

It had begun to unravel him, and Whit was spoiling for a fight before the bruises Ewan had delivered had even begun to fade.

Whit wanted to put a fist into someone's face, to remember what it was to win. To be in control. And since his sister-in-law wouldn't appreciate him coming for Devil, he'd signed up for a do-or-die, meaning he would fight all comers until he was brought low. Word had spread through the Garden like wildfire, as it always did when the Bastards offered such a show, and they'd moved the thing three times before settling on the granary, far enough away to avoid a police raid, and large enough to hold the crowd that was sure to turn up.

He'd dispatched a half-dozen comers, drunks and braggarts and two men, barely more than twenty, who'd either lost a bet or were trying to impress a lady. After them, Michael Doolan had arrived to take his thrashing, and Whit had barely controlled his fury when he'd put the man down, making sure to lift the blighter straight off his feet and remind him that if he ever threatened another woman in the Garden, Whit would throw him into the Thames and no one would ever care to look for him.

Suffice to say, Whit was barely winded when the O'Malley Trio had stepped into the ring, their arrival sending a thrill through him.

Because, while Whit loved a bout, Beast loved a fight, and the O'Malley boys were precisely the kind of fight for which he was spoiling, as he couldn't do what he really wished to do—haul off to Mayfair, find Hattie, and take her to bed for the rest of time.

To protect her, he could never see her again.

So, yes, the O'Malley brutes would do the trick nicely.

Whit dispatched the first two with haste, immediately turning his attention to the third of the brothers and the one with the heaviest fists. All had been going well, Whit ready to win the fight and prepare for the next bout when something caught his eye in the crowd, over Peter O'Malley's shoulder.

He took his eyes from his opponent for a moment, unable to place what he'd seen—nothing out of sorts, a sea of faces watching the fight, some ruddier-cheeked than others, thanks to the swill being passed around for warmth. At the far side of the circle were Felicity and Devil, her face full of serious worry, and his, bored with the whole thing. The Bastards' second-in-command, Annika, was next to them—no surprise, as she never missed a fight if she didn't have to.

Nothing out of the ordinary.

Nothing but the thing that he couldn't seem to see, and still knew was there.

What had it been?

In the midst of his distraction, Peter O'Malley had come for him, throwing a punch that Whit dodged without hesitation—a punch that, had he been paying attention, he would have seen for what it was. A trick. Before he could correct himself, Peter landed the real blow, an uppercut that snapped Whit's head back and jarred his teeth. He'd taken punches like it before, and he was turning away even as he rebounded, but Peter added a second blow, this one to the body, and Whit had no chance.

Grounded.

He caught himself, hands flat in the cold earth. He was on his knees for a second. Maybe two. Not long enough for another opponent to come for him, but more than long enough for Peter O'Malley to get the drop. He sent Whit rolling through the dirt with a kick that he would have admired if he hadn't been on its receiving end.

And that's when he'd heard her scream.

At first, he thought he was wrong—thought that the blow to his head had made him imagine her there. There were other women in attendance. It could have been one of them. But the second he'd heard the sound, he'd known the truth, the pain in his ribs receding instantly, his head already turning to find her.

He didn't have far to look.

How had she found him?

She couldn't be here. If Ewan saw her . . .

She was just inside the ring, wearing trousers that fit her curves far too well and a topcoat that wasn't near warm enough for the wind. She had to be cold. That was enough for him to resolve to get to her. To take her away from this place and get her warm.

To protect her.

The thought was distracting enough to risk the fight, but then the man behind her touched her, his eyes narrowed with anger and his mouth running from drink. She turned

toward the drunk, his fingers tightening on her arm, and
Whit focused on that place, on the harsh indent of his grip,
digging into Hattie's flesh.

Whit came to his feet, the crowd roaring.

"You wantin' more, Beast?" Peter O'Malley said, spreading his arms wide, letting showmanship reign. The crowd
had come for a show, and O'Malley was superior at delivering one. But Whit didn't have time for performance. Instead, he threw a single punch, barely looking as O'Malley
dropped to the ground, already heading for Hattie, who
was reaching into her pocket—Whit hoped for a weapon.

The man who held her stiffened, and it didn't take twenty
years of fighting to know his intent. His hand fisted.

Rage clouded Whit's vision.

He started to run, to get to Hattie before the dead man
could land the punch. And he would be a dead man if he
landed the punch. Whit would kill him before he could take
another breath.

Nearly there.

Letting out a wild roar, he launched himself toward her,
pushing her down, away from the man's blow, turning mid-
tumble to take the full force of the landing, protecting her
from the hard ground.

They landed, her eyes squeezed tightly closed, and time
stopped until she opened them, a fraction away from his
own. Relief slammed through him, with more force than the
boot he'd taken earlier. He resisted the urge to kiss her—the
assembly had had enough of a spectacle. Instead, he lowered his voice and said the only thing that came to mind.

"You shouldn't be here."

She didn't miss a beat. "I came for my business."

Excitement thrummed through him. She was fucking
glorious.

She also wasn't hurt. He gave her a once-over to be certain, then rolled her to the ground and came to his feet, immediately heading for the man who'd been about to hit her.

The man whose anger had turned to fear.

"If you're looking for a bout, you'll have it with me," he growled, turning the man pale in the light from one of the nearby fires.

"I—" The man shook his head. "He pushed me first!"

Whit set his hands to the man's shoulders and pushed, the crowd parting to let him fall onto his backside. "Now *I've* pushed you. Do you intend to fight me?"

"N-no." He scrambled away like an insect.

It wasn't enough. Whit was gone, turned full Beast. He took a step toward his enemy, wanting nothing more than to end him.

A hand fell on his shoulder, the weight of it heavy and familiar. His brother.

Whit stilled.

"Let it go," Devil said, soft at his ear. "Get your girl. And get her out of here, before people sort out what just happened and start asking questions."

It was too late to prevent that—he turned to her—the woman Devil called his girl. She wasn't, of course. It didn't matter that he couldn't stop himself from protecting her. It was habit. It had nothing to do with her.

But he couldn't protect her from him.

Whit turned to find Hattie several yards away, on her feet again, with her friend Nora, who was, apparently, as much trouble as Hattie was. Felicity was fussing over her, brushing dirt from her sleeve and chattering, as though this were all perfectly normal. Nora was transfixed by Annika, who stood nearby, hip cocked, the long blade she kept there gleaming in the firelight.

As his gaze tracked Hattie, Whit went stiff with renewed anger. Her hat was askew and dirt smudged her face, her coat was torn at the shoulder—a fact that made him want to do immense damage. A wild thought came—had the man who'd touched her been sent by Ewan?

A growl sounded from low in his throat, and he started

to turn back, but Devil stayed the movement, seeming to understand. "Just a drunk." And then a single, strong word. "Her."

She was what was important. Christ. He wanted to pick her up and carry her from there like a damn Neanderthal. "She can't be seen with me."

Devil looked straight at him. "He isn't here."

"He could be."

He nodded. "He could be. But he's not."

Whit spun away, approaching the cluster of women, keenly aware of Hattie's eyes on him, widening as he closed the distance between them. "You—" she said, and the tremor in her voice nearly did him in. "You're bleeding."

He did not slow his approach even as he looked down to find a three-inch gash low on his right side. A knife wound. He looked back at her, hand still, clutching a pocketknife. "You stabbed me."

Her jaw dropped. "I did not!" She narrowed her eyes on his. "Though you certainly would have deserved it, you bastard."

Devil laughed, low enough that only Whit could hear him. "Now I know why you like her so much. She'll run you ragged."

Before Whit could argue that he did not like her, and she absolutely would *not* run him ragged because she wasn't getting anywhere near him after he saw her home tonight, Devil was looking to Sarita, the young bookmaker trying to calm the crowd, now arguing that Hattie's interruption had impacted the outcome of the fight.

"We told ya there'd be free O'Malleys in the dirt, gents, and free there are," the girl crowed, backed by two larger men from the Bastards' crew. "I've no wagers on Beast gettin' knifed by a spectator, so sod off wi' that—not that I'd pay out on it, as there 'e stands, right as rain."

Devil waved the girl over, and she came like a flash to receive her orders, cheeks glowing copper with excitement.

While they spoke, Whit did what he could to hold himself together, to keep from taking Hattie in hand, from railing at her for turning up here, where anything could have happened. What if he hadn't been here? What if he hadn't been able to protect her?

The idea was unbearable.

He rubbed a hand over his chest to ease the aggravated tightness there as Devil returned to him, pressing a linen sack filled with ice into his hands. "Take the girl home. Get yourself sorted."

Removing his coat, Devil went to his wife, handing it to her, along with his walking stick. Felicity's eyes lit with confusion and then delighted understanding. "You're to fight?" she asked, breathless.

"You could be a touch less excited by the prospect of me in the ring, wife."

"Do you plan to lose?"

Devil's affront was palpable. "I do not."

Felicity's grin widened. "I shall be certain to give you a proper prize when you win, then."

"We're tradin' one Bastard for another tonight, lads!" Sarita crowed from the center of the ring. "Who'll step forward to fight the Devil himself?"

A handful of senseless underdogs immediately lined up to have their asses handed to them, clearly thinking that Devil, long and lean and rarely in the ring, was an easier battle than Beast. They were wrong.

Devil pulled his shirt over his head, and a cluster of women to Whit's left dissolved into sighs. Not that his brother had eyes for any of them; he was already hauling his wife close, lifting her off her feet, and kissing her thoroughly before turning to the crowd, arms wide, smile on his brutally scarred face.

"You've had Beast, gents! Now Beauty takes his turn!"

The crowd went wild, charging Sarita to lay their bets.

In the melee, Whit finally found himself able to face

Hattie. Hattie, who had pushed past Devil and was coming for him, worry on her brow, unable to take her gaze from the gash on his side. She came up short, her breath coming fast, her full lips slightly parted. Her eyes lifted to his, tracking over his face. "I'm very angry, but I don't wish you dead."

He pulled her to the outskirts of the circle, away from the notice of the rest of the assembly. The crowd dropped away. She swallowed, and he was drawn to the movement of her throat, his own mouth going dry as he thought of leaning down and putting his lips there. Licking over it. Scraping his teeth across her soft skin.

He could hear the sigh she'd make. The cries he'd wring from her.

His cock throbbed with the promise it heard.

No promise. He couldn't touch her.

He was danger to her.

He met her eyes, seeing the heat there. Feeling it everywhere. "I'm taking you home."

She swallowed again, and a low growl came from deep in his throat. She looked down at the wound she'd given him. "It seems only right that I should bandage that."

A vision flashed, of her soft fingers on his body, healing him. Pleasuring him. He grunted his approval.

She cleared her throat, forced ice into her tone. "And if you think I'm leaving before we discuss your betrayal, you are quite mistaken."

He shouldn't. He should pack her off with Nik, mere feet away, and send her home. Safe. Far from him. He shook his head. "There's nothing to discuss."

Hattie's eyes flashed. "I should like to discuss your being a proper ass."

Nik coughed her amusement at the words as Nora grinned and said, "If you think she's going to let you disappear on her, you're severely misguided . . ." She paused, then said, "What should I call you?"

"Beast," he said.

Nora tilted her head. "I think I prefer bastard, what with the way you have mistreated my friend."

This time, Nik turned wide, amused eyes on Nora. "I like you two."

Nora winked at the Norwegian. "Wait until you get to know us."

That wouldn't happen.

And was that a blush on Nik's cheeks?

He didn't have time for that. Instead, he scowled at his second and growled, "See her home."

Nik nodded, no hesitation.

"First, I'm perfectly aware of the location of my home," Nora said, and Whit gritted his teeth. Deliver him from women who thought they owned the world. "And second, I'm not leaving unless she tells me she wishes to be left."

He ignored the pleasure that thrummed through him at the woman's loyalty to Hattie, who deserved it from the wide world. *As she couldn't get it from him.*

"I assume you came in one of your carriages?" he asked on a growl.

Nora tilted her head in confusion. "Yes."

He looked to Nik. "You'll have to find the gig, too."

"Someone's stolen my curricle?" Nora said, outraged.

Nik turned to her, her amusement clear. "You left a hitched carriage in this neighborhood in the dead of night. Yes. Someone's stolen it." Nora groaned as the Norwegian added, "No worries. I'll get the boys on it; they won't have taken it far."

"Perhaps I should—" Hattie made to leave him, to go with her friend, and Whit gritted his teeth, wanting to pull her back, to keep her close, but resisting the urge. He wanted her to leave. He wanted her far away. He wanted her safe.

He wanted her.

Nora shook her head and waved Hattie back, her eyes

on Nik. "I shall be fine with—" She turned a questioning gaze on Nik.

"Annika."

"Annika," Nora said softly. "It is very nice to meet you." If it hadn't been a blush before, it was a blush now.

Nora pulled her gaze away from Nik and said to Hattie, "You came for a purpose." A knowing smile flashed. "And now you leave with it."

Hattie looked dead into Whit's eyes. "I *came* to tell him what he could do with his attempt at strong-arming my father and reneging on our deal."

"You should tell him then." She lowered her voice. "Leave nothing out. He deserves it all." *And more.* "And I shall see you in the morning."

Whit's mouth went dry at the words. At the vision that came with them. At the gift of them—a whole night, until sunrise. He shouldn't take it.

But how was he to resist it? A night with her?

Their first night.

Their last.

He couldn't. They were in his carriage in minutes, Whit taking the seat across from her, setting the ice Devil had delivered to his eye—which would be black for a day or two after the bout.

He let out a long breath once the door was closed, keeping them a secret from the world. Keeping her out of view. Safe.

Safe from all, except him.

She watched him in silence, making him wonder what she was thinking. Making him want to strip her of thought, entirely—while stripping her naked and giving them both what they wanted.

Because the silence was not simply silence.

It was full of her thoughts, wild enough to speed her breath, which he listened to, faster and faster, more and more erratic, reminding him of how she sounded with his hands and mouth on her. He'd tried not to stare at her, tried not to make out her breasts beneath what he had decided was some sort of ancient torture device she'd donned to disappear them—as though the magnificent things could be disappeared.

He tried not to think about removing that device, along with all the other clothes—clothes that seemed to do nothing to diminish his desire for her, beautiful and lush and smelling like almond sweets on the other side of the too-small carriage.

He tried not to think of her touch as she reached forward, halfway through their journey, and lifted the long strip of unmoored linen that dangled from his right fist. Tried to ignore the thrum of anticipation that sizzled through him as she used her teeth to pull the gentleman's gloves from her hands.

Her fucking teeth.

What else would she use those teeth for? What would they feel like on his skin? Scraping over his shoulder, nipping at his chest? Christ, this woman was undoing him. Did she know? Was that her plan?

He'd give her everything she wanted if she'd put her mouth on him.

She didn't. Instead, she wrapped the linen around his knuckles, carefully, as though she were preparing him for battle. As though he were a knight, and she the maiden fair, bestowing her favor.

When she was finished, she tied a perfect knot and carefully tucked the end inside the wraps before running her thumb over his knuckles and whispering, so soft he barely heard it, "There."

But he did hear it. The gentle gift of that little word.

The satisfaction in it.

After an evening of violence, he'd never felt the sting of pleasure more keenly—and he feared he lacked the capacity to endure it.

She took a deep breath and said, "Now, about my business."

He leaned his head back against the cushion of the coach, letting the cold ice pack do its work. "*My* business."

She watched him for a long moment, the clatter of the cobblestones the only sound. "Your betrayal." She couldn't know how the words stung. "What will you do with Sedley Shipping?"

Keep you safe. "Whatever I like."

Silence. Then, "Why?"

The word nearly finished the job of the ring tonight. It was small and perplexed and devastating. And in it, he heard the truth. He'd hurt her.

And it had been his only choice.

When he didn't reply, she narrowed her gaze on him and said, "You're a bastard."

"Yes," he replied, trying to ignore the disdain in her words. "What do you want from me?"

"Nothing." It was true. *I want you happy. I want you safe.*

"Look at me."

He obeyed the command without hesitation. Christ, she was stunning, sitting tall and determined, shoulders pressed back like a queen.

"You're ruining everything."

Guilt flared. "I know."

"You told me . . ." She looked out the window, into the darkness of the streets beyond. "You told me you believed in me." She looked back at him. "I believed you."

He'd face the O'Malley brothers a thousand times over this.

I do believe in you.

"Is it—" She stopped, then started again. "Is it because you don't think I can do it?"

"No." Christ. No.

She looked as though she had something to say—as though she had a thousand somethings to say. And he wanted to pull her across the carriage and onto his lap and tell her all the ways he thought she was remarkable.

But that was impossible if he was to keep her apart from him.

"Why?" She hesitated. "Why would you want us out of business? Is it just to punish Augie? He was ready to tell you about his partner—who I imagine is much more of an employer than a partner."

"His partner is no longer relevant," he said, too quickly. He didn't want Hattie anywhere near Ewan. Not now that he knew how far the duke would go to punish him. To hurt her. "Maybe we want to go straight. Start a business above-board."

She scowled. "Don't lie to me. It's beneath you."

It wasn't. But he didn't want her to see that.

"You're doing this to punish me. No one purchases every ship they use."

"We do." They didn't.

"That's bollocks," she retorted. "You can't afford to own boats, or the Crown will discover you're moving contraband every two weeks."

His brows went up at the astute assessment.

She smirked. "Surprised by my intelligence?"

"No." Not surprised. Tempted.

He wanted to take her to bed and have her school him on shipping. Lading bills and tide tables and whatever else she wanted to talk to him about.

Which was utter madness.

Before he could take the mad action, she looked him dead in the eye and slung a wicked blow. "I trusted you. I believed you. I thought you were better than this." She paused. "I thought we were . . ."

Don't finish that sentence.

He wasn't sure he could survive it. He could barely breathe for that *we*, for the way it tied them together. For the way he wanted it to. For a single, wild moment, he almost gave in.

Almost turned it all over to her. Gave her the business and the Docklands and his aid. But then he remembered Ewan, mad in the darkness, vowing to punish him via Hattie.

You'll give her up. Or I'll take her.

The memory ran like ice through him.

It wasn't possible. There could be no deal. She couldn't have her business and her safety. And he couldn't have her. Not as long as Ewan drew breath.

The carriage stopped. He reached for the door, out onto the street before the thing stopped rocking, reaching back to hand her down. A mistake. Her hands were bare now, and her skin impossibly soft against his—so soft it made him wonder if his touch might do her damage.

Of course it would. His touch would do her nothing but damage.

He tightened his grip on her anyway. He'd be damned if he'd let her go.

Not tonight.

One night.

He ignored the thought and pulled her into the house, thankful for the late hour and the lack of servants. After Devil had left to build a home with Felicity, Whit hadn't had the heart to let any of the servants go. He had more than he needed, which meant that the house was beautifully cared for; someone had left a lamp burning in the entryway for him, one he happily took up as he led Hattie up the stairs to his apartments, still the only part of the house he thought of as entirely his own.

She followed, and he could hear her curiosity as they climbed the stairs. He felt it as he turned down a long, dark hallway, in the way she slowed, her head craning to look in the other direction.

Finally, the chatterbox couldn't remain silent. "Where are you taking me?"

He didn't reply.

"You know your silence is maddening, do you not?"

As though the sound of her voice, lyric and lovely, weren't the same. He put one hand on the door to his rooms and looked over his shoulder. "I assumed you wanted to continue our discussion."

A beat, and then her reply. "I said we should do that after you're bandaged."

They both looked down to find that he'd bled through his shirt. Whit was not the type to ask for care, and yet he could not stop the low rumble that came at the idea. "Mmm."

He expected trepidation from her. Hesitation. Nerves. But he'd forgotten this was Hattie—brazen and bold.

Her violet eyes lit on his hand, frozen on the door handle, and her delicious lips curved into a considering smile. "And inside?" she asked. "Your lair?"

He exhaled a little laugh and inclined his head. "No plants."

"You're going to keep the business."

"Yes," he said. He had no choice.

"You understand I shan't go down without a fight."

"I wouldn't imagine it any other way." He imagined the fight she gave him would be the best he'd ever had. But she'd never beat him. This was his world. His game.

And he'd never wanted a win the way he wanted the one that kept Hattie safe.

Still, when one side of her mouth kicked up in a wry smile, dimple flashing, he felt it like a blow, and it made him punch drunk.

She straightened the lapels of the ridiculous topcoat she wore, smoothing the lines of the jacket over the curves it did not hide before she straightened. "There is no deal, then. We are rivals."

The way she said it, simply, as though there were no hard feelings—no harm in it—it made him want her more than ever.

"There is one deal left." He didn't know why he said it. He knew exactly why he said it.

Understanding flared in her eyes along with anticipation. "Body."

Whit went tight as a bow. He could give her one night. He could keep her safe for one night. One night, and he would let her go.

One night, and he would be able to.

"Go on then," she whispered, a nod at the door. "Open it."

Chapter Eighteen

She shouldn't have enjoyed the back-and-forth with him. She shouldn't have stayed after he admitted he had no interest in aiding any of her plans. She should have left this man who had gone from tentative partner to absolute rival in less than a week.

But she didn't want to. She was not through with him, either in business or in pleasure, and when she'd vowed she would triumph in both—it set her free.

That freedom, coupled with the truth between them, made desire all that mattered.

She crossed the threshold into rooms that smelled of honey and lemon and a touch of bay, making her think of a warm summer sun, and let herself sink into the moment—one that existed purely in service of her desire.

And that was the most magnificent freedom Hattie had ever experienced.

He moved away almost immediately, leaving her to her quiet inspection—an impossible task, as the only light source was a flickering orange glow through a door at the far end of the room. She stepped toward it, her feet sinking into a thick carpet—thick enough to explain the sound of the space, quiet and lush in the darkness. She could hear the fullness of the chamber, and she wondered what was there, around her, cocooning her from the outside world.

That was what the room felt like, even in darkness—a cocoon. Protection from everything beyond—anything that might threaten. Anything that did not promise pleasure.

It should have been cold, for the way darkness and wind had arrived outside, but it wasn't. She supposed she should not have been surprised about that—was anything about him ever cold?

Hattie could make out his shape at the far side of the room, his broad shoulders shrugging out of his coat before he tossed it over the arm of a chair, revealing narrow hips and long legs. Her mouth went dry as he crouched low at the fireplace, where glowing coals turned to cinder in the hearth. He stoked the fire and tossed wood onto it, then rose to light a half-dozen candles on the mantel.

More of the space revealed itself, and Hattie discovered she was in the most decadent room she'd ever seen. The walls were covered in rich paisley silk in blues and greens, and it was filled with a collection of extravagantly stuffed furniture, each piece larger and more welcoming than anything she'd ever experienced—a burgundy loveseat that was double the depth of any other in London, a cream-colored high winged chair with a cushion that she ached to sit upon. Rich, sapphire satin covered a chaise in the far corner, laden with pillows in myriad colors to rival the collection of a king.

More cushions were scattered before the fireplace, as though they'd been dropped there for comfort by someone whiling away the hours warming their toes.

The colors were outrageous—the hues of summer and autumn, their lushness rivaling only the lushness of the textiles themselves. Hattie's fingers itched to explore, to touch every inch of the room and revel in its pure decadence.

If he'd noticed her response, he ignored it. Or, perhaps, he angled for more of it, moving from the mantelpiece, match in hand, to light a dozen more candles, their flickering light setting the fabrics to shimmer. And then he stepped up onto a raised stool, setting the flame to a dozen more candles in a stunning brass wall sconce that climbed the wall like a vine, planted by the gods.

She took a step toward him, the softness beneath her feet drawing her attention to the floor, where a half-dozen carpets were overlapped throughout the room in a manner in which someone who did not know Whit would have thought haphazard. Hattie didn't imagine for a moment she knew Whit—not well, at least—but she knew without question that there was nothing haphazard about this room.

It was, without a doubt, his lair.

He'd told the truth about it. There were no plants, exotic or otherwise. But there were books *everywhere*.

They were piled on end tables and next to the loveseat; a stack teetered by the fireplace. In the corner nearest the door, a heavy credenza held at least twenty of them, piled like teacakes next to a decanter of scotch or bourbon or whatever the amber liquid within was. She drew closer, reaching for one of the haphazard stacks, letting her fingers trail over the spines. Margaret Cavendish's *Philosophical and Physical Opinions*, Jane Austen's *Emma*, a biography of Zenobia, a collection of work by Lucrezia Marinella, and something called *Dell'Infinità d'Amore*. A handsome copy of Christine de Pizan's *City of Ladies* topped the stack, along with a pair of *spectacles*.

This was not a library. There was no extravagant woodwork. No shelving, nowhere to display a book. These books were for reading.

And this man—this was where he read. *With spectacles*.

In her whole life, Hattie had never imagined spectacles to be tempting. But there she was, resisting the urge to ask him to put them on.

It was the most revealing peek into another person's life

Hattie had ever experienced. Revealing and delicious and so thoroughly *unexpected* that she wanted to spend the next week investigating every nook and cranny, until she understood the man who'd filled them.

Except she had a suspicion she'd never fully understand him.

"This room," she said. "It's—"

Perfect.

He was already gone—disappeared into the chamber on the far side of this magnificent space. She couldn't see him, but still, he pulled her to him as though she were on a string.

"Whit?" she called out as she stepped through into the room beyond, an odd shape, longer than it was wide, with three enormous circular windows along the far wall, each turned into a mirror by the moonless night beyond and the firelight within.

The one farthest to the left reflected a massive copper bathtub, half full of water, set to one side of the fireplace, and Hattie's attention was instantly drawn to the enormous piece—larger than any bath she'd ever seen. Heat rose from the water inside, hinting that servants had been there mere minutes earlier.

Inside the hearth, two large kettles piped happily, as though they'd been waiting all day for their master to return—as though they would continue to do so until he bathed.

She inhaled sharply, desire thrumming through her, chased by nerves. She'd been so proud of her bravery earlier, but now, faced with the wild intimacy of his rooms and now his bath . . . she was growing less so. She willed herself strong and said, "Do you intend to bathe?"

He was at a basin beyond, unraveling the strip of linen from his left hand, and for a moment, Hattie was transfixed by the movement, a deft hand-over-hand motion that revealed strength and size and dexterity. "I do," he said, as he repeated his actions with his right hand before leaning over the basin and washing his hands, scrubbing them with meticulous care.

She swallowed, her mouth dry. Tried for casual indifference. "Oh." The squeak was neither casual, nor indifferent, and she'd never been so grateful to be staring at another person's back. She cleared her throat. "That's good. You are bleeding."

Was she reminding herself or him?

He looked over his shoulder at her. Was that humor in his gaze? "Not anymore. You shall have to aim truer during our next battle."

Her brows shot together. "I never intended to—" She stopped. If she'd thought for a moment that he'd be hurt, she never would have taken the knife from her pocket. "I thought I might have to protect myself."

He stilled, and she wondered what he was thinking even as she knew he'd never speak it.

She forced a little laugh. "I didn't expect that you would protect me."

He looked at her then, over his shoulder, his amber eyes like fire, and she imagined him saying something magnificent. Like, *I'll always protect you.*

Which was mad, of course. Hadn't he just stolen her business? Turned them into rivals? She cleared her throat. "It should be cleaned and bandaged, nevertheless."

He dried his hands on a length of cloth and moved away from the table, heading for the hot water in the hearth. "The attacker becomes the nurse."

She swallowed at the words, the vision they wrought. The way they made her fingers itch to touch him. The way they set her on edge—making her feel thoroughly in over her head. When she had implemented the Year of Hattie, intending to follow a simple step-by-step plan to take her life in her own hands, she'd been prepared and polished, ready to claim the world.

No longer. He'd run riot over that plan.

Now he threatened to run riot over the rest of her, as well.

And what was worse . . . she found she wanted it.

"I shall do my best to make amends," she said, the words quieter than she intended, the room muting them.

He heard, hesitating as he reached for the second kettle—the pause barely noticeable if one wasn't watching carefully. But Hattie watched more carefully than she'd ever watched anything, so when he gave a little grunt that she might have once thought was dismissive, she heard something else. Something categorical.

Desire.

It wasn't possible, was it? He hadn't touched her tonight. They'd been in the carriage for an age. Alone, in the darkness. And she'd ached for him to touch her. Been ready to scream for him to kiss her.

And he'd done nothing of the sort.

But now . . . Hattie's heart began to race. Impossibly, he wanted her.

He tossed the garment—stained beyond reason after the events of the night—to the floor and moved to sit in a near high-backed chair and remove his boots.

She couldn't stop marveling at him, at the way his body folded into the seat, revealing muscles that she was fairly certain ordinary, everyday humans did not have, flexing and stretching. She bit back a sigh, which would have been more than embarrassing if he'd heard it.

He bent over to remove a boot, and winced. It was barely there—gone before someone might notice, at least someone who was not riveted to his every movement.

She stepped forward, not liking him in pain. "May I help?"

He froze at the question, going so still, Hattie thought perhaps she'd made a terrible mistake. He didn't look at her when he shook his head and said, impossibly quiet, "No."

The boot came off in a rush, and he winced again, ignoring whatever warning his body was providing to immediately tackle the second. She stepped forward again, and he did look up then. Repeated himself, this time louder. "*No.*"

When his second boot was discarded, he stood, reaching into his pocket and extracting his watch. Watches.

Two watches. Always.

He set them on a small table, next to a basket filled with bandages and thread, presumably because he required mending regularly after fights. Hattie was transfixed by the metal disks. Without looking away from them, she said, "Why do you carry two watches?"

There was a pause long enough for her to think he might not answer. His hands came to the waistband of his trousers. "I don't like to be late."

She shook her head. "I don't . . ."

The words trailed off as he worked the buttons of his trousers. She kept her eyes on his, not wanting to be rude, but she could count the buttons from the rough movements of shoulders as he unfastened them. Three. Four. Five.

She couldn't stop herself. She looked. *Of course* she looked. The dim light in the room made it impossible to see anything but a dark V of shadow, framed by his strong hands, thumbs tucked into the fabric as though he could stand there, under her gaze, forever, if she wished it.

She wished it.

And between those thumbs, a hint of something else. Skin. She swallowed, tearing her gaze from it, cheeks blazing. He was watching her, amber eyes gleaming in the firelight, and for a single, wild moment, she wondered what he would do if she went to him and touched him. If she added her hands to his, there, in the shadows.

As quickly as she thought it, he changed, relaxing into himself, his eyes going hooded, as though he, too, was thinking it. As though he would welcome her touch if she offered it.

He still owed her a ruination.

Every other time they'd been together, time or location

had impeded the delivery on their arrangement. But now—here—

He could ruin her, properly.

She wanted it. And giving in to her own want was a magnificent freedom.

Not that she would voice it.

He filled her silence, low and dark, as though the words were scraped through gravel on their way past his lips. "Did you have something to ask?"

She shook her head, finding words difficult. "No."

A knowing smile played over his lips and he turned away, as though this were all perfectly normal, pushing his trousers down his hips as he made for the bath. At the flash of buttocks, Hattie looked away, past him, to the window beyond the bathtub, now a mirror, revealing—

Oh, my.

She turned her back on the scene instantly. "Is this how you ordinarily conduct business?"

Silence met the question. No. Not silence. Too much sound. The sound of him stepping into the bath, the water sloshing as it accepted his weight. His low growl as he settled into its indulgent heat.

The sound was pure hedonism, and desire pooled deep, spreading heat through her, as though she, too, were in a bath.

As though she were with him in his.

What if she were?

She gave a little laugh at the thought, unable to fathom a scenario in which she would be brave enough to shed her clothing without hesitation. Unable to imagine being the kind of woman who invited herself into a man's bath.

Another splash came, and she resisted the urge to turn and look, to see what he'd done to cause it. She focused on the bright light in the room beyond, the edges of the carpets, overlapping.

Once he was settled, he spoke. "Did you not promise me a fight?"

She was so surprised by the teasing question that she turned to face him, unprepared for the vision of him, relaxed, his arms resting on the edge of the copper tub, head tilted back, eyes closed, his dark hair wet and slicked back from his beautiful face, the dried blood now gone from his cheek, a small cut all that remained, surrounded by a fast-darkening bruise.

It should have marred his beauty. It didn't. Instead, it brought him into reach, down to earth, among the mere mortals. It made Hattie want to touch him. It made her want to claim him. It made her want to—

"You've already had a fight tonight," she said softly.

His eyes flew open, instantly finding hers. "And so? What do you offer?"

"I just want to . . ." She looked to the window, to the tableau reflected in the blackness there. She, in men's clothing, eyes wide, and he, broad and bronzed in the bathtub. What didn't she offer? There was so much she wanted from him. Touch. Words. Pleasure. And something else . . . something she didn't dare name.

Something she couldn't have.

She tore her gaze away from the window. Looked to him. "I want to care for you." Like that, his relaxation was gone. His jaw set and the muscles in his shoulders tensed. She added quickly, "I shouldn't want to care for you, of course. We are enemies."

"Are we?" He reached for the length of linen draped over the tub, pulling it into the water with more force than necessary.

"I plan to give you quite a fight for my business."

"And I shall meet you toe-to-toe," he said. "Tomorrow."

A thrill shot through her at the word. At the way it freed her. Freed them both. Tomorrow was not tonight.

"I shan't like you tomorrow," she said, feeling it was important to say so.

He nodded. "I will not blame you."

Except she would like him, she feared. Even though she had absolutely no reason to like him. Even though he'd lied to her. And hurt her. But now—he did not seem like that man. He seemed . . .

Good.

His movements beneath the water were quick and perfunctory, and Hattie worried that he might aggravate his bruises. She stepped forward, holding a hand out as though she could stop him. He snapped his attention to her, and the focus in his eyes was enough to set her back on her heels.

"Tomorrow, then," she said, suddenly breathless.

The only sound in the room was the smooth movement of the water as he finished bathing. Until he asked, quietly enough that at first, she almost did not believe he'd said it out loud. "How would you care for me tonight, warrior?"

She blushed. "I told you."

"Did you?"

"I would bandage you."

"And when that is done?"

She swallowed. "I—I don't know. Thank you, I suppose. For protecting me."

He shook his head. "I don't deserve your gratitude. I don't want one thing that happens tonight to be because of your gratitude. I want it to be because you want it."

She wanted it.

"All right."

"Tell me what you're thinking," he said.

"I'm thinking I should like to talk about the deal."

He leaned forward, the sound of the water in the bath like gunfire in the room. "Say it."

She swallowed. "The pleasure."

"You want the ruination still."

She nodded. "Please."

He did not hesitate. "Tonight."

Anticipation rioted through her. She couldn't remain still any longer, simply waiting for him to finish his bath. She nodded. "Tonight. Or do you intend to renege on that, as well?"

One dark brow arched at the question, and with the bruise on his cheek, he looked like a proper rogue. Had she really said it? She couldn't believe she'd challenged him. But what was done was done, and excitement coursed through her, threatening to overflow when he let out a long "aaah," that sounded at once like pain and pleasure. "No, love," he growled, setting his hands to the edges of the bath again. "I don't renege."

He stood, the water sluicing down his torso, running along the ridges and valleys, down the deep-cut V of his abdomen. Her eyes widened at the thick length of him, straight and smooth and—*gone*. Her eyes flew to his as he wrapped a length of cloth low over his hips, shielding himself from view.

He raised a brow at her, and she heard the dry question in it. *Disappointed?*

Yes. Yes, she was.

She swallowed as he reached for another towel, drying the rest of himself with sure, leisurely strokes, as though this were all perfectly ordinary. And perhaps it was. Perhaps he spent his evenings bathing for a collection of women, each more eager than the next to watch.

"I suppose you do this often," she said, regretting the words immediately. Surely such an observation was not appropriate for this situation.

His brows rose. "Do what?"

She shook her head, but still the words came. "Bathe in front of women. Bring them here like a prince in a palace." The corner of his mouth twitched, and Hattie's nerves frayed. "Don't you dare laugh at me," she said, pointing a finger at him. "You don't know what it's like to be the inexperienced one. To be the one who has to know that you've done this a hundred times with a hundred other women . . . all very beautiful and very demure and all of whom wore undergarments designed for—"

She stopped, her eyes going wide at her words.

He dropped the towel to the floor, not taking his eyes from her. "Don't stop now, Hattie. Tell me more about the undergarments."

He was challenging her, this man whom she would loathe if she did not like him so much. She narrowed her gaze. "I'm sure they're beautiful. All frill and frippery. Mine are . . . not."

What was she doing?

"No?" He turned away to fetch a fresh pair of trousers from a low chair nearby.

She looked away as he pulled them on, the words pouring out of her mouth. "Mine serve a different kind of purpose. I mean, when I wear them."

He looked over his shoulder, that almost-smile playing on his lips again.

She closed her eyes. "You know what I mean."

"I swear I don't."

"I mean, I'm wearing them, but it's a different sort of thing when one is wearing . . ." She waved a hand over her body.

He tracked the movement and his eyes went hooded for a moment, as though he was considering all the possible undergarments available to Hattie while she was in men's clothing.

Dear God. Men's clothing did not exactly recommend her, did it?

She cleared her throat. "At any rate, I'm sure you do this often and with far more qualified people."

And, like that, he was coming for her, all long strides and perfect muscles, and his trousers not even fully buttoned, stalking her backward across the room, all predatory grace, until she came to her senses and realized she did not want to escape.

She stopped. Wonderfully, he didn't.

He barely stopped when he reached her, knocking the cap from her head, taking her face in his hands, dipping down to kiss her without hesitation, his lips firm and impossibly soft, stealing her gasp as he tilted her chin up and took her lips, his tongue coming out to stroke along her top lip, coaxing her open with the promise of it until she was on her toes, meeting him, aching for him.

When he knew he had her—how could he not, as she clung to his warm shoulders, her hands sliding over the thick muscle of his arms—he smiled against her lips, offering her a little growl as he hauled her close, realigning their mouths and finally, finally, stroking deep, giving her everything she wanted, again and again, until they were both panting from the caress.

He let them up for air, and Hattie opened her eyes, feeling kiss-drunk, making an effort to focus on him.

"I am happy you brought up qualifications," he said, his voice soft and low and delicious.

"You are?"

"Mmm." He stared into her eyes for a long moment, as though he were searching for something. "Because I am afraid I don't meet yours."

What?

Before she could ask, he leaned down toward her. When he whispered the next, he was so close, she could feel the words on her lips. "Shall I get the list? I can't make myself medium height or medium build, love . . . nor can I make myself fair-haired."

Heat raged on her cheeks at the reference to the list she'd provided the brothel what seemed like an age ago, but she refused to let embarrassment stop her from taking this moment. She lifted a hand to settle on his shoulder, bare and smooth and hot like the sun. They both sucked in air at the touch. "You're far too handsome, as well. But I suppose I shall have to make do."

He grunted, one hand coming to her cheek, his thumb stroking over the flush there. "I'm not charming, either. Or affable."

She didn't care. She tilted her face to his, and he pulled back, refusing her the kiss she desperately wanted. "But you don't want any of that, do you?"

"No," she said softly, aching for him to kiss her.

His fingers tightened in her hair. "What do you want?"

She went up on her toes and whispered against his lips, braver than she'd ever been, "I want you."

"And I want you," he said, meeting her kiss with his own, long and lush, his thumb tracing over the soft skin of her cheek as he licked at her mouth, stroking slow and lingering, a delicious taste of what might come. And then, at her lips, "Shall I tell you what I _can_ promise?"

"Please."

"I shall be _very_ thorough."

She smiled at the words, pleasure thrumming through her. "Exceedingly, even?"

He growled his assent and kissed her again, his tongue sweet and tart as it stroked over her own.

Hattie's fingers traced down his torso, the flat of her palm sliding over the magnificent ridges of his body, reveling in the heat of him until she reached the bruises on his side and he sucked in a breath of his own. She instantly released him. He reached for her, pulling her back to his heat. "Don't think about it."

She pressed her hands flat to his chest. "Don't think about the fact that you are bruised?" She resisted. "You took a boot to the side, dammit. Not to mention my blade. You'll let me have a look."

He smiled at her insistence. "I did not know you were a medical professional."

She cut him an irritated look. "I find I do not like it when you are talkative."

He gave a little bark of laughter and stole a small, delicious kiss. "You cannot blame me for having less interest in my bruises than in your body, Hattie."

She went soft at the words. "Really?"

"It's your own fault . . . now I'm curious about your undergarments."

She resisted the excitement and amusement that came at the words, instead affecting her most serious look. "But *I* am interested in your bruises."

A pause, and then a barely-there grunt of acceptance. "If I let you tend to my wounds, will you let me ruin you?"

There it was again, the temptation of freedom. The answer that she did not have to hesitate over.

She met his eyes, loving the fire in them. "Yes."

Chapter Nineteen

Contrary to Hattie's belief, Whit had never had a woman in his rooms.

The house had a massive ground floor receiving area and an office for Whit and Devil, so there'd never been reason to have Annika or any of the other women from the warehouse in his rooms. Grace had been in them a half-dozen times, but only long enough to mock his extravagant decor and leave.

As for other women—Whit never brought them here. He didn't want to answer questions about the space. Didn't want to defend the odd-shaped garret filled with the things he loved most in the world. And he certainly didn't want to give another person such access to his private pleasures.

But he had not hesitated to bring Hattie inside, even though the act of welcoming her into the space she called his lair had left him far more exposed than he'd felt when he'd bathed in front of her.

Bathing in front of her had only made him want to pull her into the bathtub with him, strip her out of her ridiculous disguise, and wash her until they were both panting with desire and he had no choice but to make her come until she screamed.

Whit thought he'd been immensely measured in not doing just that, honestly.

And then the woman had started talking about undergarments. He should be fucking sainted for stopping the sinful kiss they'd shared, full of heat and exploration and promise, and letting her tend to him with bandages and ointments when what he needed was her lips and hands.

He thought he showed immense restraint, when all he wished to do was prove that there was nothing at all impeding about the bruises, and he was quite capable of tossing her over his shoulder and taking her to bed.

But he didn't. Instead, he sat and watched as she selected a wide strip of bandage and a pot of ointment, coming to sit beside him. "Turn toward the light," she said, staring at his naked torso, as perfunctory as any doctor.

He did, and she reached out, slowly and tentatively. "I'm going to . . ."

"Touch me," he growled. He didn't think he could go much longer without her soft fingers on him.

She did as he asked, and they both sucked in a breath. Her gaze flew to his, and she lifted her hand as though she'd been burned. "I'm sorry."

"No," he said, catching her fingers and returning them to his skin. "Don't stop."

Don't ever stop.

She didn't, smoothing over the mottled skin there. "This is a wicked bruise."

He grunted, trying to ignore the pleasure that came with the sting.

"You should see a surgeon. Do you have a surgeon?"

"I don't need a surgeon," he said.

I need this. I need you.

She traced her fingers over the darkest part of the bruise. "I think you might have broken a rib."

He nodded. "It wouldn't be the first."

Her brows shot together. "I don't like that."

Pleasure was not enough of a word to describe the way her stern reply coursed through him, untethered and electric. He sucked in a breath at the sensation, wanting to assuage her worry. "They heal."

She didn't look convinced, but opened the pot of salve, lifting it to her nose. "Bay," she said softly before meeting his eyes. "You use this frequently."

"I fight frequently."

She winced at the words and he wished he could take them back. "Why?"

He didn't reply as she spread the ointment over his torso, her movements smooth and sure, and gentle enough to make him ache in an entirely different way. When was the last time he'd been tended to?

Not for decades.

He found he did not want to go back, not now that he knew the feel of her hands on him. Her soothing touch. The way she awakened every inch of him as she cocooned them in lemon and bay.

"What is in it?" she asked. "How does it work?"

"Willow bark and bay leaf." If anyone else had asked, Whit would have ended his reply there. But this was Hattie, and everything was different with her. "My mother used to make something similar. She called it *suave de sauce*. Rubbed it on her hands before bed."

"They ached from the needlework."

He hated how easily she understood something it had taken him years to work out. Hated the guilt that racked him. "I did what I could to bring money in, so she didn't have to work so hard, but she didn't want me on the streets. She paid for me to take lessons in the back room of a haberdasher off Saint Clement's Lane. Insisted I learn to read. Some weeks, the candles cost more than the money from her work." It was a lesson Whit had never forgotten. One he thought of every time he lit the candles in this room—more than he'd ever need, as though he could light that room for his mother if he tried hard enough. "Every time I told her I wanted to work, she would remind me that the lessons were already paid for. Used to say that if—"

He stopped.

Hattie's touch didn't waver. He focused on the smooth, wonderful strokes.

"She used to say that if it killed her, I'd grow up to be a gentleman."

It was why he'd left her. How his father had kept him fighting for a dukedom he'd never been meant to inherit.

And it had killed her.

He swallowed the thought, letting the bitterness settle before he added softly, "What she would think of me now."

Hattie was quiet for a long moment—long enough for Whit to think that she might not reply. But she did, because she always knew what to say. "I think she'd be proud of you."

"No, she wouldn't," he said. His mother would have loathed his life. She would have hated the violence he lived daily, the filth of his world. And she would have found the way he'd betrayed Hattie unconscionable. "She'd have hated everything but the books."

She smiled at the words, her touch unwavering. "There are a lot of books."

"We couldn't afford them." He didn't want to tell her that. It wasn't her business. And somehow, he couldn't stop talking. "She couldn't read, but she revered them." He cast a look around the room. "She couldn't afford them, and I don't even keep them in a bookcase." Another way he'd failed his mother.

Hattie didn't look up from her work. "Seems to me that the best way for you to honor her reverence is to read them. And these all look well-read."

He grunted.

She smiled. "That meant you'd like to change the subject." She looked up through her lashes at him, and her sweet smile was a welcome distraction. "I'm learning your sounds."

Her fingers smoothed over his ribs, where a purple bruise bloomed fast and furious, and he sucked in a breath. "I don't have to be a good student to know what that one meant." She lifted her hand, her task complete. "May I bandage you?"

Another grunt, and she smiled, lifting the roll of linen at her side. "I'm taking that as a yes."

"Yes," he said.

She began to roll the strip around his body carefully, her touch a constant temptation. On the third pass, her lips parted, and her breath began to come more quickly. She spoke to the bandage. "Why would you do this? You're rich beyond measure and have the respect of every man from the Thames to Oxford Street—and beyond. Why would you let them hurt you?"

Because he deserved it.

He didn't tell her that. Instead, he said, "It's how we survived."

Her touch stuttered. "Your brother and sister? And you?"

He looked down, watching her long fingers roll out the bandage. Marveled at them. At her. At the way she summoned his words. "We ran from our father. And from our . . . brother." He hated even speaking Ewan into existence with her now, as he threatened like a specter.

"Why?" This wonderful, compassionate woman, with a brother she protected even though he'd ruined everything for her.

She wouldn't understand the truth about his past, but he spoke it anyway. "We endangered everything the old man lived for. Everything the young one had worked for. And Ewan—he was willing to do *anything* for my father's love." He gave a little humorless laugh. "Not that there was any love in the bastard to give."

Her brow furrowed. "He was even willing to see you flee?"

"He *made sure* we fled." His gaze fell to the basket of

bandages and ointments. "That night, he'd come for Grace. Devil stopped him—took the knife for them both."

She gasped. "His face. The scar."

"A gift from our brother. And our father."

Loathing flashed in her beautiful eyes. "I should like to have a word with both of them."

"My father is dead."

"Good." She lifted a pair of sewing scissors and he raised a brow—she looked prepared to do battle with the tiny blades. Considering her anger, Whit might even wager on her. "And your brother?"

He shook his head. "Not dead."

Too alive. Too close.

She finished the bandaging, tying off the ends in a perfect knot. "Well, he'd best not find me in a dark alley." Whit might have been amused if he weren't so irrationally unsettled by the idea of Hattie in the way of Ewan.

You'll give her up. Or I'll take her.

He set his hands to her shoulders, urging her to look to him. "Listen to me. If you ever have cause to meet my brother, you run the other way."

Her eyes went wide at the words, at the seriousness in them. "How did you escape?"

"I didn't." Memory flashed. The dark night and Grace screaming—he and Devil breaking down a door to find their brother with a massive knife, their father at the edge of the room, watching. Pride and something else on his face—delight.

Fucking monsters.

Whit had leapt into the fray, but Ewan had been too strong. He'd always been the strong one. The perfect manifestation of ducal blood. Devil had been too hotheaded. Whit, too small. But Ewan had been strong enough to lay Whit flat, and with enough force that he couldn't get up.

Devil had leapt in. Taken the blow meant for Grace.

And it had been Grace who put Ewan down.

"Devil and Grace dragged me away. Into the night. I'd be nowhere without them."

"You were children."

"Fourteen. All of us born on the same day. Ewan, too." She tilted her head, the obvious question in her eyes. "Different mothers. And Grace, the luckiest of the bunch—different father, too. She's never had to suffer the idea of his blood in her veins."

"So, not your sister."

"Sister where it counts," he said, remembering the red-haired, square-jawed girl who'd protected them without hesitation, even as she lost more than they'd ever had. Even as she'd lost the only boy she'd ever loved. "We ran. We ran, and we didn't stop until we reached London. Once we were here we had no choice but to sleep on the street. But sleep wasn't enough. We had to eat, too."

She was still as stone, which was the only reason why he kept talking. "Devil thieved us some bread. I scavenged the cores of a half-dozen apples. But it wasn't enough. We had to survive, and that would take more."

He could still feel the bone-deep ache of the damp streets of the Rookery, the only thing that rivaled the aching loss of his mother. But he didn't tell her that. Didn't want to sully her with that.

He didn't even understand why he was telling her any of it.

He didn't want her close. *Lie.*

He couldn't have her close.

Instead, he turned the conversation to the fights. "On our third night, Digger turned up." He met her gaze. "He was another kind of bastard. Ruthless and out for no one more than himself, but he ran a dice game and a street ring and needed fighters."

Her brows knit together. "You were children."

Every time she said it, he was reminded of how different they were. How he could do nothing but sully her. He clung to the thought. To the hope that it would keep him from doing something mad. "Fourteen is more than old enough to throw a punch, Hattie."

Her attention flickered to the cut on his swelling cheek. "And what of catching them?"

One side of his mouth went up in a cocky grin. "Don' 'ave to if yer fast 'nough to get out the way."

She smiled at the way his voice slid into the Garden. "And were you very fast?"

"I had to be. I wasn't anything near strong. The runt of the litter."

She made a show of assessing his broad frame. "I find that very difficult to believe."

He lifted one shoulder and dropped it. "I grew."

"I noticed."

He felt the pleasure in the words keenly, and he went hard with a speed that surprised him. Before he could act on it, she said, "Go on," and he had no choice but to obey.

"Devil and I were middling fighters. We could bob and weave, and when we landed a punch we knew how to put force behind it. We didn't always win, but we always gave the crowd a show." The tale should have been bleak—the story of brothers given no other choice but to fight for their beds and their supper—but it wasn't. The fights were some of the best memories of those years.

"And now he is married to Felicity Faircloth."

Surprise flared and faded. "I forget she was a toff."

Hattie grinned. "I was always a bit jealous of her for being able to leave it. And for having such a good reason." A pause, and then, "You have the same eyes."

The Marwick eyes.

"I wish I'd spoken to him."

"Dev?" He shook his head. "He's not for you."

She was vaguely insulted. "Why not?"

"He's not good enough for you."

Lips curved in a smile that nearly stole his breath. "And you are?"

"Not by miles."

She lifted one hand at the words, slowly, as though she was afraid he might flee. Whit almost laughed at the idea. There was nothing that would take him from this moment. Nothing that he wouldn't do to keep her there. To strip her bare and have her. Finally. And when her fingertips brushed his temple just barely, just enough to push a lock of hair back from his face, he held his breath, wanting her to pull him close. Wanting her to kiss him.

Instead, she said, "Bareknuckle Bastards. That's how the two of you got your name."

"Three of us."

It took her a moment to understand. "Grace?"

"You've never seen a fighter like Gracie. She could take down a string of brutes and not break a sweat, and when she stepped into the ring, her opponents quaked. The world thinks us Kings of Covent Garden? It's all bollocks. We'd be nowhere without Grace. She was born to rule it." He smiled, small and private. "She gave me my first knife. Taught me to throw it—a weapon that didn't require me to be the biggest or the strongest."

Admiration flared in her violet eyes. "I rescind my earlier remarks about meeting your brother. I should much prefer to meet your sister."

"Devil would be deeply offended to hear that." He met Hattie's gaze. "But Grace would enjoy meeting you. Of that I have no doubt."

She smiled, and for a heartbeat, he wondered what it would be like if he'd met this woman in a different place, at a different time. If he'd gone to his lessons like his mother had asked. If he'd refused to leave with his father and fight for a dukedom he'd never had a chance at winning. Would he have become a merchant? A shopkeep? Something simple that kept food in their bellies and a roof over their heads?

And would he have convinced this woman so far above him he could barely see her that he was a worthy match?

Would he have come home each night, tired and happy, and found comfort with Hattie, read a book by the fire, shared a sack of sweets as they discussed the weather, or the noise of the market, or the news, or whatever normal people did on a normal day.

What might have been.

An ache bloomed in his chest at the thought, one that came with a desire so keen for something so impossible that he should have put an end to the evening right then. Because he was suddenly, acutely aware of the fact that he might ache forever if he let Hattie Sedley come closer.

Of course, by the time he realized that, he was too desperate to have her.

And so instead of sending her home, he leveled her with a long look—long enough to set another blush on her pretty round cheeks, and have her looking away with an embarrassed smile on her wide, welcome mouth.

He wanted her.

And she wanted him.

And tonight, that was all that mattered.

"Hattie," he said softly, not wanting to scare her with his eagerness.

She looked up, her violet eyes enormous. "Yes?"

"Are you through tending me?"

Her attention skittered down to the bandage around his torso. "Yes."

He reached a hand out, trailing his fingers over her cheek, the skin smooth as silk. "Do we still have a deal?"

She nodded. "Yes."

His fingers caught a loose lock of hair, like spun gold in the firelight, and he tucked it back behind her ear. She leaned toward the touch, and he caught her face, leaning closer, lowering his head to breathe her in. "Christ, you smell sweet. You're like cakes in a shop window."

She huffed a little laugh. "Thank you?"

"When I was a boy, there was a sweet shop in Holborn that made the most delicious almond sponge—I only ever had it once. The baker was a proper Belgian bastard, and he'd chase us with a broom if we darkened the doorstep, but if you stood in just the right spot across the street and down a bit, you could smell those cakes every time the door opened."

He leaned close and brushed his nose over her temple, lowering his voice to a whisper. "In my whole life, I've never had temptation like those cakes. Until you." He pressed his lips to her warm skin and told her the truth. "I've never wanted anything like I want you."

She put her hand to his shoulder, her long fingers curving up, around his neck, and for a heartbeat he panicked—thinking she might push him away. But she didn't. Instead, she turned her head and kissed him, setting her ruination in motion.

And his own.

"Whit," she whispered, the sound soft and full of sin, and there was no question of resistance. He reached for her, unbuttoning her coat, sliding his hand beneath the warm wool to her—warmer, hotter. He reveled in the feel of her body, the swell of her waist, the round curve of her hip, her strong thighs as he pulled her closer, turning, lifting her so she straddled him.

She gasped her pleasure as he settled her over his thighs, and he leaned back, one hand in her hair, just far enough to meet her eyes as she stared down from above him. A furrow crossed her brow as she resisted giving him her weight. "I'm too—"

"You're fucking perfect," he said, leaning up to steal her lips and prove it.

After a long moment, he released her lips and she pulled back to look at him, her hair askew and her mouth kiss-stung, and the uncertainty that had been in her gaze entirely gone—replaced by excitement. And delight. She smiled a tiny, demure smile, her dimple flashing as she worried the plump flesh of her bottom lip.

Christ, she was beautiful.

He shook his head. "No."

Doubt flashed. "No?"

He spread one hand over her round bottom and pulled her closer, seating her more firmly as he fisted his other hand in her hair and pulled her down to him. "That lip is not yours tonight, love. It's mine."

He leaned up to capture it, nipped her before running his tongue over it in one long lick. Her hands came to his shoulders and she gave herself over to the caress. Whit responded with a deep growl, stroking deep, sucking slow, loving the taste of her, sweet and tart and better than any candy he'd ever had.

How would he give her up?

Ignoring the thought, he focused on her, on her fingers tangling in his hair, holding him still as she gave in to the kiss. She writhed against him and he reveled in her unbridled desire—tightening his fingers around her hips as she rocked against him where he was already hard and made harder by the sweet sounds in her throat, the soft slide of her thighs against his, the heat of her against his cock.

He'd never give this up.

He grunted and grabbed her, stilling her, sitting her up so he could take her in, watch her above him like a goddess. Unable to stop himself, he thrust his hips into hers, watching as her lids lowered and she sucked in a breath.

He spread her coat wide, shucking it off her, reveling in the way her body moved as she helped him, twisting and stretching, revealing the curves she'd been teasing him with all night. No. Not all of them. He slid one hand from her curving hip up her side, until he felt the ridges of fabric beneath her shirtsleeves.

Like lightning, he fisted his hand in the fabric at her back, pulling it from the waist of her trousers. "Hattie . . ."

Her eyes went wide as he repeated the motion in front, tugging, revealing bare torso. She immediately caught the hem of the shirt and tugged it down. "No."

The word stung. "No?"

She shook her head. "It's very—bright."

He smiled. "I know."

She shook her head, her gaze flickering to the doorway to the next room. "Do you not have a bed somewhere? Somewhere dark?"

He did. But that wasn't what she was saying. "Hattie. Let me see."

She closed her eyes. "I'd rather you not."

He leaned back against the loveseat, refusing to remove his hands from her, letting his fingers slide over her thighs and play at the tops of her leather boots. "Shall I tell you what I wish to do?"

Her eyes flew open and he almost laughed—he had her attention. His curious girl wouldn't be able to resist his telling her precisely what he wished to do to her. In full detail. "I wish to remove this shirt that is too plain for you," he said softly, his fingers sliding back up to the lawn hem, not stopping until they were underneath the fabric, on her warm skin.

He teased along the soft strip just above her trousers, and whispered, "I need to remove it, you see, because I can't taste you until I have." Her lips fell open on a little intake of air. "You'd like that, wouldn't you? Me tasting you?"

"I . . ." She hesitated.

"I'd like to run my tongue over you here," he said, his hand splaying wide over the soft curve of her stomach, his cock growing harder with every new inch of her. Had anything ever felt as good as the silk of her skin? The curve of her body?

He sat up, burying his nose in the curve of her neck as

he wrapped his arms around her. "Let me," he whispered at her ear before capturing the lobe between his teeth. "Let me taste you."

She exhaled her "yes," as though it was the only word she could find.

He pressed a wet kiss just beneath her ear and released her, his hands returning to the hem of her shirt and pulling it over her head, sending it sailing across the room, forgotten before it hit the ground, because he was too focused on what he'd discovered.

The vision of those bindings, the way they disappeared her beautiful breasts—they made him want to do damage. He set a finger to the uppermost edge of the bandages, where her skin was straining white against the binds. "You know, my lady, when you spoke of undergarments, I did not expect—"

She gave a little breathless laugh, and he was grateful for it . . . for the way it pulled her from whatever doubt she had been having. "I don't imagine you did."

"Mmm," he grunted before leaning forward and tracing the pale line just above the too-tight bandages with his tongue.

"Oh, my," she whispered, her hands coming to his head, threading into his hair. "That feels—"

It was nothing compared to what he was going to make her feel. He found the end of the linen and untucked it, pulling it free before beginning the work of unbinding her.

She reached to help him.

"No," he said, as he worked to lay her body bare. "This is for me. You, on my lap, wrapped like a parcel. It's like Christmas."

She flushed at the words. "Is it?"

He slowed, holding her gaze for a long moment before he answered, "How could you not know?" The strips fell away and her eyes went hooded with the pleasure of their loss—so keen that Whit felt it like a blow, his mind going blank but for the single goal of making her feel a pleasure to rival it again and again, forever.

She returned to her senses too soon—almost immediately—and instantly moved to cover herself, an impossible task as the beautiful globes overflowed her hands. The vision was the most erotic thing Whit had ever seen, and he could not contain the growl that came from low in his throat as he leaned forward and pressed a kiss to the straining flesh above each hand, licking slowly over the red, worried skin there.

"Poor love," he whispered. "You must take better care."

He covered her hands with his own, threading their fingers together as he tracked the red lines that crisscrossed her breasts. Another kiss, and another, and another, soothing her sensitive skin with soft, gentle kisses and lingering licks and tiny sucks at the impossibly soft outermost edge of one breast. Then the other.

He worshipped her until she was rocking against him once more, until she forgot her embarrassment. Until she forgot her nerves. Until she moved her hands—and his—and revealed herself to him.

Stealing his breath.

Her skin was red and mottled by the bindings, but her nipples, pink and perfect, strained in the cool air in the room, and he took one stunning peak in his mouth and licking over it with his tongue before sucking gently, again and again, until she was panting with pleasure, her hands fisted in his hair.

Whit reveled in the sting of her hold, even as he turned his attention to the other breast, repeating his actions. He scraped his teeth across the peak, then soothed it with tongue and lips. She cried out, and for a wild moment, Whit thought he might come in his trousers like a boy.

He released her, needing to collect himself—to tamp down the riot of emotion he felt with this woman in his arms—eventually dragging his attention to her eyes once more, reading the desire there, and the uncertainty. He wanted to destroy one and flame the other, and so he did the only thing he could think to do; he lifted her in his arms and carried her to the pillows strewn before the fireplace.

He followed her down, loving the way her body turned itself over to him, relaxing into his. One of his hands stroked down her now naked torso, toying at the waist of her trousers. "More wrapping," he said quietly, his fingers at the fastening.

"I wish I were wearing something more exciting," she replied.

"I don't," he said, leaning over her to nip at the line of her jaw before reaching to pull off her boots in quick succession. "These trousers have been teasing me all night, tracing every inch of you. Making promises that I very much hope you intend to keep." He grasped the waistband and tugged, and magnificently, she let him strip them from her.

He lost his breath at the vision of her, bare and beautiful, the peaks and valleys of her body, her soft curves made stunning in the flickering firelight, and there, at the apex of her beautiful thighs, a thatch of curls that had his mouth watering. "Christ, Hattie. You're the most beautiful thing I've ever seen."

She smiled, shy and sweet, her hands coming to cover herself. "You make me nearly believe that."

He slid his hands up her legs, leaning over, unable to stop himself from pressing a lingering kiss to the back of her hand where it blocked his view, the sweet scent of her turning his words into a growl, as he continued up her body. "I'm not letting you up until you believe it, entirely."

"That might take some time," she said softly, almost too soft for him to hear.

"I have a lifetime."

Her head was turned toward the fire, staring at the flame. Somewhere along the way she'd lost her hairpins, and her beautiful blond mane spread out on the pillows like silk thread. Whit wanted to bury himself in it, in *her*. "You have tonight."

He hated the words, not liking the truth of them and the knowledge that, after tonight, nothing would be the same. Instead, he pressed a kiss to the soft swell of her rounded stomach, then licked up to the curve of her breast, reveling in the taste of her.

A night would not be enough time to explore. "Then I shall have to make it feel like a lifetime."

He sucked a nipple between his lips, loving the way it hardened against his tongue, the way she gasped at the sensation, her hips rocking back into the silken cushions. "Whit," she whispered, one hand coming to his hair, the tremor of it echoed in her voice when she added, "Please."

Anything. He'd give her anything she asked.

His cock throbbed against the buttons of his trousers, desperate to be released. Desperate for her.

Slow, he thought. It was her first time.

Christ, it was her first time.

Another man, a gentleman, would pack her up and send her home at this point. A better man. A stronger one. He didn't have any business being a part of this. Of ruining her. She deserved better than a boy from Holborn who'd lived on scraps and fought for everything he had.

He knew it . . . but he wasn't sending her home.

He wasn't called Beast for nothing.

Chapter Twenty

In all the time she'd prepared for this moment and all the times she'd imagined what it might be like, Hattie had never imagined how much she would *feel*.

She wasn't a fool, of course—she knew there was a certain amount of sensation to be expected. She knew the basics of the act, and had heard that there would be possibly pleasure and likely some pain, but she hadn't expected the way her whole being would vibrate with awareness.

She hadn't expected to be bombarded with it—with the soft silk of the cushions at her back, the heat of the fire on one side of her, and him, hot like the sun on the other. She hadn't expected his hands—the rough stroke of them over all the curves and swells that she'd spent a lifetime trying to hide and diminish. And she hadn't expected his lips, following those magnificent hands, tracking them as though she was what he'd said. As though she was *beautiful*.

That's what he'd called her.

She didn't believe him—Hattie had eyes in the head on her shoulders, and she knew what beautiful women looked like. She knew she wasn't what they were. But still . . . now, as he stroked one large, warm hand over her skin, she came alive. "Whit," she whispered, summoning his stunning amber gaze to hers, loving the way it sharpened, reading her thoughts.

"Tell me what you feel," he said, low and dark and filled with promise.

One of her hands dropped to his, riding the long strokes he passed up and down her body, in sure, firm exploration. "I feel . . ." She trailed off, searching for an answer. "I feel *alive*. No one has ever touched me like this."

A low grunt. "Good."

She smiled. "That's very primitive of you, considering we met in a brothel."

"I cannot help it. I want to be the first to touch you. Here." He stroked over her stomach, up to her breasts. "Here." He cupped her breast, ran a thumb over her straining nipple once, twice, until she arched her back and pressed herself more firmly into his hand. He released her almost instantly, and she sighed her frustration as he reversed his path, moving lower until he slid his fingers beneath hers where they covered her most private place. "Here."

She didn't stop him. Why would she ever stop him? Everything he did set her aflame with pleasure. Instead, she lifted her own hand and gave herself to his touch, barely anything, really. He simply cradled her with one strong hand, his eyes raking over her body. "I want to be the first to know everything you like," he said, lowering his lips to the curve of her shoulder. "I want to be the first to watch your body flush with pleasure." He kissed down the slope of her breast, suckled on its tip. "I want to be the first you command to give it to you."

His fingers flexed against her core, and she lifted her hips to him. "I'm not sure I could command you."

"No?" Another suck. Another little flex, hinting at more.

She closed her eyes and shook her head. "I wouldn't know what to ask."

He was barely moving at the heat of her. She rocked against the cushions. "No? You've nothing to ask?"

She bit her lip. "No," she lied.

A lick along the curve of her breast. Another gentle stroke of his hand—not enough. Not near enough. She let her legs fall open.

The pleasure in his low, rumbled "Hmm," was enough to send desire pooling deep in her, where that maddening hand now rubbed in unhurried circles, as though he hadn't considered the possibility of ever moving faster.

She ran a hand down his arm, to that hand. Added pressure.

The man laughed at her ear. "Seems like there's something you'd like to ask." He was doing it on purpose. And though she should be frustrated, she wasn't. She was *delighted*.

Perhaps a little frustrated.

"*Whit*," she said, lifting her hips to meet their combined touch.

"Hattie?" he asked at her ear, letting one finger slide, just barely, nearly close enough to what she wanted.

Her eyes flew open and she met his gaze. "You know."

"I want you to say it."

Another woman would have missed the hitch in his voice, the desire in it. The proof that he was not unmoved. But Hattie—perhaps because she'd never heard such a sound before—did not miss it. And she found she rather liked it. With her free hand, she reached for him, pulling his lips to hers, kissing him like the wanton she'd become with him. And when she pulled back from the caress, their breathing harsh, she became that woman. "You wish me to command you?"

He didn't look away. Wouldn't let her. His fingers, wicked and wonderful, kept stroking over her. "I do."

This time, when she applied pressure, he did the same.

Her gasp was punctuated by his long curse, scandalous and delicious. He leaned down and kissed her neck, scraping his teeth over her skin as he growled, "Christ, that's perfect." She rocked her hips at the words, and he bit her gently, the sting a perfect complement to the soft pleasure below. "Use me."

She did, guiding him until the pressure was perfect, letting her thighs fall open as he learned her pleasure, the weight of it, the speed of it, the way it wound her tighter and tighter.

She gasped his name. "Please."

He lifted his head, finding her eyes as he found a spot she'd never discovered on her own. "Ahh," he said. "Right there, isn't it?" One of his long fingers slid deep inside her, his thumb swirling at the point where every bit of her pleasure had distilled. "So pretty and wet, my gorgeous girl," he whispered, and she was lost to his low, lush words, pouring from him as she moved against him.

Her fingers wrapped tightly around his wrist. "Don't stop."

"Not for anything, love." He leaned down and whispered in her ear, "I've never seen anything like you taking your pleasure. Like you riding my touch until you own it. It's enough to put a man to his knees."

She closed her eyes at the words, at the way they rioted through her, winding the spring tighter. "Please," she panted.

"Once you've found it, I'm going to give it to you again."

She clung to him. "Harder."

He pressed more firmly, swirled in a tighter circle. "With my mouth . . ."

"Faster."

Faster.

"More."

More.

"And after my mouth . . . I'm going to make you come on my cock."

"Oh, God," she gasped. Pleasure slammed through her, nearly impossible to believe, and she was clinging to him, desperate for it to go on forever even as she begged for it to stop. He somehow knew what to do—stopping but not leaving her, pressing the heel of his palm tightly to the center of her pleasure as she went boneless beneath him.

He kissed her, long and slow as she returned to the moment, ending the caress in a delicious suck that had her sighing. "That was the most beautiful thing I've ever seen," he said, leaning down to suck one aching nipple.

She turned toward him, her fingers coming to play in his hair. "Thank you."

He laughed against her skin, the breath of the sound sending a delicious shiver through her. "Don't thank me, love. It was a fucking gift."

She didn't have time to blush at the foul language, as he began to move down her body, pressing kisses over her skin as he settled between her thighs. Hattie's eyes opened. "You can't—"

"Mmm," he said, ignoring the words as he parted her folds, meeting her gaze over her body. "You cannot believe I would see you here, laid out for me like a banquet, and not want to feast. You cannot believe I would not feast for days."

She caught her breath, the memory of the pleasure she'd experienced at his mouth impossible to ignore. "Yes," she said, her hand sliding over his head.

His eyes went heavy with desire as she fisted her fingers in his hair.

She smiled. "You like that."

He didn't respond, instead setting his mouth to her, pressing his tongue into her softness in a long, lingering lick that had her serving herself to him. He groaned, settling in, savoring her taste, making love to her with slow, nearly unbearable strokes.

"Whit," she whispered, writhing beneath him, pulling him tight to her, unable to stop herself as he found the aching point of her with long, slow, gentle licks that set her on fire. "More."

She was greedy for him, for his touch, for his kiss as he grasped her bottom, lifting her up to his mouth. Her eyes opened, and she met his gaze over her body, the view of him, worshipping her, threatening to send her over the edge instantly. She started to close her eyes, and he shook his head, growling his insistence that she remain with him. And she did, forgetting what ladies were supposed to be, what virgins were supposed to be. Forgetting everything but him, here, with her.

She was writhing against him, unable to stop herself from moving, and he placed one hand, large and brown from the sun, against her belly, holding her still as he worked her—stealing her breath and her thought with his stunning kisses, over and over, again and again, faster and faster until—

She flew apart beneath him, unable to keep her eyes open, letting them slide shut as he growled his displeasure—but he didn't stop. Glorious, magnificent man . . . he didn't stop. Instead, he held her through the wild orgasm—like nothing she'd ever experienced. He'd somehow taken pure pleasure and distilled it further. Pleasure incarnate.

He guided her back to earth, as though he were there for nothing more than to keep her safe. And, for a mad moment, Hattie imagined what it would be like for this man to keep her safe, forever. For him to want her, forever. For him to love her, forever.

Impossible.

Tears sprang, and he lifted his head, the muscles of his shoulders and arms tensing as worry crossed his brow. "Hattie?" Her name was harsh on his lips. He leaned over her, one hand coming to cradle her face. "What's wrong?"

She shook her head. "Nothing."

He ran that hand down her body and back up. "Christ. Did I hurt you?"

She couldn't help the laugh that came. "No. *No*," she said. "No. My God, you made me feel—" The tears again, threatening. "Whit, you made me feel *wonderful*. So wonderful that . . . I wish—"

He didn't seem to believe her. He was too focused on her face, his beautiful eyes tracking hers, seeing everything.

"I wish—" she tried again.

"Tell me," he said softly. "Tell me what you wish."

I wish we could have more than tonight.

She reached for him, kissing him deep, leading the caress in a way she'd never done before. Putting every bit of herself into it—Hattie who resisted the past, Hattie who dreamed of a future, and Hattie who wanted a man like this to love her the way she'd always dreamed, quietly, in the darkness, when no one was looking.

She kissed him until they couldn't speak, because she was too afraid to speak—too afraid that she might tell him that she wished for something he could not give her. Too afraid that he would leave her before she had the last taste of him. Before she had all of him. And when they pulled apart, she whispered against his lips, "I wish for the rest."

He watched her for a long moment, and her heart stopped as she considered the possibility that he might not give it to her.

She slid a hand down the front of him, over his bandages, until she reached the waistband of his trousers, left unbuttoned when he'd pulled them on. She hesitated there, at the edge of the dark, tempting opening, knowing that another woman would move with more certainty.

As Hattie hesitated, so, too, did Whit, freezing above her, his breath stilling. She met his gaze. Asked a silent question.

"Now," he said. "Do it."

And she did, sliding her hand inside the dark, promising V of the fabric, reveling in his quick inhale when she touched him. "Does that feel—"

"Yes."

She smiled. "I didn't finish the question."

"It feels like heaven, love."

She shook her head. "But it can feel better."

He closed his eyes. "I don't think I can bear it feeling better."

She leaned up and kissed the sharp line of his jaw. "I think you'll do fine. Show me."

His attention flew to hers. "You're not a warrior. You're a fucking goddess. Did you know that?"

She liked that very much. Unable to keep the smile from her lips, she repeated herself. "Show me."

He did, placing his hand on hers, showing her just how he liked to be touched, the firm, smooth heat of him sliding over her palm as she stroked him. "You're so soft," she whispered, her eyes on their hands in the V of his trousers. "So hard."

He grunted. "Never harder."

She met his eyes. "Is that true?"

"Yes."

She wanted to touch him, to learn him, to give him all the pleasure that he gave her. "Show me how. Teach me." He let her push his trousers aside, revealing him—full, thick, strong, and, "Beautiful."

He swore softly and grew impossibly harder at the word, guiding her touch, squeezing her around him, almost too rough, until she stroked him and he growled, the sound like a gift. She smiled, watching their joined hands work him. "You like this."

"So much," he said, the rough words drawing her attention to his face, where the muscles in his jaw clenched and he looked like he was barely hanging on to control.

She stroked him again. Down. Up. His throat worked at

the sensation, and then she paused, rubbing the pad of her thumb across the tip of him, and he closed his eyes, throwing his head back. "*Fuck*, Hattie."

She grinned. She couldn't stop herself. "You like that *very much*." She did it again, and he groaned, pulling her to him for a long kiss, tongue stroking deep as she put her lessons into action. She'd never felt so powerful.

After too short a time, he pulled her away from him. "Stop."

"But . . ." She paused. "I was enjoying that."

He huffed a little laugh. "As was I. But you asked for the rest, did you not?"

The honest words had excitement coursing through her. "You promised me the rest."

He stilled, his fingers tracing over her temple, pushing her hair back from her face as he searched her eyes, suddenly serious beyond words. "Be certain. Be certain that you choose this. That you choose me." His thumb traced over her cheek and his voice lowered to a whisper. "Be certain that you are willing to give this up to me, because I will take it and I will keep it and you can never have it back."

And in that moment, as the words settled between them in that remarkable, decadent room, filled with silks and sin, Hattie knew the truth—that she would never want this back. She would treasure this night and this moment forever. Because she would never want another the way she wanted him.

Even though she knew, without question, that she would never have more of him.

She closed her eyes at the realization, taking a deep breath before she spoke. "In my life, I've been a daughter and a sister and a friend. I've had love and respect, and lived a happier life than many . . . than most." She paused. "But I have never been an equal. Even as I fought for all the things

I wanted, I never had a choice. Not really. I always had a father or a brother or friends to tell me what I should choose. What I could have. Who I am."

She met his eyes, their amber fire unwavering on her. "And then I met you. And from the very start, you offered me choice. You never told me what I should want. What I could and could not have. You made me your equal." She smiled.

His brows snapped together. "And then I took it from you."

She nodded. "And tomorrow, we shall be rivals. But here is the truth; I could not be your rival if I were not your equal. If I were not your . . . match."

Her hand settled to his chest, and she felt the strong, sure beat of his heart beneath her palm. And she wondered, madly, what it would be like if she were his match in all things.

It didn't matter. "I have never been more certain of anything." She leaned in for his kiss, and he met her halfway. "Ruin me."

He didn't speak, instead giving her the kiss for which she asked, moving over her, kissing down her neck and over her breasts, lingering at the tight buds there until her fingers were in his hair and tugging him back up for more lingering kisses, slow and languid and setting her aflame.

She opened her thighs and he settled between them. They both gasped at the sensation, the smooth head of him cradled against the warmth of her, and he held himself up over her, not touching her anywhere else, his weight on his massive arms. "I have never done this," he whispered.

She smiled. "I don't believe you."

He shook his head. "Not like this. Not so important. Not with such a goal." He rocked into her, the hard length of him pressed perfectly at her heat, and she sighed. "I want you to remember it."

"I will," she said, her hands coming to his hips. "How could I not?"

How would she ever forget the look of him? His beauti-

ful face and his eyes like flame and the chiseled warmth of
his body?

"Well, love," he said. "I want you to remember it well."

She reached up to him, sliding her hands into his hair,
holding his eyes. "I shall. How could I forget this? The way
you look at me? Like I'm . . ."

Beautiful.

Perfect.

". . . Like I'm precious."

He swore and kissed her, his tongue stroking against
hers, slow and deep before he pulled back and pressed his
forehead to hers. "You are precious, Hattie. More precious
than you know."

*Don't say it. Not like that. Don't make me want more
than I can have.*

As though she wasn't impossibly far gone on that front.

As though she hadn't made the terrible mistake of falling
in love with this man who was too much for her.

"I don't want to be precious," she said softly. Precious
things weren't beloved. They were protected. She wanted
to be the thing he couldn't bear to part with. She wanted to
be loved. She wanted to be threadbare.

"What, then?"

She swallowed back the words. "I want to be wanted."
She pressed up against him, and they both groaned as he
slid over her, once. Twice.

He was staring into her eyes, the truth laid bare in them,
stealing her breath. "I've never wanted anything the way I
want you."

She stroked a hand down his side, reveling in his smooth
skin. "Prove it."

And he did, easing into her gently, just barely pushing
inside, filling her with the broad, hot tip of him, stretching her in the strangest, most delicious way. Her eyes went
wide at the sensation and she wriggled beneath him. "Is
this—this is—"

She moved again, and he growled. "Fuck. That's good. You're so soft. So wet." One of his hands came to her hip, his fingers curving into the flesh there, lifting her thigh to ease his movement, but he did not move. His beautiful eyes were on her face, filled with concern. "How does it feel?"

She smiled at him. "I thought it was supposed to hurt?"

He gave a little laugh. "It's not supposed to hurt." He leaned down and kissed her again. "It's never supposed to hurt, do you understand? It's supposed to feel glorious." She wiggled again, and he added, through his teeth, "Christ. Like that."

Hattie grinned. "Is there more?"

Concern gave way to surprise. "I—what?"

"I'm told there's more. Is there?"

Surprise gave way to understanding. Then a laugh. "Yes, my lady. There is more."

She lifted her brows. "And would you be so kind as to show me?"

For a moment, Hattie thought that she might have gone too far. After all, coitus was supposed to be a serious affair, she'd always thought. But this didn't seem like it should be serious. This seemed like it should be entertaining. This seemed like it should be enjoyed.

Did he agree?

One side of his full mouth lifted up in a winning smile. "More," he said, and sank into her, slow and smooth, until he was seated to the hilt and breathing as though he'd just come out of a fight.

Hattie hissed in a breath at the sensation—tight and full, and not entirely comfortable, but not entirely uncomfortable, either.

"Hattie," he panted, searching her face. "Talk to me, love."

"I . . ." She hesitated, considering. And then, "What if I—" She lifted her hips, sliding just a touch higher on him, then back. "*Ohhh*."

"Mmm," he grumbled. "My thought exactly."

She did it again, a tiny little thrust. "That is—" And again—this time, with him helping her. "Oh."

He cursed. "You liked that."

She smiled. "How did you know?"

He met her gaze, his eyes full of sin. "There are no secrets in this. I can feel it." He rocked his hips into her, leaning down to lick the skin of her neck until she sighed. "The lady likes short strokes."

She did. Very much. "And the gentleman?"

He stole her lips for a lingering kiss. "I like what you like."

What a delicious thing for him to say.

Before she could tell him so, he was speaking. That was the best part—the sensations were wonderful, but she might never get over the pleasure of having him talk to her.

Especially when the things he said were so scandalous. "I like how tight you are around me—impossibly tight," he said, the last almost to himself. "I like how your eyes go hooded when I do this—" He thrust, just barely, just enough to sear her nerves. "I like how your lips soften for my kisses, and your fingers tighten on my body." Another thrust, and another and another, and her sighs turned to cries, and she never wanted it to end.

And it didn't, not as he moved with surer strokes, deeper and deeper, until she was clinging to him, a sheen of sweat on both their bodies as they discovered each other's pleasure.

"But the thing I like the most . . ." He paused, holding himself on one arm as he reached between them, low, then lower, until he found the aching bud at her core. ". . . is making you come." He rubbed a slow, languid circle over her, timing it with his smooth, short thrusts, and she began to writhe beneath him.

"You like it, too," he growled.

"So much," she admitted, loving the way the admission shook him. He stole her lips, and moved, pulling out nearly until he'd left her, until she thought she would weep from the loss of him, and then joining her again, slow and steady. Her eyes went wide at the magnificent feeling. "Again." His thumb worked her. "*Again.*"

"My greedy girl."

Greedy for you, she wanted to say. *For all of you. For every part of you. For everything we might be together.* But she held her tongue, and instead, she said, "I am greedy. You've made me greedy."

He grunted his approval. "I'll give you everything you want."

Yes. "All of it?"

"Every bit." He was moving harder now, deeper, and his fingers still stroked where she ached for them and nothing felt strange any longer. Now it felt perfect. He felt perfect. "There's nothing more beautiful than you in ecstasy, love, nothing feels softer, nothing tastes sweeter . . . nothing is more . . ."

He lost the word to sensation, but she heard it anyway. *Perfect.*

"More," she said, the only word that would come.

"All of it," he replied, and it was perfect. They were perfect together. And then it was there, that knife's point of tension, coiled tight, tighter, tightest, and Hattie closed her eyes, her back bowing to him, as he worked her, making good on his promise, giving her everything she wanted. A vision flashed in Hattie's mind, a keen memory of dancing at the ball, when he'd collected her into his arms and his grace had become hers.

And now, she felt it again, the slow, wonderful thrust of him, the smooth press of his hips, the way he drove her higher and higher until she could no longer feel the pull of the earth beneath them.

"Please," she cried, desperate for the release she knew only he could give her.

And then he growled, "Come for me, love," and thrust deep into her, in one long, stunning stroke, rocking his thumb over her once, twice, and then . . . "*Now.*"

She was lost to his touch. To his movements. To *him*. Pleasure rioted through her, so hard that it came with an edge of fear, and she clung to him. He caught her up in his arms and held her while she came apart, his low voice in her ear: "Take it. It's for you. It's all for you."

She did, bearing down on him, convulsing around him, milking the hard length of him over and over, until she had finished and he held her in his strong arms, protecting her. When reason returned, she sighed, magnificently sated, like she'd never been before.

He pressed a kiss to her temple and moved to her side, pulling her to him; she lay against him, listening to his heart pound, fully, wonderfully satisfied. If this was ruination, she absolutely didn't understand why anyone would choose to live a proper life.

Perhaps she could convince him to do it again before tomorrow. Before they went back to being rivals. And on the heels of that thought came another—*perhaps they didn't have to be rivals*. Perhaps everything she thought she could not have was in play once more.

After all, surely what had just occurred between them was uncommon. If it were common, why would people ever leave their bedchambers?

Perhaps they could love each other.

She smiled at the thought, curving into him, rubbing one leg over his. She froze, realization crashing through her.

He hadn't finished.

A cold uncertainty flooded her as she reached for him, still hard and hot against her. "Whit—"

He caught her hand before she could get close. "Don't."

"But you—"

He lifted her hand to his lips, pressing a kiss to her fingers. "It was for you. Not for me."

She stilled, the relaxed delight that had infused her moments earlier now gone, replaced with confusion and a hint of something far more dangerous. "But why didn't you—"

"I'm for body, Hattie," he said. "Not future."

She shook her head. "Future?"

Body. Business. Home. Fortune. Future.

He grunted.

"No grunts. Not now," she said, irritation growing. "Why didn't you—"

Oh, God. Had he not enjoyed it?

Her eyes went wide.

Had she pushed him to do something he had not wished to do?

Doubt slammed through her, followed by panic and horror, and Hattie sat up, desperate to cover herself. How had she misread this situation, thinking he was enjoying himself?

Thinking he'd been enjoying himself because she'd been so thoroughly enjoying herself.

Because she'd been so lost in love with him.

No. Not *with*.

He didn't want her.

She closed her eyes against the thought, and the mortification that came with it. "I have to leave."

He sat up, as well. "Hattie."

She shook her head, tears threatening. Oh, no. She couldn't let him see her cry. She snatched her trousers in one hand and went around the edge of the loveseat to find her shirt, blessedly long enough to cover all the essential bits while she fetched her boots. She pulled on her trousers. "Thank you very much for your . . . service."

"My *what*?" he asked, coming instantly to his feet.

Hattie increased the speed of her dressing. "That's what it was, wasn't it? I mean, you didn't even . . ." She waved a hand at his erection, still evident.

"Hattie—" He started toward her, then stopped. Collected himself. "I didn't want you pregnant."

She turned to him, her mouth opening, then closing. And it was her turn to say, "What?"

"You wanted a ruined reputation. Not a ruined life," he said. "I didn't want you with child."

With child.

A vision flashed, a little boy with dark hair and amber eyes. A little girl with a wide smile and a dimple in her chin. "A child wouldn't ruin my life," she said. "I would never think such a thing." The words surprised her—somehow never imagined and then fully formed, as though they'd been there the whole time.

As though she'd been dreaming of a life with this man since birth.

But it didn't matter.

And even if it did, there were other ways to prevent pregnancy and still find pleasure. French letters. A method she'd heard about in the ladies' salon at a ball once which, at the time, had sounded rather messy, but tonight would have been something rather more . . . exciting.

If Hattie had *heard* of such a solution, she expected Whit had *used* it.

"A child would have tied you to me," he replied. "And I can't let that happen."

The words stung. She hadn't even thought of that. A child came with a child's mother. And he didn't want that. It made sense. Why would he? With a woman he'd thought of as nothing more than an agreement. An arrangement. A woman he didn't want.

He didn't want her.

Hadn't he just proved it?

"I grew up without a father," he added. "I know how difficult it is for a mother to provide alone. I would never do that to you. Or to a child."

She shook her head. "I never would have imagined you would."

He seemed to cast about for something to say. "Girls like you don't marry boys like me, Hattie. Boys raised in the Rookery muck, living every day with the stink of it."

"What proper horseshit," she said, the words out of her mouth before she could stop them, startling them both. But she was furious. "There are a thousand reasons why I wouldn't marry you, and where you were raised doesn't even rank," she said, and it was the truth. She'd met men born far above him in station and living far below him in character. She pulled on one boot. "There's nothing wrong with your past."

"There's everything wrong with it. Look at my face, Hattie. The shiner'll be bigger tomorrow."

"And you got it by choice, not by chance. Don't for a second think I pity you, Saviour Whittington."

He stilled. "Don't ever call me that."

"Why?" she snapped, pulling on the second boot. "Are you afraid you'll have to come out from behind the Beast and face the world as a man?"

His gaze narrowed on her. Good, let him glower. She wasn't about to fear him. How dare he ruin her and then ruin her night? "I can't keep you safe," he said, the words sounding like they were tortured from him. "I can't love you."

The words were a cold slap, doubling down on the shame she already felt. She knew it, of course. She wasn't for loving. She wasn't even for sex.

Good old Hattie.

"I've never asked you to keep me safe." She had to get out of this place before she died of embarrassment or found one of his famed blades and stabbed him. "I never asked you for love," she said, grateful that he wouldn't see the lie. She held up a hand before he could speak. "None of this matters, anyway. You made certain it wouldn't. I am happy one of us was able to remain disconnected from the events of the evening."

He ran his hands through his hair in fury and frustration, and Hattie tried very hard not to notice how all his muscles bunched and rippled with the movement. She almost succeeded. "I wasn't disconnected."

"No. Of course not," she said, donning her coat, grateful to be covered up, finally. "Everyone knows that men deeply engaged in coitus often fail to complete the task."

Anger and shock warred in his narrow gaze. "I completed the task, Lady Henrietta. Three times, by my count."

"But I didn't!" she cried, feeling like a proper failure. Dear God—all that pleasure he'd delivered her and she couldn't do the same for him? Was she *that* undesirable that he could simply ignore the pleasure that had nearly destroyed her?

She'd never been so humiliated.

He didn't respond, and Hattie used the silence to transform her frustration into anger. Fury coursed through her and she reveled in the way it incinerated her embarrassment. "You know, I wish I'd known it would be this way. I would have returned to the brothel."

He growled. "What the fuck does that mean?"

"At least there, I would have known precisely what the arrangement entailed." She paused. "At least there, I could have paid for the privilege of not being made to feel like a chore."

The muscle in his jaw ticked again and again as he watched her. "Nothing about tonight was a chore."

She'd never wanted to believe anything more in her life.

Her lips began to tremble. No. She would be damned if she'd show him how hurt he'd made her. She reached into the pocket of her coat and extracted the packet of sweets she'd taken from the shipment earlier that day. "Well, it's over now." She tossed the pouch to the settee. "I thought you might like those."

He did not look at it.

"Right then," she said, betrayal running through her once more. Hotter. Angrier. "Rivals it is."

Silence.

She nodded, and headed for the door.

Chapter Twenty-One

"Beast."

Whit looked up from his quiet sentry on the rooftops high above the offices of Sedley Shipping to find Devil standing several feet away. His brother had clearly said more than his name, and was waiting for acknowledgment, but Whit had been too focused on the street below, where a steady stream of dockworkers entered and exited the building—no doubt to receive their final payment from the business—all while a dozen Sedley employees hurried in and out of the warehouse, boxes and bins and paperwork in hand, preparing it for its new owner.

Not knowing that he stood high above, observing his recent acquisition.

Loathing himself for acquiring it.

"How did you find me?"

"You've put every available lookout we have to work searching for signs of Ewan. You think I would not know you would be here? Watching over her?"

Hattie.

It had been three days since she'd left him alone in his

home, having destroyed it with the specter of her presence. He couldn't do anything in the house—not eat or bathe or light a fucking candle—without thinking of her. Without reliving her, smelling like almond cakes and looking like sin.

So, he hadn't gone home in three days.

Instead, he kept watch over her. He'd followed her at a distance from the moment she'd left him three nights earlier—to her home in Mayfair, to the Docklands, to the warehouse, in Nora's curricle.

He watched as she kept her shoulders straight and her head high, as though he hadn't hurt her. As though he hadn't destroyed the Year of Hattie unequivocally, for no reason she could divine, but because he was a monster.

Because he couldn't tell her the truth. If he did, Whit had no doubt his brazen warrior would seek Ewan out herself. And he couldn't have that.

So, he watched without her knowing—ensuring her safety. Ensuring that Ewan couldn't make good on his threat.

And it was devastating punishment, because he knew he'd hurt her. And that was worse than the loss of her. Almost worse than the memory of her smooth skin and her low laugh and the taste of her, and the feel of her coming apart beneath him, and the enormous feat of strength required *not* to stay inside her and share in her pleasure and take his own.

And somehow, in that act—an act that had ensured that he gave her only what she wished and nothing more—the act that ensured that she obtain ruination, but not regret, Whit had been the one pummeled with regret.

Because the moment he'd had Hattie Sedley naked before him, all he'd wanted was to keep her there forever.

But he couldn't. He couldn't protect her.

Devil came to his side at the roof's edge. "Is she in there?"

Whit didn't reply.

"The boys tell me you've been here all day."

"So has she." She'd come early this morning, looking like

sunshine. She'd entered the building and not exited, and so he'd waited, stillness and uncertainty a wicked test, like Orpheus walking out of hell. "Have we found him?"

Devil shook his head, sadness in his eyes. "No. But the rooftops are watching. If he turns up here or at the docks, they'll get him." He straightened. "And you've got eyes on your lady." *Not mine.* "He shan't hurt her."

It was an empty promise. Ewan was wild with grief and anger, and every movement he made was out of passion, not sense. Whit was beginning to understand. "Not once we find him," he said. "I'll kill him myself."

"And claim your lady?"

No. He would destroy Ewan for threatening Hattie. But it wouldn't change anything—there would always be an enemy. Always a threat. And he would never be able to keep her safe. He looked back to the street, watching as a pair of dockworkers left the warehouse, hooks on their shoulders and smiles on their faces.

Envy coursed through him. *Had they seen her?*

Devil leaned back on the low wall that marked the edge of the roof. The brothers stood in silence for long minutes, and from a distance, an observer would have marveled at the strength of them, one long and lethal, the other a broad bruiser. "You cannot watch her forever, Beast."

But he could. He could watch her until she found herself a new life, in Mayfair, far from him. He could watch her until she found another path to a different future. One with another man.

He clenched his fists at the thought, loathing it even as he knew that it was best.

That another man would save her from the danger that Whit could not help but bring down upon her.

He swallowed, watching a pair of men exit the building below, boxes in hand, to deposit them in Hattie's father's coach. "What do you want?"

Devil tapped his stick against his boot. "Jamie has received a clean bill of health. The doctor has cleared him to work. He wants onto a delivery rig."

"No." The boy had been shot in the side and was at death's door the last time Whit saw him; he couldn't possibly be at full health, no matter how good the doctor was. He'd let Jamie return to the rigs once he'd seen for himself that Jamie was at full capacity. "He works the warehouse until he's ready for the rigs."

Devil nodded. "That's what I told him. He doesn't like it."

"Tell him to come see me."

"Ever the protector," Devil said dryly, flipping up his collar. "Christ, it's cold." When Whit did not reply, he added, "Tonight's wagons are ready." They had a ship in harbor, filled to the brim with ice and alcohol, playing cards and glass—everything waiting to be moved to the warehouse, then parceled out overland to the rest of Britain. A half-dozen wagons would run to and from the docks tonight to empty the hauler.

Whit extracted his watches from his pocket. *Half past six.* He looked over the rooftops toward the dock, where a line of ships sat quiet, gilded in the late afternoon sunlight. "And the ice moves when?"

"Nik's checking the melt, but it's been draining for two days, and we've booked every available hook for half-nine." Devil pointed across the river, where clouds loomed grey and ominous. "Looks like we'll have some cloud cover. We hold it for a week." A pause. "Assuming you think it's safe to move it."

The question was in the words—would Ewan come for it?

"He isn't after the goods. He never was." Devil remained silent, but tapped his infernal stick. Whit looked to him. "Whatever you've got to say, say it."

"I'm not only worried about Ewan."

Whit growled. "What does that mean?"

"They're saying the Bastards have gone soft, because Beast has found a lady."

I did find a lady. And then I lost her.

"If they worry I've gone soft, they can come find me." He looked back to the Sedley warehouse. "I diversified our business."

"For business? Or personal?"

"Both," Whit said, knowing the words were a lie. "It keeps her safe. And now we can ship . . ."

Devil raised a brow. "What?"

"I don't know. Tinned salmon. Or tulip bulbs."

"What horseshit. What in hell do you know about tulip bulbs?"

Whit's eyes narrowed to slits. "I'm getting a bit tired of being told I'm talking horseshit."

Devil's brows shot up. "Oh? Who besides me is speaking truth to you?" His eyes lit, and a smile split his long face. "I'll tell you what, bruv, I do like her."

Whit shot him a look. "Don't like her. She's not for liking."

"Is she for loving?"

Memory flashed, unpleasant. *I can't love you,* he'd said to her, as she'd dressed with all possible speed, desperate to leave his house after he'd ruined the night they'd had. What kind of an imbecile of a man said such a thing to a woman after making love to her?

Surely, there'd been another way to keep her safe. Something other than insulting her. Christ. He should run himself through as punishment.

It didn't matter that it was the truth. "Another man would be lucky to love her."

"Why not you?"

He leveled Devil with a look. "Ewan threatened her, Devil. Outright."

Devil watched him for a long minute, tapping that infernal walking stick against the toe of his outstretched boot. Then, "If we're *diversifying*, we're going to have to have a conversation about the ships."

"Why?"

"Well, first, we'd better learn a bit about tinned salmon and tulips, but besides that, they're sitting empty in the berths, which is bad for them."

"What do you know about what's bad for boats?"

"I don't know a damn thing, but now that we own a fucking fleet of them, I think one of us ought to start, don't you? Seems like we might need to seek out a boat expert." A pause. Then, "Do you know anyone with a love of boats?"

Whit turned on his brother then. "What do you want from me?"

"You cocked it up," Devil said.

"You think I don't fucking know that?" Whit resisted the urge to put a fist in his brother's face for no good reason. "He threatened to *kill* her."

"And you stole her business out from under her. You punished her for the sins of men—it's familiar." It was the plan Devil had implemented before he fell in love with Felicity. "Christ, the things we do to women."

"It's bollocks," Whit said. "But how else do I keep her safe?"

"You don't," Devil said. "Keeping her safe requires locking her up. And if I know one thing—it's that women don't care for locks."

"She's brilliant. And she should be running the business. She should have been running it from the start, but her father wouldn't give it to her."

Devil nodded once. "Then let her husband give it to her." The meaning slammed through him, even before his brother added, "Marry her."

There was an irony in the way the words came, as though marriage were a neat solution that Whit simply hadn't considered. As though he hadn't been consumed by the idea of marrying her. As though he hadn't imagined that marriage would keep her close.

But it wouldn't keep her safe. "I seem to recall recommending such a thing to you not long ago, and you taking the suggestion . . . poorly."

Devil leaned back and crossed his arms over his chest with the calm certainty of a man well loved. "Once I came around to it, it worked out very well."

Whit shook his head. "Marriage isn't an option."

"Why? You might as well marry her if you're going to follow her around like a guard dog for the rest of your days. You want the girl, Whit. I saw you go for her at the fight the other night. I saw the way she strung you tight."

Of course he wanted her. Christ. Any man in his right mind would want her. She was brilliant and bold and strong and beautiful, and when she came, she moved against a man like sin.

But how could he bring her into this world? Put her in danger?

Devil raised a black brow. "Do you wish to know what I think?"

"No."

"Does she want you?"

There are a thousand reasons why I wouldn't marry you, and where you were raised doesn't even rank.

He could still hear Hattie's anger in the words.

"No." *Not anymore.*

His brother's brows shot together. "Why not? You're rich as sin, strong as an ox, and nearly as handsome as I am."

Whit raised a brow. "That's all it takes?"

"Well, if she's as brilliant as you say, she's definitely too good for you, but that didn't stop Felicity from marrying me."

"Felicity made a mistake."

"Don't you ever tell her that," Devil said, a stupid smile flashing before he grew serious once more. "Answer me. Does she want you?"

Silence.

"Ah. So that *is* why you bought the business—and the boats."

"No!" Whit said, resisting the niggling truth in the back of his mind. "I bought them to keep her safe. Like we discussed."

"At the risk of repeating myself: horseshit." Devil smirked. "You bought the business—and the boats—for Henrietta Sedley. Like the time when we were boys when you tried to get that girl's attention by buying the teacake she'd been eyeing all afternoon." He paused, distracted by the memory. "What was her name?"

"Sally Sasser," Whit said, immediately on the defensive. "And I gave that teacake to her!"

"But you bought it to get her attention, instead of just telling her you wanted to go for a walk, or whatever. Like an imbecile."

"You nearly destroyed your wife's reputation for sport," Whit pointed out.

"Aha!" Devil grinned. "So you admit you want to marry the girl."

I can't love you.

She'd be another person to care for. Another to protect.

Another to lose.

"I admit no such thing," Whit said, frustration pouring through him. "I bought them to get her far from the Bastards. I bought them because it would keep her safe."

"Fine. Why have you kept them?"

"Because I've barely owned them a week!"

"Nah. Why have you kept them, bruv?"

Whit stopped.

For her.

Christ. Whit rubbed a hand over his face.

He'd kept them for her. Because she'd told him she wanted a shipping business. And he'd wanted to give her what she wanted.

Because hope was a fickle bitch.

"There it is."

"Fuck off," Whit said. "You were nearly dead in a ditch before you realized how much you cocked it up with Felicity."

"And here you sit, hale and healthy. You should thank me for the wisdom I impart to you." Devil smirked. "Now, tell me how you cocked it up, so I can impart additional wisdom as your older, wiser, brother."

"We were born on the same day."

"Yes, but it's clear my soul is wiser."

"Get stuffed." Devil didn't move, letting silence fall between them, knowing that silence was never silence if Whit was there. Silence was thought, miles a minute. Finally, he said, "She is too good for me."

There was no denial in Devil's eyes. No humor, either.

"I am nothing like what she deserves. Born the bastard son of the worst kind of man, raised in a bed-sit in Holborn, then raised again in the filth and fights of the gutter." He paused. Then, "And Ewan. I can't ask her to live in his shadow."

One of Devil's dark brows kicked up. "I'm not sure Henrietta Sedley is the kind of woman who lives in anyone's shadow. I heard she nearly took out Michael Doolan with a blade stolen from you."

"She was ready to slice him to bits."

Devil smirked. "Good thing you came along."

"Don't twist it," he said. "She's not like us. She doesn't fight dirty. She's so clean, it's impossible to imagine how I wouldn't drag her into the gutter if I touched her."

"So far above you, you can barely see her," Devil said softly. The words full of memory.

"Yes," Whit said, looking down at the empty street below. "And what does the lady say?"

How could I forget this? Had she known what they'd had? How rare it had been? It didn't matter, because he'd ruined it. He'd made her feel like a chore.

As though he wouldn't spend the rest of his days chasing the pleasure he'd felt with her.

I can't love you.

I never asked you for love.

"Have you told her?" Devil interrupted. "About the past?"

He met his brother's eyes. "I'm not good enough for her."

Devil shook his head. "You're wrong, but I've never been able to convince you of it. Neither has Grace. But listen to me, bruv. You're the best of the lot of us."

Shame flared at the words and Whit looked away. "That's not true. I couldn't keep you safe." He stopped, thinking of the night they'd run. "I couldn't keep my mother safe. And I can't keep Hattie safe."

Devil sighed. "Ewan is an ass, but he's always been the smartest of the three of us. And he's always known where our weaknesses lie." A pause, and then, "I thought I was like the duke."

Whit's head snapped up at the confession. "You're nothing like him."

"Most days, I know that. And here is what I wish you could see." His amber eyes glittered with frustration and insistence. "I wish you could see that the Mad Duke of Marwick is threatening your happiness for the second time in your life, and this time you have something far more devastating on the line."

Hattie.

"And I wish you could see that you didn't simply punish yourself in the last few days; you punished Hattie. And worse, you made her choice for her." He reached a hand to his brother's shoulder. "You are more than our savior."

Whit closed his eyes, remembering the night they'd run. "I could barely move. You should have left me."

"No." Devil came to his full height. "You were one of us. Ewan came for us all that night. Ewan, who is lost, and the duke, who is dead, and it is time for you to realize that without you, Grace and I would be nowhere. It's time for you to realize that without you, the Rookery would be nowhere. The men wouldn't have jobs and the women wouldn't have pride and the children wouldn't have lemon ice every time we have a ship in harbor. And that's you. I didn't build that. I was too angry and too vengeful. *You* built it. Because you've always looked out for us. And you shall always be the best of us."

The words hung between them, until Devil added, "Henrietta Sedley might be the best woman the world has ever seen, but don't for one second believe that you are not her equal."

You made me your equal.

Hattie's words, full of awe.

Whit's own disbelief.

"I can't convince you of it," Devil said softly, wrapping his hand around Whit's head and pulling him close, until their foreheads touched. "And, sadly, neither can she."

Whit took a deep breath. "I can't keep her safe."

"No." Devil shook his head. "It's the worst truth. But loving them is the best."

Loving Hattie.

"I'm sorry to break up what looks like a beautiful moment, but we've a problem."

The brothers looked up to find Annika crossing the rooftop, tall and blond, her coat billowing in the wind and her brow furrowed like she was in the midst of an Oslo winter.

"Nik!" Devil said, releasing Whit from his grasp, turning with a wide grin on his face. "You will not believe the rumors I've been hearing."

Nik's didn't look to him. "I don't care."

"I hear you've a new friend."

The Norwegian stilled and looked to Whit, pleading in her eyes. "Tell him to shut up."

Whit couldn't help his own smile, welcome after the

events of the last few days. "Where were you twenty minutes ago when he came up here? I would have liked for him
to do the same."

"One of the boys told me you brought a certain fast driver
up to the roof to show her the stars last night," Devil said.

Nik cleared her throat. "It was to make amends for your
fledgling criminals stealing her gig in the first place."

Understanding dawned. Nik and Nora. Not that Whit
could blame the woman before him—if Nora was anything
like her friend, she was irresistible. But first things first.
"You tell the lady that I'll remove the wheels from every
one of her vehicles if she doesn't learn to drive with more
caution."

Nik rolled her eyes and shot Devil a look. "Was it Brixton? That boy needs to stop running his mouth."

"It wasn't Brixton, as a matter of fact," Devil said, casually tapping the end of his walking stick against his boot.
"And you needn't be embarrassed; I only mentioned it because Felicity and I have found ourselves on that roof more
than once." He looked to Whit. "Perhaps you should bring
Lady Henrietta up there."

The idea of bringing Hattie to the rooftops and laying her
bare beneath the stars was devastating.

Whit scowled at his brother. "You're an ass." He looked
to their second, resisting the urge to gape at her bright pink
cheeks. "What's the problem?"

Gratitude flashed in her eyes. "We're to have forty able-
bodied men on the docks tonight, to help with unloading."

Whit nodded.

"But there aren't forty to be had," she said. "There aren't
four."

Whit wasn't concerned. Not yet. But he was puzzled.
"What's that mean?"

She waved a long arm toward the docks in the distance.
"It's quiet on the docks."

"Because Whit bought all the boats," Devil quipped. "I've

already had a word with him about it. We're getting it sorted. What do you know about tinned salmon?"

Nik's brow furrowed in confusion for a heartbeat before she shook her head and returned to the matter at hand. "That's not why. There's no one to do the work."

Devil gave a little huff of laughter. "That's impossible."

"I swear to you it isn't," Nik said. "There's no one working the docks. There are no hooks to be had. And we've ninety tons of ice melting in the hold every moment we think about what might or mightn't be possible."

"I've seen dockworkers all day," Whit said, lifting his chin toward the warehouse across the street. "They've been in and out of Sedley, collecting their pay."

"Be that as it may . . ." She reached into her coat, extracting a piece of paper and extending it to Whit. "There are no men to work the cargo on the docks. And if I had to guess, I'd say you're the reason why."

He took the letter.

> *Beast—*
> *Congratulations on your new business.*
> *Good luck finding men willing to work for you.*
> *I await your reply.*
>
> Yrs, etc.,
> *Lady Henrietta Sedley*
> *Future proprietress, Sedley Shipping*

Whit gave a little, shocked laugh and looked to Nik. "Where'd you get this?"

"Sarita says she nailed it to the mast of the *Siren* not an hour ago."

His brows knit together. "What is the *Siren*?"

"One of your new haulers."

"Impossible. She hasn't left the warehouse since she arrived."

"Seems she has." She raised a brow in the direction of

the note. "We found it flapping in the breeze, virtually the only sound on the docks."

Those docks were full whenever there was a ship in berth, men flocking, knowing there was money to be had for anyone with a strong back and a steady hand. He looked down at the note. "No hooks to be had?"

Nik shook her head. "Nowhere. We've our men—but nowhere near enough to empty that ship as quickly as we need tonight."

How had she done it?

Devil whistled, long and low. "I thought you said she didn't play dirty."

Whit's heart began to pound. He had said that, hadn't he? But this was dirty. Wonderfully, wickedly dirty. He lifted the paper to his nose, reveling in the soft scent of almonds on it.

"She doesn't need to be kept safe," Devil said, his words full of dry humor. "Christ, we all need to be kept safe from *her*. She's been waging war right beneath your nose."

"You've got to get your girl, Beast. She risks the whole shipment; I don't have to tell you how many months it will take to replenish the amount of champagne we've got in that hold if it gets stolen."

Whit should have been furious. And he was. She'd put herself in danger to best him. But he was also vibrating with excitement. He hadn't lost her. This was a shot over the bow.

His warrior wasn't through with him.

"She promised me a rivalry."

Another long, low whistle from Devil, and then, "This is proof that watching isn't enough, bruv. If you want her safe, your best shot is standing by her side."

Chapter Twenty-Two

After a childhood on and off the decks of ships, trailing behind her father, Hattie was rarely more comfortable than when she was on the water, even when the water in question was a barely-there lift from the Thames as the tide ebbed. She stood on the raised deck at the prow of the hauler, lantern at her feet, staring out at the black river, marveling at the silence of the dock at dusk on a night when a ship was in port and ready to be unloaded.

She'd done it.

It had taken three days, a fair amount of funds, every favor she'd ever accrued while working for Sedley Shipping, and every ounce of goodwill she'd ever gained from the men and women here on the docks, but Hattie had locked up every available hook in the Docklands tonight, and Whit would have no choice but to come for her.

She knew it was silly, but she wanted him to come for her. Because as embarrassed and ashamed as she'd been when she'd left his rooms three evenings earlier, she still wanted to prove to him that she was a powerful adversary. A respected rival.

Lie.

She wanted him to see that they were perfectly matched.
I can't love you.

Luckily, she didn't have to face the memory of his words, because he arrived. She felt him before he spoke, his presence changing the air around her—making her feel simultaneously breathless and powerful.

She turned to face him, excitement running through her as she lifted her chin, the cool breeze whipping up the Thames, billowing her skirts around her legs. She willed herself to look as strong as she felt in that moment. And she was strong. Stronger, as he approached.

Her rival.

Her match.

More. Could he not feel it?

His long strides consumed the deck, his gaze unwavering. She did not move, and for a small, wonderful moment, the whole world fell away and she was full of triumph, as though her plans for the Year of Hattie hadn't gone utterly sideways.

After all, she'd summoned him to her.

He stopped at the foot of the steps leading up to her. "You're trespassing."

She raised a brow. "And you are here to dispatch me with all haste?"

"This is my boat, Lady Henrietta."

The words were firm and unyielding, spoken in a tone that had no doubt set legions of men to cowing. But Hattie was not a man. And it did not make her want to cow. It made her want to reign. "This *ship*"—she exaggerated the correction—"is sitting in this harbor, empty and rotting."

He cursed under his breath and looked up to the sky. "I've owned the damn boats for a week, so there's no need to plan a funeral for them right now."

"We needn't plan a funeral at all," she said, lifting the lantern at her feet and moving to the top of the steps where he stood. "If you trade them to me."

He raised a brow. "For what?"

"For the men I've locked down—the ones you need to save your hold full of ice. The ones you came for."

He raised a brow. "You can't lock them down forever."

"I can lock them down long enough for"—she looked down the row of ships to the hauler that sat lower in the water than all the others, assessing it for a moment—"eighty-some tons of ice to melt."

"Ninety-some," he corrected her.

"Not for long," she said. "What's inside the ice, hopefully dry? More of that bourbon you like so much?"

Something flared in his gaze. Surprise. Admiration.

And Hattie resisted the urge to grin her triumph. "I don't care about the real cargo, but thieves will. You don't want these ships, and I do. And I think you may find it very difficult indeed to run a shipping business from these docks—with these men—if I don't wish you to."

"You don't know who you play with."

"It seems I'm playing with my match, if you ask me." He raised a brow, and excitement threaded through her. "After all, I just locked up every hook from here to Wapping, and none of your other rivals have ever done that. What are your options now?"

He watched her, silent. Then, "You're very proud of yourself, aren't you, warrior?"

She grinned. "I am, rather. You must admit, this is a magnificent move."

He didn't reply, but she saw the small twitch at his lips, a movement that made her want to throw herself into his arms and kiss him, despite his being the enemy.

She resisted the urge and changed tack. "Do you know why ships have figureheads?"

"I do not."

She smiled, lifting the lantern at her feet. "They've had them since the dawn of sailing, all across the word. The Vikings. Rome and Greece. Every culture that is known to have sailed open water used figureheads."

She came to stand at the top of the steps, staring down at him. "Ancient Norse sailors believed that the figurehead was fate made manifest. A ship of size might have had eight or ten of them, taking up valuable weight and cargo space. They were made to guard and protect for every eventuality of seafaring—one for calm seas, one for storms, one to appease the winds. If there was a plague on a boat? There was a figurehead for that."

Still, he did not speak.

"When a storm would appear on open water, the crew would rush to batten hatches and tie back sails—to prepare for rough seas. But there were crewmembers whose job it was to change the figurehead—one that would ward against evil, protect against storms, and lead sailors to paradise if the worst happened." She watched him carefully. "It is said that if a ship sinks without a figurehead, the sailors who die haunt the sea."

She stopped. His eyes gleamed. "Go on."

He always listened to her. He could make her feel like she was the only other person in the wide world. "Those? The ones that faced the storms? The ones that shepherded the sailors to their death? They were always women."

She looked out at the black river, where the tide ebbed and the ships settled into the silty riverbed. "When I was younger, I thought it was wonderful—after all, it was bad luck for girls to sail, but every ship had half a dozen women in the hold, just waiting to meet the sea." She paused, remembering the sailing myths her father used to share.

"Only when you were younger?"

She met his eyes. "Now I understand that girls being bad luck on a ship is a bollocks thing that people say to keep women from living the lives they wish."

He nodded. "Tell me the rest."

"It's just a story," she said. "A story designed to convince young men to take to the sea and give up their lives. A legend passed from man to man, so when they met their inevitable death, it seemed like it was just that, inevitable. And also, not so bad, because they expected it."

"And so?"

"We believe stories, especially when they seem as though they can't possibly be true." She began to descend the stairs, toward him. He didn't move. "The hijacking isn't the stuff of legend. The knock to the head?" She waved it away. "You've had a thousand of those." She landed on the final step, just high enough to bring them eye to eye. "But . . . the night the docks went silent?"

He huffed a little laugh. "A story for the ages."

"That story makes me a queen. The woman who tamed the Beast."

His lids lowered, and for a moment, his eyes filled with sin. And then he said, low and dark, "You like that."

Yes. She did. *But only if she was his queen.*

She ignored the impossible thought. "If you relinquish your hold on these ships, your cargo is emptied tonight, as planned. And no one ever need know I locked them down. But if you don't . . ."

"That's blackmail," he said.

"Nonsense," she said. "It's negotiation. Between rivals."

"Ahh," he said softly, and she realized that if she leaned in, just a bit, she would be close enough to touch him. He didn't seem to be interested in such a thing.

Hating the thought, she added, "If you don't like the negotiation, I also have a proposal."

His brows rose in question. "I'm listening."

"You've the power in Covent Garden, and tonight, I've proven mine lies in the Docklands." She stopped.

"A partnership."

She nodded. "Business."

"All aboveboard," he said.

"Well, my part of it, at least," she replied, loving the way his lips twitched. Loving him. Wishing she could propose a bigger partnership. One that ended with them together in the evenings as well as the days.

Wishing he could love her.

Whit pulled his watches from his pocket, considering the two metal disks before returning them. He looked away, shifting on his feet, and for a moment, Hattie thought he might leave. But he didn't. Instead, he took a deep breath and let it out long and slow. And then, as though he'd been carrying the words around for an age, he spoke. "I was born at St. Thomas's, Southwark."

She stilled, the shock of the words—of his personal revelation—overwhelming. His mother had been unmarried. St. Thomas's was a lying-in hospital for unwed mothers, a miserable place. Most of the babies born there were shipped to orphanages around the city—their mothers shamed into believing that raising their families alone would place such a stigma on the babies that they were dooming them to a fate worse than the hospital itself.

As though orphanages were better than homes, poor or otherwise. As though institutions were better than families, however they came.

"Saviour," she whispered, unable to stop herself.

Don't ever call me that.

The echo of his anger the other night, when she'd tossed his name back into his face, was quick and unpleasant, and Hattie immediately added, "I'm sorry. I didn't mean to—"

"No," he said, a little smile on his lips, as though he was trying to put her at ease. "You're right. Named for the place where I was born and the man who founded the hospital. My mother's payment for a bed. There are a hundred of me. A thousand."

Hattie itched to reach for him, knowing he would not allow it. "And your mother? What was her name?"

"María." He looked past her, toward the dark river, where a half-dozen rowboats made their way through fog and low tide, the lanterns set inside them turning them into floating clouds. "María de Santibáñez. It's been twenty years since I said that aloud." He exhaled. "She used to tell me she shared the name with some ancient relative—lady-in-waiting to a queen." His voice turned to disdain. "Like it meant something."

"It did, to her."

"She'd be beside herself if she knew I was here. Speaking to the daughter of an earl."

"Daughter of an earl by luck," she reminded him. "Once my father dies, that all goes away. And I stand on my own merit again."

"In the short weeks I've known you, Henrietta Sedley, I have come to see that your merit is superior to all others. They should give you the earldom."

She scoffed. "I don't care about the title."

"My father was a duke."

Hattie's jaw dropped at the words, spoken like they were taking a turn about a Mayfair ballroom. She shook her head as though to clear it. "Did you say . . ."

Another humorless laugh. "Twenty years since I've said my mother's name, and I've never said that. But yes, my father was a duke."

"And you were born at St. Thomas's."

"My mother's parents came from Spain to work the estate of my father's father." He paused, as though, for the first time, it occurred to him—"My grandfather." After a moment, he continued. "My mother's father was a great horseman. He was brought from Madrid to keep the stables on the estate. My mother was born there, raised a stone's throw from glory."

Raised on a ducal estate in England, daughter to the stable master, she would have been happy and content—destined for a life as a wife and mother, married well. Whit would have been born into a life that was nothing like the rookeries of Covent Garden.

"What happened?"

"Her parents died young and she was given a place in the main house."

Dread pooled deep in Hattie. She'd heard the story a thousand times. Men of means, and the way they destroyed the young women around them. "Whit—" She reached for him, but he stepped away.

"She never said a bad word about him. Used to make excuses for what he did. He was duke, after all, and she a servant, and one did not marry the other. But she was beautiful, and he was charming . . . and men were men . . ." He trailed off, and Hattie mapped the high cheekbones and full lips that had robbed her of speech when she'd first met him. She had no difficulty believing that his mother was a great beauty.

When he looked at her, there was something in those beautiful amber eyes—the ones he shared with his brother and so must have come from his father. "In my life, I have done many things. Things that shall send me straight to hell. But I have never repeated the sins of my father."

"I know that." Without question, she knew that.

He took a deep breath. "I was young, and I did not understand. I believed her—I believed that we'd left the estate because that was what was done, and that we should be grateful for our flea-infested mattress in Holborn and for the money we had that was not even enough to light candles for her to see properly. But now . . ." He trailed off, and she waited. Hating the story. Desperate for it.

"I know now that she ran from that hospital. That she ran so they wouldn't take her from me." Hattie's chest tightened at the anguish in his voice. "They would have called it taking me from her. But it wouldn't have been that. That would have been good for her. That would have saved her. And instead, she sacrificed herself for me."

It wasn't true. "She didn't."

"She did," he said, lost in the memories of a woman who

must have loved him desperately. "When he found us, he didn't even look at her. He came for me."

"He took her from you," she said softly.

He met her eyes, something like gratitude in them, before he turned away. Hattie followed, like she was on a string. When he got to the center mast of the ship, he reached up to touch the scarred wood there, where over a lifetime, a thousand things had been nailed to the wood.

He spoke to the mast. "You left my note here."

She did not hesitate at the change of topic. "I have a flair for the dramatic."

He looked over his shoulder at her. "The Year of Hattie."

"It's going absolutely terribly."

"Things take time," he said.

"I've waited quite a bit of time already."

He nodded, shoving his hands in his pockets and leaning back against the mast, his hat low over his brow, his greatcoat blowing about his legs, making him look the very portrait of a roguish sailor, and for a moment, Hattie wondered what it would be like if she were his. If she didn't have to battle him. If he would simply wrap her in his coat and let her revel in his warmth and put her arms about his neck and . . .

Love him.

What if this remarkable man let her love him?

"I want to tell you the rest."

"I want to hear it." His gaze flew to hers, narrow and assessing, as though she'd surprised him. "It is going to be awful, isn't it?"

"Yes," he said.

She nodded. "And you've never told anyone else."

"No." He wouldn't have.

"Let me bear some of it."

He looked up to the mast, where the sails were tightly wrapped and tied. "Why would you want that?"

Because I love you.

She couldn't say that. So, instead, she took a step closer, coming near enough that her skirts billowed around his legs, and said, "Because I can."

And that seemed to be enough.

"There were four of us."

She nodded. "All born on the same day." He'd told her that much.

"Devil's mother was a sailor's wife. Mine a servant. Ewan's was a courtesan. And Grace's—she was a duchess."

Hattie's eyes went wide. "She is legitimate? But I thought you said—"

"Grace's father was not ours, but her mother was the duchess, increasing alongside our mothers—or, at least, in time with them." Hattie stayed silent, marveling at the madness that came with title and privilege. "The duke was desperate for an heir, and he knew his best chance at one was the babe in his wife's belly, even though the child wasn't his by blood."

"Why not wait and get the duchess with child again? Try for a boy? One of his own?"

Whit smiled at that, wide and winning enough that Hattie was dazzled by it. "Because the duchess had made it impossible for him to sire more heirs."

"How?" His smile was contagious.

"She shot him."

"Dead?" It wasn't possible.

"No. In the bollocks."

"No!" Hattie's eyes went wide, then narrowed with loathing. "Good."

"Grace inherited her mother's aim, if you are curious."

"I am indeed, and I should like to come back to that, if we may."

"With pleasure." Hattie warmed at the way the reply made it feel as though they had a lifetime of conversation before them. He continued. "So. The duchess produced a babe, but it was a girl. And my bastard of a father baptized her the heir, claimed she was a boy, and shipped her and her mother off to the country."

Hattie shook her head. "That's illegal. It's betraying the line."

"It is, indeed," Whit said. "And it's punishable by death if a false heir is seated."

She met his eyes. "That's why you had to run. Because you knew. And he was worried you would tell people."

"Clever girl," he said softly, admiration in his eyes. "And he was right. I am telling you, am I not?"

But no one else. Not ever. "I don't understand . . ." She hesitated. "Who did he intend for heir?"

"The duke was greedy and prideful. And he wanted an heir to mold in his imagine. To pass his legacy on. He had three sons. But what we did not know was that we had him. He'd been watching us. Devil in the orphanage, Ewan in a Covent Garden brothel, and . . ." He trailed off.

"And you," she said. "With your mother." A woman who loved him. A home that was safe. Reading lessons. Her chest grew tight.

"Not for long," he replied. "He brought us to the country—to the seat of the dukedom. And he told us the plan. One of us would be his heir. That boy would inherit everything. Money, power, land, education. He would never want for anything." A pause. And then, "And neither would his family."

She had known the words would come. Known that, eventually, this mad, monstrous duke would threaten the only thing Whit held dear. His mother.

"How?" she asked, the word on a whisper. She didn't want to know.

"We fought for it. A hundred ways. A thousand. It started easy. Footraces and dancing." The waltz. He'd said his father had made him learn to waltz. "Tests on proper forms of address. Proper silverware. The location of the correct crystal. And then, as he sorted us out, it became clear he didn't care about any of that. What he wanted was a strong son who would carry on his line and impress the wide world."

If ever there was a man who could be those things—could do those things—it was Whit. "What did he make you do?"

"There is a reason that when we got to London, we were good fighters."

Her eyes went wide. "He made you fight each other?"

He nodded. "Even that was easy. We might not have known each other, but we were brothers, and we were happy to scrap when necessary. We learned quickly how to throw a punch and make it look like it would hurt, but pull it at the last moment, so we never did real damage. Ewan was better at that than all of us," he marveled. "You'd see it coming like a boulder, and it would land feather light."

For a heartbeat, Hattie found gratitude for this man she knew would become the villain of the play. The one who would try to kill Grace, and take a blade to Devil's cheek.

"We thought we were brilliant, working together to bring down our father. We didn't know it was all part of the plan. He'd been making us a team so he could use us against each other. And he did. He started to toy with us. He'd threaten one of us to get the others to fight." He looked away. "The threats were wild. If two of us didn't fight until one was on the ground, the third would get the switch until we did."

"You wanted to save them."

"Yes," he said. "Of course."

Saviour. Not just his name. His whole being.

"He'd give us treats, then take them away. Gifts. Toys. Animals. Anything we liked. He loved forcing us to beg for what we loved." Whit looked to her. "You tease me about my lemon sweets? They're because of him. Thank you for the raspberries."

"Of course." She nodded. She wished she could keep him in sweets forever. She wished she could pull him close and hold him tight, but he wouldn't allow it, this proud, wonderful man.

"I couldn't keep up after a while, and I started making plans to escape. I knew that if I could make it back here— back to Holborn—I could find my mother. And we could run. That was my plan. To get back here and run."

Hattie would have given anything she had. Business, boats, fortune, future—all of it—to change what he was about to say. But still, it came. "He told me that if I stayed, he would keep her alive. It became clear I wasn't there to win. That I was never in the running to be duke. He hated that I took after my mother. Raged that I was too small. Too dark. He brought me to train the others. I was there for Devil and Ewan to fight, and if I did it well, if I took the beatings, if I lost the competition, I would be able to go home to my mother, and with money to save her from the life into which she'd been forced."

He went quiet for a long time, and Hattie ached in the silence for the beautiful boy he'd been, and the magnificent man he'd become.

"I would be able to save her." It had been a lie. Hattie didn't need the confirmation. She knew in her soul that it had been a lie.

"He was a monster," she said. "A fetid, rotten, coward of a man."

Whit looked surprised. "You're angry."

"Of course I am! You were children! And he was a grown man with money and power. What kind of a person manipulates children! His own children!"

"One who wants an heir."

"Heirs are nothing once you are a corpse," she snapped before realization dawned. "Wait. Heirs. You ran. With Devil. And Grace."

He nodded.

"Ewan became heir. A duke. *He betrayed you.*"

Another nod.

"And now? Where is he?"

"I don't know." The words were full of frustration.

Understanding flared. "But he's here. Close."

A muscle twitched in his jaw. "I won't let him hurt you. I will keep you safe."

And there it was. Her answer. "That's what this is; you keep me safe from him."

He met her eyes. "Until my dying breath."

She shook her head. "I am not afraid of him."

"You should be. I am."

"It is he who should be afraid of me," she vowed, fury coming hot and powerful. "I should like to have a good go at him with my bare hands."

His eyes went wide, and he huffed a little, surprised laugh. "You are very angry."

"Don't you dare laugh. This isn't amusing. Don't you see? They have taken enough from you. I shan't let him take from me, too." She was vibrating with rage, unable to control herself or the tears that came around the wicked knot in her throat. "I should like to find them and destroy them. I should like to take one of your very sharpest knives and seat it directly into their black hearts."

He reached for her. "Love, don't cry. It's in the past."

"It's not," she said, batting his hand away. "You've carried this for years. You'll carry it forever. And I *loathe* it. I loathe them. You cannot possibly think I would hear this story, about the man I love and the people *he* loves, and not wish to do severe bodily harm to everyone who thought to cross him."

He stilled. "Hattie."

She didn't notice. She was too far gone. "Ruining the lives of *children*? For a goddamn title? What utter nonsense. My only consolation is that your father, I am happy to say, is rotting quite miserably in hell."

"Hattie," he said, low and tight, as though he had something urgent to say.

"What?" she asked, her breath fast and furious.

"You love me?"

Heat flashed through her, followed by cold, and then pure panic. "What? No. What?" She paused, her breath coming harsh. "What?"

His beautiful eyes lit in amusement. "You said you loved me, Hattie. Do you love me?"

"I didn't say that." She hadn't. Had she?

"You did, but that's not the relevant issue at this point."

"What is?"

"Do you love me?"

"I . . ." She paused. "I hate your father."

He smiled. "Well, he is dead. So you win on that score." He reached for her then, pulling her close.

"Was it a very painful death?" She spoke to his shoulder, loving the way his arms wrapped around her. She was desperate for his touch—for the proof that he'd survived the hell of his childhood and stood here, healthy and strong.

He pressed a kiss to her temple. "Agonizing. Tell me you love me."

She sank into his heat, unable to resist the hard, welcome planes of him. He was so big, and she liked it far too much. She liked *him* far too much. Loved him more than she should, as he would never reciprocate. "No," she whispered.

He tilted her chin up to face him. "Please?"

"No." She shook her head.

He leaned down and kissed her, small and soft and perfect. "Why not?"

Because you don't love me back. The words he'd spoken in his rooms the other night were etched in her memory. *I can't love you.* She wouldn't say it to him. Not if he couldn't say it back.

"Because I don't want to be more of a burden."

"How would that ever burden me?"

"You've spent your whole life protecting people. Feeling responsible for them. Saving them. Giving of yourself, even when you needn't. And I don't want to be a part of that. I don't want to be another person you feel responsible to. I don't want to be another person you belong to, because you can't help yourself." She took a deep breath, wishing for calm. "I don't want to be a chore."

He stiffened, the cool breeze whipping around them, and for a moment Hattie thought that he might release her. She supposed that was reasonable. She supposed she should pull away from him, as she'd just made the very important point that she didn't want to be his burden.

But the truth was, she didn't want to pull away from him.

She wanted to stay with him.

Forever.

Because she loved him. Because she wanted to keep him safe.

His arms tightened around her, and she inhaled, filling her lungs with him—lemon and bay and his delicious warm spice. She closed her eyes and gave herself up to him, the mast at his back making an already sturdy, strong man even sturdier. Even stronger.

"The *Siren*," he said after an age. The words lost in the breeze coming off the river, but there, at her ear. "The ship is called the *Siren*."

She nodded. "It's the largest of the six you bought to punish me."

"Not to punish you." He pressed a kiss to her temple. Spoke to her hair. "You must believe I didn't do it to hurt you."

She wanted to. But none of it made sense.

Before she could ask, he was talking. "The Siren. Beautiful women who could make a man throw himself into the sea. Temptation incarnate. Singing men's deepest desires,

making the impossible seem possible. They could make you
believe your dreams had come true."

"And poor Odysseus, stumbling across the wicked women,"
she quipped. "If only he'd taken the long way round the is-
land."

He laughed, the low rumble a beautiful temptation. "Ah,
but Odysseus didn't stumble across them. He went looking
for them, knowing what he was in for." He looked down at
her, his amber eyes glittering in the lantern light. "Like all
the rest of us, he thought he could have a taste and not be
lost."

The story had Hattie thrumming with pleasure, fairly
vibrating with desire for him to touch her. A Siren in his
own right. And then he said, "It's an apt name for a ship of
yours."

"Is it?" she asked. "I rather thought it seemed the opposite." He tilted his head in silent question, and she said,
"I am not exactly known for my feminine wiles. I lack the
skill of temptation entirely, it seems."

He gave a little grunt. Acknowledgment? Disagreement?
It was impossible to know. "Hattie . . ." he said, her name
trailing off into a low growl. "You cannot possibly think that.
I've never in my life been tempted the way you tempt me."

"And you have a keen fondness for sweets," she quipped.
He didn't laugh. "It's the truth."

"That's very kind." She smiled, though she didn't feel
it. "But you didn't cede to it, and so you'll certainly allow
that I could be a better temptress. And I've leagues to go
before I approach Sirenhood." She laughed, small and self-
deprecating. "No man will ever toss himself into the sea for
a shot at good old Hattie."

"That's bollocks," he said, and there was something in
his growl that she'd never heard before.

"Odysseus had to have himself tied to his mast to avoid
the temptation of the Sirens. Tighter and tighter, until he

was bleeding from the ropes and screaming for his men to release him, so he could get to them. They tempted him to *death*." She stepped back, out of his arms, away from him, knowing she wouldn't be able to do battle with him again. Not now that she knew him. Not now that she wanted him so much. Not now that she loved him so much.

She would lose her boats, and she would lose her business.

But that seemed minuscule compared to losing him. *And she'd never even had him.*

She met his eyes and said, to herself as much as to him, "I couldn't even tempt you to pleasure."

She turned to leave, to find her way off this boat, away from him. But he came for her, her name on his lips, his fingers capturing hers and spinning her back as he caught her face in his hands and kissed her, long and lush and frantic, as though he was afraid that if he didn't, she might disappear forever.

Hattie gasped at the sensation, and he pulled her tighter, stealing the sound, licking over her lips and claiming her mouth in long, slow, lovely sweeps until her knees were weak and she was loose in his arms and drunk with him. Only then did he release her lips—without releasing her—trailing kisses over her cheek to her ear, where he said, hot and devastating, "You tempted me. You have tempted me every second since I woke in your carriage, tied in knots." He bit her earlobe hard enough to sting, then sucked on it until she clung to him. "You've tempted me to pleasure a thousand times. I've wanted to strip you of your clothes a thousand times. To lay you naked under the sun and the moon and the stars and worship you until we've both forgotten our names."

She was wild with the words. With the way they set her aflame. "I thought you didn't want me. I thought you didn't care . . ."

He bit her neck this time, a sharp punishment chased

with the pleasure of his slow tongue. "Lack of want does not leave a man hard for days."

"Were you?" She swallowed, simultaneously embarrassed and thrilled. "Hard for days?" *It wasn't possible.*

"I've been hard since the first time I heard your voice." One hand roamed down her side, pulling her to him by the waist. "Since the first time I touched your body."

She pulled back to look into his dark, promising eyes. "Really?"

He raised a brow. "Are you happy to hear of the affliction?"

"Yes."

He laughed at her instant reply. "Well then, yes, Hattie. I was hard with the thought of you, with being inside you, with coming inside you, with staying inside you forever. And I wanted you back so I could tell you just how much I wanted you, and just how little of a chore making love to you would be."

She smirked. "That sounds quite excellent."

"I am happy to have had a chance to delight you, my lady." He pulled her close for another kiss. "But you should know, Odysseus was a hero. And I am not." And another. "He wanted to resist. I don't. I want it all. I want every inch of you. It's all I've thought of since the moment you left. Since before." He pressed his forehead to hers. "Christ, Hattie. I want all of it. I would happily be tied to a mast if it meant I could have a taste of my deepest fantasies. Which all feature you."

She went hot at the words, at the vision they heralded, of this magnificent man, tied to the mast not three feet away. Her gaze flickered to it, and when she looked back at him, he groaned his pleasure. "Fuck, Hattie. You're imagining it. I can see it in your eyes."

She looked to him, knowing she should deny it. Instead, she said, "I am quite good with knots."

He exhaled a long "Ahhhh . . ." And then, impossibly, flashed her a dark grin. "Prove it."

Her eyes went wide. "You cannot mean . . ."

He pulled her close. "The other night, it was for you. But tonight. This . . . what if I told you it was for me?" The words became a low rumble. "Tie me to the mast, Siren; let me hear you sing."

Chapter Twenty-Three

It wasn't forever, she knew. She kept telling herself that as he backed away from her, without taking his eyes off her.

She followed without hesitation. *It wasn't forever*, she reminded herself, again and again, because this man—this magnificent man—was making her feel like forever might be possible. Like their past and her family's actions and the fact that he was in the way of all of her dreams didn't matter in the least, because he was about to let her take her pleasure in ways she'd never imagined.

Never imagined, because she'd never even known such a man, such a moment, was possible. But they *were* possible. They were possible right now, as he stripped his greatcoat away with a lack of care, letting it fall to the deck.

She cast a look about the ship, grateful for the lowered center deck and the darkness of the docks, emptied of people that night. And still, she said, "We could be seen."

"Unlikely, as someone has cleared the docks for this particular temptation." He dropped his topcoat at his feet, revealing his knives, the leather holster crisscrossing his vest and the lawn shirt beneath. Unable to stop herself, Hattie reached for him; he froze as her fingers traced the leather straps.

"You're missing one." He stiffened, and she wondered where he'd left it. Why. But there would be time for that later. Now, there was only time for this. She met his gaze. "Let me?"

He sucked in a breath as she stroked along the wide band crossing his torso to work at the brass buckle there with a firm, sure touch, as though she'd done it a hundred times before. She'd certainly dreamed of doing it a hundred times before. When it was done, she slid the straps from his broad shoulders and down his strong arms, and settled the weapons carefully at their feet.

She stepped back, assessing him, and he swore in the darkness. "Hattie, you look like you've plans for me."

She lifted her eyes to his. "In fact, I do."

He exhaled harshly. "Make haste, love."

She came forward and pulled his shirt from his trousers, loving the way he moved with her, helping, his muscles flexing with pleasure at every brush of her fingers. He took it from her hands, pulling it over his head and dropping it to the deck, and reached for her, pulling her in for another kiss. She gave herself up to it, her hands roaming down over his chest, her palm sliding flat along his skin until his stomach muscles tightened beneath her touch and he hissed his desire.

She nipped at his full bottom lip and pulled back. "Aren't you cold?"

"I'm hot as the fucking sun," he said, hauling her in for another kiss. "Now, about those plans . . ."

She laughed and slid her fingers through his own, lifting them over their heads, to a hook on the mast, where the trailing ends of the ropes that worked the mainsails were neatly coiled. She didn't have to tell him to clasp that hook. Didn't have to tell him to keep his hands there. Not even when she backed away from him.

"Where are you going?" he growled, not liking the way she pulled away from him.

Hattie smiled, circling the mast until she found what she was looking for, a length of rope that had come unmoored since the ship had been docked. Returning to face him, close enough to feel his heat, she leaned up and wrapped the rope around his wrists, carefully, so it did not chafe even as she tied a perfect knot.

He grunted as she stepped away and he tested the bindings, his eyes coming to hers. "You like this."

"Very, very much." There was nothing not to like. He was the most beautiful thing she'd ever seen, all long limbs and thick muscles, the image of him making her mouth water—and the desire in his eyes making her ache to touch him again.

"Stop looking, Siren." She lifted her eyes to his. "It's time for you to take what you want."

She approached. "What do you want?"

"All of it." The response was instant. "I want everything you want."

She shook her head. "That's not enough. This is for you."

"Pleasing you is for me." He'd said it before, in his rooms. And she hadn't believed him. But tonight, she nearly did.

She stepped closer, no longer able to be apart from him. "What would the Sirens sing to you, Beast?" Her hand slid over his chest, her thumb stroking over the flat disk of his nipple. He sucked in a breath. She caught his gaze. Stroked again. Saw the flex of his jaw. She leaned in and pressed a kiss there, lingering, stroking, until he let out a harsh "Ahhh."

She smiled against his skin. "I like that."

"As do I."

Her hands stroked up his arms, then down, down over his chest and torso, over his smooth skin, brushed with soft hair, lower and lower, to his waist, where that hair disappeared beneath his trousers. She worked the first button there, then the second and third. "When I saw you the other night?" she said quietly. "I thought you might touch yourself here. For me."

A low rumble sounded in his chest.

She pressed a soft kiss to his broad chest as she worked his trousers open, and another as she pushed them down past his hips, revealing the hard length of him. His breath came in harsh pants when she reached for him, and then stopped altogether when she took the smooth length of him in her hand. "So hot," she said. "So hard."

"For you, love." The words were wrenched from him, followed by a low, thick groan when she rubbed her thumb gently over the broad head of him.

She smiled at his chest. "You like that."

He exhaled harshly. "I do."

She looked up at him. "What else do you like?"

He threw his head back against the mast, staring up at the stars. "All of it. My God, Hattie." She pressed another kiss to his chest, fisting him in her hand—down, then up again, until he cursed softly in the darkness. "I want to touch you."

She shook her head, licking over the nipple she'd missed earlier. "Not right now. I'm busy tempting you." Another stroke of her fist. "You like this."

"Yes."

"Tell me what else you like?"

His eyes opened and desire pooled deep in her at the look of him, wild with pleasure. "No."

She leaned up and kissed him, and he was ravenous, eating at her mouth with his own. When she pulled away again, he grated, "Untie me."

She smiled. "Do you think this was how Odysseus felt?"

"I don't care. Untie me. I want to touch you."

She shook her head, lowering her attention to the steel length of him in her hand. He looked, too, and they watched as she stroked him, over and over, until the ropes above them creaked with his resistance. Their sound, combined with the rhythm of their breath and the smooth slide of him, was enough to make Hattie ache. "You won't tell me?"

He bit back a groan. "What?"

"What you want?" She met his eyes.

He shook his head, but did not look away from her. "This is for you."

She smiled, feeling like a queen. "And if I told you that I, too, want it?"

His exhale burst from him like he was in pain, but she was already moving, sliding down his body, to her knees. "Fuck, Hattie," he said softly. "You don't have to—"

She smiled at the words, pressing a kiss to the muscle above his thigh that plunged in a V toward the straining length of him. "I liked this very much when you did it to me."

"So did I, love," he growled.

"Will you like it, too?"

"Yes." The word was a breath. "God, yes."

"May I?" she asked quietly.

He grunted, his hips moving toward her. A silent plea.

She opened her lips over the hard, straining tip of him, licking her tongue gently over him, gently, tentatively, uncertain what he would like. He pulled tight against the ropes, his back bowing at the touch, and he shouted her name in the darkness.

He liked it.

Hattie did, too. The feel and taste of him, the strength of him beneath her hands and against her tongue, and the pure, unmatched power he gave her. Hattie had never felt this way—so certain. So strong. So desired, it felt like he might do anything to have her.

It was need.

She took him into her, the salt and sweet of him like nothing she'd ever experienced as he talked from his place above her, this strong, silent man who seemed to only ever have words in the throes of pleasure. He whispered wicked words—words like *harder* and *deeper*—words like *tongue* and *suck* and *fuck, Hattie, just like that.* And she followed where he led, took him slow and deep, reveling in his pleasure. In her own.

She liked this.

She liked him.

She loved him.

He was pulsing against her tongue as she found a rhythm that made them both mad—and then he was making filthy promises, like *please, Hattie . . . more, Hattie . . . if you don't stop, I shall come . . .* but she didn't want to stop, especially not when he lost all words—every word but one.

"Hattie . . ." Again and again, over and over, until she, too, forgot everything else, and then he was giving himself over to pleasure, and to her, and, finally, to release, loud and unbridled and glorious, just them and the ship and the docks and the sky.

And when she released him, she was full of a single thought.

More.

More of this power, this pleasure, this partnership. She was greedy for it.

For him.

She opened her eyes and looked up at him, his eyes riveted to her, unwavering. Her heart pounded. "Untie me." The words were harsh and nearly broken, and Hattie wondered if she'd gone too far.

Was he angry?

"Now. Untie me." She scrambled to her feet, reaching for the knot, requiring her to get close to him. Close enough for him to dip his head and suck at the soft skin of her neck and send shivers through her. Close enough for him to scrape his teeth along the curve of her jaw. To sink his teeth into her earlobe before hissing, "I am going to make love to you, finally. Properly."

The sheer need in his voice had her fingers fumbling

at the ropes, her gaze flying to his, gone mad with desire. He thrashed against the bindings, wild, like the Beast for which he'd been named. And then he added, pure cold command in his voice, "Now."

"Yes," she said, breathless with want, but her fingers wouldn't work, and he was growling his frustration, and she was echoing him, and then she remembered . . . She pulled back and met his wild eyes. "You glorious man. You have knives."

She pulled one from the holster at their feet and in an instant he was free, his arms coming around her, the knife she'd used spinning across the deck—neither of them caring as he lifted her in his arms as though she weighed nothing, upending her balance—her whole world—until her back was against his clothes piled beneath them.

He kissed her lips, then down her neck before he loomed over her, the lantern casting him in golden light, his bare shoulders flexing and his hands working to pull her skirts up, up, up, until he found the slit in her pantaloons and met her eyes. "I like these undergarments less than the ones the other night."

She nodded.

"No more of them." And with a wicked rip, they were gone, and—

"Ohh," she sighed as he growled at her neck.

"So wet." His fingers sank into her and he met her eyes, watching her as he stroked deep. "I like that."

She smiled at the echo from earlier. "So do I."

"Mmm." He lowered his head to kiss her, long and slow, until desire pooled, setting her body aflame. She lifted her hips, meeting his strokes, and he sat back, watching her for a moment, "Show me how much." She did, meeting his beautiful amber eyes as they mapped her body, her movements. As they made her believe he wanted her as he'd said. Beyond reason. "You're so beautiful. I could watch you do that forever."

She thrust against his fingers, and he set his thumb to the straining bud nestled above them, rubbing once, twice, until she groaned. "Whit!"

He smiled, wolfish. "That's what it feels like when you touch me."

She cut him a look. "Do it again. So I can remember."

He laughed, low and deep, and did, the movement sending fire rolling through her like a tide. "My brazen, greedy beauty." He stroked deep, over and over, slowly and perfectly, wonderfully steady, until she was writhing against him.

And then he released her, and she gasped her displeasure. "Wait!"

"Mmm." He licked his fingers and leaned over her, kissing her long and slow. "No. You wait, now."

He reached for the laces on her dress, untying the ribbons and loosening the bodice, opening it to reveal her chemise and corset, undressing her carefully until she was bare beneath him and he could suckle the tip of one breast, and then the other, until she was hard and aching, and her fingers were tight in his hair. "Please, Whit. Please."

He kissed her again, lowering himself over her, blocking the cool breeze from the Thames with his impossibly warm body. "Please what, love?"

"You promised to make love to me." She spread her thighs, knowing she shouldn't. Knowing ladies didn't. Not caring. "Finally," she repeated his earlier words, loving the way he settled into her, the long, smooth length of him sliding through her, the tip of him notching just where she ached to be touched again. He groaned at the sensation, and triumph flooded her. "Properly."

He laughed, harshly. "I want to, love." He rocked against her again, and she sighed at the pleasure. "So much. I have never felt anything like the feel of you coming around me." Another slide. Another notch. Another gasp.

"Do it," she said, moving on the next slide, until he froze, the tip of him kissing her aching opening.

He cursed, low and thick. "Hattie. God. You *are* a Siren."

She lifted her hips, and they both groaned as the head of him slid inside her, just barely, just enough to tempt them both. She slid her fingers into his hair. "Now," she whispered. "Please, Whit. Now."

He gave it to her, sliding into her with a single, slow, sure press, no hesitation like there had been the first time, as though he knew she could take whatever he gave her. And she could. At least, she could take the sensation . . . but the pleasure . . . the feeling . . . the knowledge of what was to come . . . she wasn't sure that wouldn't make her mad.

"You are so hard," she said, when he was seated deep inside her, unable to keep the awe from her voice. "So full."

He bit her shoulder with a little growl. "Hard for you, love. Only for you."

She smiled. "Mmm."

He barked a little laugh. "I'll never get tired of the way you take your pleasure, love. Like you deserve it."

She met his gaze, bold and brazen. "I do deserve it."

He nodded. "You do. And all I want to do is give it to you."

She smiled. "You like it."

"I like you."

Her heart skipped. What a magnificent man. What a strong and decent and beautiful, magnificent man. Tears sprang, and he noticed—of course he noticed—and worry marred his brow. "Love, does it hurt? Should I—"

"No," she said, clutching his arms. "No. Don't you dare leave me."

He stilled.

"I . . ." She shook her head, unable to stop herself from whispering, "I love you."

He bowed his head at that, meeting her forehead with his. "I don't deserve it."

What a lie it was. Her hands came to the back of his neck, fingers sliding into his hair. "You do."

"I don't," he whispered. "But I'm taking it."

He began to move, and Hattie was lost in the long, lovely strokes that stole her breath and her thought, and all she could do was sigh his name. He watched her, reading her pleasure, altering his rhythm until everything fell away—the dock and the ship and the world beyond them. Beyond *him*.

He kissed her neck. The line of her jaw. Her lips. "My Hattie. My beautiful Hattie."

And she believed it, meeting a long stroke with a tilt of her hips, and sending a jolt of pleasure through them both. Their gazes met. "I liked that," she said, shy and teasing.

"Mmm. Let's see if we can find it again."

They did, the thrum of desire fading into laughter. Was this what it was like for everyone? Was it always so bright? Like the sun had risen and cleared out all the darkness?

"Hattie," he whispered. Her gaze snapped to his. "Tell me again."

You shall lose your heart.

He rocked into her. "Please."

Her heart was already gone. "I love you."

He thrust into her. "Again."

"I love you." She clung to him, and he reached between them, finding the straining bud just above where they were joined. "Yes. Whit."

"I can't wait much longer, love. I'm desperate to come in you."

"Don't wait," she said, his touch winding her tighter and tighter, sending her higher and higher. "Please, love. Please, don't wait."

"Again," he whispered. "Just once more."

"I love you." She gave him the words a heartbeat before she was lost to the pleasure, flying apart beneath him and the London sky, and she was crying his name and clinging to him as he worked her in a beautiful, undeniable rhythm, carrying her through one release, and then another, before he gave up his own with a low, loud groan, the most delicious sound she'd ever heard.

When they returned to the moment, their breath in harsh symphony, the river tide lapping against the side of the ship, Whit pulled her tight against him, turning to put his back to the deck and cover them with his greatcoat. He pressed a kiss to her temple and exhaled, long and lovely. "Beauty."

The word sent warmth through her, and she cuddled nearer to him.

He pressed a kiss to her shoulder. "I do not deserve you."

She smiled at the words. "I think you can agree that I am almost as much trouble as I am delight."

He did not reply, his broad, rough fingertips painting designs across her bare shoulder, soft and sure and mesmerizing enough to make Hattie forget where they were, and who they were, and all the reasons they could not be together. She tracked those movements, the slow slide of his fingers and the feel of his breath in her hair, slow and even, until her eyes became heavy, and she wondered what might happen if she fell asleep here, in his arms, on the riverfront.

And just as she decided that she didn't much care what would happen if she did just that, because he didn't seem to be interested in moving, either, he spoke, the words a soft rumble beneath her ear.

"Marry me."

Chapter Twenty-Four

$\mathcal{O}$f course he was going to marry her.

He'd been planning to marry her from the moment he stepped onto the damn ship and saw her standing on the raised prow, looking every inch a warrior, waiting to do battle. *His* warrior, waiting to take him as spoil.

As though he wouldn't go willingly into her arms. Especially after she'd told him she'd like to murder both his father and his brother. And capped the whole thing off perfectly by telling him she loved him.

She loved him.

If Whit never heard it again, he would remember that moment forever. When he took his last breath, it would be with Hattie's indignant fury in his memories, and *the man I love* in his ears.

She loved him, and that changed everything; it made her his, unquestionably.

And then she'd tied him to the mast and made him hers, after making him wild with desire and filling him with pleasure and satisfaction and calm certainty. For the first time in his life, Whit hadn't doubted. He'd known.

He was going to marry Henrietta Sedley.

Nothing had changed, and somehow everything had.

So it was unfortunate but expected that, when he suggested the idea, it was less of a question and more of a command, but he certainly hadn't expected what came next. He hadn't expected her to go still against him, as though the words had been a blow. And he hadn't expected her to lift her head slowly, moving the way one might around a rabid dog.

And he certainly hadn't expected her to say, simply, as though he'd asked her if she would like tea, "No."

What in hell?

"Why not?"

"Because I love you."

His breath caught at the words, the ones he'd wanted so desperately earlier, but he could not bask in the pleasure of them. He was too concerned about the rest. "Dammit, that's a reason to marry me, Hattie."

"Not if you can't love me back." She paused. "Not if you can't love me as your equal. Can you?"

Yes. No.

Not the way she wanted.

Goddammit.

Fear spread through him, hot and unpleasant. He knew what she meant by equal. He'd heard her proposal of partnership.

But if they were partners, he couldn't keep her safe—not from Ewan, and not from anything else.

If he loved her, he'd lose her.

She sat up in his silence, reaching for her clothes, and he hated that they were here again—her dressing and him feeling like he'd been smacked over the head with a tea service in a blow he absolutely deserved.

Coming to her knees, she tugged her skirts over her full hips and pulled the bodice around her before saying, quietly, "I don't wish to force the issue. I don't wish to be the person you maybe love. The one it takes thought to know you love." She paused. "I wish to be the answer that pours from your lips—no matter how stoic you are. I wish to be the person you cannot save for high days and holidays, because you want me by your side on all the other days."

She was too precious for the other days.

"I deserve that. Partnership. Equality. You taught me that." She gave him a little smile. "I know that's impossible. And so, no . . . I won't marry you."

There was such emotion in the words, sadness and resignation and honesty, as though she'd known these words long before she'd had cause to speak them. As though she'd been prepared for them. God, he hated the idea that she'd been prepared for them.

"Hattie." He stood, pulling his trousers up and finding his shirt, pulling it on over his head. "You don't understand."

She sighed and said, "I don't wish to be rivals. I wish to be . . ." She shook her head, and he loathed it. "I shall release the men tomorrow." She waved in the direction of his pocket. "I assume you have a watch to confirm it, but I imagine it is too late to bring all the hooks back to work tonight."

He extracted a watch, barely registering the warm metal that backed it as he read the time. "It's six minutes to ten."

She looked up from tightening the lacing of her bodice to look down the dock to the ship sitting lower in the water than all the others. "You should be half done with your unloading—all that ice on wagons trundling through the city."

"Not half. But you're not far off. Hattie—"

She cut him off. "I'll release them tomorrow," she said again.

"How did you do it? Lock them down?"

She smiled. "You're not the only one with loyal friends, Beast."

The moniker thrummed through him. "I believe that

without question." He wished she counted him among them. "It's not often someone calls me that without fear in the word."

"I am not afraid of you."

He knew that. And it gave him more pleasure than he could say. He cast about for the right words. "You have always been fearless. Always knowing what you want and how you intend to get it. Never allowing others to set you on a path." He paused, then told her the truth. "I have never had that fearlessness."

Her brow furrowed and he pressed on, shaking his head. "All I am is fear. I was forged in it. Made in the terror that one day, someone I love would face danger, and I would not be able to save them." He exhaled on a shuddering breath. "I can't keep you safe."

Her beautiful violet eyes did not waver. "Of course you can't." The words cut through him like a blade. "There is nothing fearless about me. I am scared *every* day. I fear the wide world and the way it stares at me and sneers at me and whispers about me when it thinks I cannot hear. I fear a life of half measures, full of shadows of emotions and hints of possibilities and a thousand things I might have had if only I'd reached a bit farther."

He shook his head. "That's not a life you'll ever have."

He'd make sure of it.

Tears sprang in her beautiful violet eyes, and an ache started in Whit's chest. *Why was she crying?* "There was a time when I wanted marriage, you know. When I wanted children and domestic idyll. Of course I did. It's what women are told we should want from birth. Our fathers tell us, and our brothers, and the world around us. Except, when you're like me—too loud and too big and with too many ideas— you can't have the dreams everyone insists you must have. Because they aren't really for you."

He resisted the urge to tell her to stop. He hated how she

qualified herself. Hated how she always made herself seem less, when she was so infinitely more.

But he understood those qualifications better than anyone.

Instead, he whispered, "Hattie," her name coming soft on his lips as he ran a hand over his chest.

She ignored him, pressing on. "It wasn't hard to convince myself I didn't want it—the marriage, the companionship. After all, plenty of women age into spinsterhood. Plenty of men remain bachelors. And I had a plan."

He nodded. "The Year of Hattie."

She smiled at him. "That's all a bit nonsense now, isn't it?"

I'll give you a year. I'll give you a lifetime.

She seemed to hear the thoughts, as though he'd spoken them aloud. "I don't want it from you."

The words stung.

"I learned to adapt. I learned to want the business and to want to be captain of my own fate. I learned to accept that I could not have it all."

But she could. He would make sure she had it all. She loved him, and he was willing to give her everything she wanted. The boats, the business . . . and all the bits she'd been told she could not have.

Before he could say it, she added, "And then you turned up." She shook her head. "You turned up and you threatened all the things I wanted. You threatened the business I'd helped to build—the one I'd planned to sustain. You threatened the future I'd so carefully planned out."

He shook his head. Not anymore. Had he not just offered it to her?

She looked at him and took a deep breath, then said, "But worse than all that, you made me want the rest. All the bits I told myself I had not wanted before. You made me want them. And not from just anyone. You made me want them from you." She paused. "Not instead of. In addition to. All of it. Every bit of life that I might have. Vibrant and wild and full of mornings in the Covent Garden market and evenings on the docks and nights in your beautiful rooms, surrounded by candles and books and cushions in every color."

She looked into the distance, where a lantern bobbed in the wind on the deck of the ship that held the Bastards' most recent shipment, and she added, so soft that the words were lost on the wind, "I know it sounds mad. Like the wild dreams of a girl with no sense. But it's not mad. I don't need protection from it. I need a partner for it. I want it all."

The words were not lost to Whit. He heard them. He heard them, and they rioted through him on a vision of her living that life. He could see Hattie's skirts billowing in the riverfront breeze, as she watched over the men and their hooks—the men she'd already proven adored her by the way she'd plucked them from his reach that night. And they would adore her still—they would look to her for guidance and for direction and she would reign over them like a queen.

Like *his* queen. Because he would be by her side. He would be at her back, keeping the wind at bay. And perhaps, in time, there would be children, too, learning to climb on their mother's boats and playing hide-and-seek in their father's warehouse—little girls with violet eyes, shouting down at him from the rigging, and boys with bright smiles and a taste for raspberry sweets and lemon ice.

He reached for her, pulling her to him, loving the way she came without hesitation, even now, even as she denied him the thing he wanted most in the world. "Take it then. All of it. I give it, freely. Everything you want."

Her eyes found his, the lantern light making them glitter. "I want love. And you cannot both love me and keep me locked away, precious and protected from the world. You cannot keep me safe and let me stand by your side."

The words froze him. How many times had he told himself that he could save the world if only he did not love it? He couldn't have another weakness. Not one that racked him with fear that he might one day not be able to protect her.

She was already enough of a weakness.

She'd already laid him low.

If he loved her—he'd never be free of his need for her.

Too late.

She shook her head and pulled away, out of his embrace. "I don't want any of it in half measures. Not the business, not the fortune, not the future. And certainly not you."

She stepped away, out of reach, wrapping her arms about her, and Whit's heart began to pound, his mind resisting the movement, self-loathing filling him to his core. She was protecting *herself*.

From him.

And he wanted to scream at the realization. He wanted to scream, and go to her, and take her in his arms and promise her everything she wanted. The whole life. Himself included. He would love her.

And they would face the world—Ewan—all of it—together.

Perfectly matched.

And in the realization—something else.

He moved toward her, marveling at her strength, at the way she held her ground, his brave, brazen beauty. He could see so much in her eyes. Doubt, yes, and concern, no doubt out of fear that he'd been an ass before, and what was to stop him now? But there was something more there. Something that lit when he moved toward her. Something that he recognized, because he felt it so keenly himself.

Hope.

But before he could give voice to it, before he could make his case, before he could beg her to give him a chance, before he could tell her he could learn, before he could tempt her with all the things she'd wanted . . . all the things *he* wanted . . .

An explosion cut through the night, setting the docks ablaze.

---

fore he could tell her he could learn, before he could tempt her with all the things she'd wanted . . . all the things he wanted.

An explosion, thunderous, mighty, settling the deck of the place.

Chapter Twenty-Five

Hattie watched him come for her, slow and deliberate, his eyes clear and a smile teasing at his lips, dreading his wonderful touch, his soft words, the promises she knew would tempt her to believe that he might be able to give her everything she asked. She steeled herself for whatever he was about to say, knowing that it would be impossible to resist him—this man she had come to love beyond reason— knowing he was about to touch her with soft strokes and warm kisses, and worrying she would not be able to bear it even as she wanted it *badly*.

But he didn't touch her as she expected. Instead, when the thunderous explosion rocked the docks, he flew toward her, his eyes filled with terror, knocking her down, rolling her mid-air, collecting her in his arms, and bearing the brunt of impact as they slid across the deck and into the side wall of the ship.

When they came to a stop, Hattie was immediately turning to face him. "Are you—"

His hands were everywhere, sliding over her arms and her torso, "You're not hurt?"

"No." She shook her head, her own hand against his

chest, feeling his heart thundering beneath her touch. "You shouldn't have done that. You'll have wicked splinters from the deck."

"You think I give a shit about splinters when you might have been—" He reached for her, pulling her closer, squeezing her tightly. "We have to get you out of here."

"What's happened?" She pulled away and looked up to the sky, where sparks floated into the night. Shouts rang out from down the dock. "Something's been attacked."

"Stay here." He moved across the deck like lightning, fetching his holster and strapping it on before turning to investigate. He assessed the situation in seconds. "The shipment."

Cold dread settled. "My brother?"

He did not meet her eyes. "No. Mine."

Her eyes went wide. "Ewan."

He came for her, reaching down to catch her hand and help her up. "We've got to get you out of here."

"Absolutely not." Shock flared. "I'm going to help."

"No." He grasped her hand and pulled her to the gangway, and down the slip to solid ground, where men were already pouring into the docks to stem the fire. "If he's here, you're in danger."

Hattie looked toward the ship burning in the berth. "How many men?"

He wasn't paying attention, too focused on the crowd amassing nearby. "What?"

"How many men were on the ship?"

He turned to her, met her gaze. "I don't know." He grabbed a boy running by, nearly lifting him from his feet. "Brixton."

"Beast! Yer a'right!" The boy's eyes went wide. "Sarita said she saw you comin' down 'ere, but ye didn't leave."

"I'm all right, bruv," he said, and Hattie saw the relief in the boy's eyes. Understood it. She would have come running for him, too. "Get gone. 'S not safe here."

"No, boss." Brixton looked to the boats and lifted his chin. "I'm goin' to help."

"Who's on the watch?"

"It's ten o'clock, Beast," the boy said, and she heard the fear in his voice. "Yeah?"

Whit stiffened, and she saw the hesitation in his frame. Saw him resist something primal. "Yeah. Get in there. But if anything seems wrong, you get out."

The boy smiled, reckless and far too young. "Anyfin' like a Derry and Tom?"

Whit cuffed the boy on the chin at the Cockney slang for bomb. "Yeah. Like a Derry and Tom."

He released the boy and turned for Hattie, grabbing her hand and pulling her away from the crowd. "Come."

Away from the fire.

"What? Why?" He didn't respond, pulling her into a narrow passageway leading up between a tavern and a sail shop. She tugged at her hand, but his grip only grew tighter. "Where are you taking me? What does ten o'clock mean?"

He didn't slow. "On nights when we're not moving cargo, the guard changes at ten."

Understanding, quick and painful. "Double the number of men at the ship."

He grunted.

"Oh, my God, Whit. I did this. I locked up the hooks. If I hadn't, this wouldn't have happened."

He didn't turn back. "Or we'd have two dozen dead men down there instead of whatever we have."

She stopped, digging her heels into the cobblestones. "We have to go back."

"No." Unequivocal.

She straightened her shoulders. "I am responsible for whatever happened there tonight. I shall help. I *can* help."

He cursed under his breath and looked up at the sky. "You're not going back there. There's been an explosion large enough to decimate a hauler, I've got a hold full of ice and contraband aflame and Ewan has already said he's willing to hurt you to get to me."

"He shan't hurt me with half the docks watching!" she said. "Let me make it right!"

"These are not your sins, Hattie," he said. "You're going home."

"Of course they're not my sins!" she shouted. "You think I don't know that? But this is my world, too! This is my turf, too! If you are worried, I am worried. If you are there, I am there. And let Ewan come. We shall face him together. *Together.*"

He turned away from her, raising a hand to flag down a hack. "We will do no such thing. I don't want you near him. He'll come for you to punish me. And I can't have that."

"Why?"

"Because I took the only thing he ever cared about from him."

"What? What could possibly be more valuable than his brothers?" She thought back to the docks. "Than the lives of the men and women who work for them?"

"Not what. Who."

Understanding came swift and certain. "*Grace.*"

"Clever girl," he said softly.

The hack pulled to a stop nearby, its horses huffing in the night. The driver looked to the orange light flickering over the rooftops, then to the knives strapped to Whit's chest, nervously. "All right, milord?"

"Better when you get her far from here," Whit growled as he pulled the door open.

"No," she said, fury raging. "I am not leaving you here to face an inferno and a madman and whatever else is down there."

He met her eyes, a small smile on his lips. "You plan to fight my battles for me, love?"

She shook her head. "Never *for* you. *Alongside* you."

He smiled, sad. "Ever my warrior."

He wasn't going to let her. He was going to put her into

this carriage and be off to a fight that could leave him destroyed. Worse. "Don't do this. Believe in me."

Believe in us.

"You don't have to protect me."

The words seemed to unlock him, filling him with determination. Lengthening him. Broadening him. Steeling him. "I do, though. It's all I must do. You've asked me why I carry two watches," he said, quick and stern, as though he was giving her directions to an impossibly difficult location. And perhaps he was. "I am never late. I am never late, because I was too late to save my mother. She was dead when I arrived, of whatever plague had ripped through the rooming house that week. Dead and alone. And I couldn't protect her."

"Oh, no . . ." Hattie said softly, reaching for him, her fingertips brushing the leather straps of the holster that caged him. The weapons he kept close.

"But I can protect you," he went on. "I can protect you forever. I can keep you away from my brother. And I can keep you away from all of this."

"This is part of it!" she said. "It's part of the world I wish. Part of the life I wish. *With you.*" She shook her head. "Don't you see? I'd rather have a night with you than a lifetime without you."

He shook his head. "No. I'll never see you into danger."

Tears sprang, frustrated and angry. "You don't get to decide. I do."

"Goddammit, this isn't the Year of Hattie anymore, this is your life! This is my sanity!" He closed his eyes. "Please. Get in the fucking hack. Now."

She narrowed her gaze. "Make me."

And he did, the wretched man, lifting her from her feet like she was a sack of grain and tossing her into the conveyance. Making sure she was unbalanced enough that she wouldn't be able to stop him from closing the door.

She heard the thump of his fist on the side of the hack, barely sounded before the wheels were in motion. Outrage and fury flared as Hattie sat up, looking out the window, barely able to make out the shape of him, running back to the docks. Back to danger.

She banged on the roof of the hack. "Stop this carriage right now!"

"Can't help!" came the muffled reply from the driver. "The man gave me a quid to take you to Mayfair!"

"A quid to abduct me, you mean!"

"If I was abductin' you, lady, I wouldn't be takin' ye to Berkeley Square!"

She didn't even live in Berkeley Square, but that was a moot point. "I'll pay you to stop!"

Hesitation. "Seems like whatever was going on at the docks wasn't for you, luv!"

So now the hack driver had decided to find his sense of right and wrong. "Argh! Men!" Hattie pounded on the roof of the carriage. She didn't need protection from this stranger or from the man who'd just tossed her into his carriage. Dammit, hadn't it been Hattie who'd tossed Whit *out* of a carriage all those nights ago?

"Dammit, dammit," she screamed, moving to the door, watching the buildings sail past. She'd never felt as useless as in those moments as the carriage raced from the docks, where Whit and his men raced against water and flame.

She belonged there. With him. Alongside him.

Marry me. Join me.

Had he honestly believed that if she agreed to his offer, she wouldn't stand with him? Did he not see that being a wife meant being a partner? Being an equal? Did he not know that if he was going to share his life with her, she wanted all of it? Even this bit?

Especially this bit.

The carriage decelerated, and she looked out the window. They were coming up on a collection of taverns where people flooded the streets, making high speed impossible . . . now was her chance.

The hack slowed to a crawl, and Hattie measured the curve in the street. She took a deep breath and pushed open the door, closing her eyes and leaping.

She tumbled, a heavyset black man with a wide-brimmed hat and a big beard breaking her fall with a loud "Oof!" followed by a "Christ, gel! What in hell would possess you?" And then . . . "Wait! Yer the Sedley gel. The one who bought up the hooks tonight."

She nodded, already righting herself and turning to return to the docks in question. "Hattie Sedley."

He smiled. "Bollocks of brass, goin' in against the Bastards."

"Not against," she said. "*With*. I simply needed to get their attention."

He laughed, full and deep, and said, "Beast's lady, then?"

"If he'd come to his senses," she tossed over her shoulder, already leaving him, heading back to the docks, as quickly as she could.

She wove her way in and out of the streets and alleys of the neighborhood until she landed back where she'd come from, where Whit had left her. Turning a corner, she passed through the crowd that had assembled outside a popular drinking hole on one end of the dock, tankards in hand and each man with a theory on what had happened a hundred yards away. "I heard the Bastards are fighting each other. Beast don't like Devil's bride." What utter nonsense.

"That ain't it. I heard another group wants in on the ice business." Hattie nearly laughed at that, as though the trade in frozen water was cutthroat enough to involve explosives.

"Must be somefin' to do with Sedley payin' the dockworkers not to work tonight. Too much of a coincidence—no one local on the dock to get 'urt when a damn bomb sinks the Bastards' cargo."

"Tide's out," came a reply. "There ain't no sinkin' to be done. Ice'll just slide out the hold and melt into the river."

"Winter freeze'll come early this year," came a loud masculine guffaw.

Hattie rolled her eyes, having no patience for the gawkers and gossipers who knew nothing but seemed to enjoy fabricating plenty. She looked to one of the quieter observers. "Has anyone been hurt?"

"Three men taken to the Bastards' surgeon in the Garden. Beast refused to let the dockside butcher touch 'em."

Of course he had. Whit would have rather cut off his own arm than let a leech with a bloody apron and a sturdy saw see to his men. Hattie increased her pace, eager to find him. She could see the ship now, lit by the flames still burning but now under better control—managed by a line of men working in unison—lifting river water by the bucketful, working to combat the fire that threatened the whole dock. The men moved quickly and with steady control, as though they'd done this precise thing a dozen times before. More.

And they had. The landing saw its fair share of gunpowder and rifle ships—and fire. Confident in the men's work, she pushed forward, aiming for the burning ship. For the man she loved.

"Lady Henrietta?"

She turned at the sound of her name as a man stepped from a doorway in the darkness, tall and fair. Recognition flared. He was the Duke of Marwick—recognizable to any self-respecting spinster in the *ton*, even unshaven and wildeyed. Hattie did not for a moment believe that this particular duke was simply taking a late night stroll on the London docks, no matter how mad society thought him to be.

Rage came tight in her throat and she slipped her hand into her pocket, feeling her pocketknife there, heavy and warm. "Ewan."

Surprise flashed in his eyes. "He told you about me."

"He told me he had another brother who was a monster." She tightened her fist on her knife. "You look the part."

A shout came from down the dock, and she looked to it,

two men racing past, unaware of the two conversing in the darkness. Returning her attention to Ewan, she said, "This is your doing."

"Yes." His words were devoid of emotion.

"And it's not enough? Three men to the surgeon? Another shipment destroyed? Now you think to what . . . come for me?"

"Do I?"

"Isn't that what you do? Threaten your brothers and their livelihoods and their future?"

"And you are Saviour's future?"

The wind picked up, and Hattie's skirts billowed out around her. Her hair came loose from its pins. "I want to be," she said, and there was no sorrow in the words. Only fury. "I have spent a great deal of my life fighting for the things I desire—and the things I deserve. And now I fight for *my* future, and you threaten that, too. And for what?" She paused, watching him. "Some cheap revenge."

He stepped toward her, his amber eyes—at once so familiar and so foreign—flashing. "There is nothing cheap about my revenge. They took everything from me."

She scowled at him. "They took nothing from you. They built a kingdom from nothing—a world of good people who know your brothers' kindness and generosity and loyalty. Loyalty of which you can only dream. And you . . ." she spat. "You have tried to strip them of it. And I won't have it."

Surprise flashed. "You won't?"

The wind whipped her skirts about her legs as she came to her full height. "I won't. Whit has spent a lifetime worrying about what might happen when you come for him. And here is the truth of it—you would do well to heed it—it is you who should worry. Because if you harm them, these good men with good hearts and strong minds, *I* will come for *you*. And there is no past between us to keep you safe."

"Saviour always lived his life as though name was destiny," he said with a little laugh. "And here you are, protecting him. Like a guardian angel."

"I think you'll find I'm far less angel than I am warrior." She extracted her knife and took a step toward the awful man. "It is time for you to go, Ewan."

His gaze fell to the blade, and he reached into his coat, extracting one of his own. No. Not his own. Whit's. The missing blade she'd noticed earlier. She looked up at the duke, their enemy, fear rioting through her. And still, fury won out. "That doesn't belong to you."

"Does it belong to you?" He flipped it in his hand, offering her the hilt. She reached for it. Took it in hand, and he let it go. "Perhaps you are a gift to all of us."

She heard hope in the words. A plea. Something else. "I can see why he loves you."

In that moment, Hattie realized that Whit did love her. And she wasn't leaving these docks until he told her. And this man was in the way of it. "Then you can see why I won't let you take that from him."

"Tonight"—he looked down the docks, past the empty boats to the massive cargo ship being unloaded—"this . . . none of it matters to them."

She shook her head. "You taught them that. Money does not make power. Title does not make might. And none of it—none of it makes happiness."

"Not like love."

There was a truth in the words, clear and sad, and if it had been anyone else speaking them, Hattie would have ached with sympathy for him. But this man had spent a lifetime threatening the man she loved, and he could sod off. "Do you doubt my willingness to put a knife in you if you come for him again?"

"No."

"My ability to do it?" She fairly itched to do it.

"I told him to give you up," Ewan said. "Threatened to take you from him if he didn't."

The confession was unexpected and somehow utterly obvious. Of course Whit had pushed her away. He would have done anything to protect her. *Her savior.* Her gaze narrowed. "That was misjudgment."

He nodded. "He wouldn't do it."

She shook her head. "No. *I* wouldn't. You aren't a specter to me. You aren't my past. And you aren't my future. I don't fear you. And I will never give him up."

Silence fell between them. And then, "You remind me of her."

Grace. "From what I hear, that is a great compliment."

"He told you about her?"

"Of course," she said softly. "She is his sister."

Something shifted in Ewan at that—something that Hattie could not explain except to say that he seemed to settle. "She was their sister," he said. "But she was my heart." His eyes flew to hers, and in the wild depths she saw his aching sadness. "He had a life with her, and now a life with you, and I had nothing."

"You chose nothing."

He looked to the docks, his gaze unfocused. "I chose *her*."

Hattie did not reply. She didn't have to. He was lost to thought. To *memory*. And after a long moment, he looked to her—his amber eyes so like Whit's, and so empty of Whit's passion—and said, "It's over."

Hattie let out a long breath. Relief coursing through her. "You won't come for him again."

"I thought I would know . . ." he said, trailing off. Then, again, the words rougher than before. More broken. "It's over."

The Duke of Marwick turned from her and walked away, as though he'd never been there at all. She watched him leave, tracking his movements until he was swallowed by the night and she could no longer see him.

She turned back to the docks, slipping the knife in her palm into her pockets, and made for the ship where men worked seamlessly to salvage what they could from the cargo of the ruined ship. Men she knew would stand shoulder to shoulder with Whit and Devil and the Bareknuckle Bastards any time.

She marveled at the long line of them, doing their back-breaking work, heaving ice and cargo, and there, silhouetted by the flames, and wielding a hook like he'd been born with it in hand, their leader. The man she loved, leading his troops.

A single word coursed through her as she traced his strong, broad form with her gaze.

Mine.

He disappeared, presumably down into the hold, to save more of the wreck, and Hattie made for him, crossing the long, barren dock to the ship, a hundred yards away, more resolute than ever.

She didn't want the boats; she wanted him. She wanted him, and she wanted this life, next to him, on this burning dock. She wanted to be next to him on that burning boat. And if he refused to have her there, she would battle for him, reminding him every day that she did not need a protector. She only needed him.

She increased her pace, eager to close the distance between them and tell him just that.

Hattie had already crossed to the docks, walking close to the line of empty ships when she heard the shout behind her. Turning, she saw Ewan running toward her. She slid her hand into her pocket, palming Whit's onyx blade, wondering what his enemy was going to do, prepared to sink it into his thigh, his shoulder, his chest—whatever was required.

He hadn't reached her when the second explosion detonated—breaking the ship behind her into pieces, and sending them both flying.

Chapter Twenty-Six

The ship might be aflame topside, but below deck there were more than seventy tons of ice and cargo still salvage-able in one way or another, assuming the men moved quickly.

Once he'd been certain Hattie was being safely ferried away from the docks, Whit had returned to the ship. Nik had arrived with the promise that Devil was on his way, ostensibly to assess the damage, but Whit knew better than anyone that the damage to the ship was irreparable. The contents, however, were a different story.

After checking on the men who'd been sent to the Rook-ery infirmary, Whit had collected a heavy iron box hook and set to work on the line of men who were working in unison, heaving crates up and passing them from man to man, until they'd saved as much cargo as they could. The men had come quickly from the taverns along the docks, forgetting that Hattie had paid them not to work that night—knowing that there was a difference between a deal made for rivalry and a tragedy requiring assistance.

When he'd assessed the hold, finally, he'd acknowledged a bit of loss—several cases of brandy had been smashed in the reverberations of the explosion, but Whit had been impressed with the security of the cargo.

He'd heard a second explosion in the distance while below deck, the sound tearing a wicked curse from him. The report had come quickly. Another boat. An empty one. Nothing that required his attention. Tonight, this hold required his attention, and quickly—before the ice, which had been carefully packed and cared for on the Oslo end of the journey, melted enough to make it difficult to move the contraband.

The Bastards smuggled inside ice, so as not to risk discovery—not even on a night like tonight, when it seemed every alternate plan should have been in play.

Instead, Whit worked at the head of the line, slowly and methodically, deciding which blocks were moved, which stayed, and which cargo left the hold when. He'd be damned if he'd see their carefully imported, untaxed product suddenly compromised by too much fear and the same amount of speed.

He hooked two crates of bourbon in quick succession, passing them along the line before collecting a block of ice, and then a second. The man working alongside him groaned under the weight of the heavy blocks.

"Those are clear enough to sell," Whit said of the ice blocks, raising his voice to make sure Nik heard him from her place deep in the hold. "And there's a half dozen here that are the same—untouched by the explosion."

The Norwegian nodded, then smirked in his direction. "And would you like them to be sold?"

"No."

She grinned. "You save them for raspberry ices. How sweet."

The children of the Rookery got sweets when there was ice in port. Whit saw no reason why that should change because of the evening's disaster.

"Tell me, Nik," he intoned as he hefted another block. "Does the Lady Nora have a sweet tooth?"

The men on the line laughed at the question, especially when Nik threw Whit an insulting hand gesture. Whit smiled and returned to his work, letting the rhythm of the line lull him into calm. Into thoughts of Hattie. He wondered if she preferred lemon or raspberry ice; imagined the sounds she would make if he fed her the sugary treat. If he dropped a spoonful of it between her breasts. How long he'd be able to resist the urge to lick it from her skin.

He grunted as he moved a cask of ale, passing it down the line.

I want it all.

Hattie's strong, sweet voice, demanding everything she desired. Everything she deserved. Insisting that he be her equal partner or nothing at all.

Christ, he wanted it, too.

But tonight this world had almost killed her, and he hadn't been able to protect her. Ewan had come for them— Whit had no doubt his brother was behind the explosion— but even if the lookouts tracked him and found him, threats would keep coming. The threat was the wide world. And Whit knew, without question, that though he could barely conceive of a life without Hattie, he absolutely could not live without her safe.

He'd been right to push her away. To put her in the hack.

Don't do this. Believe in me.

He resisted her words, still echoing through him.

You don't have to protect me.

Of course he did. He had.

"Beast!"

The call came from a distance, from above the hold, and he didn't reply, not wanting to leave his work, the strain of the casks and crates burning his muscles and keeping the pain of sending Hattie away at bay.

Devil dropped down into the hold behind him nevertheless, pushing his way through the line. "Beast," he repeated, and that's when Whit heard the strange tenor of his brother's voice. Familiar. Unsettling.

Something had happened. Something had gone terribly wrong.

He turned to face Devil, the taller man's lean face all angles in the lamplight, cheeks shadowed, eyes focused in the darkness. Devil was in shirtsleeves—as was Whit—but he was missing his cane sword. The loss of it was like the loss of a limb, and Whit noticed instantly. He stayed his movement, coming to his full height in the low-ceilinged space. "What's happened?"

A moment, then Devil shook his head.

Whit cursed in the darkness. "Goddammit." It could only be news of the men they'd sent to the infirmary earlier. "Abraham? Mark? Robert?" They'd all been conscious—none of them with wounds that had struck Whit as terminal. But things did not always work out the way they seemed. "Did someone not make it? Which one?" He stepped toward his brother. "I shall tear London apart by the bricks until we find Ewan. He dies."

It never got easier. How many had they seen die? Dozens? A score? A hundred? When one grew up on the streets of Covent Garden, death was a part of life, like violence and illness, but it never got easier.

"Who is it?" he asked again.

Devil shook his head, his eyes filled with something awful. Something Whit didn't understand. What then? What else could it—

"Whit." Devil wasn't angry. It wasn't frustration in his words, thick with the accent of their past. Thick with sorrow. "Bruv. It's Hattie."

Whit stilled, his brother's face coming into sharp focus. Full of sadness. Fear, too. Fear of what might happen when Whit understood everything. And something else—fear that it might one day happen to him.

And that fear—tinged with the hot, panicked relief of a man who had dodged a bullet—brought the truth. Whit froze, understanding crashing through him. A third explosion. One that did more damage than the others.

Nik came toward him, horror on her pale face. "Beast," she said softly. Entirely un-Nik-like.

He dropped the hook to the floor of the hold, his step toward Devil the only movement, no one working, everything stopped, like time. Like his heart. "No."

Devil nodded. "The boys found her on the docks, a hundred yards from here."

Whit looked over his shoulder to where Nik stood sentry, several feet away, her brow furrowed. He shook his head. "It's not her. I put her in a hack."

He'd paid the driver. Sent her to Mayfair.

Sent her away, not wanting her here. In danger.

Protecting her.

And she'd begged him to stay. *Believe in me.*

If he had—she would have been with him. *Safe.*

"She came back," his brother said. "The second explosion must have—"

Whit slid a hand into his pocket, running a thumb over the pocket watch within. His warrior wouldn't have waited half a block before finding a way back if she wanted to be here.

She'd found a way back. To stand beside him. His equal.

Would you know if she were dead?

Ewan's question the night he'd threatened Hattie. The night he'd promised to take her from Whit if he didn't give her up.

Would you know if she were dead?

He'd know. He'd know that the whole world was upended. He'd know the light had gone out. He'd know.

He shook his head. *He'd know.* "Where is she?"

"They're bringing her to the surgeon."

The surgeon.

"I have to get to her." He couldn't be late this time.

Devil nodded. "Yes. But—Whit . . ."

Fuck that. He wasn't losing her. Not now. Not ever. "No."

No. Whatever his brother was trying to say, Whit wasn't hearing it. He was already tearing out of the hold to get to Hattie.

HIGH ON THE rooftops above the docks, the third Bareknuckle Bastard crouched low, watching as her brother exited the hold of the burning ship, fresh with the news that his love was lost. She saw the fear in his gait, the determination, too, the way his expression flattened into stoic, strong resolve, as though he could go up against death.

As though he would, if it meant keeping her.

She watched as he landed on the firm ground, his mind fracturing just as his life would if Henrietta Sedley didn't survive, into two halves—like a mast in a storm—before and after Hattie.

Grace watched, and she ached for Beast, and for his love.

She knew what it was to lose the most important person in the world.

She knew what it was to have him ripped from you.

And she knew what it was to survive it.

But she was through with mere survival. And she was through with the boy she'd lost—the boy they'd all lost—toying with them for sport.

She came to her full height, her long coat billowing out behind her, hat low over her brow. "This ends now," she said to the pair of women who stood at her side. "As it should have ended years ago."

Her lieutenants stood in silent sentry, watching the tableau below, blades at their belts. Grace pointed to the darkness, to the doorway where the wounded man had dragged himself into hiding after the blast. Where he'd watched as the Bastards' lookouts had collected Hattie.

"Bring him to her." He couldn't—

He'd waited for a ghost for twenty years.

Tonight, the Duke of Marwick got his wish.

SHE WOULDN'T WAKE. So he kept vigil.

Whit didn't remember how he got to the infirmary, didn't remember the path he'd taken, whether he'd come via hack or on foot. Didn't remember if he'd met anyone else along the way, nor how he got inside. Had he knocked on the door or kicked it in? Had he been led here? To this bed in a poorly lit corner of the main room of the Rookery hospital, where a single candle burned on a nearby table—the only thing that kept the darkness at bay?

It didn't matter.

None of it mattered but her.

Hattie—still as stone in the bed, eyes closed, chest barely rising and falling, as life and death battled for her. Life and death . . . and Whit.

He didn't remember seeing the doctor. Didn't remember whatever useless words he'd offered—some explanation of her lack of consciousness. Some reference to a blow to the head. Something about ice and swelling and the mysteries of the human brain.

Something about trauma.

Trauma, Whit remembered, as it coursed through him, too, as he stared at her, as he came to his knees by her bedside and took her cool hand in his own, bringing it to his lips to kiss it, memorizing the weight of it. The feel of it, the softness of it.

Someone brought him a chair, but he didn't use it. Whit had never thought much of God—but he knew what prayer looked like, and if staying on his knees would bring Hattie back, he'd stay there forever. And he did pray, in those moments, kissing her knuckles one by one, and willing her strong. Willing her fingers to tighten.

He prayed to God, yes, but mostly, he prayed to Hattie. And he prayed out loud, using all the words he could find, as though in giving them to her, he might keep her alive. It was a mad thought, but the only one in Whit's head, and so for the first time in his life, he talked . . . without thought, without knowing when he would stop.

Because he would talk forever if it meant he could keep her there, with him.

Kneeling by her side, looking down at her perfect, beautiful face, made gold in the candlelight, he told her all his truths.

He began with the most important one. "I love you."

Regret thrummed through him, opening a wide space between them, and he clung to her hand and refused to take his eyes from her as he repeated himself. "I love you, and I should have told you that before. I should have told you the night at the fights." He swallowed, fighting for words. "I should have told you before then—in Covent Garden when you went after my best broad-tosser and found the queen."

He paused, then, the words catching in his throat. "I found the queen that night, too. I found you, and I should have told you that I loved you. I should have told you how beautiful you are. I should have told you how I am laid low by your impossible eyes and your wide, wonderful smile." He closed his eyes and set his forehead to her hand. "I should like to make you smile again, love. I should like to make you smile every minute of every hour of every day for the rest of our life until you tire of it and I have no choice but to kiss it from your lips and give you respite. And I should like very much for that life to be so long that we grow old next to each other, rattling about in our home, with our children and grandchildren coming and going and rolling their eyes at how I never stopped being a fool over you."

His gaze tracked her face for movement, running over her full cheeks and her long nose and the twin slash of her brows—which rose and fell with every excitement she felt—a barometer of her emotion, now unmoving. Whit rubbed a hand over his face, panic and anguish running through him. "My brother nearly had to die before he realized how much he loved his wife . . . But this . . ." He didn't think he could bear it.

"I'd die a thousand times over to prevent this. To prevent you, here . . . I'd trade places with you in a moment. The world doesn't need me like it needs you. Who will buy up all the extra flowers in the market at the end of the day? Who will hold the loyalty of the London docks like you? Who will—" He swallowed around the knot in his throat. "Who will teach my daughters to tie a decent knot?" His voice cracked on the last, and he bowed his head to the bed, broken by the moment. "Christ, Hattie. Please don't leave me. Please don't go."

People came and Whit barely noticed—Devil and Felicity first, filled with concern, Felicity instantly going to her knees beside him, her strong hand firm on his arm. He didn't look at her. He couldn't look into the face of her worry. Instead, he stared into Hattie's face and said, quietly, "She's locked away."

Felicity's fingers squeezed his arm, strong and sure, but he heard the tears in her voice when she said, "No lock is unpickable."

But Hattie wasn't clockwork and steel. She was flesh and bone and love, and if Whit knew anything, he knew those were the most fragile of things, there and gone in an instant.

His brother approached, settling a hand on his shoulder. "The crew is outside, standing guard. Twenty of them, more by the minute."

Keeping vigil.

"They should be moving cargo."

"You let me worry about that. They should be here. With you."

"They don't know her." He turned to his brother. "*You* don't know her."

Devil's eyes flashed. "They know *you*, Beast. They know the man who has cared for them from the start. And they cannot wait to know the woman he loves." He cleared his throat. "Neither can I."

Whit looked away, back to Hattie, racked with emotion. "I do love her."

Felicity's grip tightened.

She didn't say, *And you shall have her.*

She didn't say, *And love is enough.*

Because it wasn't true. None of it was a guarantee.

"I'm giving her the business."

"Of course," Devil said.

He did not look away from her hand in his, on her bare fingers. He lifted them to his lips, pressing kisses on her knuckles again, bribing her. "Wake up, love. I'll give it all to you. I'll prove it to you. Just wake up and let me love you."

Silence fell in the wake of the whispered words, stretching for long minutes until Devil said, "And what of you? Will you give yourself to her, as well?"

"I'll never not be hers."

Felicity pressed a kiss to his shoulder at that and stood, Devil coming forward to help her up, to pull her into his arms and hold her tight, as though he could ward off whatever evil had come for Hattie that night.

Whit met his brother's bleak gaze over his sister-in-law's head. "Don't ever let her go."

Minutes, hours, days later—time marked by nothing but Hattie's shallow breaths—dark night gave way to blinding sun, and the room revealed itself, clean and happy. The doctor's wife came and went, leaving food that Whit didn't eat and tea for Felicity and Devil, who stood watch over the other three victims of the attack—legs set, wounds bandaged, expected to mend.

And still, Hattie slept, her hand limp in Whit's.

And still, he spoke, soft and constant, the words like the tide.

The door burst open and Nora rushed in, Nik at her heels. Nora flew to Hattie's side, next to Whit, tears in her eyes. "Hattie—no!"

Guilt rioted through him, worse for her friend's anguish. "I sent her away," he confessed. "I tried to get her away from it."

She looked to him, a watery smile on her face. "Hattie would never have allowed that. She knows what she wants and will do whatever it takes to get it. She leapt back into the fray to fight alongside you. Because she wants you." She reached for him, pressing her hand against his cheek, rough from a day without a shave. "She came back for you because she loves you."

Loves.

Whit held on to the present tense in the word.

Nik turned away from the moment, to face Devil and give the most recent report. "The explosions—they were set by the bastard who worked with Sedley."

"Russell," Nora spat. "Pure garbage."

"We've got him," Nik added. "He claims Ewan paid for one of the blasts. Says the second was free."

"I shall see to him," Devil said, his voice cold with menace.

"I should like to watch," Nora said as the doctor entered and she ceded her spot.

He lifted Hattie's wrist, tracking her pulse. "It's strong and steady." He looked to Whit. "She might yet live."

"Good God," Nora said, shocked by the forthright words.

Whit cursed and turned away from him. "If that's all you can offer, get out."

Devil stepped forward. "Beast, let the man work. You know he's the best in London. Would you rather he left her to the surgeons on the docks?"

"I would never do that," the doctor said, meeting Whit's

eyes, understanding in his clear blue gaze. "I've faced worse than you, Beast, and lived to tell the tale. Here is what I can offer. There are no breaks. No bleeding. No visible swelling. A few scrapes and bruises, but nothing to go by beyond the lump on her head."

He turned away, collecting a sack full of ice from a tray nearby before placing it beneath Hattie's head. "We are lucky for two things—a strong pulse and an unending supply of ice. And I vow this: I shall do everything I can to save your lady."

My lady. Whit swallowed at the words, the knot in his throat pulsing with emotion. "Thank you."

The doctor nodded and made for the door, turning back just before he exited. "Ah. I nearly forgot." He reached behind to the waistband of his trousers. "This was in the lady's pocket, but I believe it belongs to you."

Onyx and steel shone in the light.

His blade. The missing one. Somehow now in Hattie's possession. He looked to Devil. "Ewan."

One of his brother's black brow's rose and he turned to Nik. "No sign of him?"

She shook her head. "Nothing. What does it mean?"

Whit looked back to Hattie. "It means she fought for us."

His warrior.

His savior.

He pressed a kiss to her hand. "Wake up, love. Please."

"It bears mentioning," the doctor said, casually, "that there are some who believe that in this particular state, the patient can hear. My wife tells me you've been talking to her. I suggest you keep on with that."

He should have been embarrassed, considering the audience, but Whit would have stripped himself naked in the middle of the Rookery for all the world to see if it would wake her up.

And so he kept talking.

"I should have told you how beautiful you are. I should

have said it more. I should have said it until you forgot there was a time when you didn't believe it."

Nora and Felicity sniffled in the background, but still, Hattie slept.

After flattery, he tried bribery. "I'll buy you one of Rebecca's pups. I'll buy you the whole lot of them. They can follow you along the docks during the day and sleep at your feet at night." He'd join them. "I found the French bean seller at the market—there's a standing order for fresh beans for you. You only need tell him Beast sent you."

"That's not an order, Beast, it's fearmongering," Devil said from the place he'd taken up against the far wall, as sentry. "Hattie, you should wake for no reason other than to keep Beast from shaking down every shopkeep in the Garden for you." He paused, "Also, because I'd like very much to know the woman who has my brother tracking down sellers of French beans."

Whit shook his head, but did not complain. He'd accept anything that might wake her. "I shall ask my confectioner to make you more of those raspberry drops. Others, too, if you like. Strawberry or apple. Whatever you choose. I don't know your favorite fruit." He looked to Nora. "What is her favorite fruit?"

Nora shook her head, tears in her eyes. "I'm not telling you." She lifted her voice. "Wake up and tell him yourself, Hattie."

He nodded. That was good. He wanted to hear it from her. He wanted to know everything about her, and he wanted it all to come direct from the source. He looked back to her, casting about for something else.

Striking on it.

"Devil," he said, raising his voice so his brother could hear him.

"Aye?"

"There's a house in Berkeley Square. Next to Warnick's. It's empty."

"Yeah?"

"Buy it. Put it in her name."

His brother did not hesitate over the request. He nodded. "Done."

Whit brushed her hair from her face, ran his fingers over the impossibly soft skin of her cheeks. "You see, love? We're buying your house. You'll have to wake to live in it, though. And I'd like very much to live in it with you." He reached to touch her, to brush the hair from her brow. "The Year of Hattie is shaping up."

She moved.

It was barely there, the movement. A flicker behind her eyelids. He wouldn't have noticed if he weren't so focused on her. He came up off his knees, leaning over her on the bed. "Hattie?" He moved closer, taking her hand in his again, trying not to squeeze too hard. "Hattie. Please, love."

Another flicker. "Yes. That's it, love."

The air in the room shifted, everyone coming closer, the whole assembly on a knife's point, except for Whit, who was talking again. "You have to open your eyes, Hattie. You have the most beautiful eyes. Have I told you that? I've never seen eyes like yours—so expressive. And when you told me you loved me earlier, you nearly put me to my knees. Wouldn't you like a chance to do that again? Open your eyes, love." He lowered his voice to a whisper. "Open your eyes so I can tell you how much I love you."

And she did.

Her lids opened and her gaze focused on his, and—impossibly—she smiled, as though she hadn't just been on death's door. And she did put him to his knees, because he found he did not have the strength to hold himself up.

Nora gasped, and Nik was out the door for the doctor, and Hattie tightened her hand in his, and said, "That was a very tempting offer."

He laughed at the words, unable to keep the tears from spilling down his cheeks. "I'm very happy to hear it."

Her hand came to his head, her fingers tangling in his hair, weak, but there. "Tell me," she whispered.

"I love you, Henrietta Sedley."

Her smile broadened, dimple flashing. "I like that."

He barked another laugh. "As do I, now that you're awake enough to hear it." He paused, then looked over his shoulder to the door. "Where's the damn doctor?"

She shook her head, "No doctor. Not yet," she said. "Not before I say this: I set out to claim myself—body, business, home, fortune, future. But you own it all."

"We don't have to marry," he said. "You want the business. It's yours. I'll have the papers drawn up now. The fortune you'll no doubt make with your sharp mind and your charm. Have all of it to yourself. But . . ." A plea edged into his words. "Let me share your future. Not as your husband. Not as your protector. As your partner. As your equal. However you like. I'll take whatever you'll give, as long as we're together."

She shook her head with a little wince that had him looking for the doctor again. "No, Whit. You misunderstand. You own it all. Every bit of me. And I give it, freely."

He pressed a kiss to her knuckles and then to her lips, to her cheeks and forehead and then back to her mouth. "I own nothing. Everything of mine is yours, nothing if it is not shared. My business, my life, my world, my heart."

She smiled, small, but there. "I am your protector."

He closed his eyes at the words. At the pleasure that rioted through him with them. "Yes. Christ, yes."

"Tell me again."

And he did, low and sweet against her lips. "I love you."

The doctor came and went, pronouncing her on the mend but requiring observation for several days in the infirmary. Their assembled guests left with proper introductions and relieved kisses and promises to visit daily, and moments later, a cacophonous cheer sounded from outside, shaking the windows in their seats.

Inside, Hattie's eyes went wide, and she lifted her head from where it rested on Whit's chest, as the moment they were alone, he'd climbed into bed with her and vowed not to leave the place until she did. "What was that?"

"The Rookery, cheering their lady on the mend."

She smiled at that. "Their lady?"

"*My* lady."

"My Beast." A pause and then, "Kiss me again."

He did, first gently, and then, when she pulled him closer, deeper. When he finally lifted his head, she sighed. "Tell me again."

"I love you."

Pink washed over her cheeks—a mark of her pleasure, and of her health. And then she closed her eyes and said, "Now tell me all the other things. All the things you said when I couldn't hear them."

And Beast settled in, his lady in his arms, content to spend the rest of his life doing just that.

Epilogue

One Year Later

Hattie stood at the helm of the ship, taking in her city.

The sun set over the rooftops, the whole of London burning amber in the light, the river gleaming like gold. She could hear the shouts of men and women up and down the docks, chattering and laughing and calling out to each other, late afternoon on the Docklands bursting with life. A half-dozen other ships were berthed along the quay, all owned by Sedley-Whittington Shipping, all crawling with dockworkers hauling product, all aboveboard.

But not this one. This one quiet, left only to her.

This one belonged to the Bareknuckle Bastards.

"There you are."

Hattie turned at the dark, satisfied words to find her husband crossing the deck, greatcoat billowing out behind him as his long legs and sure strides consumed the oak boards. She lifted a hand as he approached the steps leading up to where she stood. "Wait."

He did, instantly, looking up at her with a smile on his lips and a question in his eyes—eyes that glittered amber as the setting sun. His face bronzed from a summer of work on the ships—he remained breathtakingly handsome. "What is it?"

She smiled down at him. "I just like to look at you."

Whit's smile turned wolfish. "As I like to look at you, wife." He took the steps two at a time, meeting her halfway across the raised deck, taking her into his arms. "I like to touch you, as well."

He caressed down her arms, over the turquoise dress she wore. "I like this pretty frock." Lifting one hand to her hair, pushing a long lock behind her ear. "I like your beautiful eyes." And then he set his hand possessively to her belly, round and full with their first child. "And I like this more than I can say."

She blushed at the low, sinful words, at the memory of how well he had proved the last the night before. She tilted her face up to his. "And what do you think of kissing me?"

He growled low in the back of his throat and showed her just how well he liked that, too, kissing her long and lush, stroking deep until she was lost to it, giving herself up to him. Only then did he break the caress with a second, soft and sweet, and a third on her cheek, and the last in her hair as he pulled her close and breathed her in. "I love you," he whispered, the words stolen by the wind before Hattie could hear them.

But she felt them, nonetheless, curling into his warmth. "So here I am, as requested."

"Mmm," he said, holding her tight to him. "On our ship."

She smiled, turning her face into his chest, a hint of embarrassment coming with understanding. Whit had refused to allow the ship, once called the *Siren*, to become a part of Sedley-Whittington, pointing out again and again that the level of sin the vessel had hosted made it much better suited to the Bareknuckle Bastards. Hattie had rolled her eyes at the theory . . . until he'd rechristened it the *Warrior*. And then she'd rather liked that he kept it for the business that had been with him the longest.

"Nik wanted to get it out before low tide, but I told her I have plans for it tonight." The words were low and dark, and Hattie shivered at the promise in them.

"What kind of plans?" she sighed.

"The kind of plans that end with my wife naked under the stars."

Her arms wrapped about his neck, and she tucked herself into the warmth of his coat. "Well, it is my birthday."

"So it is." Whit leaned down and kissed her, nipping her full lower lip with his teeth. "I was thinking more about how it is a new year."

She raised a brow. "It's September."

"Ah, but the Year of Hattie is complete. And you've ticked off your items, have you not?" He pulled her tight and whispered at her ear. "Body."

She sighed as he nipped at her ear, then kissed down the side of her neck, and her hands came to his shoulders, clinging to him for balance. "You did very well with helping me with that one."

"I wonder if perhaps we might revisit it," he said, walking her back and lifting her up to sit on the edge of the ship, holding her tight and tucking himself between her thighs, pressing against her core.

"I think it could be arranged." She laughed as he licked at the curl of her ear. "What else?"

"Business and fortune," he growled.

"Oh, I did quite well with that. I married a rich man with a head for business."

Another grunt. "I believe it is more that he married a rich woman with a head for it."

Hattie had barely left the infirmary after Ewan's attacks on the docks when Whit produced a special license for them to marry. The wedding had been in the Covent Garden church, and was followed by a wild celebration on the docks, with lanterns and music and food and lemon ice and raspberry treats for anyone who wished them.

After that, Hattie and Saviour Whittington had built a shipping business that rivaled anything the city had seen before—employing every able body in Covent Garden and the Docklands and gaining the admiration and the envy of most of London's aristocrats and all of London's businessmen.

"One might even say Sedley-Whittington threatened to turn the Bareknuckle Bastards into upstanding gentlemen," Whit said, kissing down the column of Hattie's neck.

"Mmm. Thankfully, that threat never came to fruition." She smiled, the dimple in her right cheek flashing. Whit kissed the divot, one of his large hands coming to her belly, where their child grew, healthy and strong. And awake. Sensing its father's touch, it kicked, and Whit's eyes went wide, wider still when Hattie said, "She's preparing to be a Bareknuckle Bastard."

His laugh was perfect, and then he said, softly, "Home."

She met his eyes. "You are home."

The reply earned her another kiss, long and lingering, until she was clinging to him, and wishing they were any-where but here, and anything but clothed.

But Whit wasn't ready to be done with talking, remark-ably. "And so? What will come next? How shall we top your first Year of Hattie—a rollicking success?"

She shook her head. "It wasn't a success, you know—not a rollicking one, at least."

"What does that mean?"

"Only that there is one item left on my list." She pulled him close, the sun disappeared behind London, darkness falling over the docks, cloaking them in nothing more than each other. "Would you help me with it?"

"Anything," he whispered, holding her gaze. "Name it."

She grasped the lapels of his coat and pulled him close. "The future."

He growled, low and lush. "You've had that from the start."

Acknowledgments

When I conceived of the world of the Bareknuckle Bastards, I had no idea that I would fall so thoroughly in love with Covent Garden and the London Docklands, and I'm indebted to so many for time and knowledge. I could not have written Whit and Hattie's story without the extensive collection of the Museum of London, particularly Charles Booth's anthropological survey of *Life and Labour of the People of London*, as well as the incredibly knowledgeable staff of The Museum of the London Docklands and the Covent Garden Area Trust, and the stunning standing exhibitions of the Foundling Museum.

I'm very lucky to write with the unflagging support of the brilliant Carrie Feron and the entire team at Avon Books, including Liate Stehlik, Asanté Simons, Angela Craft, Pam Jaffee, and Kayleigh Webb. Eleanor Mikucki never fails to make me look better, and Brittani DiMare's immense patience is a tremendous gift.

Whit and Hattie would never have made it to the page without a collection of women far smarter than I am. I'm forever grateful for the brilliant minds of Louisa Edwards, Carrie Ryan, Sophie Jordan, Sierra Simone, and Tessa Gratton, and the precious friendship of Jennifer Prokop and Kate Clayborn.

For Eva Moore, Cheryl Tapper, and all the members of OSRBC: As promised, a violet-eyed heroine—I hope she is a worthy addition to the canon.

And for Eric, the silent hero of my heart—thank you for always knowing when I need your words.

Keep reading for a sneak peek at the
next Bareknuckle Bastards novel

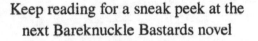

Coming 2020 from Avon Books!

Daring and the Duke

He was rescued by angels.

The explosion had sent him flying through the air, knocking him back into the shadows of the docks. He'd twisted in flight, but the landing had dislocated his shoulder, rendering his left arm useless. It was said that dislocation was one of the worst pains a man could experience, and the Duke of Marwick had suffered it twice. Twice, he'd staggered to his feet, mind reeling. Twice, he'd struggled to bear the pain. Twice, he'd sought out a place to hide from his enemy.

Twice, he'd been rescued by angels.

The first time, she'd been fresh-faced and kind, with a wild riot of red curls, a thousand freckles across her nose and cheeks, and the biggest brown eyes he'd ever seen. She'd found him in the cupboard where he hid, put a finger to her lips, and held his good hand as another—larger and stronger—had reset the joint. He'd passed out from the pain, and when he woke, she'd been there like sunlight, with a soft touch and a soft voice.

And he'd fallen in love with her.

This time, the angels who rescued him were not soft, and they did not sing. They came for him with strength and power, two of them, strong and agile, cloaks over their heads, turning their faces dark, coats billowing behind them like wings as they approached, boots clicking on the cobblestones. They came armed like Heaven's soldiers, blades at their sides made flaming swords in the light of the ship that burned on the docks—destroyed at his command, along with the woman his brother loved.

So, it seemed like justice that the angels who came were soldiers. That they would come to punish and not to save.

Still, it would be rescue.

He pushed to his feet as they approached, to face them head on, to take the punishment they would deliver. He winced at the pain in his leg that he had not noticed earlier, where a shard from the mast of the destroyed hauler had seated itself in his thigh, coating his trouser leg in blood, making it impossible to fight them.

He lost consciousness.

When he woke, it was night still—Night again? Night forever?—he was alone in a dark room, and his first thought was the one he'd had upon waking for twenty years. *Grace.*

The girl he'd loved.

The one he'd lost.

The one for whom he'd searched for a lifetime.

His shoulder had been set and his leg bandaged. He sat up, too busy hating the truth and the darkness to think of the pain that seemed to come from everywhere, within and without. His head throbbed a fog that could only come from laudanum as he reached for the low table near the bed, feeling for a candle or a flint, and knocked over a glass. The sound of liquid cascading to the floor reminding him to listen.

That's when he realized he could hear what he could not see.

A cacophony of muffled sound, shouting and laughter nearby—just beyond the room?—and a roaring din from farther away—outside the building? Inside, but at a distance? The low rumble of a crowd—something he never heard in the places he usually woke. Something he barely remembered. But memory came with the sound, from a similar distance—from farther away, from a lifetime ago.

And for the first time in twenty years, the man known to all the world as Robert Matthew Carrick, twelfth Duke of Marwick, was afraid. Because what he heard was not the world in which he'd grown.

It was the one into which he'd been born.

His heart began to pound, wild and violent in his chest, and he stood, crossing the darkness, feeling along the wall until he found a door. A handle.

Locked.

The angels had rescued him and brought him to a locked room in Covent Garden.

He did not have to cross the room to know what he would find outside, the rooftops filled with angled slate and crooked chimneys. A boy born in the Garden did not forget the sounds of it, no matter how hard he'd tried. He stumbled to the window nevertheless, pushing back the curtain. It rained, the clouds blocking the light of the moon, refusing access to the world outside. Denying him sight, so he might hear sound.

A key in the lock.

He turned. The door opened, the hallway beyond barely brighter than the room where he stood—just bright enough to reveal a woman in shadow. Tall. Lean.

She stilled and the darkness gifted him sound from the other side of the room. A little intake of breath. Barely there and somehow sharp like a gunshot.

And like that, he knew.

She was alive.

Daring and the DUKE

The Bareknuckle Bastards, Book III

Ewan and Grace's story
Coming 2020

At Avon Books, we know your passion for romance—once you finish one of our novels, you find yourself wanting more.

May we tempt you with . . .

- **Excerpts** from our upcoming releases.

- Entertaining **extras**, including authors' personal photo albums and book lists.

- Behind-the-scenes **scoop** on your favorite characters and series.

- **Sweepstakes** for the chance to win free books, romantic getaways, and other fun prizes.

- Writing **tips** from our authors and editors.

- **Blog** with our authors and find out why they love to write romance.

- **Exclusive content** that's not contained within the pages of our novels.

Join us at
www.avonbooks.com